Christmas Carol

by

Charles Dickens

The Christmas Angel

by

Abbie Farwell Brown

For additions, deletions, corrections or clarifications in future editions of this text, please e-mail Contactus@elmhillbooks.com

Published by Elm Hill Books®, an imprint of J. Countryman®, a division of Thomas Nelson, Inc. Nashville, TN 37214

Products from Elm Hill Books® may be purchased in bulk for educational, business, fundraising, or sales promotional use. For information, please email SpecialMarkets@ThomasNelson.com.

The illustrations included in *The Christmas Angel* are by Reginald B. Birch, from the Houghton Mifflin Company 1910 edition of *The Christmas Angel*. All illustrations are from the library of Joe Wheeler.

Published in association with the literary agency of WordServe Literary Group, Ltd., 10152 S. Knoll Circle, Highlands Ranch, CO 80130.

Cover design by Patti Evans
Interior by Jennifer Ross

Printed in the United States of America

A Christmas Carol Previously published by Focus on the Family Publishing, Colorado Springs, Colorado in 1997 under ISBN 1-56179-556-9

The Christmas Angel Previously published by Tyndale House Publishers, Wheaton, Illinois in 1999 under ISBN 1-56179-762-6

A Christmas Carol

In Prose
A Ghost Story of Christmas

By
Charles Dickens

With an Introduction and Afterword by
Joe L. Wheeler, Ph.D.

ELM HILL BOOKS
A Division of Thomas Nelson Publishers
Since 1798

www.thomasnelson.com

PREFACE

I have endeavored in this
Ghostly little book to raise the
Ghost of an Idea which shall
not put my readers out of
humor with themselves, with
each other, with the season,
or with me. May it haunt their
house pleasantly, and no one
wish to lay[1] it.

Their faithful Friend and Servant,
C.D.
December 1843

TABLE OF CONTENTS

SCROOGE IN THE CROSSROADS

I cannot remember when I first heard it read, nor when I first read it myself, nor when I first experienced it on film, nor even when it first engulfed me as live drama. I only know that looking back through life, somehow *A Christmas Carol* was always there.

In the century and a half since *A Christmas Carol* was published in 1843, we have come to take it for granted: We just accept it as if it had always been with us—like the Wise Men, crèches, and holly. What would the world be like without Scrooge, Marley, the Cratchits, the Three Ghosts, "Bah! Humbug!" and Tiny Tim? Well, in 1842, none of them existed.

What was the year 1843 like for Charles Dickens? Simply put, it was not good. Let me explain.

As we'll see in the author biography, Dickens endured a tough childhood. Then, at the age of twenty-five, he was catapulted to the top of his world. It is always dangerous to soar too high too young: It usually results in a strong case of hubris—unless the twenty-five-year-old is strong and wise beyond his years; unless he realizes, with Nebuchadnezzar, how quickly the God who giveth can become the God who taketh away. In other words, today's success is already unrealizingly sowing the seeds of its own destruction. This was true with Dickens. He had assumed that he had become great by his own efforts—by the sheer brilliance of his mind and force of his will.

Perhaps a baseball analogy would help. In 1863, Dickens stepped up to the plate and hit *Boz* out of the park. Next, he hit *Pickwick* out of the park. Then *Oliver Twist*, then *Nickleby*, then *The Old Curiosity Shop;* and then *Barnaby Rudge*, which just cleared the outer wall. Then came his ill-fated trip to the United States, and when his bat made contact with *American Notes*, he hit only a bloop single, not realizing that he now had a hairline crack in the bat. *American Notes* was followed by *Martin Chuzzlewit*—and with it, he broke his bat.

For the first time in seven years, Dickens was in trouble. It all began because the Americans refused to pay him his due royalties, which made Dickens angry. Because of his fame he assumed, mistakenly, that he could say anything he wanted when he traveled to the late great colony of America, so he decided to tell them what he thought of their cheapness. To put his condition in the modern vernacular, he had an attitude problem. Even his countrymen felt he had gone too far.

The result: the golden faucet that had gushed its riches upon Dickens for almost seven years slowed its flow so much that he wondered if perhaps his well was going dry. What if people would no longer buy his books?

Never a humble man, Dickens always knew, to a penny, the value of his gifts. At least, he thought he had before 1842. Now he wasn't so sure anymore.

What could he write that would improve his fortunes and help bring back his fickle public? It had to be something he could write quickly, not just another two-year book serialization. So the idea for *A Christmas Carol* came to him (see biography). For a month and a half, Dickens immersed himself in the world of Scrooge. In the process, he gradually became aware that, somewhere along the way, he had become a Scrooge himself: He had felt so secure in his gifts that he assumed he no longer needed other people—that he no longer needed to care (not just abstractly, but one-on-one) about them.

In the course of writing the story of Scrooge, Dickens was able to pull himself back from the brink and realize his need for others. He began to wonder if he had ever really known who he was. And could he ever really know without going backward in time?

The answers to those questions were a long time in coming, but *A Christmas Carol* was the first step. Dickens learned something else during the writing of this little book: He learned about the difference between writing a lean, cohesive book (written all at once) and writing the usually episodic, rambly serialization.

As a result of this no man's land between the overconfidence of his youth and the social conscience of his maturity, Dickens was able to make it through the rest of his life without being destroyed by pride. He found out things about himself that stripped away some of his arrogance. And sorrow would rock him on his heels again and again.

So it came to pass that in the last quarter of Dickens' life, in his 450 public readings (an average of one performance every twelve days for fifteen years), the story of Scrooge became as indispensable as singing the national anthem at a big league baseball game. And as Dickens' life drew to a close, a higher percentage of each evening's performance was devoted to *A Christmas Carol* and its lesson of agape love.

It is no hyperbole to say that without this one little book, the life of Charles Dickens most likely would have been very different. In a very real sense, then, we may validly say that the Christmas Carol characters conceived by this author ended up taking him on a journey that would last a lifetime.

It is our privilege to be invited along. Welcome to the timeless world of *A Christmas Carol.*

ABOUT THE INTRODUCTION

For decades, one of the few absolutes in my literature classes has been this: Never read the introduction before reading the book! Those who ignored my thundering admonition lived to regret their disobedience. Downcast, they would come to me and say, "Dr. Wheeler, I confess that I read the introduction first, and it wrecked the book for me. I couldn't enjoy the story, because all the way through I saw it through someone else's eyes. I don't agree with the editor on certain points, but those conclusions are in my head, and now I don't know what I think!"

Given that God never created a human clone, no two of us will ever perceive reality in exactly the same way—and no two of us ever should! Therefore, no matter how educated, polished, brilliant insightful or eloquent the teacher might be, don't ever permit that person to tell you how to think or respond, for that is a violation of the most sacred thing God gives us—our individuality.

My solution to the introduction problem was to split it in two: an introduction, to whet the appetite for and enrich the reading of the book; and an afterword to generate discussion and debate after the reader has arrived at his or her own conclusions about the book and is ready to challenge my (the teacher's) perceptions.

MOVIE HISTORY

Year: 1938—*A Christmas Carol*,
MGM, black-and-white and colorized, 69 min.
Cast: Reginald Owen, Gene Lockhart, Kathleen Lockhart, Terence
Kilburne, Leo G. Carroll, Lynne Carver, Ann Rutherford, Barry Mackay,
June Lockhart (screen debut)
Director: Edwin L. Martin

Year: 1951—*A Christmas Carol, or Scrooge*
(British), black-and —white and Colorized, 86 min.
Cast: Alastair Sim, Kathleen Harrison, Jack Warner, Michael Hordern,
Patrick Macnee, Mervyn Johns, Hermione Baddeley, Clifford Mollison,
George Cole, Carol Marsh, Miles Malleson, Ernest Thesiger, Hattie
Jacques, Peter Bull, Hugh Dempster
Director: Brian Desmond Hurst
Screenplay: Noel Langley
Composer: Richard Addinsell

Year: 1954—*A Christmas Carol* (musical),
black-and-white, 54 min.
Cast: Frederic March, Basil Rathbone, Ray Middleton, Bob Sweeney,
Christopher Cook

Year: 1984
Cast: George C. Scott, Nigel Davenport, Frank Finlay, Edward Woodward,
Lucy Gutteridge, Angela Pleasence, Roger Rees, David Warner,
Susannah York, Anthony Walters
Director: Clive Donner
Screenplay: Roger O. Hirson

ABOUT THE AUTHOR

Though I have studied and taught Charles Dickens throughout my teaching career, this is the first time I have dug so deeply into the various strata of his life. Two definitive biographies gave me bedrock to build on: Edgar Johnson's monumental *Charles Dickens: His Tragedy and Triumph* (New York: Viking Press, 1977; first edition, 1952); and Fred Kaplan's powerful *Dickens: A Biography* (New York: William Morrow & Company, 1988). A wealth of additional material came from E.W.F. Tomlin's engrossing *Charles Dickens: A Centennial Volume* (New York: Simon & Shuster, 1970); Jane R. Cohen's *Charles Dickens and His Original Illustrators* (Columbus: Ohio State University Press, 1980); and Michael Patrick Hearn's splendid *The Annotated Christmas Carol* (New York: Clarkson N. Potter, 1976)—Mr. Hearn has kindly given me permission to enrich this edition by the treasure trove of information appearing in the footnotes. Perhaps the ultimate dictionary of our time, invaluable for the words no longer in use, is *The Compact Edition of the Oxford English Dictionary* (New York and Glasgow: Oxford University Press, 1973). The 1946 edition of the Encyclopedia Britannica provided me with G. K. Chesterton's succinctly written biographical synthesis of Dickens' life and works. For additional enjoyment and insights, I encourage you to search out these books and read them in their entirety.

℘

There can never be another Dickens . . . If a novelist of similar genius appeared tomorrow, we could safely prophesy he would never arrive at the height of popularity Dickens held for thirty years. The Victorians wanted Dickens' novels as nobody these days really wants anybody's novels. They were the great family entertainment, with something for everybody.

(J. B. Priestly in Tomlin, p. 27)

The Victorian age was a different world than the one we live in today. First of all, print was king. Books and magazines were as exciting to those living a century and a half ago as the cinema is to us today—more so, in fact, for we have quickly become jaded to a medium that bombards us so incessantly, that gives us no peace, no blessed silence in which to think and reflect.

But not so then. The home was still central to life, and divorce was incredibly rare. Large families were the norm; they had to be, for of six children, if only two survived to adulthood, that would barely replace the mother and father, much less enable the population to grow. Since so few children received any education, and since so many children entered the workforce at such an early age (six to twelve being the norm among poorer families), large families did not cost as much, by percentage of family income, as they do today.

Fathers ruled supreme, and their word was law—as often as not, even after the children had grown up. This was especially true with the daughters: Often, a father would selfishly refuse to let a daughter marry, keeping her at home as cheap labor for life and guaranteeing him health care in old age.

There was no central heat or central air, so during the winter everyone congregated around the fireplace or the kitchen stove; and during the summer they'd find the coolest room in the house (high ceilings resulted in relative coolness on the floor level, and cross-ventilating windows helped to cool the house as well). With no televisions, no CD-ROMs, no VCRs, no videos, no cinemas, no radios even, what did people do back then? They read—and created their own entertainment.

Normally, they weren't interested in a "quick read," for the evenings were long. And they created their own inner imagery, for illustrations were few. Let me give you a fun assignment: Start your own archaeological expedition by searching out old magazines (the easiest to find are bound volumes in antique stores) and see how far back you can go. What you will find is that, before 1860, magazines carried few illustrations, and the illustrations that did appear were usually crude, simplistic or stereotyped. It's almost as if there's a huge wall separating the years before 1860 from the years after that date. Do a similar search with full-length books. Your conclusions will be the same. Thus, at that time in history, the words themselves had to provide not only the story line, but also the visual effects.

Furthermore, since full-length, bound books were expensive, few people could afford to buy them; hence, the need for story serializations that appeared weekly, every other week or monthly (the original soap operas). Most of Dickens' books were part of this tradition, being hawked on street corners, sold in bookstores or included in magazines (which were sold in the same way). Once you know this fact about early nineteenth-century publishing, you will understand a lot about the books themselves. For instance, they all have roller-coaster story lines. Each chapter is already in motion and includes deep plunges and neck-jarring turns; and each chapter ends on a high summit looking down into an abyss—that was to make sure you would toss and turn all week, waiting for the next installment.

The whole family—usually six to twelve children, mother, father, and other relatives—would gather around on an evening, and the stories would be read aloud, often being passed from one reader to the next. Thus each story became an integral part of the family psyche and memories—not just the hearing or reading of them, but also the individualized and collective responses to certain passages.

Further reinforcement came later as families put on their own dramatic skits, adding yet another dimension to the story lines. Sadly, today the entire process of passing on a story has degenerated to spoon-feeding pabulum to youngsters: Everything is so predigested and prepackaged that all one has to do is flop down on a couch, half-asleep, and let a given story wash over and into you, punctuated by potty-break commercials.

Given this difference between the nineteenth century and the late twentieth, it is small wonder that, during Dickens' time, families gathered authors into their hearts in ways unthinkable today, considering them greater than royalty or heads of state. Authors were the superstars of their age.

And for his time, Dickens was the number one box-office draw—both in the British Empire and in the United States.

Let's see how all of this came to be.

A Strange Sort of Pot to Grow In

The row house in which Charles John Huffam Dickens was born on February 7, 1812, still stands: 387 Mile End Terrace, Landport, Portsea, not far from London. Like most of the homes the boy was to know, it proved to be but a way station to something else. Before he was five months old, the family moved again, to something cheaper.

It was a most undistinguished family into which Dickens was born—none of them known to memory had ever done much to crow about. His mother, Elizabeth Barrow, born in 1788, was slim, dark-haired, hazel-eyed, pretty and loved to dance; in fact, on the night her second child was born, she attended a ball. That attitude of carelessness and devotion to self would remain unchanged through the years. Nevertheless, she was cheerful, sweet-tempered and well-educated for the time. A remarkable mimic, she had a keen sense of the ridiculous which she would have much need of, given that she was married to John Dickens.

John Dickens, born in 1785, was an eternal optimist, always perceiving his glass of life as half-full rather than half-empty. He took seriously his job as clerk in the navy pay office, which paid £176 a year. Generous, cheerful, kind, warm-hearted and hospitable—he loved to entertain. John had one flaw: His outgo was invariably more than his income. All his life, he borrowed from tomorrow to pay for today. His son was to re-create him in many forms—to Chesterton, John

Dickens was halfway between Micawber and Dorrit: "a man of wavering and unstable status, partly by his misfortunes and partly by his fault" (Britannica VII, p. 331). Ostensibly genteel, John was a wondrous talker, always seeming to be more than he was—"magniloquent," according to Johnson. In that sense, *David Copperfield's* Micawber is his portrait, etched in undying colors.

The Dickens family would always be on the move. To John and Elizabeth, it was just the way things were. Both took life as it came, never getting very upset when troubles deluged them. Their laughter always burbled through the rain.

Young Charles was to know only one short period of relative tranquility and stability: When he was five, his father was transferred to the naval yards in Chatham, a shipbuilding town that was even then becoming part of the cathedral city of Rochester. Besides his older sister, Fanny, Charles had a baby sister, Letitia. John, now earning £300 a year, moved into a three-story brick house (also part of a row-house complex) on Ordnance Terrace, overlooking the river Medway. There were small front and back gardens, a couple of hawthorn trees to climb, and fields nearby that filled with wildflowers in the spring.

The Dickenses were well enough off to afford two servants: Jane Bonny and Mary Weller. The latter, Charles never forgot because of the horrifying stories she told him at night. "One of these gory narratives concerned a certain Captain Murderer who slaughtered his successive wives, baked them in meat pies, ate them and picked their bones:" (Johnson, p. 17). Another horrific tale had to do with a Faustian figure who sold himself to the devil and ended up in a nightmare world haunted by rats. Needless to say, these stories were anything but conducive to sleep: "Little Charles would lie in bed rigid with terror" (Johnson, p. 18). Perhaps because of Mary Weller's gruesome stories, early on Charles became obsessed with cannibalism—an interest he never lost, even after he grew up.

Charles learned to read at his mother's knee, and from then on, he read voraciously. He and Fanny attended a dame school for a time; the grim old woman who ran the school, Charles would remember all his life, later portraying her as the Mrs. Pipchin who would help to make Paul Dombey's life so miserable.

It was in Chatham that Charles first fell in love. Next door lived two children, George and Lucy Stroughill. Charles would remember Lucy all his life as a "peach-faced creature with a blue sash" (Johnson, p. 19).

Fanny and Charles enjoyed singing comic songs together, and the proud father would often hoist his son onto the table and have him entertain guests in his high childish treble. Charles would also sing sea duets with Fanny while both stood on the dining room table.

Introduction

Sometimes in life, apparently simple acts have far-reaching results. Oftentimes Charles and his father would walk together on the Gravesend to Rochester road; as they'd cross the Rochester Bridge, up ahead like a fairyland palace on top of Gad's Hill would rise a brick Georgian mansion, with bow windows and a small white bell turret. One day his father, noting a look of dreamy longing on his son's face, said, "If you are very prospering and work very hard, you may someday come to live in it" (Johnson p. 11). Charles, a veteran of cramped living quarters, considered that statement in partial disbelief and in partial hope, then stored away the moment among the rest of his young dreams. Through the long years ahead, the glow of that one vision of Gad's Hill Place would remain in his mind as a beacon of the possible.

Great windjammer battleships riding proudly at anchor in the Chatham Naval Yard, the narrow streets climbing up to towering Rochester Cathedral, the romantic ruins of a once great castle, the verdant hills of Kent and the gilded river Medway meandering its way down to the English Channel across from France . . . these images represented Dickens' personal Eden, the sanctuary to which he could retreat when his world darkened. It was a time when he felt secure and loved.

The streets of Chatham—filled as they were with jostling tradesmen, shopping women, convict laborers, sailors and soldiers—always excited Dickens. Downriver a ways, great ship hulks housed prisoners when they were not working. When one of them escaped, guns were fired, warning everyone to lock their doors. But it was the river that most filled young Charles' dreams. Hour after hour, he would wander down its banks, listening to the tide come in and go out, watching the boats, barges and ships as he daydreamed.

Because the whole family was musical and loved drama, their home life was filled with both. Fanny was already taking piano and voice lessons, preparing for a musical career. The theater, in those pre-media days, was everywhere. But the first escape into that world that Charles could remember was "the delights—the ten thousand million delights of a pantomime . . . [to] which a long row of small boys, with frills as white as they could be washed and hands as clean as they would come, were taken to behold the glories . . . What mattered it that the stage was three yards wide, and four deep? We never saw it. We had no eyes, ears or corporeal sense but for the pantomime" (Kaplan, p. 27). He was seven when he first heard the great Grimaldi perform in London.

To his home, Charles brought the theater—charades, pantomimes, comedies, melodrama, magic-lantern shows. He could direct as well as act in everything. He could even write his own dramas. But in the famed Rochester Theatre Royale, he saw the great actors of the age—including, the tragedian Edmund Kean and the comedian Charles Matthews—tread the boards. It was in this theater that Charles first shuddered at the evil of Richard III and the witches in Macbeth. Oliver Goldsmith and William Shakespeare were his two theatrical idols.

And his stage-struck father, on their long walks together, would thunder out or whisper memorable lines from the great dramas—all of which the child absorbed as parched ground does drops of rain.

At home, Charles had long since graduated from "Jack and the Bean Stalk," "The Yellow Dwarf," "Robin Hood," "Red Riding Hood" and "Valentine and Orson" to his parents' books: *Roderick Random, Peregrine Pickle, Humphrey Clinker, Tom Jones, Don Quixote, Gil Blas* and *Robinson Crusoe.* Remembering years later, he wrote,

> *When I think of it, the picture always arises in my mind of a summer evening, the boys at play in the churchyard and I sitting on my bed, reading as if for life. Every barn in the neighborhood, every stone in the church, and every foot of the churchyard, had some association of its own, in my mind, connected with these books, and stood for some locality made famous in them. I have seen Tom Pipes go climbing up the church steeple; I have watched Strap, with the knapsack on his back, stopping to rest upon the wicket-gate; and I know that Commodore Trinnion held that club with Mr. Pickle in the parlour of our little village alehouse.*
>
> (Johnson, pp. 23-24)

But there was a darker side even here. Charles' mother was more willing to have children than to commune with them once they were born. The maids would spend time with him, walking with him, telling him stories, listening to him and entering his world. So would his father, as work permitted—but not so his mother. Charles was to grow up soul-hungry for a mother, and that never-to-be-filled void radically altered both his art and his life.

Dickens would also experience death at an early age. In today's society, most of our deaths occur from crime, self-induced diseases like lung cancer, automobile accidents and from old-age afflictions. Charles' world was quite different: Crime-related deaths paled in significance when compared with deaths in childbirth or from childbirth complications (both mother and baby) and childhood diseases—all too often, they proved fatal; also, diseases such as smallpox, cholera, tuberculosis, diphtheria, measles, scarlet fever, whopping cough and dysentery, as well as those resulting from antiquated medical care, abysmal sanitation, lack of fresh air and poor hygiene, claimed thousands of victims.

Early on, young Charles perceived this fragility of life. Mary Weller often took him along with her when she went to lyings-in (in those days, babies were born at home) in her capacity as midwife. Charles couldn't help but notice that babies died as often as they lived. "In one instance, a multiple birth had produced four or five dead infants, who were laid out, 'side by side, on a clean cloth on a chest of drawers,' which reminded him of pigs' feet as they are usually displayed at a neat tripe-shop" (Kaplan, p. 29). He would, of course, experience death again and again in his own family.

For a while, Charles attended nearby Giles School, where he felt he was on his way to becoming a gentleman. He studied penmanship, elocution, vocabulary, arithmetic, history, geography and Latin—and he even won a prize for a recitation.

But in June 1822, without warning, John Dickens was transferred back to London.

Adrift in London

To a child, moves are rather a lark—as long as things go well with Mother and Father, for they represent the home, not bricks, board, steel and glass. Consequently, Charles saw nothing ominous in another move.

But it didn't take long to unravel the secure blanket he had warmed his heart with in Rochester. He was permitted to stay one last summer in Kent, after which the ten-year-old boy was packed into a smelly coach—he was the only passenger—and sent to Cheapside in the rain. It was a most dreary ride. But arrival home was not much better. Everything was disorganized and confused, not only in the house itself but in that protective wall of fiscal solvency that parents erect around their children's sense of well-being. A bond was due, and John Dickens didn't have the money to pay it. The only way he could avoid disaster was to borrow more and cut back on expenses.

One of the first expenses to go was Charles' education: He was not permitted to return to school. Charles was desolate, for school had been opening up a new world for him. And it certainly didn't help when his parents, somehow, found enough money to send Fanny off to the Royal Academy of Music but had none left for him.

All the while, there were continual knocks on the door as merchants and moneylenders demanded their money. And here and there, credit for the family's necessities began to be denied. John and Elizabeth appeared not to be unduly bothered by it all: He always felt "something would turn up" (à la Micawber), and she was so disorganized that one more problem wasn't enough for her to lose sleep over. But it was not so with Charles and Fanny—they were deeply humiliated by these fissures in their home walls. The very floor under their feet began to shake—and Charles, because he wasn't able to attend school, felt it most.

No one paid much attention to him, leaving him to putter around, do chores, watch over the younger children (there were now five in all) and run errands. He began to wander the streets of London—and these streets began to teach him a different kind of lesson. He saw "dirty men, filthy women, squalid children, fluttering shuttlecocks, noisy battledores, reeking pipes, bad fruit, more than doubtful oysters, attenuated cats, depressed dogs, anatomical fowls . . . and rotting cabbage. He began writing character sketches of those he observed" (Kaplan, pp. 35-36).

Neither John nor Elizabeth knew how to dig themselves out of their mess. Each had constructed a way of life. He tried to live as a gentleman, and she expected to live as she had as a child—a pampered member of the upper-middle class. In spite of their money woes, Elizabeth still perceived herself to be a woman of beauty and high culture, entitled to a comfortable life. Kaplan notes that neither was especially intelligent or hard-working; and they had neither strong religious convictions nor clear professional goals to help them establish long-range plans. Furthermore, they refused to recognize that self-denial was essential to survival.

When taxes came due, and they could not come up with what they owed, a summons was issued. And then another. At this juncture, George Lamert, an uncle, offered eleven-year-old Charles a job in his shoe-polish factory and warehouse; there, he could earn six shillings a week for the family coffers. His parents accepted the job for him.

Now Charles' dream of success and gentility seemed dead for sure. Two days after his twelfth birthday, the boy, stunned and in despair, reported for work. Some middle-class boys, less high-strung and sensitive than he, might have thrived in such an environment—but not Charles. Looking back a quarter of a century later, Dickens wondered how he could have been so cavalierly cast out of his home and why "no one had compassion enough on me—a child of singular abilities, quick, eager, delicate and soon hurt, bodily or mentally—to suggest that something might have been spared, as certainly it might have been, to place me at any common school. Our friends, I take it, were tired out. No one made any sign. My father and mother were quite satisfied. They could hardly have been more so, if I had been twenty years of age, distinguished at a grammar-school, and going to Cambridge" (Johnson, p. 31).

In truth, such child labor was the usual thing in nineteenth-century England. And the hours were anything but short: At the factory, the boys began work at 8 a.m. and didn't get to quit until twelve hours later, at 8 p.m; they had only two breaks all day. The factory itself was a dilapidated old building on the Thames. It was filthy, and the smell of decay was omnipresent. There were rats everywhere: in the wainscoted rooms, in the rotten floors, in the crumbling stairway—and they could be heard continually as they swarmed throughout the building.

Charles had no idea of how desperate his parents' financial condition was and what a relief it was to increase their cash flow, even by the small amount his work brought in. And on their part, they did not realize that their child was dying inside from the shame of having to work in a factory. It was not the job itself that humiliated him—"cover the pots of paste-blacking; first with a piece of oil paper, and then with a bit of blue paper; to tie them around with a string; and then to clip the paper close and neat, all round, until it looked as smart as a pot of ointment from an apothecary's shop" (Johnson, p. 32). On the finished product he pasted a printed label. No, his shame wasn't because of the job; it was because his father had always encouraged him to be a gentleman.

Since the other boys had no pretensions of gentility, they felt instantly that Charles would not mesh—in fact, they called him "the young gentleman." In his autobiography, Dickens cried out,

> No words can express the secret agony of my soul, as I sunk into this companionship; compared these every day associates with those of my happier childhood, and felt my early hopes of growing up to be a learned and distinguished man crushed in my breast. The deep remembrance of the sense I had of being utterly neglected and hopeless; of the shame I felt in my position; of the misery it was to my young heart to believe that, day by day, what I had learned, and thought, and delighted in . . . , was passing away from me, never to be brought back anymore; cannot be written. My whole nature was so penetrated with the grief and humiliation of such considerations, that even now, famous and caressed and happy, I often forget in my dreams that I have a dear wife and children; even that I am a man; and wander desolately back to that time of my life.

> (Johnson, pp. 32-33)

Eleven days after Charles began work at the blacking factory, his father was arrested for debt. He would spend the first three nights in what they called a "sponging house," trying to raise money and avoid imprisonment. Charles, his eyes filled with tears, spent the weekend shuttling messages back and forth for his weeping father. But it was all in vain: On Friday, February 20, John Dickens was taken to Marshalsea Prison. His last words to his son, before the gates closed behind him, were these: "The sun has set on me forever" (Johnson, p. 33).

At twelve years of age, the son had already exchanged roles with the father—never again could his father be to him what he had once been. For Charles, the two experiences of beginning work at the factory and having his father imprisoned for debt had taken the rest of his childhood away from him.

To this darkest period of his life, Charles would return later, in books such as the autobiographical *David Copperfield* and try to exorcise the demons left within by these two experiences. But with Charles, nothing was ever lost: For he stored faces and mannerisms in his nearly photographic memory, to be held there until he had need of them—as sooner or later he almost always would. Even in debtor's prison, images were captured for the future: For instance, when his father sent him to the next floor to beg loan of a knife and fork, Charles saw "a very dirty lady in [the captain's] dirty room; and two wan girls, his daughters, with shock heads of hair. I thought I should not have liked to borrow Captain Porter's comb" (Johnson, p. 33). As Charles stood there, burning the scene into his mind, he instinctively knew that the two dirty little girls were the captain's "natural children" and the dirty lady was not his wife.

Though in prison, John Dickens retained his ornate, florid speech, but he was "dreadfully shaken. He became tremulously tragic; it may have been at this time that his son observed in his father that fluttering and frightened motion of the fingers about the lips that he later attributed to William Dorrit in the same misfortune" (Johnson, p. 34). And he had reason to be frightened. Either he remained here in Prison—for he had no means to pay his debts—or he publicly admitted he could not handle money and availed himself of the last resort: the Insolvent Debtors Act. Of course, if he pursued the latter option, gone would be any chance he had of getting his job back: "Income, pension possibilities, all hopes, would vanish" (Johnson, p. 34). In desperation, John applied for early retirement on the basis of a chronic urinary problem.

Meanwhile, at home (if one could call it that), Charles' "distracted mother tried to keep things going and the whimpering children fed by pawning brooches and spoons [even the beloved books] and gradually stripping the rooms bare of furniture. At last there was nothing left in Gower Street but a few chairs, a kitchen table, and some beds; and the family camped out in the two parlours of the emptied house" (Johnson, p. 34).

Finally, it became clear that declaring insolvency was the only way out. The Dickenses would have to prove absolute destitution. One of the most humiliating days of Charles' life was having to report to the insolvency appraiser to see if what he wore would fall within the guidelines. He was deathly afraid they'd take his grandfather's silver watch ticking away in his pocket, but the official took one long look at the shabbily dressed boy and waved him out. It only took a moment, but that was seared into Dickens' consciousness for all time.

What came next, however, was even harder for the proud boy to accept. His mother and the four younger children left the now virtually empty Gower Street house and moved into Marshalsea Prison. True, it was crowded there—but it was also cheaper. And even more important, they were temporarily relieved from having to deal with all the irate, importuning creditors who laid siege to their home. In prison, the rest of the family could come and go at will—as long as they were back in before the outer prison doors were locked for the night.

Charles, however, was not included with the rest of the family; instead, a place was found for him to dwell, with a Mrs. Roylance, who unbeknownst to her, "unconsciously began to sit for Mrs. Pipchin in Dombey when she took me in" (Johnson, p. 35). Though his father paid for his lodging, all of Charles' food had to come out of the six shillings he earned at the factory.

So there he was: a smallish twelve-year-old boy adrift in one of the world's greatest cities. Years later, he wrote of these days that he had "no advice, no counsel, no encouragement, no consolation, no support, from anyone . . . I know that, but for the mercy of God, I might easily have been, for any care that was taken of me, a little robber or a little vagabond" (Johnson, pp.35-36). Undoubtedly, one of the reasons he remained so bitter at his mother was that here, during the darkest days of his life, his own mother had thrown him into the streets to sink or swim, drift into crime or stay above it, on his own. She didn't seem to care.

Not having to be accountable to anyone, Charles began roaming the streets like Harun al-Rashid of Baghdad, a thousand years earlier and O'Henry of New York, almost a hundred years later. He peered into every crevice, listened intently to every conversation, took stock of every characteristic and assimilated every nuance of the great city.

On Sunday, his one day off, he would call for fourteen-year-old Fanny at the Academy of Music, and together they'd walk across Westminster Bridge en route to the prison, there to spend the day. On one of these evenings, he broke down completely. Listening to his broken sobs, his father emerged from his own troubles long enough to consider those of his son. As a result, he had Charles moved into a back attic close to Marshalsea; and from that point on, the boy was able to eat both breakfast (very early) and supper (very late) in the prison. Not even in his new home did Charles fail to observe the people around him: His new landlord was "a fat, lame old gentleman with a quiet old wife and an innocent grown-up son who was also lame"

(Johnson, p. 37). The trio later became the Garlands in *The Old Curiosity Shop*.

Back in Marshalsea, John did not remain depressed for long. He assumed his usual lordly air, as if instead of being an inmate of the prison, he was actually the warden. The other debtors, most impressed, elected him chairman of the committee that did run their part of the prison. He did a superb job at it, treating with noblesse oblige "everyone from the turnkeys to the humblest inmate" (Johnson, p. 38). Dickens was good at this sort of thing. It was his own affairs that he couldn't manage. In spite of all the odds to the contrary, he blithely announced that things "were looking up." Strangely enough, he was right: His mother died, leaving him a legacy of £450. Thus John Dickens left prison a little over three months after he had entered it.

The Dickenses returned to Camden Town and took up temporary lodging. From there they moved to their shabbiest place yet. For some strange reason, during this period, Dickens was able to resume work at his old job at the navy office. Chesterton noted that Charles, by this time, "was no longer a normal boy, let alone a child. He called his wandering parent the Prodigal Father; and there was something of the same fantastic family inversion in the very existence of so watchful and critical a son. We are struck at once with an almost malicious maturity of satire; some of the best passages of prison life of the Pickwicks and Dorrits occur in private letters about his own early life" (*Britannica* VII, p. 331).

Week after week passed—and still Charles continued in his daily hell. To a child, today is all the time there is; both yesterday and tomorrow are irrelevant and meaningless. Thus to the sad boy, the boot-polish existence appeared to be eternal. But one day his father chanced to come into the factory at a time when Charles and coworker Bob Fagin were racing to see who could tie up the most pots in a short amount of time. Since they were the two fastest boys there, Lamert installed them next to one of the windows (he had moved the company to Covent Garden), so they could attract crowds.

Something about seeing his son in such a public role spoke to the father's pride, or perhaps even appealed to his sense of pity; at any rate, he wrote a zinger of a letter to Lamert. Now that he had a legacy from his mother, he could write such a caustic letter and not get hurt by it. Characteristically, he didn't confront Lamert personally but had his son hand-deliver the letter and thus receive the full, undiluted brunt of Lamert's anger. The upshot was that—to his great joy!—Charles was sent home.

But that was not the end of it, for his mother took an entirely different view of the matter. They needed the extra money, and who knew how long John's navy job would last? So, Elizabeth took it upon herself to go to Lamert and see if she could smooth over the quarrel and have Charles reinstated. She succeeded so well that she brought back an invitation for him to return to work the next day.

For once in his life, however, John Dickens bowed his back: Charles would not go back to that place—instead he would go to school. The battle raged, but father held his ground. Many years later, Dickens drained some of the long-harbored venom he had for his mother by writing these words that even then were wracked with remembered anguish: "I do not write resentfully or angrily, for I know how all these things have worked to make me what I am: but I never afterwards forgot, I never shall forget, I never can forget, that my mother was warm for my being sent back [to the factory]" (Johnson, pp. 39-40).

So deeply was this burning memory buried that neither Dickens' wife nor his children ever heard of it until after he was dead. One thing is unquestionably true. So profound were the effects and so deep the rage, shame, humiliation and raw pain experienced from the four to five months spent at the blacking factory and from the three months his family spent at Marshalsea that these intertwining dark valleys represent the dividing line between the child and the man. Charles was never able to think as a child or act as a child again. He determined that never again was anyone going to have such power over him. Most of his rage resulted from his parents' inability to handle their money wisely.

Up to this time, Charles had loved and respected them, in varying degrees. But now, he, first of all, no longer loved them as unreservedly as he once had; and second, he had lost most of his respect for them—and without respect, love rarely flourishes. Dickens, once he made up his mind on something, rarely looked back, and even more rarely did he change his mind. It was to this crucial watershed of his life that he first fully realized that if he was to become the success he dreamed of being, he could not expect much help from his father; and worse, still, he could not expect any empathy from his mother, the one person from whom he ought to expect the most. And there was no question that if he did not direct his own destiny and control his own earnings versus debt ratio, he would have no more future than his father did.

In essence, this twelve-year-old boy decided, on his own, that from this point forward, he was taking command of his own destiny.

Taking Charge

For a brief period, there was relative peace in Charles' life. His father enrolled him in Wellington House Academy, and there he studied for a couple of years. The school was probably neither better nor worse than most, but in terms of character contributions, Charles was able to add (in part or whole) "the vicious Squeers of *Nicholas Nickleby*, the fuming Creakle, the gentle Nell and the absent-minded Dr. Strong of *David Copperfield*, the murderous

M'Choakumchild of *Hard Times* and the explosively repressed Bradley Headstone of *Our Mutual Friend*" (Kaplan, p.45). The curriculum included Latin, composition, penmanship, geography, arithmetic and French. Oh yes, and the value of money.

Meanwhile, at home, John and Elizabeth continued in the same jovial fiscal irresponsibility and mismanagement. In spite of two bequests, the Dickenses were continually being harassed by creditors, who attached just about everything John Dickens and his family owned. Always, it seemed they were on the run— keeping intact the family record of fleeing to another dwelling about once a year.

Charles was fifteen when his mother, always in need of money, arranged to have him drop out of school and become a law clerk at Ellis and Blackmore. Thus ended his life's formal schooling. Brief though it was, it was more than most children of that time received.

Charles was not impressed with the legal profession. About the only real benefit, resulting from his rather boring job of registering wills, serving processes and carrying documents back and forth, was that he became ever more knowledgeable about every building, byway, and forsaken corner of London. Not only did he study the different sections of the city—from "Tower Hill to the Strand, from Hampton Court to Greenwich—but he also paid careful attention to the people themselves.

> He had seen the drunken revelers staggering home at early dawn and women bringing in baskets of fruit to Covent Garden Market, and long past midnight, watched the baked potato men and kidney-pie vendors closing their stalls in the neighborhood around Marsh Gate, and the Royal Coburg Theatre. "I thought I knew something of the town," said George Lear, remembering their days together at Ellis and Blackmore's, "but after a little talk with Dickens I found that I knew nothing. He knew it all from Bow to Brentford . . . . He could imitate, in a manner that I never saw equaled . . . the low population of the streets of London in all their varieties, whether mere loafers or sellers of fruit, vegetables, or anything else, and, besides these, all the leading actors and popular singers of the day, comic or patriotic."
>
> (Johnson, pp. 47-48)

While all this was happening, John Dickens permanently lost his navy office job; however, on the basis of twenty years of work and six children, he was granted a half-pension. But at forty-one, he couldn't live on that, so he set about learning shorthand; so enthusiastically did he throw himself into this new career that a year later he had become one of the elite Parliamentary Corps (transcribers) for the British Press. Charles was impressed enough with his father's efforts to shell out half a guinea for Gurney's shorthand textbook for himself.

Shorthand was only a tool for advancement, however. Drama, on the other hand, was life itself. Virtually every night found Charles in one of the cheap theater seats somewhere in London—from the major theaters at Covent Garden, Drury Lane and Haymarket, to the "minor" theaters, and besides these, theaters of every possible kind.

Meanwhile, finding his salary frozen at Ellis and Blackmore, Charles moved on to Charles Molloy, a solicitor. But here, too, he was a young man in a hurry. Two months short of his seventeenth birthday, he concluded he could now hold his own with the best shorthand competitor, so he quit Molloy and joined a distant cousin on the Consistory Court of Doctors' Commons. Here he continued the apprenticeship in law that would one day make possible that judicial masterpiece, *Bleak House*, for the Doctors' Commons included "the Admiralty Court; the Prerogative Office, where wills were registered and filed; the Prerogative Court, which dealt with Testamentary matters in the dioceses; the Court of Arches, which was the provincial court of the Archbishop of Canterbury; and the Consistory Court, which was the diocesan court of the Bishop of London" (Johnson, p. 40). Most of Charles' work was for the latter three.

His law apprenticeship represented only one part of Dickens' education. Another was made possible when he reached his eighteenth birthday: Finally he could secure a British Museum's reader's ticket. During the next three to four years, (his real college education), Charles immersed himself in Shakespeare, Addison, Goldsmith, Berges, Symonds and other great thinkers, and he dug deeply into the history of England.

Along the way, he fell hopelessly in love with a bewitching little blonde beauty named Maria Beadnell. He was seventeen, hence still a bit naïve about the world and the odds against his success. Given his low income and her higher station in life (her father was a moderately wealthy banker), he faced stiff odds. Unpropitiously, Dickens' father chose this period to declare insolvency again—not the best son-in-law recommendation to a hard-nosed banker.

Like most immature males of his age, Charles did not really know what he wanted—nay, needed—in a wife. Maria (two years older than he) was everything he should have avoided matrimonially. For one thing, she was too much like his mother: self-centered and frivolous. Though Dickens would obsessively pursue

A Christmas Carol

Maria for four years, clearly there never was much of a chance that her parents would sanction a marriage that socially appeared so undesirable.

Maria was flattered by Dickens' obvious surrender to her charms and his intensely eager courtship; he was also fun, intelligent, widely read, witty, a great conversationalist and a hilarious mimic. All in all, he was a real asset in the parlor room. But she agreed with her parents about the unsuitability of the match.

At a party in 1833, Maria effectively squelched Charles' ardor by referring to him as a boy. "The word scorched my brain," Dickens recalled later (Kaplan, p. 53). Even so, Charles had benefited from his association with her because, in trying to win her, he had worked even harder at moving quickly up the career ladder.

All of his life—perhaps because he got so little from his mother—Charles yearned for love and appreciation. He had an insatiable need to daily be assured that he was worthy of being loved and appreciated. It was not enough that he had been told so yesterday: he had to be told again today!

Perhaps the theater could provide the daily adulation he craved. In March 1832, Charles made an appointment with George Bartley, manager of Covent Garden. In his request for an audition, Charles expressed belief in his gifts: "I have a strong perception of character and oddity and a natural power of reproducing in my own person what I observe in others" (Kaplan, p. 54). Fanny, now an instructor at the Royal Academy, agreed to accompany her brother with his repertoire of comic stories, songs and skits.

But on the day of the audition, Dickens was laid up with a terrible cold—even his face was inflames—so he was unable to audition. Writing Bartley, Charles thanked him and said he would resubmit his application for an audition the following season. In the meantime, he continued to produce and perform in dramatic productions, most often involving his family and friends. His father, now a portly journalist, always reveled in such things: performing as well as watching.

Dickens' final break with coquettish Maria Beadnell took place in May 1833. He would use her in his fiction, however, just as he would use almost everyone with whom the interacted. Dickens would portray Maria as a younger version of his mother: "the prototype of the flighty, self-indulgent coquette whose feelings never run deep enough to know and express real love" (Kaplan p. 57). Kaplan notes that Dickens was attracted equally to two types of women: The Maria type "whose physical beauty and domineering manner attracted him erotically. Pain and pleasure, rejection and acceptance, were closely allied in his emotional life. Against that attraction, against women like Maria and his mother, he needed and antidote, a pure sister, an ideal wife" (Kaplan p. 57).

Dickens had come a long way from the little boy who had reeled from the dual onslaughts of the blacking factory and the imprisonment of the father. But four years of unrequited love for Maria had taken their toll on him—and it did not assuage the bitter pain of rejection to know that, had his family status been higher and his career prospects brighter, she might indeed have become his wife. In fact, twenty-five years later she had the audacity to tell him so. At the very time when the entire Beadnell family began to blow frostily upon his suit, had they only known it and waited a short time, the most famous author in the English-speaking world could have been part of their family.

But there is no question about one thing: Dickens had changed dramatically from the boy he had once been. Had his mother given him the love he so desperately needed, had Maria cared more for him than she did for status, then he might have been able to give a different kind of love than he did to his wife and parents. As it was, the crucible of pain and anguish resulting from a stingy dose of mother love; the insolvency, imprisonment and continual humiliation attendant to his parents' inability to handle money; the terrible spirit-blighting of the blacking factory; and the rejection of the sincerest, purest and most intense romantic love he would have in his lifetime prepared him to write the kind of books that achieve immortality. In November 1834, John Dickens was again arrested for nonpayment of a bill he owed a merchant; at the same time, he admitted to the family that because of nonpayment of the house rent, once again they were being evicted.

Charles concluded it was time to leave home for good.

"Boz"

The stenography expertise started it all. Two years after Charles began that career, he started another one. In 1831, John Henry Barrow, one of his uncles, asked Dickens if he'd be interested in contributing to his magazine, *Mirror of Parliament*, which printed transcripts of political debates much as the *Congressional Record* does today in the United States. Shortly after he began writing for the *Mirror*, Dickens also began to write for the *True Sun* (a liberal paper whose views he normally agreed with). But it was in *Mirror of Parliament* that he experienced the most rapid progress—not only in what he was paid but also in being offered editorial positions.

About this time, the chief secretary of the United Kingdom, Edward Stanley, had given a major speech dealing with conditions in Ireland. In fact, so long was the speech that the *Mirror* had eight reporters assigned to taking it down (with Dickens doing the beginning and the end of it). When the speech appeared in print, Stanley found errors everywhere—except in the first and last parts; he asked Barrow to send the reporter to him who so superbly recorded those parts of his speech. The praise given him by the secretary represented the high point of Dickens' life up to this time.

Parliamentary debate alternated between utter boredom and spine-tingling drama. The next debate after the Irish Coercion Bill became law had to do with the aftermath of Secretary Stanley's Bill for the Abolition of Slavery in the Colonies. During this memorable debate, Dickens recorded young Mr. Gladstone's maiden speech as well as memorable speeches by Edward Bulwer-Lytton, Daniel O'Connell and others.

Although Dickens faithfully and accurately recorded these debates, he was gradually becoming more and more disillusioned with the political process. So much of it was bombast and mere rhetoric—and so little of it improved the lot of the average person.

Along the way, Dickens, having a little extra time on his hands, began to write short fictional sketches based on people he had met and observed in and around London. One night he mailed to the Mirror a sketch satirizing a local politician. Not long after that, Dickens purchased the latest number of the magazine in a Strand bookstore. As he walked out, his heart was pounding: Would his piece have been considered good enough for inclusion? Turning a page, he saw his sketch there in all its glory.

So agitated was he that he walked on and on until he found a place of privacy in Westminster Hall. And there "for half an hour he paced the stone floor 'my eyes so dimmed with pride and joy that they could not bear the street, and were not fit to be seen'" (Johnson, p. 72).

The editor, Captain Holland, liked Dickens' sketch so much that, in the next edition, he asked for the author to submit "more papers" (free, of course). Dickens did so, and five more were published during the following seven months. The earlier sketches carried no author identification, but starting with the August sketch, Dickens attached as his nom de plum "Boz." How did he come up with it? According to Johnson, it "had arisen out of Dickens' jesting nickname for his seven-year-old brother Augustus . . . whose nasal mispronunciation of Moses as 'Boses' was facetiously adapted and shortened to 'Bose' by the time Dickens borrowed it for his own pseudonym: 'Boz was a very familiar household word to me, long before I was an author'" (Johnson, p. 73).

The very same month that "Boz" was born, Dickens had begun work for the *Morning Chronicle*. The editor, John Black, was a scholarly but determined philo-

Introduction

sophical radical. Within only a couple of years—no small thanks to the popularity of Dickens' writing—he was able to increase the daily paper's circulation 600 per-cent—to 66,000, making it second in circulation only to the famed *London Times*. From this time on, Dickens' life became more interesting, as Black had him cover the most significant stories of the day, some taking him as far away as Scotland. By now, Dickens had seen and recorded so much that government offi-cials no longer impressed him—so he felt free to inject humor into stories deal-ing with them. As a case in point: "At another public dinner, when the Earl of Lincoln floundered through a few halting words and resumed his seat in confu-sion, Dickens reported: 'Lord Lincoln broke down, and sat down'" (Johnson, p. 75).

By late 1834, the identity of the increasing popular "Boz" sketches was no longer secret, and Dickens was pointed out as a young man who would go far. But even his £275 salary proved insufficient to cover his and his family's expens-es. It didn't help much that his "prodigal father" had done it again: His recent employers had let him go, and now he owed so much that arrest was imminent. Characteristically, the good man fled, leaving his wife and children to face what-ever music was performed by the creditors. Poor Charles decided that, like it or not, he'd have to step in and salvage something out of the mess. At the consider-able sacrifice and tightening of his own budget, he worked out a solution: For the rest of his life, he would pay his parents' bills.

On January 31, 1835, a far-reaching event occurred, but not for the reason one might expect: The proprietors of the *Morning Chronicle* launched another paper, which they called the Evening Chronicle. George Hogarth, music critic for the morning paper, was chosen as the editor. One of Hogarth's first decisions was to ask Dickens if he would be willing to submit sketches similar to his "Street Sketches." Dickens agreed. Hogarth had been a writer to the Signet (an elite law practitioner) in Scotland and was a friend of Robert Burns and Sir Walter Scott—in fact, his sister had married James Ballantyne, one of Scott's closest business asso-ciates. Hogarth had had his eye on Dickens for some time, so now, with Dickens agreeing to submit twenty sketches during the next seven months, the friendship deepened. Hogarth invited Charles to visit his family at home—not an entirely altruistic gesture, as he had ten children, among whom were three attractive daughters: Catherine (the oldest at nineteen), Mary (at fifteen), and Georgina (at seven). Johnson describes Catherine as being "a pretty girl with a rosy complexion, heavy-lidded blue eyes, and a slightly retroussé nose" (Johnson, p. 78). Kaplan describes the eldest in more detail: "With heavy-lidded eyes and turned-up nose,

Catherine had a becoming tendency to carry her shortness into full-figured plumpness. Though not quick of wit or foot, she was warm, engaging, eager to please and to be pleased and clearly on the marriageable side of adolescence. Unlike Maria [Beadnell], she was not flirtatious or fickle" (Kaplan, pp. 66-67).

Dickens now had more clearly defined marital goals and expectations than had been true when he courted Maria: First of all, he wanted a woman who would consider him to be the center of her life; second, recognizing that he was marrying more than a wife, he wanted her family to provide an intimacy and stability that was lacking in his and, if possible, to also be one in which the world of the mind and the arts was central. Furthermore, having had enough rejection to last a lifetime, he wanted someone who would not be likely to refuse him. All these elements, he found in Catherine (Kate) and the Hogarth family.

Dickens was not at all concerned that Catherine would be incapable of keeping up with him in terms of imaginative thought. He was twenty-three now, and raising rapidly professionally; it was time for him to marry. "With a strong sense of having been deprived of a familial hearth, he used the Hogarths' as the threshold of his own. Marriage to an amiable, conventional, sweet-tempered and domestic woman, who would cooperate with his desire to be master of his own home, to be in control of his life and work, to have compliant, contained and unthreatening sexual relations, to have children with whom to express his own familial needs, was strongly attractive" (Kaplan, pp. 67-68). Charles proposed, and Catherine accepted. As it turned out, in Catherine and the Hogarths, Dickens got everything he wanted. The package was responsible for the explosion of creativity ahead; unfortunately, it was also responsible for a different kind of explosion at the end.

Dickens was sincere in his commitment to Catherine: In return for having a bedrock of faithfulness at home (on which he would build a life, a career, a legacy and an estate), he would be faithful to her. Catherine was correct in her assumption that she—her heart, soul, mind and dreams—was not as central to him as he was to her. But she married him anyway. Dickens leased some rooms next door to the Hogarths and alleviated space constraints with the two families by adding to his household his brother, Fred and her sister, Mary. Charles and Catherine were married at St. Like's Church, Chelsea, on April 2, 1836. Dickens' close friend, Thomas Beard, served as best man.

The ceremony, wedding breakfast and one-week honeymoon to Gravesend Road in the little village of Chalk (near Chatham) were alike—simple. Dickens chose Chalk because it was in Kent, and the site of the only Shangri-La he had ever known. His bride was very different from "the tiny and teasing charmer with enchanting ringlets" Maria Beadnell, for Catherine was "a full-bosomed lass with long, dark hair and a sleepy voluptuousness" (Johnson, p. 89) that perhaps helped account for the fact that she was pregnant before the week was over and would be pregnant—seemingly almost continuously—throughout their marriage. Ten children would survive.

Mary, Catherine's younger sister, idolized her brilliant brother-in-law. She, it turns out, might very well have been the perfect wife for him instead of her more prosaic sister. To Dickens, Mary possessed the ingredients missing in Catherine: intelligence, the ability to understand and empathize with his creative genius, numerous virtues, unquestioned loyalty and budding beauty. "She became," Dickens said, "the grace and life of our home; so perfect a creature . . . never breathed" (Johnson, p. 94). She was the ideal girl-wife.

Meanwhile, exciting things were happening to Dickens. All his life, he would juggle a thousand-and-one projects, manuscripts, involvements, responsibilities and deadlines. At this time, his newspaper and magazine reporting kept him forever on the go—politically, nothing happened that he wasn't a part of, in one way or another.

However, for three years, the "Boz" sketches had been building an audience for him. Late in 1835, Dickens and Beard put together a collection of the best of the sketches and landed George Cruikshank as the artist. That was no mean coup, because Burne Jones, the Rossettis, Sickert, Whistler and others prophesied that Cruikshank would someday be know as the greatest English artist of the nineteenth century.

Although Cruikshank would illustrate only five Dickens books (twenty-four would be illustrated with pictures) out of the nearly 900 he would illustrate over his long and impressive career, both men profited by their brief (1835-1841) association. Today, Cruikshank's fame rests more on his Dickens illustrations than on any others he did. Sadly, their egos eventually wrecked their relationship. Before "Boz," Cruikshank, the idol of millions, was so famous that he was paid not to caricature kings. Though Dickens knew what his characters ought to look like, Cruikshank had his own ideas. A terrific struggle for control ensued. Dickens won, and his star continued to rise; Cruikshank lost, and his star began to sink.

Sketches by Boz: Illustrative of Every-Day Life and Every-Day People was published by John Macrone on February 7, 1836, Dickens' twenty-fourth birthday. In the two volumes were sixteen Cruikshank illustrations. Macrone paid Dickens £150 for all rights; he received no royalties. Copies were sent to VIPs such as Lord (Edward John) Stanley, members of Parliament such as Thomas Noon Talfourd and many editors. While reviews were favorable, the best were Hogarth's and John Forster's (who would become one of Dickens' closest friends). Snatches from these reviews include:

> "He can sympathize with the underpaid milliners' and staymakers' [corsets'] apprentices, and pity the scantily clad ballad singer with the wailing child whose only reward from the passing crowd is 'a brutal laugh at her weak voice.' Such sights, he says, 'will make your heart ache—always supposing,' he bitterly adds, 'that you are neither a philosopher nor a political economist.' Well-bred ladies and gentlemen might do something more generous and useful than recoil from the sixteen-year-old streetwalker whose features are already branded with depravity 'as legibly as if a red-hot iron had seared them' and whose later career 'in crime will be as rapid as the flight of a pestilence . . . in its baneful influence and wide-spreading infection.'"

(Johnson, p. 84)

Such commentary was prophetic, for Dickens would go on to become perhaps the most powerful social critic of the age.

By August, *Sketches* had gone into its second printing, and during 1837 it went through two more. Even more important, the success of the book attracted the attention of two gentlemen whose fortunes would intertwine with those of Dickens: the publishers Edward Chapman and William Hall. They came to him with a proposal: Would he like to collaborate on a project with well-know illustrator Robert Seymour? Seymour, born out of wedlock, was a slightly unbalanced but extremely talented artist, best known for his slashing caricatures of the hunting set—those wealthy Englishmen who had nothing better to do with their time than ride around slaughtering birds and animals.

The project Chapman and Hall had in mind was a series of plates illustrating the adventures and misadventures of the mythical Nimrod Club (a group of amateur sportsmen); the central figure would be "Mr. Nathaniel Winkle." Seymour's sketches would be the meat of the work; Dickens' text would provide pleasing commentary. Several other writers had already turned down the commission before it was offered to Dickens.

But Dickens was no pushover. In fact, he brashly seized control of the project, suggesting that, instead of his writing Seymour-induced commentary, Seymour should illustrate Dickens' prose. And central to his prose would be Pickwick instead of Winkle. The result was more than a bit fun, for Dickens thought

Introduction

Seymour was illustrating his prose and Seymour thought Dickens was describing his art. But there was one serendipity: Seymour did depict *Pickwick* so vividly that he gave him immortality—"made him a reality"—and Dickens' text had given him precious little to go on. As the tug-of-war continued, Seymour, already furious about a non-Dickens-related situation where he had been publicly ridiculed, went over the edge and took his life. Hablôt Knight Browne (known as "Phiz") took over and thereby rose to fame with Dickens on the astounding success of *The Pickwick Papers*. For the rest of Dickens' life, Seymour's widow continued to demand additional recognition and money; he, however, adamantly refused to help her.

Pickwick began life inauspiciously, as Chapman and Hall only gambled 400 copies in the first printing. Subsequent sales continued in the doldrums, and Dickens filled the waiting time with projects such as writing the lyrics for John Braham's "The Village Coquettes." As late as the fourth issue (almost all of Dickens' books were first issued serially), *Pickwick's* sales were still sluggish—but in that fourth installment, Dickens, in a stroke of genius, introduced Sam Weller. By July, interest in *Pickwick* began to build—then it became a torrent, with 40,000 copies sold of every issue. Reviewers now raved about it, and it became the rage of the season.

Johnson notes that "readers in every class of society became Mr. Pickwick's devoted admirers and followed his adventures from month to month with roars of loving laughter" (Johnson, p. 110). Dickens had created a new literary form, a fairy tale that was simultaneously humorous, heroic and realistic. Pickwick was "a beaming fairy godfather to almost all the world, forever rescuing maidens and bestowing them on their true loves, succoring the oppressed, showering even the cheats and petty tricksters with his kindness. His very existence and personality represent[ed] a kind of magic; if not that of an ugly duckling turned into a swan, [than that of] a very foolish goose transformed into an angel in gaiters" (Johnson, p. 110).

By the time the last green-covered number of Pickwick had hit the stands, "they had become a mania. Nothing like it had ever happened before . . . It is doubtful if any other single work of letters has ever aroused such will and widespread enthusiasm. *Barely past the age of twenty-five, Charles Dickens had become world-famous, beaten upon by a fierce limelight which never left him for the remainder of his life*" (Johnson, pp. 110-11, emphasis added).

Olympus

The world was at Dickens' door. The son of an insolvent ne'er-do-well was now the toast of London—and soon, the world! It was a heady feeling for such a young man.

About this time, Charles' marriage to Catherine began to unravel. Had they started out marriage alone—just the two of them—they might have bonded. But with two strangers in the house—Fred and Mary—family member or not, a tension was created that might otherwise not have been there.

While Charles courted Catherine, Mary had become like a sister to him. Apparently, always happy and so helpful she rapidly proved to be indispensable; Mary soon became the joy of the household. Usually, in a marriage a husband and wife need to work through their differences, but, as Johnson points out, a monkey wrench had been thrown into the Dickenses' marital machinery: "When the third member [Fred had left earlier] of the family is a beautiful and adoring young girl who admires her sister's husband beyond measure, it is easy for him to believe that any flaws in the serenity of his home are no fault of his, and it is easy for him, too, without quite realizing that he is doing so, to exalt the younger sister at the expense of the other" (Johnson, p. 97). Exacerbating the situation even more was Catherine's amazing fecundity: The bloating we associate with pregnancy often puts a strain on a marriage, for the wife loses the figure she had before, especially as she nears full-term. If she no sooner delivers one than she becomes pregnant with the next—and a beautiful sister is there to shine in her stead, trouble is likely to result. To his credit, Dickens remained faithful to his wife—that did not turn out to be the problem.

It was a Saturday evening, May 7, 1837, and Dickens' new comedy, *Is She His Wife?* was being performed in the St. James Theatre. Mary never looked lovelier than she did that night as she leaned "her sweet face" over the edge of the box. The play had to do with two intertwining young marriages that weren't going well—certainly reflected by lines such as, "how little did I think when I married you six months [ago] that I should be exposed to so much wretchedness," and "If you are perpetually yawning and complaining of ennui a few months after marriage, what am I to suppose you'll become in a few years?" (Kaplan, p. 93). The marital bickering at home must have come to mind as Mary watched the drama unfold—though not, perhaps, as bad as to warrant Dickens' contention many years later that "Mary . . . understood . . . in the first months of our marriage 'that the marriage was as miserable a one as ever was'" (Kaplan, p. 93).

After the performance was over, they returned home. Soon after midnight, Mary became violently ill. Doctors were called in, and the Hogarths came from next door. Mrs. Hogarth was almost hysterical with fear. The doctors concluded that Mary had a weakened heart and had experienced a stroke. Charles, Catherine and Mrs. Hogarth stayed with her all night. Sunday afternoon, Charles administered some brandy to Mary as he held her in his arms. Before sinking into a gentle sleep, she whispered to him, and her very last words were of him, he later wrote. She died at three that afternoon. "The light and life of our happy circle . . . passed quietly away to an immortality of happiness and joy," wrote Dickens. Catherine was more succinct: "I never saw her look so lovely and the next [day] she was dead'" (Kaplan, p. 93).

Mary's death almost destroyed Dickens, for she had indeed been the light of their lives. Pickwick came to an absolute halt—in fact, Dickens could not write a word. It was the only time in his life that he was incapable of meeting a deadline. Three months pregnant, Catherine miscarried.

As for Dickens, he never completely recovered from his sister-in-law's death. To him, it was just another form of rejection: The first had been his mother's maternal rejection; and the second, Maria Beadnell's romantic rejection. "Idealized as the female who genuinely loved him and whom he could trust, Mary had been elevated into the perfect sister; She had sympathized 'with all my thoughts and feelings more than anyone I knew ever did or will'" (Kaplan p. 94). Significantly, Kaplan notes that the "faultless Mary had been a better mother, a better sister, an alternative Catherine, a completion of Catherine, adding insight, sympathy and intelligent understanding" (Kaplan, p. 94).

The terrible downside for the stricken Catherine, had she fully realized it, was that her sister would prove to be a far greater rival in death than she ever could have been had she lived and gotten older, for she was frozen at maximum beauty and perfection—for all time. Now nothing Catherine could ever say, do or be could possibly compare with the image Dickens retained in his heart and mind of this lost sister.

It is a measure of his grief that Dickens worded Mary's tombstone as he did:

MARY SCOTT HOGARTH
Died 7th May 1837
Young, Beautiful, and Good
God in His Mercy
Numbered Her with His Angels
At the Early Age of
Seventeen

For years, Dickens hoped that when he died, he might be buried with her.

The memory of Mary would powerfully affect the books Dickens wrote. A good example of this is *Oliver Twist*, which Dickens began five months before Mary died, the same month his first son, Charles Culliford Boz Dickens, was born. *Oliver* (published in 1839) was, in fact, the first book in which he came up with a plot before he wrote the story. Most of it was written in the year and a half after Mary's death and is extremely autobiographical. It was a voyage in which Dickens traced his own pattern of early and continual rejection; in his fiction, this rejection is usually portrayed in the person of an orphan (Oliver, Pip, Little Nell, David Copperfield, Ester Summerson) or a child who has lost one parent (Nicholas Nickleby, Florence Dombey, Amy Dorrit). Oliver's mother, unlike his own, dies in childbirth, "young, beautiful, and good"—to Dickens, the perfect expression of unqualified love (Kaplan, p. 96).

About a year after Mary's death, Dickens introduced the beautiful seventeen-year-old Rose Maylie into *Oliver Twist.* She represents Dickens' lost angelic sister; too good, too sweet, too pure, to be long for this earth. Yet, in the end, Dickens cannot let Rose go and lets her live instead. As Johnson puts it: "When he was drawing near the end of *Oliver Twist,* he found himself unable to carry out his original intention of having Rose Maylie die. He could not bear to describe the fair young creature breathing her last amid the blossoms of May" (Johnson, p. 127).

But *Oliver Twist* is far more than a memorial to Mary—and a far cry from rollicking *Pickwick*—for in it, for the first time, Dickens moves in his biggest reform guns, aimed primarily at England's antiquated and inhumane Poor Law and at the heartbreaking conditions endured by those forced to exist in London's appalling slums. The book does have comedy, but it is a comedy that bites. Johnson points out that it took courage for Dickens to abandon a sure thing in Pickwick and follow up that lighthearted book with such a somber, bitter and serious portrayal of the darker side of urban life. In *Oliver Twist,* Dickens hit his stride, for the readers loathed Fagin and Sikes with all the intensity that they had loved Pickwick and Weller.

G. K. Chesterton notes that Oliver is "not only the first of [Dickens'] nightmare novels, but also the first of his social tracts." And that, furthermore, Dickens was already showing his mastery of unforgettable lines, such as "in that intolerable repetition throbbing in the murderer's ears: 'will wash out mud-stains, blood-stains'" (*Britannica* VII, p. 332). Oliver Twist was the first book for which Dickens used his own name. From then on, his real name and "Boz" were used interchangeably.

For some time, Dickens had been gathering his forces for an attack on Yorkshire schools. Though they claimed to be offering a quality education at bargain prices, in reality they were "notorious for negligence, cruelty and pedagogical incompetence" (Johnson, p. 137). Other "schools" were actually dead-end hellholes for illegitimate and other unwanted children. Dickens gathered information for this book by traveling under an assumed name and doing on-the-spot research. Titled *Nicholas Nickleby*, the book sold 50,000 copies on the first day it appeared in print.

Interestingly enough, *Nicholas Nickleby* was a synthesis of *Pickwick* and Oliver: According to Chesterton, "Pickwick has a prevailing tint of gaiety and *Oliver Twist* of gravity, not to say grimness; but with *Nicholas Nickleby* (1839) we have the new method, which is like a pattern of light and dark stripes" (*Britannica* VII, p. 333). "Vain, ineffectual and verbally comic" Mrs. Nickleby, by the way, is patterned after Dickens' own mother (Kaplan, p. 119).

Chesterton also notes that, though the book has major weaknesses in it, it is saved by the marvelous characters with whom Dickens peoples it—for example, Vincent Crummles, Miss Snevellici and her "incomparable" father and Mr. Mantalini.

Off and on during his life, Dickens turned back to the format of a magazine, in order to broaden his financial net even more. (He had signed a lucrative agreement with Chapman and Hall, having learned much about his marketability, since his naïve beginning when he'd take what ever was offered.) In 1840, Dickens started a new weekly magazine titled *Master Humphrey's Clock*. Although sales started briskly, they dropped off precipitously when readers discovered there was no ongoing serialized story. In order to recapture them, in June of that year, Dickens began a new novel, *The Old Curiosity Shop*. It was a sentimental age, and Dickens took full advantage of that fact with this particular book. Little Nell became one of his most famous characters, both in England and in the United States. As the story progressed and Dickens neared her probable death, readers became more and more apprehensive, begging him to not let her die. And he, remembering again the death of Mary, found it difficult to continue the story.

The Old Curiosity Shop has much to say about nineteenth-century greed and speculation—especially on the stock exchange. Thanks to the tear-inducing addition of this story, *Master Humphrey's Clock* came back to life again. As it neared its end, up to 100,000 copies of each issue were being sold.

Kaplan notes that Little Nell's improvident grandfather is yet another in a long line of failed fathers in Dickens' fictional gallery. As a result, the orphaned Little Nell is forced to father her grandfather and to become both mother and father to herself, mirroring Dickens' own childhood.

Meanwhile, much had been happening in Dickens' personal life. His closest circle of companions now included writers such as John Forster, Thomas Carlyle,

Lord Edward Bulwer-Lytton, William Makepeace Thackeray, Wilkie Collins, Leigh Hunt and Harrison Ainsworth; artists such as John Leech, George Cruikshank, Daniel Maclise, Hablôt Knight Browne; actors such as William Charles Macready and Walter Savage Landor; journalist such as Thomas Beard, William Henry Wills and Mark Lemon; and politicians such as Thomas Noon Talfourd and Charles and Edward Landseer.

At home, life was generally serene. By the mid-1830s, his parents had only their youngest, Augustus, at home. As for his mother, according to Kaplan, by the early 1840s, "she balanced matriarchal stoutness with some affectations of youthfulness, particularly 'the juvenility of her dress' and her semi-comic confusions of speech. Her son described her wardrobe as 'the attempt of a middle-aged mutton to dress itself lamb fashion'" (Kaplan, pp. 118-121). Although he frequently had his folks over for dinner on Sundays and holidays, Dickens kept his emotional distance from his mother.

As for his father—much as he loved him, Dickens was often enraged by his finding ever new ways of trading on his son's fame in order to secure extra transfusions of money. Occasionally, father and son would endure stormy sessions, scenes in which his father played the role of the prodigal son. Dickens accurately described his father as 'an optimist—he was like a cork—if he was pushed under water in one place, he always bobbed up to time cheerfully in another, and felt none the worse for the dip'" (Kaplan, p. 103). Finally, reaching the end of the proverbial rope, Dickens decided to exile the "governor" and his lady to an attractive little house in the beautiful but quiet countryside of Alphington, near Exeter. Dickens gave them an allowance that should have covered all their needs. For them, though, who were by now a bit afraid of their famous son, it seemed like rejection and the remote location like an exile. "For him, it was self-protection with a touch of revenge" (Kaplan, p. 105).

As Dickens' own family grew, he periodically moved them to larger quarters. In March 1838, his first daughter was born—he named her Mary (Mamie) Hogarth Dickens; eighteen months later, Catherine (Katey) Macready Dickens followed her. Catherine usually had tough pregnancies and was often ill during and after them. Her sister's death had deeply affected her, and for a long time afterward, she was in a deep depression. After her daughter Mary's birth in 1838, she was "alarmingly ill" for some time. But the children kept coming: Walter Savage Landor Dickens came next, in 1841.

Every summer, Dickens would take his family to the seaside (to towns like Brighton and Broadstairs), to the country or across the Channel to the

Introduction

Continent. These vacations were not just for the immediate family; they often included extended family and friends as well.

Back in London, Dickens was involved in many clubs: the Trio Club, the Cerberus Club, the Shakespeare Club, the Parthenon Club, the Garrick, the Athenaeum Club and so on. Founded in 1824, the Athenaeum Club invited only the elite to its membership: the leading scholars, men of letters, artists, along with such men as Macready and Charles Darwin. Thackeray had to wait until he was forty to be invited in, Browning until he was fifty-six.

In June 1841, Dickens and Catherine traveled to her native Edinburgh, where he was treated like a monarch at a public banquet. He was introduced as "perhaps the most popular author now alive" (Kaplan, p. 113). After dinner, Catherine led 200 ladies to the gallery to hear the toasts and speeches. It was so crowded that people were turned away. "As Dickens came through the door, and entered the hall, the orchestra struck up, to 'tumultuous applause' and 'shouts of delight,' the popular music-hall song, 'Charley Is my Darling'" (Kaplan, p. 116). The rest was a royal progress.

In his negotiations with publishers, illustrators and other members of the literary field, Dickens developed into a shrewd and almost brutal bargainer. According to Johnson, Dickens never surrendered even the smallest point to his adversary. In his obsession to win, he was relentless. This iron-gloved determination would make him the wealthiest writer in the British Empire—but it would also make him unnecessary enemies and bring him great sorrow.

Twisting the Sword

The Old Curiosity Shop was followed by *Barnaby Rudge* in 1841. This book was Dickens' first attempt at historic fiction. It's also unique in that it is considered to be the first detective novel. Closest perhaps to Scott's *The Heart of Midlothian*, it deals with the historic Gordon riots and the burning of the Newgate Prison by an infuriated mob. Dickens treated his protagonist Lord George Gordon, whom he drew from English history, better than many felt he deserved. Describing the writing process, Johnson notes that "as his imagination plunged into the surging tumults of the riots themselves, Dickens' emotions boiled up in a strange turmoil. Fear and horror of the ferocities of mob violence struggled with his fierce sympathy for the wrongs of the oppressed rising like fiends to avenge themselves in destruction. He obviously shared with the rioters an orgiastic joy in the flaming demolition of Newgate amid clamor and smoke. He shuddered and at the same time he exulted in this overflow of authority" (Johnson, p. 183).

A Christmas Carol

Coloring the picture, undoubtedly, was the image of Marshalsea Prison staining his childhood. The actual riots of 1780 were the historical basis for the story, but his contemporary readers saw in it current events—such as the deep industrial depression, the Chartist movement for universal suffrage and equal representation in Parliament, the riots of Welsh miners in 1839, the empty cotton mills and their jobless workers walking the streets and the entire north of England on a great strike that was dispersed only by troops firing point-blank into the crowds.

But in this book, Dickens was doing more than merely entertaining. He had just read "with anger and horror" the report of the Children's Employment Commission, which gave accounts of dark mining tunnels reeking with poisoned air, in which seven-year-old children were chained to heavy carts and brutally forced to drag them; of "girls clad only in ragged trousers working in the dark, often up to their knees in water and carrying heavy loads of coal up steep ladders a distance exceeding the height of St. Paul's Cathedral; of dreadful accidents constantly occurring; of deformed and stunted boys toiling fourteen hours a day, fed on offal, struck with bars, burned by showers of sparks from red-hot iron, pulled by the ears until the blood ran down: (Johnson, pp. 184-85).

Barnaby Rudge is grimly prophetic, and in it Dickens tells England's power brokers that unless they voluntarily make reforms now, it will later prove too late as they are swept away in a tidal wave of blood à la French Revolution.

Now occurred an event of far-reaching significance: In 1842, Dickens decided to visit the United States. Catherine went with him. He was thirty years old and as famous in America as he was in England. However, the United States caused Dickens to grind his teeth in frustration because of the nation's refusal to honor international copyright laws and pay him royalties. Beginning in 1834, pirated editions of Dickens' books had begun to be sold in immense quantities in America. He was hopeful, however, that the United States would prove to be a utopia, a community of friends, a model of Christian rhetoric put into everyday practice. In short, everything England was not. Dickens and Washington Irving had been corresponding for some time, so they both looked forward to meeting each other. Dickens hoped Irving would guide him to the nation's most congenial thought-leaders.

All of America turned out to honor Dickens, and he was besieged by fans wherever he went. He quickly discovered that Americans, unlike the English, neither understood nor respected personal space. In fact, Dickens felt more like a captured lion than an honored quest. The newspapers sensationalized his every move. "Soon he felt so beset, waylaid, hustled, sat upon, beaten about, trampled down, mashed, bruised and pounded by crowds" that he felt everything was out of control (Kaplan, p. 127).

While Dickens was sitting for a portrait in Boston, "ladies pressed into the studio to stare at him until Dickens bolted for the door, only to be mobbed there and forced to retreat and lock himself within. When hunger obliged him to emerge for lunch they were still besieging the doorway and surged about him instantly again, clinging to him while they furtively snipped bits of fur from his [buffalo] coat as souvenirs and filling the passage with a soprano clamor of adulation" (Johnson, pp. 202-203).

Letters poured into such an extent that within three days, Dickens had to hire a secretary, George W. Putnam. Even while eating, Dickens would sign autographs. Though he never turned down a request for an autograph, "he drew the line at gratifying the numerous young ladies who wanted locks of his hair" (Johnson, p. 203).

Dickens initially planned to write a positive book on Americans and the United States. He was most impressed by the Perkins Institute for the Blind—especially that the children were not forced to wear ugly uniforms. And he was "deeply moved by the loving success with which Dr. Samuel Gridley Howe and his helpers taught blind, deaf and dumb children how to communicate with their fellows and develop into intelligent and cheerful human beings. He was strongly impressed by the use of kindness and of occupational therapy in the State Hospital of the Insane" (Johnson, p. 205). Especially did he note the thoughtful touch of potted plants in the windows. Longfellow and Charles Sumner personally conducted him on a walking tour of Boston, visiting the waterfront, Paul Reverie's house and the Bunker Hill monument; and before parting, Longfellow invited Dickens to breakfast with him at the Craigie House the following Friday.

Determined to see more of the United States than just Boston and New York, Dickens set out on a hectic trip through rural America. He began by taking the train to Philadelphia, Baltimore and Washington. Along the way, he was appalled at American hygiene—or, rather, the lack of it—especially the widespread habit of spitting saliva and tobacco juice into spittoons, but not caring too much where the nasty stuff landed. The sides of trains tended to be speckled with spit much as if a monstrous flock of birds had paid their compliments. And whenever the train stopped, heads popped in, "bawling out, 'Is Mr. Dickens here?'" (Johnson, p.209). During Dickens' New York stay, Irving came down the Hudson and hauled him up to his Tarrytown estate, Sunnyside; William Cullen Bryant was there, too.

Used to fresh air and milder winters, Dickens had a tough time dealing with overheated interiors, for Americans evidently didn't believe in opening windows during the winter. Franklin stoves were everywhere, heating rooms to a most uncomfortable level for the British couple.

In Baltimore, Dickens had a long chat with Edgar Allen Poe. In Washington—which the British had burned almost to the ground thirty years earlier—Dickens met Henry Clay, former president John Quincy Adams and Daniel Webster; he also had a private audience with President Tyler. To Dickens' disgust, even in the White House, visitors picked their teeth and constantly spat tobacco juice on the carpet.

In the South, Dickens felt as if he were in prison because of the treatment of slaves. He could hardly wait to get away from that region. Going west, Dickens and his wife took the train twelve miles outside of Baltimore, where the track ended. From there, the couple traveled by stagecoach or steamboat. At Harrisburg, they boarded a canal boat, headed to Pittsburgh, then took a steamboat to Cincinnati; from there, they went to St. Louis, Missouri; to Cairo, Illinois; then north to Toronto, Montreal, and Quebec. At the end of 1842, they stood by Niagara Falls, of which Dickens rhapsodized: "This great place . . . the most wonderful and beautiful in the world" (Kaplan, pp. 136-139). On one leg of the journey, poor Catherine was showered all night with flying tobacco spittle from a well-dressed man sitting next to them. Dickens decided they could not handle another experience like that, so at Columbus, he hired a carriage just for them. This form of transportation proved to be not much of an improvement. The roads were rough, and the Dickenses were constantly being tossed into the roof of the carriage, slammed against the sides and ignominiously heaved onto the floor. As for Catherine, she was unmoved by most things—except the bedbugs—and even Niagara Falls, to her, was only so much water.

Then it was back to New York, via stagecoach, steamboat and railroad. From there, they boarded a ship for home, having been gone half a year. "On shipboard, [Dickens] played perpetually on an accordion that he had bought in March and on which every night he had played 'Home Sweet Home' as they had traveled through America" (Kaplan, p. 142).

On the way home, Dickens realized that he had not won the victory over the greedy interests that were against copyright reciprocity with England. In fact, it would not be until twenty-one years after his death that the United States, kicking and screaming, finally joined the larger world community and began paying authors royalties.

Just before leaving Montreal, Dickens had written Forster: "As the time draws nearer, we get FEVERED with anxiety for home . . . Kiss our darlings for us. We shall soon meet, please God, and be happier and merrier than ever we were, in all our lives . . . Oh home—home—home—home—home—home HOME!!!!!!!!!!!!" (Johnson, p. 235).

Once home, they were engulfed by the children, and Dickens spent hour after hour playing games with them, rocking the younger ones on his knee—in a rocker he brought over from the United States—and singing silly songs to them.

A parting gift in America had been Timber Doodle, a little white Havana spaniel. When he reached home, Dickens renamed the dog "Snittle Timberry" and gave each of the children a loony name, too: Charley became "Flaster Floby," a corruption of "Master Toby"; to her infinite amusement, quiet little Mamie he dubbed "Mild Glo'ster"; fiery-tempered Katey became "Katey Lucifer Box"; and baby Walter, because of high cheekbones, was christened "Young Skull."

Then Dickens went to work on American Notes, his account of and reactions to the United States and Americans. Most of the book was Boz-like: a series of impressions. Dickens minced no words about the things he didn't like—especially slavery and the copyright pirating. Friends were concerned about the reception such a book might receive—as well they should have been, knowing Dickens' tendency, once opposed on something, to bull-headedly do it anyway. They were afraid that Americans, still being new to the family of nations, would be thin-skinned about his criticism.

Longfellow arrived for a visit and had a wonderful time with everyone—especially the children (who loved him) and the Dickenses' "pet" raven, Grip, "a talkative and rambunctious bird . . . who alarmed the children and lady visitors by pecking at their ankles" (Johnson, p. 175). The bird served as a model for his namesake in *Barnaby Rudge*. When Grip died, Dickens wrote some of his friends about the last touching moments: "A bird fancier was first called in to administer a powerful dose of castor oil. The next morning, much better, Grip 'so far recovered his spirits as to be able to bite the groom severely.' But he had a relapse, in which he talked to himself incoherently. 'On the clock striking twelve he appeared slightly agitated, but he soon recovered, walked twice or thrice along the coach-house, stopped to bark, staggered, exclaimed Halloa old girl (his favorite expression) and died'" (Johnson, p. 240).

While the Dickenses had been gone, Catherine's youngest sister, Georgina (now fifteen), had spent a lot of time with the children. So much did they rave about her and clamor for her that she was invited to become part of the family, just as Mary had been—and she quickly proved herself indispensable to all.

At the same time that he was wrestling with *American Notes*, Dickens was trying to bring his next novel to life. He had a terrible time finding just the right name for the book and its hero: "Sweezleden," "Sweezlewag," "Chuzzletoe," "Chuzzleboy," "Chubblewig" and Chuzzlewig were considered and discarded en route to "Martin Chuzzlewit."

As originally conceived, there was a theme of selfishness and the vices that are spawned by it—and, in spite of the book's many turns and twists, that theme remained a constant. Johnson feels that "the vast gallery of multiple perspectives on selfishness is dazzling—young Martin, thoughtless and self-indulgent; his domineering grandfather; an entire tribe of snapping, snarling, greedy Chuzzlewits, salivating for the family fortune; hypocritical and pontifical Pecksniff; the brassily glittering swindler Trigg Montague; the fraudulent land speculator Zephaniah Scadder; . . . the menacing frontier bully, Hannibal Chollop" and so on, make this an incredibly riveting saga (Johnson, pp. 242-243). But the two characters that really run away with the story are "the snuff-stained and feisty Sairey Gamp and the bland and unctuous Pecksniff" (Johnson, p. 244).

Despite the concerns, *American Notes*, sold like wildfire on both sides of the Atlantic. In New York, 50,000 sold in two days, and in Philadelphia, 3,000 sold in thirty minutes. Reviews were mixed: Many thought Dickens' picture of America was too harsh.

In contrast to *American Notes*, the British sales for Chuzzlewit were sluggish. Since American Notes was selling well in the United States, Dickens decided to hurl Chuzzlewit across the water to American and leave him there to see if he could thereby help to sell more books in England.

If certainly appeared that Dickens was biting the hand that had fed and entertained him in that new nation. *American Notes* was bad enough, but to stir in the ugly greed of *Chuzzlewit* was twisting the sword in the wound with a vengeance. In the United States, the book aroused a veritable firestorm of fury. Even though Dickens had expected to stir the Americans up, he had not expected such virulence or outrage. All he had done in *Chuzzlewit* was to portray American culture as "essentially materialistic, immoral, greedy, hypocritical and debased" (Kaplan, p. 157). Surely they couldn't be upset over a little thing like that?

But there was another part of the fallout from the sluggish British sales of *Chuzzlewit* that was rather sad. In an unwise moment, William Hall groused about the low sales and muttered something about maybe reducing Dickens' royalties proportionally. Always thin-skinned about money, Dickens, upon hearing Hall's remark, began to think of changing publishers, which he did after *A*

Christmas Carol was out. Though Chapman and Hall had always been fair to Dickens, and the three men had become dear friends, Dickens would not return to them for sixteen years. To Dickens, friendship came second in any business deal. There was more than a little of Chuzzlewit in his own dealings.

During all these years, Dickens reveled in his family. He loved to celebrate, and his joie du vivre was most infectious. For instance, he put on a big celebration each year, tying in his oldest son's birthday, Christmas and Twelfth Night with a professionally done extravaganza of "charades, magic shows, pantomimes and elaborate amateur theatricals." Since Dickens loved to dance, dancing was very much a part of the agenda as well. And no Twelfth Night celebration was complete without Dickens putting on a magic show, with Forster playing the straight man.

Itchy Feet

It is indeed ironic how sometimes the work we put into the "smaller" projects during life turns out, in retrospect, to be the most significant. After *Chuzzlewit's* sales refused to rise, Dickens needed money, and he cast about for a quick way to earn some. *A Christmas Carol* was the result. The irony comes from the inescapable fact that if every other story he wrote should fall out of favor, *Carol* would survive.

Strangely enough, at the time Dickens wrote *Carol*, the old Christmas traditions were on the decline and actually in danger of being lost. Dickens has been credited with almost single-handedly bringing them back (Hearn, p. 1).

The year 1843 was a strange time in Dickens' life to have written such a Christmas book: The American tour had not been a success; even less so—at least in terms of readership and critical response—had been the slashing anti-American attacks in *American Notes* and *Chuzzlewit;* to say nothing of the undeniable fact that the latter represented the first significant ebb in book success for Dickens in quite a few years. For the first time, he had to face the possibility that he might have peaked and that the rest of his life would be all downhill. His family expenses were high—and now Catherine was pregnant again, with their fifth child.

But Dickens' life and career had one constant: He never ceased caring. Especially did he care about the poor, the downtrodden, the disadvantaged and the children. On October 5, 1843, he had shared the Athenaeum stage with the man who would go on to become one of the British Empire's greatest prime ministers: Benjamin Disraeli. The subject of the day was the poor and the need for education. The audience's applause was so enthusiastic and supportive that Dickens couldn't get the subject out of his head. Wasn't there some way he could do more?

During a three-day visit to Manchester, Dickens' mind kept returning to want and ignorance. One evening, en route to an appointment, the story concept of *A Christmas Carol* was born. Hearn notes that "on his return home, this inspiration so possessed him that over the book's writing he 'wept and laughed and wept again, and excited himself in a most extraordinary manner in the composition; and thinking whereof he walked about the back streets of London, fifteen and twenty miles many a night, when all sober folks had gone to bed: (Hearn, pp. 8-9).

For the root of the story, Dickens relied on his own earlier narrative, "The Goblins Who Stole a Sexton," wherein Gabriel Grub, a mean-spirited gravedigger, is taken by goblins to their den, and there they reveal to him, through panoramic imagery, how Christmas really ought to be observed. Dickens borrows, too, from his Christmas writings in *Pickwick Papers* and *Sketches by Boz.*

But Carol moves on from there into uncharted waters. The theme Dickens articulates, and which he never lets the reader forget, is that Christmas "is a time of all others, when Want is keenly felt, and Abundance rejoices" (Hearn, p. 13). In this story, finally Dickens had a vehicle for an appeal to the people of England on behalf of the poor man's child.

Having chosen the theme, Dickens created Scrooge next; in his boyhood state—even to the books he loves—Scrooge is Dickens himself. The pathos of Tiny Tim, Dickens drew from those in his own family who had died as children or teenagers. The Ghost of Christmas Present clearly articulates the plight of children in mines and schools like the ones in Yorkshire that Dickens had studied firsthand.

As momentum increased, Dickens dropped everything else in his obsession to stay with his characters—for his characters were every bit as real to him as any friends or loved ones in actual life. For a month and a half, he lived, slept and dreamed the story, delivering it to Chapman and Hall in mid-November. Apparently, neither partner was optimistic about potential sales for the book, so they proposed a cheap edition. In the end, Dickens decided to take all the risks himself, including the cost of the illustrations (color and black-and-white). Compounding the earnings problem, Dickens insisted that the lovely little book (russet binding, stamped in gold, colored endpapers, gilt edges and the title page printed in two colors) be sold for only five shillings so it would be available to everyone.

A question some might ask is this: What effect did finishing the book have on Dickens himself? According to Hearn, "At the completion of the manuscript, the Christmas fervor still burned within him, and when the holidays did arrive, he celebrated them with an exuberance that his friends (including Forster, Thackeray and Carlyle) had not witnessed before. 'Such dinings, such dancing, such conjurings, such blind-man's bluffings, such theatre-goings, such kissingsout-of-old-years and kissings-in-of-new-ones, never took place in these parts before,' he wrote Felton" (Hearn, p. 14).

He did not have long to wait for the reading public's verdict: The sales were tremendous—on Christmas Day alone, 6,000 copies were sold. Reviewers were kind as well. Edgar Johnson summed up the book's philosophy in these words: "Dickens insists that no way of life is sound or rewarding that leaves out men's need of loving and being loved. A Christmas Carol is a serio-comic parable of social redemption, and Scrooge's conversion is the conversion for which Dickens hopes among mankind" (Johnson, p. 257).

Because of the double whammy of a luxurious book for a pauper's price, Dickens' original profits were almost nil—and he badly needed the money. He was devastated. His entire earnings for his first Christmas season added up to only £726.

Having established the Christmas genre, during the next few years, Dickens followed Carol up with *The Chimes* (1844), *The Cricket on the Hearth* (1845), *The Battle of Life* (1846) and *The Haunted Man* (1848). The second and third titles did well; the last two considerably less so. But Dickens was never again to write a Christmas story anywhere near as powerful as the story of Scrooge and Marley.

Eventually, the combination of the trip to America, changing publishers (to Bradbury and Evans) and undulating sales, plus the itch to try something new, all combined to give Dickens the worst case of wanderlust yet. Then, too, pirates really moved in on *Carol*. Dickens took them to court, but lost money, as most of the culprits merely folded and ran away with their earnings. As a result, Dickens tended, in the future, to just bite his lip and let it go when other unscrupulous publishers stole from him.

Frances Jeffrey Dickens was born in January 1844. By now, Dickens was complaining about the regularity with which new mouths and appetites arrived at his door, and he blamed poor Catherine: "I hope my missus won't do so never more" (Kaplan, p. 158). He never seemed to feel it necessary to acknowledge that he might have had a tad to do with this increase himself.

So, they decided to go to Italy. The caravan consisted of (according to Dickens):

1. The inimitable Boz;
2. The other half ditto;
3. The sister of ditto ditto;
4. Four babies, ranging from two years and a half to seven and a half;
5. Three women servants, commanded by Anne of Broadstairs. [The baby (the fifth child) was added to the party at the last minute.] (Johnson, p. 266)

On July 2, 1844, the entourage set out, complete with Snittle Timberry, barking excitedly. Dickens was in high spirits, like a boy out of school and delighted to be leaving society. He was "aweary of it, despise[d] it, hate[d] it and reject[ed] it" (Johnson, p. 269). Other than that, society was fine.

Once across the Channel, Dickens secured a behemoth of a coach for £45. Soon it, with the Dickens' entourage inside, was on the way to Paris. Describing it, he wrote Forster: "Let me see—it is about the size of your library; with night-lamps and day-lamps and pockets and imperials and leathern cellars and the most extraordinary contrivances" (Johnson, p. 269). Their passage caused all the excitement a 100-cannon windjammer would generate in a quiet harbor. The eleventh day out saw them on a grimy vessel crossing the Rhone.

Arriving at Marseilles, their carriage was hoisted to the deck of the *Marie Antoinette* "amid a Vesuvius of Profanity" as it bumped against everything around it (Johnson, p. 271). In time, they disembarked at Genoa and were dismayed at the filth and stench of the streets. Since the streets were narrow and their carriage wasn't, it was forever scraping or jamming. At last they came to their long-anticipated palazzo: "an archway with a rusty and sagging gate opening on a rank, dull, weedy courtyard attached to a building that looked, Dickens reflected, like a pink jail. His heart sank. This 'lonely, rusty, stagnant old staggerer of a domain' was the Villa de Bella Vista! (Johnson, p. 272).

The next day, they discovered that if you didn't shut the lattice blinds—which took away your view of the Mediterranean—"the sun would drive you mad; and after sunset the window had to be shut, 'or the mosquitoes would tempt you to suicide'" (Johnson, p. 273). They survived Villa de Bella Vista (Villa of the Beautiful View) until late September, when they moved to the Palazzo Peschiere (Palace of Fishponds), which had seven fountains, each with fish. Inside was the grand sala, fifty feet high, and two bedrooms larger than any in Windsor Castle. It was a veritable wonderland for the children to play in.

In this idyllic setting, Dickens continued to cast around for a story line. Suddenly, it seemed as if all the church bells of Genoa were clanging at once. Thus was born his second Christmas book, *The Chimes,* a story pleading for charity and justice for the dead-end poor.

Upon completing the manuscript in November, Dickens decided to deliver it personally to his publisher in England. Leaving his family behind, he traveled to Parma, Bologna—and then Venice, which dazzled him as had few wonders during his lifetime: "The wildest visions of the Arabian Nights are nothing to the Piazza of Saint Mark and the first impression of the inside of the church. The gorgeous and wonderful reality of Venice is beyond the fancy of the wildest dreamer" (Johnson, p. 281).

From there he went to Milan, across the Alps by moonlight, through Paris, and across the Channel to England again. After seeing that his manuscript was in good hands, Dickens took a ship to Genoa and was back with his family in time for Christmas.

Dickens was not to find writing as easy in Italy as in noisy, turbulent London. They decided to travel some more. Upon seeing Rome, Dickens initially was not impressed—but then he saw the Coliseum, and from that time on, he began to fall under the spell of the Eternal City. Later, the Dickenses moved on to Naples; they climbed Vesuvius and looked down into the boiling cauldron. By mid-June, they were back in England again, complete with a manuscript titled "Pictures from Italy."

Alfred D'Orsay Tennyson Dickens was born on October 28, 1845; both the Count D'Orsay and Tennyson were there, godfathering the christening celebration.

But Dickens' dry spell continued—in fact, it was one of the longest of his career. During these years, he and his family traveled some more throughout Europe, but the muse seemed gone from him. Finally, in Lausanne, on June 28, 1846, Dickens was able to write Forster and tell him the good news: BEGAN DOMBEY! He began it with a determination to use it as a vehicle for getting back his audience. Because of that goal, he didn't take chances: He incorporated into the plot only what had heretofore worked for him. Chesterton puts it this way: "[I]t has very much the character of the winding up of an old business, like the winding up of the Dombey firm at the end of it. It is as comic as the earlier books were comic, and no praise can be higher; it is as conventional as the earlier plots were conventional, and never really pretended to be anything else" (*Britannica* VII, p. 334).

Dombey represents the first time Dickens chose the protagonist from the aristocracy rather than from the people. It bridges back to *Chuzzlewit* in that the story reveals that the power of love is ultimately greater than the power of money. Dombey is a powerful symbol of the money-centered society Dickens knew and the belief that money can buy everything.

Captain Cuttle and Mr. Toots are among the great portraits in the book. Florence Dombey, like Ruth Pinch in Chuzzlewit, is another reincarnation of the loving spirit of the long-since-departed Mary Hogarth; and the pathos of Paul Dombey's life also is in the same almost—too-good-for-this-world vein. Yet, at the same time, much of Paul Dombey is autobiographical and hence bridges to David Copperfield.

A Christmas Carol

Dombey was written in different parts of Europe—key sections were completed in Genoa, Switzerland, and Paris, where Dickens met his idol, Victor Hugo, as well as Alexandre Dumás and Eugène Sue. Along the way, Catherine gave birth to their seventh child, Sydney Smith Haldimand Dickens.

Dombey roared along, becoming ever more successful, as the various installments hit the streets. Never again was Dickens to have money problems. But an ominous note surfaced during the last part of the book: the disintegration of Dombey's marital relationship was being mirrored by his own. As Catherine got older and experienced one pregnancy after another, her appearance suffered, and she began to appear, in Dickens' own words, "tremendously fat" (Kaplan, p. 237). Just as bad, husband and wife communicated poorly—so much so that Dickens began to despair as he looked down through the years and saw nothing ahead but loneliness of mind. He certainly could have found plenty of beautiful women who would have eased that loneliness for him, but unlike many of his closest friends who did have affairs, his moral code was more rigid than theirs.

The House on Gad's Hill

Dombey reminded Dickens of himself as he once was, and the birth of the dreams that had taken him to his unparalleled eminence. With his next book, Dickens would go even deeper, to see if he could find not only his earlier self but perhaps the answers to the questions that were gnawing on his happiness. So it was that in 1849—at the age of thirty-seven—Dickens began one of his greatest books: *David Copperfield*. Chesterton describes the book as a "romantic biography"— which is not bad, "for romance is a very real part of life and perhaps the most real part of youth. Dickens had turned the telescope around or was looking through the other end of it; looking perhaps into a mirror, looking in any case out of a new window. It was life as he knew it, and even as he had lived it. In other words, it is fanciful but it is not fictitious; because not merely invented in the manner of fiction" (*Britannica* VII, p. 334). Chesterton goes on to point out that the way Dickens breathed life into stock characters, as he did in *Pickwick* and *Nickleby*, was quite different from what he did in *David Copperfield*. The way Dickens perceived the key characters in the book was the way any youth would have seen them, for young people have a different perspective on life than do adults: "There are men like Steerforth and girls like Dora; they are not as boys see them; but boys do see them so. This passionate autobiography, though it stiffens into greater conventionality at the real period of passion, is really, in the dismally battered phrase, a human document" (*Britannica* VII, p. 334). Chesterton then wraps up his analysis of *Copperfield* with a most provocative addendum: Evidently, *Copperfield* must have accomplished what Dickens hoped it would, for never again would Dickens replow that old ground. The book represents the dividing line between what Dickens was and what he was becoming.

One of Dickens' key motivations to look backward almost certainly was the untimely death of Fanny, his closet sibling, of tuberculosis in 1848. She had been dying for two years. By May 1848, she was coughing incessantly and could only achieve temporary relief by taking morphine. During her last weeks, Dickens haunted her bedside—as did their father. Dickens wrote Catherine that "no words . . . can express the terrible aspect of suffering and suffocation—the appalling noise in her throat—and the agonizing looks around" (Johnson, pp. 338-339). Fanny died on September 2nd. She was thirty-eight years old.

In 1849, Henry Fielding Dickens (child number eight) was born on January 15. That same year, Dickens completed a little book—today virtually unknown—that is significant to Christians: *The Life of Our Lord.* In it, he tried to portray to his children, and to other readers, what Christ's love and ministry were all about.

Dickens did not return to *David Copperfield* until after Fanny died. The protagonist of the story was originally called "Thomas Mag"—then "David Mag"—and finally "David Copperfield." Dickens had perfect pitch when it came to deciding on names for his characters. He was startled when Forster pointed out that the initials were his own, reversed. The Micawbers are, of course, immortal—especially Mr. Micawber (so much of his father is poured into his "cork-ship"). Dora is Maria Beadnell, only sweet and gentle. In no other book he ever wrote did he dare to reveal so much of himself and of this he always remained conscious: "'Like many fond parents,' he said, 'I have a favourite child. And his name is David Copperfield'" (Johnson, p. 355).

When Dickens finished the book on October 21, 1850, he wrote Forster, expressing his ambivalence—his oscillation between joy and pain. He concluded the letter with: "Oh, my dear Forster, if I were to say half of what Copperfield makes me think to-nighttonight, how strangely, even to you, I should be turned inside out! I seem to be sending some part of myself into the shadowy world" (Johnson, p. 355).

Dickens' ninth child, Dora Annie Dickens, was born in August 1850.

The next year, 1851, was rough: Dora was gravely ill, Catherine was ill both physically and psychologically and Dickens' father was dying. On March 31, after enduring a horribly painful and bloody prostate operation—without the benefit of chloroform—John Dickens died. Dickens was there in time, but his father was past recognizing him. Johnson poignantly observes, "As he looked at his father's dead face, where were the grandiloquence, the improvident borrowings, the irresponsibility, the disappearances to escape the bailiff? He could remember only the hard work, the irrepressible gusto, the old companionship of walks to Gad's Hill, the loving pride in a small boy's singing, the tenderness that throughout many a night had nursed a sick child" (Johnson, p. 376).

Barely two weeks later, after having appeared to recover, little Dora suddenly died in convulsions.

On May 16, Dickens and his theatrical company put on Bulwer-Lytton's play *We're Not as Bad as We Seem*—it had been postponed because of Dora's death—for Queen Victoria and Prince Albert.

In March 1852, Dickens' tenth and last child, and one of his favorite, was born: Edward Bulwer Lytton Dickens (nicknamed Plorn: mercifully abbreviated from Plornishghenter).

On the heels of *Copperfield* came *Bleak House*, as powerful an attack on the British legal system and bureaucratic gobbledygook as has ever been written. Its beginning is famous for the greatest extended metaphor of weather—in this case, fog—ever featured in a work of literature. The fog's counterpart is the Court of Chancery, an institution Dickens knew well from his court-reporting days. The case, based on an actual one, has to do with a legal duel over the considerable assets left to two children (in the book, the case is known as Jarndyce and Jarndyce). Though it takes them three generations, the lawyers manage to milk every last penny out of the "inheritance." The novel is all-encompassing and the attack is multidimensional.

Mrs. Jellyby is one of Dickens' most wondrous creations: the wealthy do-gooder who drives everyone bonkers with her fund-raising for overseas charity needs; yet she couldn't see a real one at home if it ran over her. Esther Summerson is a synthesis of Mary and Georgina. All three sisters ended up giving their lives to Dickens. Georgina, too, was captivated by his genius and, in time, became the keeper of the sacred flame, proving herself absolutely indispensable to him.

One of the really tough aspects about the writing of *Bleak House* has to do with Dickens' use of two first-person narrators: one male, one female. Wilkie Collins declared that it "contains . . . some of the finest passages he has ever written . . . brought out with such pathos, delicacy and truth, as no living writer has ever rivaled, or even approached" (Kaplan, p. 288).

Johnson's capsulization of the book is itself a work of art (keeping in mind that when Dickens was writing the last pages of *Bleak House* in August 1853, there was a siege of stormy weather at the same time):

Introduction

There is a poetic fitness about this nocturnal violence that marked the close of Bleak House, *for it is a dark and tempestuous book. The fog choking its opening scene, the rain swirling over Ghost's Walk at Chesney Wold amid the dripping funeral urns on the balustrade, the black and verminous ruins of Tom-all-Alone's crashing at intervals with a cloud of dust, the besmeared archway and iron-barred gate that lead to the rat-infested graveyard, insinuate their oppressive gloom even amid the genial sunlit scenes. A turbulent and furious hostility to vested evils storms savagely through it pages.*

(Johnson, pp. 396-397)

So exhausted was Dickens after finishing *Bleak House* that he, Wilkie Collins and Augustus Egg left on a two-month holiday in Switzerland and Italy. Upon his return, Dickens put on the first public readings from his works: He read for three hours from *A Christmas Carol,* in front of 2,000 spellbound listeners, followed by another three hours from *The Cricket on the Hearth.* He did Carol again on November 29, specifically for 2,500 poorer workers.

After *Bleak House* came another powerful social novel, *Hard Times* (1854), Dickens' first story of outright social protest. Earlier books had contained sections of social criticism, but this book was a frontal attack. Dedicated to another critic of contemporary society, Thomas Carlyle, it is based on personal observations of life in Manchester, one of England's great manufacturing centers. Unfortunately for Dickens' credibility, however, the bad guys are such monsters that they seem stereotypical rather than real. As to the conditions that caused Dickens to write the book, here is what Johnson has to say:

Chimneys smutted the sky and killed grass and trees, chemical waste fouled the streams, bleak miles of tenements spread like a cancerous blight over the countryside. Row upon row of flimsy houses, three quarters of them with no privies, crammed thousands of human beings into damp rooms and cellars. Heaps of ordure and garbage outside drained into ditches which provided the only water people had to drink. The owners of the factories fought by every evasion against obedience to the Ten Hours Bill, cynically defied sanitary regulations in unventilated workrooms, and recklessly ignored the law requiring that dangerous machinery be fenced in.

(Johnson, p. 405)

A Christmas Carol

Dickens was irate enough about the conditions themselves, but what made him livid was the deliberate ignoring of the landmark legislation that was supposed to protect workers from the industrialists who considered human life to be less important than making money. Dickens wrote *Hard Times*, a 100,000-word book, in one nonstop whirlwind of energy and concern, finishing on July 17, 1854.

In the book are revealed other fissures in Dickens' house, such as female dependency (reminding one of that experienced by Mamie, Katey, Georgina and Mary). John Dickens can be seen in the redemption of Thomas Gradgrind, as well as in the negative picture of Mr. Bounderby; Mrs. Sparsit is another revealing picture of his mother. Catherine can be seen in Stephen Blackpool's wife: her "incompetence, clumsiness, withdrawal from responsibility and unsuitability" (Kaplan, p. 310).

On his forty-third birthday, with snow four to six feet high on either side of the road, Dickens once again cast eyes on his childhood dream house, the Georgian mansion that crowned Gad's Hill. And it was for sale! Dickens had never owned property before—wouldn't it be fitting, his life being the fairy tale it was, if he could own it? He set about to buy it and then spent additional money bringing it up to his exacting specifications.

It is said that there are two tragedies in life: when one's dreams fail to come true, and when one's dreams do come true. Both chose this moment to coalesce.

Here was Dickens—after a lifetime of living in houses, large and small, comfortable and cramped, at last having the opportunity to not only live in but also buy his childhood dream home. What more could one ask life to give him? Two days after his birthday, he chanced to look down at some mail, looked away, then swiveled back: There was something familiar about that handwriting! He had seen it before—long, long ago. Yes, no question about it. It was a letter from Maria Beadnell. "Three or four and twenty years vanished like a dream, and I opened [her letter] with the touch of my young friend David Copperfield when he was in love" (Kaplan, p. 323).

As Johnson tells the story, Dickens opened the letter with a shaking hand. He did remember hearing that Maria had not married until the ripe old age of thirty-five, and to a man who was neither distinguished nor wealthy. Now the shoe was on the other foot, and she was writing to him, asking if they could reestablish the old friendship. She was still married and had two little girls; but that hadn't kept her from trying to rekindle a long-dead flame with one of the most famous men in the world. He must see her! Over the next few weeks, they corresponded, before finally setting up a time and place to meet—privately. Dickens did not really intend to reignite a romance with her—that was long since dead. But it would be delightful to perhaps flirt a little. Considering the dying of his love for Catherine, who knew what might happen . . . if the chemistry was still there. In one of his letters, Dickens told Maria that she had been the catalyst for all he had become. Finally, the day came for their meeting. He had expected her to look older—after all, she was forty-five:

> *Nevertheless, for all her warning, he was surprised to find her so undeniably fat. But it was not the physical change that was shattering. The gay little laugh had turned into a silly giggle. The delightful little voice, running on in such enchanting nonsense, had become a muddleheaded and disjointed volubility. The pretty pettish flirtatious little ways, the arch glances and tones of voice that suggested a secret understanding, were merely ridiculous affections in a middle-aged woman. What had happened to the fascination that had captivated him? Or, still worse, was it possible that Maria had always been this absurd and brainless chatterer, that her angelic charm had been only the radiant hallucination of youth?*
>
> (Johnson, p. 419)

Even more terrifying, this stout monster, "tossing her head with a caricature of her girlish manner, throwing him the most distressing imitations of the old glances, behaved as if this private meeting involved them in some intimate agreement. But 'this grotesque revival' of what had 'once been prettily natural to her,' was now like an attempt to resuscitate an old play 'when the stage was dusty, when the scenery was faded, when the youthful actors were dead, when the orchestra was empty, when the lights were out'" (Johnson, p. 419).

These were the words to describe the impact on him of seeing Maria Beadnell again after all those years—only the name he gave her was Flora Finching and the book (his next) was *Little Dorrit*.

It would have been better for Dickens—certainly, better for his family—had he learned his lesson from this attempt to rewrite the past. But it was not to be: The letter from Maria Beadnell is the Pandora's box of the rest of his life. The letter set in motion feelings that perhaps might otherwise have died still-born, or at least have been unacted upon. And he had had to follow through, meet with her family, listen to her twaddle as she chirped by his side, even catch her cold, and then find ways to avoid being cruel as she attempted to resume the old relationship.

Originally, Dickens had intended to call the new story *Nobody's Fault*—but moments before publication, he switched to *Little Dorrit*. The experience with Maria had profoundly shaken him, unsettled his equilibrium, and forced him to reexamine his rosiest contentions.

Today a book dealing with imprisonment for debt would appear far-fetched, but to readers of Dickens' day it was no joke. Of course the book was much more than a mere re-creation of Marshalsea: It was an attack on a vast, disembodied bureaucracy that apparently had to be accountable to no one. Dickens also stirred in rack-renting of the poor, extortion and sinister collusion at the top.

Dickens wrote part of *Little Dorrit* in England (in the middle of bull-headed government resistance to reform and corrupt and inefficient administration of the bloody Crimean War) and part of it in Paris (in the middle of a speculative frenzy). The result was a brooding darkness. And by the time he got to the revisionist portrayal of Maria Winter née Beadnell as portrayed by Flora Finching, he was beginning to chortle at the drollness of the whole thing. Of course he couldn't laugh too much, for Maria didn't look much different now from Catherine. Both were fat, and both, he felt, were difficult to communicate with. Little Dorrit herself is yet another re-creation of Mary and Georgina Hogarth.

For the first time since Pickwick, Dickens returned to a debtor's prison as a setting. For years, rather than see it, he would detour. Even though John Dickens is not William Dorrit, there was enough of his father in the character to disturb him. And Mrs. Clennam is perhaps the most horrible is the most horrible and frightening example of bad mothering in all his fiction.

On May 11, 1857, *Little Dorrit* was completed.

Best of Times, Worst of Times

We now come to a play coauthored by Wilkie Collins and Dickens that really became a play with a play. Collins' name was on it and the title was The Frozen Deep, a melodrama based on the ill-fated polar expedition of Sir John Franklin—all the members had died of starvation or exposure. Dickens played the romantic lead, as Richard Wardour, a rejected suitor of Clara Burnham. Presaging *A Tale of Two Cities*, Wardour rescues his successful rival, Frank Aldersley, and then dies with Clara's tears raining down on his face. Its first performance was on January 6, 1857.

Meanwhile, Gad's Hill was finally his! The Dickenses began moving in. One of their first guests was Hans Christian Andersen, who stayed a bit too long: five weeks (four weeks and four days longer than Benjamin Franklin's proverbial three-day limit).

Introduction

Queen Victoria, Prince Albert, and the king of the Belgians were given a private performance of *The Frozen Deep*. But then, in late August, the play was to be performed in an immense auditorium; so large, in fact, that only an experienced actress could "make her actions seen and her voice heard"; consequently, substitutes had to be found for Katey and Mamie, as well as for most of the other female members of the cast. The suggestion was made that Dickens consider "the well-known actress Mrs. Ternan and her two daughters, Maria Ternan and Ellen Lawless Ternan" (Johnson, p. 445). Dickens (as stage manager) assigned the part of Nurse Ester to Mrs. Ternan, the part of Clara Burnham (the heroine) to Maria (the more experienced of the two sisters), and Lucy Crawford (a minor role) to Ellen. At the performance, Dickens surpassed himself, leaving the audience in tears. The second night—with 3,000 in the audience—was just as powerful.

The play coincided with a period of deep despair for Dickens—despair because he felt he was living in a loveless marriage and could not get out. Divorce, in Victorian England, was unthinkable. Furthermore, he and his writings represented part of the rock upon which societal morality was based. To all other appearances, Dickens seemed to have a perfect everything—especially his home life. Dickens wrote Forster, saying, "Poor Catherine and I are not made for each other, and there is no help for it. It is not only that she makes me uneasy and unhappy, but that I make her so too—and much more so" (Johnson, p. 448). Then Dickens went on to admit that this state of affairs had existed ever since the days when Mary, his first child, was born.

Forster countered that there were no perfect marriages—most people had problems of some kind. But Dickens would not accept such a solution in his case: "Too late to say 'put the curb on, and don't rush at hills,' Dickens responded wearily, '— the wrong man to say it to. I have now no relief but in action. I am incapable of rest. I am quite confident I should rust, break and die, if I spared myself. Much better to die, doing'" (Johnson, p. 449).

This is a sad part of Dickens' story. Suffice it to say that shortly after moving to the dream mansion on Gad's Hill, the Dickenses separated. The marriage was not dissolved; she and the children had visitation rights, and Georgina stayed on as de facto mother and person in charge of day-to-day activities and events (for she was extremely capable where Catherine was not).

Unquestionably, however, this separation had a major impact on the children, resulting in Katey's escaping into a loveless marriage within a short time after the breakup. Of this period, Katey would later write: "My father was like a madman when my mother left home . . . This affair brought out all that was worst—all that was weakest in him. He [seemingly] did not care what happened to any of us. *Nothing could surpass the misery and unhappiness of our home*" (Kaplan, p. 399, emphasis added).

Family life was never the same—for that matter, neither was Dickens. There was another woman: beautiful eighteen-year-old Ellen Ternan, who had performed in *The Frozen Deep* with him; but she never came to live at Gad's Hill. And sadly, Dickens forced many of their friends to take sides. In his treatment during this period of Catherine, his children, his extended family and his friends, he exhibited an unbecoming ruthlessness and unkindness.

Certainly, all this unhappiness shortened his life. It definitely aged him.

Meanwhile, because of a change of publishers, Dickens changed the name of his magazine to *All the Year Round*; and because of his story serializations, its sales skyrocketed from 40,000 an issue to 300,000 during the next ten years.

The core idea for A Tale of Two Cities had come to Dickens during the torment of 1858, when his personal world appeared to be caving in on him. Somewhere between his disintegrating marriage and the vicarious sacrifice in The Frozen Deep, to say nothing of a new love, the story had come to him. For some years, Dickens had experienced recurring dreams of being a prisoner, manacled and behind walls—for that was how his marriage had seemed to him. And Paris was, next to London, perhaps his favorite city. He had learned French, and since his books had been translated into French, he was almost as well known there as he was in London. So, in the wrenching drama of The Frozen Deep, with one sister's tears cascading down on him, and the other, her heart in her eyes, standing to the side, with the whole Franklin party imprisoned in ice and dying there, Dr. Manette's long imprisonment in the Bastille and Sidney Carton's renunciation and great sacrifice amid the holocaust of the Terror was born. Johnson notes that Dickens had thought of his own life with Catherine as an iron-bound and stone-walled misery, weighed down by adamantine chains. It is not strange that in the fantasy from which imagination is born Dickens should dream of a prisoner bitterly immured for years and at last set free, and of a despairing love rising to a noble height of sacrifice. The story as a whole reflected Dickens anguished sense of the grandeur of renunciation, his longing for the ultimate woman and his rebellion against the imprisoning codes of society that inflicted the most hideous sufferings on mankind.

Dickens had wrestled with a number of possible titles for this story: *One of These Days, Buried Alive, The Thread of Gold, The Doctor of Beauvais.* But he was not really satisfied with any of them. There was quite a waiting period anyhow,

Introduction

for in the seismic shocks of the year, he had not been able to concentrate on writing at all.

He turned to his dear friend Carlyle for ideas. Carlyle's landmark *French Revolution* was one of the most significant historical works of the age, and Dickens drew heavily from it. Carlyle took him so seriously that he buried him in two cartloads of books from the London Library. "The more Dickens waded through them, however, the more he felt with amazed admiration that Carlyle had torn out their vitals and fused them into his fulminous masterpiece, which was aflame with the very essence of the conflagration" (Johnson, p. 479).

By March, Dickens' unerring sense of title appropriateness had brought him to *A Tale of Two Cities,* and with the door slammed on the title search, he was ready to go on. With an eye on profits, he decided to issue the story monthly as well as weekly.

By the time he reached "The Track of the Storm" section, Dickens was caught up in the action and whirled along like a chip carried aloft on the crest of a tidal wave: "The boiling cauldron of the Terror was a macrocosm filled with huge and flaming projections of his own raging emotions" (Johnson, p. 479). Dickens found it difficult to choose sides: "He pities the victims, but his deepest understanding is with a people driven mad. Though he sickens at the cruelty of mass murder, in his heart there is also a sympathy for these frenzied mobs, turned wolfish by oppression, that rises to a fierce exultation" (Johnson, p. 480).

As for the female protagonist, that portrait would not have been possible without Ellen Ternan. The story itself began as "Richard Wardour lay on the ground, dying and seeing Ellen out of the corner of his eye." Even the description of Lucie Nanette is unquestionably a real-life description of Ellen. The two patriarchal figures, Dr. Manett and Jarvis Lorry, represent significant growth in Dickens' ability to construct more balanced father-figures.

The crackling electricity of the tale comes from the two men who love Lucie: Sydney Carton and Charles Darnay. According to Kaplan, they are both Dickens. Darnay, like Dickens, has renounced his family's past and is starting over. Carton, on the other hand, has wasted his life and feels semi-damned—and can be redeemed only through renunciation.

The opening lines are considered perhaps the greatest in all literature:

It was the best of times, it was the worst of times, it was the age of wisdom, it was the age of foolishness, it was the epoch of belief, it was the epoch of incredulity, it was the season of Light, it was the season of Darkness, it was the spring of hope, it was the winter of despair, we had everything before us, we had nothing before us, we were all going direct to heaven, we were all going the other way—in short, the period was so far like the present period, that some of its noisiest authorities insisted on its being received, for good or for evil in the superlative degree of comparison only.

And how incredible the odds against such a beginning being tacked to one of the greatest book endings in all literature: "It is a far, far better thing that I do than I have ever done: it is a far, far better rest that I go to than I have ever known."

As the story hit its stride and began to thunder into full speed, smashing into kindling anything that stood in its way, Dickens sighed with satisfaction: "'The best story I have written, [it] has greatly moved and excited me in the doing, and Heaven knows I have done my best and believed in it.' The public was dazzled by the sureness of style, the firmness of tone, the combination of literary qualities and noble feeling whose ultimate referent was the model of Christ" (Kaplan, p. 415).

At home—if it could be called that anymore—things were different. Dickens had imagined that if he could only sever the shackles that bound him to Catherine and capture his beautiful Ellen, he would be happy at last. Ruefully, he discovered that that was not to be true. Katey's wedding breakfast brought the reality home to him. She was lovely, all in white, but he felt certain she did not love Charles Allston Collins—very much a mama's boy (even at thirty-one). Her mother was not there; neither were her grandmothers—Georgina was the only member of the large Hogarth family attending. After the wedding breakfast, Katey came out, dressed for her honeymoon—in black (appropriately, as it turned out, since apparently there was to be no consummation). Before leaving, she cried bitterly on her father's shoulder. "When the house was quiet and empty, Mary [her father refused to permit her to marry the man she loved] found her father in Katey's bedroom alone. He was on his knees, sobbing, with his head buried in her wedding gown, 'But for me,' he wept brokenly, 'Katey would not have left home'" (Johnson, pp. 485-86).

Ten days after the bride in black left on her sad honeymoon, Dickens' brother Alfred died. He was thirty-eight, just as Fanny had been when she died. Although Dickens was the eldest, he would outlive all of his brothers. Of the two remaining brothers, one would die just past forty and the other in his late forties.

When sales of *All the Year Round* began to drop, Dickens called an editorial caucus. What should be done? Obviously, what would help most would be another book to follow *A Tale of Two Cities*. He would title it *Great Expectations*, and it would be the same length as *Tale*.

Expectations is again autobiographical, although not nearly as much as was true with *David Copperfield*. But Pip's humiliation and griefs mirror those of Dickens as a child. Johnson maintains that "fundamentally, the novel is a reassessment of Dickens' own former subservience to false values" (Johnson, p. 490). Paradoxically, Pip's "great expectations" have to do with his dream of one day living as a gentleman on some-one else's money—without having to lift a finger himself; yet Dickens had nothing but scorn for the idle class, the aristocratic drones who made such messes of their lives.

Unquestionably, too, there is much in Pip's enslavement to Estella that mirrors Dickens' obsession with Ellen. Johnson maintains that "never before had he por-trayed a man's love for a woman with such depth or revealed its desperation of compulsive suffering. David Copperfield's heartache for Dora is without illusion, all self-absorbed need [Victorian mores precluded Dickens from discussing sexu-ality other than in generalities]; his desire for Estella is as self-centered as his desire to be a gentleman. It is the culminating symbol and the crowning indict-ment of a society dedicated to selfish ends" (Johnson, pp. 490-91). But Johnson points out that Pip is not irredeemably selfish—as the story's conclusion reveals.

Kaplan insightfully notes that "unlike [Dickens'] previous orphan heroes . . . , Pip is utterly unheroic; unromanticized, his sensibility and moral code free of the complications of talent and authorial self-glorification. He is as close to the self stripped bare as Dickens could ever get" (Kaplan, pp. 432-33).

The early setting of the book is Dickens' Kentish childhood utopia. Also from his childhood is the hulking prison from which the convict escaped. According to Kaplan, before Dickens started the book, knowing it would be heavily autobi-ographical, he reread *David Copperfield* in order to avoid duplication—and was deeply affected by it. It helped that he was now living in the house he had once dreamed of owning and could look out on the setting of the book. Like *David Copperfield*, *Expectations* was narrated in first person, G. K. Chesterton declares that "he never wrote anything better, considered as literature, than the first chapters of *Great Expectations*" (Britannica VII, p. 334).

Meanwhile, Dickens' aging mother was becoming totally dependent on him. As for friendships, almost all of his early friends were dead, thus he felt more and more alone. Those who surrounded him now were mostly—as Johnson puts it—"literary dependants" (Johnson, p. 492).

Dickens began to spend more of his time giving public readings of his works. In those days of print dominance, for an author-elocutionist to read, with dra-matic expression, from his works was as close to stage performances as one could get. Initially, it appears that Dickens went into it to test the waters, so to speak:

to see if—after separating form Catherine—he had lost his following. Clearly, those who thronged to his readings divorced their love for his books from any moral judgment of his private life.

Dickens could not have known it, but in *Our Mutual Friend* (written in 1864-65), he was writing his last complete full-length novel. It would be a book set in London—but a far cry from the joyous *Pickwick* of his youth. In a way, it was his King Lear; for, though only in his fifties, he had been battered beyond his years by the trauma in his life. In *Friend*, the great city of London cast somber shadows: It was "a hopeless city with no rent in the canopy of its sky." And, as Johnson points out, "the structure of society is one in which dominance has passed from the aristocracy to the middle class, capitalism and stock exchange. Money now seemed its only aim, pecuniary respectability its only standard" (Johnson, p. 497).

From all indications, Dickens had, over time, been able to persuade Ellen Ternan to come to Gad's Hill more often and to go places with him; but it brought neither of them much happiness, for both were torn by guilt and shame.

Meanwhile, an event occurred that jolted Dickens into apprehensions about the amount of time left to him. On June 9, 1865, he was with Mrs. Ternan and Ellen on a train from Dover to London when it crashed. All around them were mangled bodies and the cries of the wounded. Dickens climbed out of their train car, teetering precariously over a void, and helped all he could. Later he came back for the Ternans and for his precious manuscript, a segment of *Our Mutual Friend.* Ten passengers on the train—seven of them women—died, and forty were seriously wounded. Ellen's health was never the same afterward. Newspapers carried stories of the event, complete with names.

The emotional effect of the train wreck on Dickens can be seen in the story line and characters of *Our Mutual Friend.* Kaplan notes that "redemption . . . in Our Mutual Friend is a Christian affair in a frighteningly un-Christian culture. Material and psychological disintegration are constant threats—death by exploitation, death by brutalization, death by dehumanization, death by spiritual atrophy, death by one's body being inhabited by the materialism that the society promotes" (Kaplan, p. 474).

Kaplan feels that the character Bradley Headstone is perhaps "Dickens' most powerful negative self-portrait . . . the dark side of his own passion, willfulness . . . creativity . . . and self-destructiveness" (Kaplan, pp. 474-475). Having completed the manuscript, Dickens resumed his public readings—this time, at an even more killing pace. For a while, he toyed with the idea of going to Australia but finally decided against it. Now, the United States . . . that was another matter entirely:

Introduction

It was unfinished business. Friends and family alike tried to dissuade him from going, for his health was failing. After years of burning the candle at both ends, the middle had shrunk alarmingly. However, Dickens was promised £10,000 minimum (around US $2 million in today's purchasing power) to be deposited in a bank in England, if he would go. To Georgina and Mary, Dickens admitted, "I begin to feel myself drawn towards 'America, as Darnay in *A Tale of Two Cities* was attracted to the Loadstone Rock, Paris" (Johnson, p. 525).

No Relief But in Action

Dickens had always been a driven man, but about the mid-1860s, he took the governor off his engine and let her out. There was no one left in his life to challenge his absolute control—they could only weakly advise and wait for the inevitable accounting from a body and heart faithful, dependable and resilient almost beyond belief.

Other than in his Magazine, Dickens wrote little else. He did begin a new novel, *The Mystery of Edwin Drood*, but it remains a mystery to this day because he never completed it. Undoubtedly, he had finally decided to write a mystery because of his long association with Wilkie Collins, author of *The Woman* in *White* and *The Moonstone*.

As the time drew near for his second trip to the United States, Dickens began to have increasing trouble with his left foot, a physical problem dating back to the train wreck. His apprehension mounted: Should he go? Of course he would go—nothing short of death could stop him once he had made up his mind.

It was the evening of November 2, 1867, and excitement ran high in London's Freemason's Hall. Around 450 of the most distinguished men in the empire and about 100 women were there to pay tribute to Dickens, the greatest author of the age. According to Johnson, "wild enthusiasm greeted the arrival of the two most famous living novelists as Dickens entered on [Bulwer] Lytton's arm. Following the procession were Lord Chief Justice Cockburn, the Lord Mayor of London, Lord Houghton, Sir Charles Russell and an assemblage of the Royal Academicians" (Johnson, pp. 531-32).

In his tribute to Dickens, Bulwer-Lytton said, "Happy the man who makes clear his title-deeds to the royalty of genius while he yet lives . . . Seldom, I say, has that kind of royalty been quietly conceded to any man of genius until his tomb becomes his throne, and yet there is not one of us now present who thinks it strange that it is granted without a murmur to the guest whom we receive tonight" (Johnson, p. 532). When Dickens rose to acknowledge the tribute, the audience lost control. "Men leaped on chairs, tossed up napkins, waved glasses and decanters above their heads. The ladies' gallery was a flag of waving hands and handkerchiefs. Color and pallor followed each other in Dickens' face, and those wonderful eyes,' said one guest, 'flamed around like a search light'; tears streamed down his cheeks and as he tried to speak his voice faltered" (Johnson, p. 533). Though he eventually regained his composure and gave an eloquent response, many felt that the evening's climax was Dickens' silent tears.

Then it was time to say good-bye to his family—including farewell to Charley's children, his only grandchildren. When he came to little Mary Angela (whose nickname was "McKitty"), she—since he didn't like to be called "Grandfather"—hugged him and called him by her pet name, "Wenerables." On November 9, 1867, dickens left Liverpool and headed for America on the Cuba.

As it prepared for Dickens' arrival on November 19, the proud, aristocratic, staid city of Boston went into a frenzy—the streets were swept twice and the capitol building and old South Church were repainted. And there were Dickens-related souvenirs everywhere—from "Little Nell Cigars" to "Pickwick Snuff." As the *Cuba*, its whistle shrieking, steamed into port, showers of rockets lit up the night sky. When Dickens disembarked, he was met by cheers and applause from thousands of people crowding the docks and streets. He was taken immediately to the Parker House, where George Dolby (his tour manager) told him the tickets for the first four readings were already gone, thanks to a line a half a mile long. The next day, Longfellow arrived for a visit; later he brought Emerson, Holmes and Agassiz with him as well.

Dickens quickly noted that much had changed since his last visit a quarter of a century before. For one thing, most people now respected his personal space. In his daily walks (seven to ten miles), whenever he'd stop to look in a window, the people nearby stopped, too.

A most poignant day was Thanksgiving, when he dined at the Craigie House with Longfellow. In the bookshelves, he noted that there was a shelf of his own books, "and [he] said with a wink that delighted Longfellow's children, 'Ahh! I see you read the best authors!'" but throughout the meal and the visit, the house was haunted by the memory of Longfellow's beautiful wife whose dress had caught fire six years before: "She was in a blaze in an instant, rushed into his arms with a wild cry, and never spoke afterwards" (Johnson, p 535). She died within hours, in agony.

After the initial Boston readings, Dickens shuffled between East Coast cities. New York went as crazy as Boston had in anticipation of Dickens' arrival: People stood—and slept on mattresses—in line all night, with 5,000 there by morning. And at Steinway Hall, the German janitor greeted Dickens with eloquence: "'Mr.

Diggins . . . you are greed, meinherr. There is no ent to you.' Then, reopening the door and sticking his head out, 'Bedder and bedder,' he added; 'Wot negst'" (Johnson, p. 537).

Meanwhile, Dickens came down with a terrible cold, which plagued him the entire trip. But no matter how raw his throat was in the afternoon, some how he always made it through the readings. A feel for these performances can be gained from the diary of laughing Allegra, Longfellow's twelve-year-old daughter:

> *Sam Weller and Mr. Pickwick, Nicholas Nickleby and the old gentleman and the vegetable marrows over the garden wall. How he did make Aunt Betsy Trotwood snap out, "Janet, donkeys"—and David Copperfield yearn over the handsome sleeping Steerforth. How the audience loved best of all the* Christmas Carol *and how they laughed as Dickens fairly smacked his lips as there came the "smell like an eating house and a pastry cook's next door to each other, with a laundress' next door to that," As Mrs. Cratchit bore in the Christmas pudding, and how they nearly wept as Tin Tim cried, "God bless us everyone!" (Johnson, p. 538)*

By now Dickens realized that, because of his ill health, he'd have to eliminate from his tour Chicago, St. Louis and Cincinnati, which elicited howls of outrage from the Midwest. Dickens did find time to send $1,000 to Mrs. Clemm, Poe's mother-in-law, who had been suffering from need since Poe's death.

In Washington President Andrew Johnson, the chief cabinet members, the Supreme Court, ambassadors, naval and military officers, government officials, politicians and other dignitaries, all came the first night of his arrival, and many more came the following nights.

Even though the city was in an uproar over impeachment proceedings, President Johnson invited Dickens to call at the White House; later they also dined with statesman Charles Sumner and the just dismissed secretary of war Edwin Stanton. During their meal, the subject of Abraham Lincoln came up. Both Sumner and Stanton had attended a cabinet meeting the ill-fated day on which Lincoln had been assassinated, and they had been with him later as he died. Stanton, remembering that last cabinet meeting, called attention to the fact that the president—instead of lolling about as he usually did—was sitting erect in a dignified way and had told them of a recurring dream he had had: "I am on a great broad rolling river—and I am in a boat—and I drift!" (Kaplan, p. 523).

Dickens was visibly affected by the story and, for the rest of his life, he told it to anyone who would listen.

A Christmas Carol

At the Delmonico farewell dinner in New York, Dickens came in, leaning on Horace Greeley's arm. At the end of the banquet, Dickens thanked the guests, telling them, with a smile, that he had learned a few things about America over the last twenty-five years, emphasizing that on this visit, "I have been received with unsurpassable politeness, delicacy, sweet temper, hospitality, consideration and . . . respect for . . . privacy" (Kaplan, p. 528).

There was a huge crowd to see him off on April 22. Dickens limped along, for his left foot was giving him increasing pain. The trip had far exceeded his financial expectations: £20,000 instead of £10,000.

Early in May 1868, as Dickens stepped off the Graveshead train and headed home, he saw that the houses on the way to Gad's Hill were bedecked with banners and flags and that people everywhere were welcoming him home.

In his last public readings, Dickens increasingly included death scenes. For a long time, he had included "The Death of Little Nell" and other moving passages. Now he added "The Murder of Nancy." In reading such passages, women often fainted. The act of reading them took a toll on him as well. Kaplan maintains that so total was Dickens' identification with the murder of Nancy by Sikes that afterward, on his way home, he'd guiltily look back to see if police were following to arrest him. During the readings, his pulse would rise from 72 to 112.

When Dickens finally went to his doctor to ask about the pain in his left foot and the fact that he would skip words or transpose them in his readings, among other things, he was told that he had probably experienced a minor stroke.

"No more readings!" commanded the doctor.

But Dickens couldn't live without them. Kaplan takes us to the last of Dickens' 450 or so readings, on March 15, 1870. "Tired, sad, his left foot in pain, the exhausted Prospero made his dreaded final appearance on the platform. He read *A Christmas Carol* and the trial scene from Pickwick. Against expectations, finding the energy to make one last effort, he read with verve and brilliance. The applause was overwhelming, and seemed to go on and on. Finally, it was quiet again" (Kaplan, p. 548). In the silent hall, Dickens confessed how he had just brought to an end fifteen years of performing. Then, gathering his strength, he concluded with these words: "'From these garish lights I now vanish evermore, with a heartfelt, respectful, and grateful farewell.' He walked slowly from the platform into the wings, as if in deep mourning. Tumultuous applause and hand-kerchief-waving brought him back one more time. Tears rolled down his cheeks. He kissed his hands to his friends, good-bye" (Kaplan, p. 549).

On March 9, Dickens had a private audience with Queen Victoria at

Buckingham Palace. Instead of ten to fifteen minutes, it lasted close to an hour and a half. Dickens spoke of his latest works, his American tour and Lincoln's dream; and they exchanged gifts—he gave her a copy of *David Copperfield*. Later, at other dinners, he chatted with Disraeli and Gladstone (considered by many to be two of the greatest prime ministers the British Empire has ever had).

The Mystery of Edwin Drood was Dickens' swan song. Had he lived to complete it, it would, for the first time, have told the story—obliquely, it is true—of Dickens' entire life. Kaplan maintains that the book is as autobiographical as *David Copperfield*.

Early in June 1870, Dickens was back at Gad's Hill. All around him were the sights and fragrances of early summer. The new conservatory had just been finished. Joking with Katey, he pronounced, "You now see POSITIVELY the last improvement on Gad's Hill" (Johnson, p. 578). And they laughed. On Sunday, he seemed refreshed when he returned from a quiet afternoon walk. "When dinner was over, he and Katey remained sitting in the dining room to be near the flowers in the conservatory, while they listened to Mary sing in the drawing room. At eleven o'clock, Mary and Georgina retired, but Dickens and Katey sat enjoying the warm perfumed night air. He and his daughter talked long and affectionately" (Johnson, p. 578). Then he told her that he wished he had been "a better father, and a better man" (Johnson, p. 578). Later he spoke of his hopes that he might make a success of Edwin Drood, "'if, please God, I live to finish it.' Katey looked startled. 'I say if,' Dickens told her, 'because you know, my dear child, I have not been strong lately'" (Johnson, p. 578). It was 3 a.m. before they finished talking.

Katey got up late that June 4 and went out to the recently built writing chalet to tell her father good-bye (she planned to be gone till Saturday). She felt uneasy and made Georgina promise to write her the next day to reassure her that her father was still all right. But as she waited for the carriage to be brought around, she felt she must go back to him. Much later, she would write of that moment: "His head was bent low down over his work, and he turned an eager and rather flushed face towards me as I entered." Usually, Dickens would merely raise his cheek for a good-bye kiss, say a few parting words and go back to work. But not this time. When he saw her, "he pushed his chair back from the writing table, opened his arms, and took me into them." Then she hurried back to the house, saying to herself, without knowing why, *I am so glad I went—I am so glad* (Johnson, p. 579).

On Wednesday, June 6, uncharacteristically, Dickens wrote all day on the novel he would never finish. The last page he ever wrote depicts a hauntingly beautiful Rochester morning:

Changes of glorious light from morning boughs, songs of birds, scents from gardens, woods and fields—or, rather, from the one great garden of the whole cultivated island in its yielding time—penetrate the Cathedral, subdue its earthly odour and preach of the Resurrection and the Life. The cold stone tombs of centuries ago grow warm; and flecks of brightness dart into the sternest marble corners of the buildings, fluttering there like wings.

(Johnson, p. 579)

That night he intended to go to London. As he stood up to get ready, he started to fall, and Georgina helped to lower him to the floor. Doctors were sent for, and telegrams were sent to Mary, Katey, and others. Just before they had gone out for the evening, Katey had suddenly turned to Mary and said, "Mamie, I feel something is going to happen to us" (Johnson, p. 580).

Early the next morning, Charley and the London doctor arrived. The doctor pronounced it a paralytic stroke. Katey was sent to London to inform her mother, and Ellen was sent for, too. All day, members of the immediate family gathered.

"Just before six in the evening . . . Dickens' breathing grew fainter. At ten minutes past, he gave a deep sigh. His eyes were closed, but a tear welled from under his right eye and trickled down his cheek. Then he was gone. 'Like a weary factory child'" (Johnson, p. 580). He was fifty-eight.

The news of Dickens' death flashed around the world—across the vast reaches of the British Empire, to India, Australia, Canada, to the United States.

"I never knew an author's death to cause such general mourning. It is no exaggeration to say that the whole country is stricken with grief," wrote Longfellow.

In Genoa, a headline in the Italian newspaper read: *Nostro Carlo Dickens è Morto* [Our Charles Dickens Is Dead].

In the Parisian *Moniteur des Artes* were these words: "My pen trembles between my fingers at the thought of all that we—his family—have lost in Charles Dickens."

The bell of St. Stephens was just sounding nine-thirty when the procession (of three carriages only, as mandated in Dickens' will, with no public funeral, no public homage) reached the entrance to the Dean's Yard.

There was sudden silence.

Then the great bell of Westminster Abbey began to tool . . . and the vast city came to a complete halt.

Shortly afterward, at the command of the dean of Westminster (countermanding the injunction in Dickens' will), the massive doors of the great cathedral slowly opened to let the waiting people in.

And there, in Poets Corner—next to Handel, Macaulay and Johnson and not far from the busts and monuments of Milton, Spenser, Dryden, Chaucer and Shakespeare—thousands of men, women and children passed silently by Dickens' tomb, hour after hour, day after day—each leaving a flower and a tear. (The section on Dickens' death and funeral is derived from Johnson, pp. 571-83; Kaplan, pp. 553-56; and Tomlin, p. 42.)

Joseph Leininger Wheeler, Ph.D.
The Grey House
Conifer, Colorado

Works by Charles Dickens

Major Works

1836-1837	*Sketches by Boz: Illustrative of Every-Day Life And Every-Day People*
	The Pickwick Papers
1837-1839	*Oliver Twist*
	Nicholas Nickleby
1840-1841	*The Old Curiosity Shop*
	Barnaby Rudge
1842-1843	*American Notes*
1843-1844	*Martin Chuzzlewit*
	A Christmas Carol
1843	*The Chimes*
1846-1848	*The Battle of Life*
	The Cricket on the Hearth
	The Haunted Man
	Dombey and Son
	Pictures from Italy
1849-1850	*The Life of Our Lord*
	David Copperfield
1851-1853	*A Child's History of England, Vols. 1 and 2*
1854	*Hard Times*
1855-1857	*Little Dorrit*

1859-1861	*A Tale of Two Cities*
	Great Expectations
1864-1865	*Our Mutual Friend*
1870	*The Mystery of Edwin Drood (incomplete)*

Minor Works

1821	*Misnar: The Sultan of India*
1836	*"The Strange Gentleman" (lyrics)*
	"The Village Coquettes" (lyrics)
	Is She His Wife?
1838	*Memoirs of Grimaldi*
	Sketches of a Young Gentleman
	Gabriel Vardon: The Locksmith of London
1839	*Sketches of Young Couples*
1857	*Lazy Tour of Two Idle Apprentices*
	(with Wilkie Collins)

Magazines

Household Words
All the Year Round

Stave[1] One:

Marley's Ghost

Marley was dead: to begin with. There is no doubt whatever about that. The register of his burial was signed by the clergyman, the clerk, the undertaker, and the chief mourner. Scrooge signed it. And Scrooge's name was good upon The Exchange, for anything he chose to put his hand to. Old Marley was as dead as a doornail.

Mind! I don't mean to say that I know, of my own knowledge, what there is particularly dead about a doornail. I might have been inclined, myself, to regard a coffinnail as the deadest piece of ironmongery in the trade. But the wisdom of our ancestors is in the simile; and my unhallowed hands shall not disturb it, or the Country's done for. You will therefore permit me to repeat, emphatically, that Marley was as dead as a doornail.

Scrooge knew he was dead? Of course he did. How could it be otherwise? Scrooge and he were partners for I don't know how many years. Scrooge was his sole executor, his sole administrator, his sole assign, his sole residuary legatee, his sole friend and sole mourner. And even Scrooge was not so dreadfully cut up by the sad event, but that he was an excellent man of business on the very day of the funeral, and solemnized it with an undoubted bargain.

The mention of Marley's funeral brings me back to the point I started from. There is no doubt that Marley was dead. This must be distinctly understood, or nothing wonderful can come of the story I am going to relate. If we were not perfectly convinced that Hamlet's Father died before the play began, there would be nothing more remarkable in his taking a stroll at night, in an easterly wind, upon his own ramparts, than there would be in any other middle-aged gentleman rashly turning out after dark in a breezy spot—say Saint Paul's Churchyard for instance—literally to astonish his son's weak mind.

Scrooge never painted out Old Marley's name. There it stood, years afterwards, above the warehouse door: Scrooge and Marley. The firm was known as Scrooge and Marley. Sometimes people new to the business called Scrooge "Scrooge," and sometimes "Marley," but he answered to both names: it was all the same to him.

Oh! But he was a tight-fisted hand at the grind-stone, Scrooge! A squeezing, wrenching, grasping, scraping, clutching, covetous, old sinner! Hard and sharp as flint, from which no steel had ever struck out generous fire; secret, and self-contained, and solitary as an oyster. The cold within him froze his old features, nipped his pointed nose, shriveled his cheek, stiffened his gait; made his eyes red, his thin lips blue and spoke out shrewdly in his grating voice. A frosty rime was on his head, and on his eyebrows, and his wiry chin. He carried his own low temperature always about with him; he iced his office in the dog-days; and didn't thaw it one degree at Christmas.

External heat and cold had little influence on Scrooge. No warmth could warm, no wintry weather chill him. No wind that blew was bitterer than he, no falling snow was more intent upon its purpose, no pelting rain less open to entreaty. Foul weather didn't know where to have him. The heaviest rain, and snow, and hail, and sleet, could boast of the advantage over him in only one respect. They often "came down" handsomely, and Scrooge never did.

Nobody ever stopped him in the street to say, with gladsome looks, "My dear Scrooge, how are you? When will you come to see me?" No beggars implored him to bestow a trifle, no children asked him what it was o'clock, no man or woman ever once in all his life inquired the way to such and such a place, of Scrooge. Even the blind men's dogs appeared to know him; and when they saw him coming on, would tug their owners into doorways and up courts; and then would wag their tails as though they said, "No eye at all is better than an evil eye, dark master!"

But what did Scrooge care? It was the very thing he liked. To edge his way along the crowded paths of life, warning all human sympathy to keep its distance, was what the knowing ones call "nuts"[2] to Scrooge.

Once upon a time—of all the good days in the year, on Christmas Eve—old Scrooge sat busy in his counting-house. It was cold, bleak, biting weather: foggy withal: and he could hear the people in the court outside go wheezing up and down, beating their hands upon their breasts, and stamping their feet upon the pavement stones to warm them. The city clocks had only just gone three, but it was quite dark already—it had not been light all day: and candles were flaring in the windows of the neighboring offices, like ruddy smears upon the palpable brown air. The fog came pouring in at every chink and keyhole, and was so dense without, that although the court was of the narrowest, the houses opposite were mere phantoms. To see the dingy cloud come drooping down, obscuring everything, one might have thought that Nature lived hard by, and was brewing on a large scale.

The door of Scrooge's counting-house was open that he might keep his eye upon his clerk, who in a dismal little cell beyond, a sort of tank, was copying letters. Scrooge had a very small fire, but the clerk's fire was so very much smaller that it looked like one coal. But he couldn't replenish it, for Scrooge kept the coal-box in his own room; and so surely as the clerk came in with the shovel, the master predicted that it would be necessary for them to part. Wherefore the clerk put on his white comforter, and tried to warm himself at the candle; in which effort, not being a man of a strong imagination, he failed.

"A merry Christmas, uncle! God save you!" cried a cheerful voice. It was the voice of Scrooge's nephew, who came upon him so quickly that this was the first intimation he had of his approach.

"Bah!" said Scrooge, "Humbug!"

He had so heated himself with rapid walking in the fog and frost, this nephew of Scrooge's, that he was all in a glow; his face was ruddy and handsome; his eyes sparkled, and his breath smoked again.

"Christmas a humbug, uncle?" said Scrooge's nephew. "You don't mean that, I am sure."

"I do," said Scrooge. "Merry Christmas! What right have you to be merry? What reason have you to be merry? You're poor enough."

"Come, then," returned the nephew gaily. "What right have you to be dismal? What reason have you to be morose? You're rich enough."

Scrooge having no better answer ready on the spur of the moment, said "Bah!" again; and followed it up with "Humbug."

"Don't be cross, uncle!" said the nephew.

"What else can I be," returned the uncle, "when I live in such a world of fools as this? Merry Christmas! Out upon merry Christmas! What's Christmas time to you but a time for paying bills without money; a time for finding yourself a year older, but not an hour richer; a time for balancing your books and having every item in 'em through a round dozen of months presented dead against you? If I could work my will," said Scrooge indignantly, "every idiot who goes about with 'Merry Christmas' on his lips, should be boiled with his own pudding, and buried with a stake of holly through his heart. He should!"

"Uncle!" pleaded the nephew.

"Nephew!" returned the uncle, sternly, "keep Christmas in your own way, and let me keep it in mine."

"Keep it!" repeated Scrooge's nephew. "But you don't keep it."

"Let me leave it alone, then," said Scrooge. "Much good may it do you! Much good it has ever done you!"

"There are many things from which I might have derived good, by which I have not profited, I dare say," returned the nephew. "Christmas among the rest. But I am sure I have always thought of Christmas time, when it has come round—apart from the veneration due to its sacred name and origin, if anything belonging to it can be apart from that—as a good time: a kind, forgiving, charitable, pleasant time: the only time I know of, in the long calendar of the year, when men and women seem by one consent to open their shut-up hearts freely, and to think of people below them as if they really were fellow-passengers to the grave, and not another race of creatures bound on other journeys. And therefore, uncle, though it has never put a scrap of gold or silver in my pocket, I believe that it *has* done me good, and *will* do me good; and I say, God bless it!"

The clerk in the tank involuntarily applauded: becoming immediately sensible of the impropriety, he poked the fire, and extinguished the last frail spark for ever.

"Let me hear another sound from *you*," said Scrooge, "and you'll keep your Christmas by losing your situation. You're quite a powerful speaker, sir," he added, turning to his nephew. "I wonder you don't go into Parliament."

"Don't be angry, uncle. Come! Dine with us tomorrow."

Scrooge said that he would see him—yes, indeed he did. He went the whole length of the expression, and said that he would see him in that extremity[3] first.

"But why?" cried Scrooge's nephew. "Why?"

"Why did you get married?" said Scrooge.

"Because I fell in love."

"Because you fell in love!" growled Scrooge, as if that were the only one thing in the world more ridiculous than a merry Christmas. "Good afternoon!"

"Nay, uncle, but you never came to see me before that happened. Why give it as a reason for not coming now?"

"Good afternoon," said Scrooge.

"I want nothing from you; I ask nothing of you; why cannot we be friends?"

"Good afternoon," said Scrooge.

"I am sorry, with all my heart, to find you so resolute. We have never had any quarrel, to which I have been a party. But I have made the trial in homage to Christmas, and I'll keep my Christmas humor to the last. So a Merry Christmas, uncle!"

"Good afternoon," said Scrooge.

"And a Happy New Year!"

"Good afternoon!" said Scrooge.

His nephew left the room without an angry word, notwithstanding. He stopped at the outer door to bestow the greetings of the season on the clerk, who cold as he was, was warmer than Scrooge; for he returned them cordially.

"There's another fellow," muttered Scrooge; who overheard him: "my clerk, with fifteen shillings a week, and a wife and family, talking about a merry Christmas. I'll retire to Bedlam."[4]

This lunatic, in letting Scrooge's nephew out, had let two other people in. They were portly gentlemen, pleasant to behold, and now stood, with their hats off, in Scrooge's office. They had books and papers in their hands, and bowed to him.

"Scrooge and Marley's, I believe," said one of the gentlemen, referring to his list. "Have I the pleasure of addressing Mr. Scrooge, or Mr. Marley?"

"Mr. Marley has been dead these seven years," Scrooge replied. "He died seven years ago, this very night."

"We have no doubt his liberality is well represented by his surviving partner," said the gentleman, presenting his credentials.

It certainly was; for they had been two kindred spirits. At the ominous word "liberality," Scrooge frowned, and shook his head, and handed the credentials back.

"At this festive season of the year, Mr. Scrooge," said the gentleman, taking up a pen, "it is more than usually desirable that we should make some slight provision for the Poor and Destitute, who suffer greatly at the present time. Many thousands are in want of common necessaries; hundreds of thousands are in want of common comforts, sir."

"Are there no prisons?" asked Scrooge.

"Plenty of prisons," said the gentleman, laying down the pen again.

"And the Union workhouses?" demanded Scrooge. "Are they still in operation?"

"They are. Still," returned the gentleman, "I wish I could say they were not."

"The Treadmill and the Poor Law are in full vigor, then?" said Scrooge.

"Both very busy, sir."

"Oh! I was afraid, from what you said at first, that something had occurred to stop them in their useful course," said Scrooge. "I'm very glad to hear it."

"Under the impression that they scarcely furnish Christian cheer of mind or body to the multitude," returned the gentleman, "a few of us are endeavoring to raise a fund to buy the Poor some meat and drink and means of warmth. We choose this time, because it is a time, of all others, when Want is keenly felt, and Abundance rejoices. What shall I put you down for?"

"Nothing!" Scrooge replied.

"You wish to be anonymous?"

"I wish to be left alone," said Scrooge. "Since you ask me what I wish, gentlemen, that is my answer. I don't make merry myself at Christmas and I can't afford to make idle people merry. I help to support the establishments I have mentioned—they cost enough; and those who are badly off must go there."

"Many can't go there; and many would rather die."

"If they would rather die," said Scrooge, "they had better do it, and decrease the surplus population. Besides—excuse me—I don't know that."

"But you might know it," observed the gentleman.

"It's not my business," Scrooge returned. "It's enough for a man to understand his own business, and not to interfere with other people's. Mine occupies me constantly. Good afternoon, gentlemen!"

Seeing clearly that it would be useless to pursue their point, the gentlemen withdrew. Scrooge returned his labors with an improved opinion of himself, and in a more facetious temper than was usual with him. Meanwhile the fog and darkness thickened so, that people ran about with flaring links, proffering their services to go before horses in carriages, and conduct them on their way. The ancient tower of a church, whose gruff old bell was always peeping slyly down at Scrooge out of a Gothic window in the wall, became invisible, and struck the hours and quarters in the clouds, with tremulous vibrations afterwards as if its teeth were chattering in its frozen head up there. The cold became intense. In the main street at the corner of the court, some laborers were repairing the gaspipes, and had lighted a great fire in a brazier, round which a party of ragged men and boys were gathered: warming their hands and winking

their eyes before the blaze in rapture. The water-plug being left in soli-
tude, its overflowing sullenly congealed, and turned to misanthropic ice.
The brightness of the shops where holly sprigs and berries crackled in the
lamp heat of the windows, made pale faces ruddy as they passed. Poulterers'
and grocers' trades became a splendid joke; a glorious pageant, with which
it was next to impossible to believe that such dull principles as bargain
and sale had anything to do. The Lord Mayor, in the stronghold of the
mighty Mansion House, gave orders to his fifty cooks and butlers to keep
Christmas as a Lord Mayor's household should; and even the little tailor,
whom he had fined five shillings on the previous Monday for being drunk
and bloodthirsty in the streets, stirred up tomorrow's pudding in his gar-
ret, while his lean wife and the baby sallied out to buy the beef.

Foggier yet, and colder! Piercing, searching, biting cold. If the good
Saint Dunstan[5] had but nipped the Evil Spirit's nose with a touch of such
weather as that, instead of using his familiar weapons, then indeed he
would have roared to lusty purpose. The owner of one scant young nose,
gnawed and mumbled[6] by the hungry cold as bones are gnawed by dogs,
stooped down at Scrooge's keyhole to regale him with a Christmas carol:
but at the first sound of:

"God bless you, merry gentleman!

May nothing you dismay!"

Scrooge seized the ruler with such energy of action that the singer fled
in terror, leaving the keyhole to the fog and even more congenial frost.

At length, the hour of shutting up the counting-house arrived. With
an ill-will Scrooge dismounted from his stool, and tacitly admitted the
fact to the expectant clerk in the tank, who instantly snuffed his candle
out, and put on his hat.

"You'll want all day tomorrow, I suppose?" said Scrooge.

"If quite convenient, sir."

"It's not convenient," said Scrooge, "and it's not fair. If I was to stop
half-a-crown for it, you'd think yourself ill-used, I'll be bound."

The clerk smiled faintly.

"And yet," said Scrooge, "you don't think me ill-used, when I pay a day's wages for no work."

The clerk observed that it was only once a year.

"A poor excuse for picking a man's pocket every twenty-fifth of December!" said Scrooge, buttoning his great-coat to the chin. "But I suppose you must have the whole day. Be here all the earlier next morning."

The clerk promised that he would; and Scrooge walked out with a growl. The office was closed in a twinkling, and the clerk, with the long ends of his white comforter dangling below his waist (for he boasted no great-coat), went down a slide on Cornhill, at the end of a lane of boys, twenty times, in honor of its being Christmas Eve, and then ran home to Camden Town as hard as he could pelt, to play at blindman's-buff.

Scrooge took his melancholy dinner in his usual melancholy tavern; and having read all the newspapers, and beguiled the rest of the evening with his banker's-book, went home to bed. He lived in chambers which had once belonged to his deceased partner. They were a gloomy suite of rooms, in a lowering pile of building up a yard, where it had so little business to be, that one could scarcely help fancying it must have run there when it was a young house, playing at hide-and-seek with other houses, and forgotten the way out again. It was old enough now, and dreary enough, for nobody lived in it but Scrooge, the other rooms being all let out as offices. The yard was so dark that even Scrooge, who knew its every stone, was fain to grope with his hands. The fog and frost so hung about the black old gateway of the house, that it seemed as if the Genius of the Weather[7] sat in mournful meditation on the threshold.

Now, it is a fact, that there was nothing at all particular about the knocker on the door, except that it was very large. It is also a fact, that Scrooge had seen it, night and morning, during his whole residence in that place; also that Scrooge had as little of what is called fancy about him as any man in the city of London, even including—which is a bold word—the corporation, aldermen, and livery. Let it also be borne in mind that Scrooge had not bestowed one thought on Marley, since his last mention of his seven years' dead partner that afternoon. And then let any man explain to me, if he can, how it happened that Scrooge, having his key in the lock of the door, saw in the knocker, without its undergoing any intermediate process of change—not a knocker, but Marley's face.

Marley's face. It was not in impenetrable shadow as the other objects in the yard were, but had a dismal light about it, like a bad lobster in a dark cellar. It was not angry or ferocious, but looked at Scrooge as Marley used to look: with ghostly spectacles turned up on its ghostly forehead. The hair was curiously stirred, as if by breath or hot air; and, though the eyes were wide open, they were perfectly motionless. That, and its livid color, made it horrible; but its horror seemed to be in spite of the face and beyond its control, rather than a part of its own expression.

As Scrooge looked fixedly at this phenomenon, it was a knocker again.

To say that he was not startled, or that his blood was not conscious of a terrible sensation to which it had been a stranger from infancy, would be untrue. But he put his hand upon the key he had relinquished, turned it sturdily, walked in, and lighted his candle.

He did pause, with a moment's irresolution, before he shut the door; and he did look cautiously behind it first, as if he half-expected to be terrified with the sight of Marley's pigtail sticking out into the hall. But there was nothing on the back of the door, except the screws and nuts that held the knocker on, so he said "Pooh, pooh!" and closed it with a bang.

The sound resounded through the house like thunder. Every room above, and every cask in the wine-merchant's cellars below, appeared to have a separate peal of echoes of its own. Scrooge was not a man to be frightened by echoes. He fastened the door, and walked across the hall, and up the stairs; slowly too: trimming his candle as he went.

You may talk vaguely about driving a coach-and-six up a good old flight of stairs, or through a bad young Act of Parliament; but I mean to say you might have got a hearse up that staircase, and taken it broadwise, with the splinter-bar[8] towards the wall and the door towards the balustrades: and done it easy. There was plenty of width for that, and room to spare; which is perhaps the reason why Scrooge thought he saw a locomotive hearse going on before him in the gloom. Half a dozen gas-lamps out of the street wouldn't have lighted the entry too well, so you may suppose that it was pretty dark with Scrooge's dip.

Up Scrooge went, not caring a button for that. Darkness is cheap, and Scrooge liked it. But before he shut his heavy door, he walked through his rooms to see that all was right. He had just enough recollection of the face to desire to do that.

Sitting-room, bedroom, lumber-room.⁹ All as they should be. Nobody under the table, nobody under the sofa; a small fire in the grate; spoon and basin ready; and the little saucepan of gruel (Scrooge had a cold in his head) upon the hob. Nobody under the bed; nobody in the closet; nobody in his dressing-gown, which was hanging up in a suspicious attitude against the wall. Lumber-room as usual. Old fire-guards, old shoes, two fish-baskets, washing-stand on three legs, and a poker.

Quite satisfied, he closed his door, and locked himself in; double-locked himself in, which was not his custom. Thus secured against surprise, he took off his cravat; put on his dressing-gown and slippers, and his nightcap; and sat down before the fire to take his gruel.

It was a very low fire indeed; nothing on such a bitter night. He was obliged to sit close to it, and brood over it, before he could extract the least sensation of warmth from such a handful of fuel. The fireplace was an old one, built by some Dutch merchant long ago, and paved all round with quaint Dutch tiles, designed to illustrate the Scriptures. There were Cains and Abels, Pharaohs' daughters; Queens of Sheba, Angelic messengers descending through the air on clouds like feather-beds, Abrahams, Belshazzars, Apostles putting off to sea in butter-boats, hundreds of figures to attract his thoughts—and yet that face of Marley, seven years dead, came like the ancient Prophet's rod, and swallowed up the whole. If each smooth tile had been blank at first, with power to shape some picture on its surface from the disjointed fragments of his thoughts, there would have been a copy of old Marley's head on every one.

"Humbug!" said Scrooge; and walked across the room.

After several turns, he sat down again. As he threw his head back in the chair, his glance happened to rest upon a bell, a disused bell, that hung in the room, and communicated for some purpose now forgotten with a chamber in the highest story of the building. It was with great astonishment, and with a strange, inexplicable dread, that as he looked, he saw this bell begin to swing. It swung so softly in the outset that it scarcely made a sound; but soon it rang out loudly, and so did every bell in the house.

This might have lasted half a minute, or a minute, but it seemed an hour. The bells ceased as they had begun, together. They were succeeded by a clanking noise, deep down below; as if some person were dragging a heavy chain over the casks in the wine merchant's cellar. Scrooge then remembered to have heard that ghosts in haunted houses were described as dragging chains.

The cellar-door flew open with a booming sound, and then he heard the noise much louder, on the floors below; then coming up the stairs; then coming straight towards his door.

"It"s humbug still!" said Scrooge. "I won't believe it."

His color changed though, when, without a pause, it came on through the heavy door, and passed into the room before his eyes. Upon its coming in, the dying flame leaped up, as though it cried, "I know him; Marley's Ghost!" and fell again.

The same face: the very same. Marley in his pigtail, usual waistcoat, tights and boots; the tassels on the latter bristling, like his pigtail, and his coat-skirts, and the hair upon his head. The chain he drew was clasped about his middle. It was long, and wound about him like a tail; and it was made (for Scrooge observed it closely) of cash-boxes, keys, padlocks, ledgers, deeds, and heavy purses wrought in steel. His body was transparent, so that Scrooge, observing him, and looking through his waistcoat, could see the two buttons on his coat behind.

Scrooge had often heard it said that Marley had no bowels,[10] but he had never believed it until now.

No, nor did he believe it even now. Though he looked the phantom through and through, and saw it standing before him; though he felt the chilling influence of its death-cold eyes; and marked the very texture of the folded kerchief bound about its head and chin, which wrapper he had not observed before: he was still incredulous, and fought against his senses.

"How now!" said Scrooge, caustic and cold as ever. "What do you want with me?"

"Much!"—Marley's voice, no doubt about it.

"Who are you?"

"Ask me who I *was*."

"Who *were* you then?" said Scrooge, raising his voice. "You're particular, for a shade." "He was going to say "to a shade," but substituted this, as more appropriate.

"In life I was your partner, Jacob Marley."

"Can you—can you sit down?" asked Scrooge, looking doubtfully at him.

"I can."

"Do it then."

Scrooge asked the question, because he didn't know whether a ghost so transparent might find himself in a condition to take a chair; and felt that in the event of its being impossible, it might involve the necessity of an embarrassing explanation. But the ghost sat down on the opposite side of the fireplace, as if he were quite used to it.

"You don't believe in me," observed the Ghost.

"I don't." said Scrooge.

"What evidence would you have of my reality, beyond that of your senses?"

"I don't know," said Scrooge.

"Why do you doubt your senses?"

"Because," said Scrooge, "a little thing[12] affects them. A slight disorder of the stomach makes them cheats. You may be an undigested bit of beef, a blot of mustard, a crumb of cheese, a fragment of an underdone potato. There's more of gravy than of grave about you, whatever you are!"

Scrooge was not much in the habit of cracking jokes, nor did he feel, in his heart, by any means waggish then. The truth is that he tried to be smart, as a means of distracting his own attention, and keeping down his terror; for the specter's voice disturbed the very marrow in his bones.

To sit, staring at those fixed glazed eyes, in silence for a moment, would play, Scrooge felt, the very deuce with him. There was something very awful, too, in the specter's being provided with an infernal atmosphere of its own. Scrooge could not feel it himself, but this was clearly the case; for though the Ghost sat perfectly motionless, its hair, and skirts, and tassels, were still agitated as by the hot vapor from an oven.

"You see this toothpick?" said Scrooge, returning quickly to the charge, for the reason just assigned; and wishing, though it were only for a second, to divert the vision's stony gaze from himself.

"I do," replied the Ghost.

"You are not looking at it," said Scrooge.

"But I see it," said the Ghost, "notwithstanding."

"Well!" returned Scrooge, "I have but to swallow this, and be for the rest of my days persecuted by a legion of goblins, all of my own creation. Humbug, I tell you! Humbug!"

At this the spirit raised a frightful cry, and shook its chain with such a dismal and appalling noise, that Scrooge held on tight to his chair, to save himself from falling in a swoon. But how much greater was his horror, when the phantom taking off the bandage round its head, as if it were too warm to wear indoors, released its lower jaw, which dropped[13] down upon its breast!

Scrooge fell upon his knees, and clasped his hands before his face.

"Mercy!" he said. "Dreadful apparition, why do you trouble me?"

"Man of the worldly mind!" replied the Ghost, "Do you believe in me or not?"

"I do," said Scrooge. "I must. But why do spirits walk the earth, and why do they come to me?"

"It is required of every man," the Ghost returned, "that the spirit within him should walk abroad among his fellowmen, and travel far and wide; and if that spirit goes not forth in life, it is condemned to do so after death. It is doomed to wander through the world—oh, woe is me!—and witness what it cannot share, but might have shared on earth, and turned to happiness!"

Again the specter raised a cry, and shook its chain and wrung its shadowy hands.

"You are fettered," said Scrooge, trembling. "Tell me why?"

"I wear the chain I forged in life," replied the Ghost. "I made it link by link, and yard by yard; I girded it on of my own free will, and of my own free will I wore it. Is its pattern strange to you?"

Scrooge trembled more and more.

"Or would you know," pursued the Ghost, "the weight and length of the strong coil you bear yourself? It was as full as heavy and as long as this, seven Christmas Eves ago. You have labored on it, since. It is a ponderous chain!"

Scrooge glanced about him on the floor, in the expectation of finding himself surrounded by some fifty or sixty fathoms of iron cable: but he could see nothing.

"Jacob," he said, imploringly. "Old Jacob Marley, tell me more. Speak comfort to me, Jacob!"

"I have none to give," the Ghost replied. "It comes from other regions,[14] Ebenezer Scrooge, and is conveyed by other ministers, to other kinds of men. Nor can I tell you what I would. A very little more, is all permitted to me. I cannot rest, I cannot stay, I cannot linger anywhere. My spirit never walked beyond our counting-house—mark me!—in life my spirit never roved beyond the narrow limits of our money-changing hole; and weary journeys lie before me!"

It was a habit with Scrooge, whenever he became thoughtful, to put his hands in his breeches pockets. Pondering on what the Ghost had said, he did so now, but without lifting up his eyes, or getting off his knees.

"You must have been very slow about it, Jacob," Scrooge observed, in a business-like manner, though with humility and deference.

"Slow!" the Ghost repeated.

"Seven years dead," mused Scrooge. "And travelling all the time!"

SCROOGE'S LOOKOUT

"The whole time," said the Ghost. "No rest, no peace. Incessant torture of remorse."

"You travel fast?" said Scrooge.

"On the wings of the wind," replied the Ghost.

"You might have got over a great quantity of ground in seven years," said Scrooge.

The Ghost, on hearing this, set up another cry, and clanked its chain so hideously in the dead silence of the night, that the ward[15] would have been justified in indicting it for a nuisance.

"O blind man, blind man!"[16] cried the phantom, "not to know, that ages of incessant labor, by immortal creatures, for this earth must pass into eternity before the good of which it is susceptible is all developed. Not to know that any Christian spirit working kindly in its little sphere, whatever it may be, will find its mortal life too short for its vast means of usefulness. Not to know that no space of regret can make amends for one life's opportunity misused! Yet such was I! Oh! Such was I!"

"But you were always a good man of business, Jacob," faltered Scrooge, who now began to apply this to himself.

"Business!" cried the Ghost, wringing its hands again. "Mankind was my business. The common welfare was my business; charity, mercy, forbearance, and benevolence, were all my business. The dealings of my trade were but a drop of water in the comprehensive ocean of my business!"

It held up its chain at arm's length, as if that were the cause of all its unavailing grief, and flung it heavily upon the ground again.

"At this time of the rolling year," the specter said "I suffer most. Why did I walk through crowds of fellow-beings with my eyes turned down, and never raise them to that blessed Star which led the Wise Men to a poor abode! Were there no poor homes to which its light would have conducted me?"

Scrooge was very much dismayed to hear the specter going on at this rate, and began to quake exceedingly.

"Hear me!" cried the Ghost. "My time is nearly gone."

"I will," said Scrooge. "But don't be hard upon me! Don't be flowery, Jacob! Pray!"

"How it is that I appear before you in a shape that you can see, I may not tell. I have sat invisible beside you many and many a day."

It was not an agreeable idea. Scrooge shivered, and wiped the perspiration from his brow.

"That is no light part of my penance," pursued the Ghost. "I am here tonight to warn you, that you have yet a chance and hope of escaping my fate. A chance and hope of my procuring, Ebenezer."

"You were always a good friend to me," said Scrooge. "Thank 'ee!"

"You will be haunted," resumed the Ghost, "by Three Spirits."

Scrooge's countenance fell almost as low as the Ghost's had done.

"Is that the chance and hope you mentioned, Jacob?" he demanded, in a faltering voice.

"It is."

"I—I think I'd rather not," said Scrooge.

"Without their visits," said the Ghost, "you cannot hope to shun the path I tread. Expect the first tomorrow, when the bell tolls one."

"Couldn't I take 'em all at once, and have it over, Jacob?" hinted Scrooge.

"Expect the second on the next night at the same hour. The third upon the next night when the last stroke of twelve has ceased to vibrate. Look to see me no more; and look that, for your own sake, you remember what has passed between us!"

When it had said these words, the specter took its wrapper from the table, and bound it round its head, as before. Scrooge knew this, by the smart sound its teeth made, when the jaws were brought together by the bandage. He ventured to raise his eyes again, and found his supernatural visitor confronting him in an erect attitude, with its chain wound over and about its arm.

The apparition walked backward from him; and at every step it took, the window raised itself a little, so that when the specter reached it, it was wide open. It beckoned Scrooge to approach, which he did. When they were within two paces of each other, Marley's Ghost held up its hand, warning him to come no nearer. Scrooge stopped.

Not so much in obedience, as in surprise and fear: for on the raising of the hand, he became sensible of confused noises in the air; incoherent sounds of lamentation and regret; wailings inexpressibly sorrowful and self-accusatory. The specter, after listening for a moment, joined in the mournful dirge; and floated out upon the bleak, dark night.

Scrooge followed to the window: desperate in his curiosity. He looked out.

The air was filled with phantoms, wandering hither and thither in restless haste, and moaning as they went. Every one of them wore chains like Marley's Ghost; some few (they might be guilty governments) were linked together; none were free. Many had been personally known to Scrooge in their lives. He had been quite familiar with one old ghost, in a white waistcoat, with a monstrous iron safe attached to its ankle, who cried piteously at being unable to assist a wretched woman with an infant, whom it saw below, upon a door-step. The misery with them all was, clearly, that they sought to interfere, for good, in human matters, and had lost the power forever.

Whether these creatures faded into mist, or mist enshrouded them, he could not tell. But they and their spirit voices faded together; and the night became as it had been when he walked home.

Scrooge closed the window, and examined the door by which the Ghost had entered. It was double-locked, as he had locked it with his own hands, and the bolts were undisturbed. He tried to say "Humbug!" but stopped at the first syllable. And being, from the emotion he had undergone, or the fatigues of the day, or his glimpse of the Invisible World, or the dull conversation of the Ghost, or the lateness of the hour, much in need of repose; went straight to bed, without undressing, and fell asleep upon the instant.

Stave One Footnotes:

1 Used as "stanza" of a carol.

2 Agreeable, gratifying; a source of pleasure or delight.

3 The very hot place, for those damned for their sins.

4 A famous London insane asylum.

5 An English monk who, according to legend, once grabbed hold of the devil's nose with red-hot pincers.

6 Bit gently, with mouth closed.

7 Guardian, attendant spirit, or clerk, of the weather.

8 Front crossbar that supports the springs.

9 A room used for firewood and general storage.

10 At one time, bowels were thought to be the seat of compassion—see 1 John 3:17 (King James).

11 A ghost; a degree.

12 It was believed that dreams—and ghosts—were often induced by indigestion (in effect, hallucinations).

13 The dead were often bound around the chin and head to keep the mouth closed.

14 According to Hearn, Dickens was influenced here by Dante: Just as the poet Virgil is the guide to the poet Dante, just so the miserly Marley is the guide to the miser Scrooge. Both visions apparently took place over a three-day period (Dante's at Easter, Scrooge's at Christmas). In Dante's Fourth Circle, the avaricious are condemned to roll great weights, hence Marley's similiar punishment. As with Dante, both spirits speak in "veiled speech," as Christ cannot be spoken of in the infernal world.

15 An officer, watchman, or policeman of the ward (26 wards or parishes in London at that time, according to Hearn).

16 Hearn notes that Dickens was dissatisfied with the "Oh! Captive, bound, and double-ironed!" line and hence substituted these words in his later-public readings.

Stave Two:

The First of the Three Spirits

When Scrooge awoke, it was so dark, that looking out of bed, he could scarcely distinguish the transparent window from the opaque walls of his chamber. He was endeavoring to pierce the darkness with his ferret eyes, when the chimes of a neighboring church[1] struck the four quarters. So he listened for the hour.

To his great astonishment the heavy bell went on from six to seven, and from seven to eight, and regularly up to twelve; then stopped. Twelve. It was past two when he went to bed. The clock was wrong. An icicle must have got into the works. Twelve.

He touched the spring of his repeater,[2] to correct this most preposterous clock. Its rapid little pulse beat twelve: and stopped.

"Why, it isn't possible," said Scrooge, "that I can have slept through a whole day and far into another night. It isn't possible that anything has happened to the sun, and this is twelve at noon."

The idea being an alarming one, he scrambled out of bed, and groped his way to the window. He was obliged to rub the frost off with the sleeve of his dressing-gown before he could see anything; and could see very little then. All he could make out was that it was still very foggy and extremely cold, and that there was no noise of people running to and fro, and making a great stir, as there unquestionably would have been if night had beaten off bright day, and taken possession of the world. This was a great relief, because "three days after sight of this First of Exchange pay to Mr. Ebenezer Scrooge or his order,"[3] and so forth, would have become a mere United States' security[4] if there were no days to count by.

Scrooge went to bed again, and thought, and thought, and thought it over and over and over, and could make nothing of it. The more he thought, the more perplexed he was; and the more he endeavored not to think, the more he thought. Marley's Ghost bothered him exceedingly.

Every time he resolved within himself, after mature inquiry, that it was all a dream, his mind flew back again, like a strong spring released, to its first position, and presented the same problem to be worked all through, "Was it a dream or not?"

Scrooge lay in this state until the chimes had gone three quarters more, when he remembered, on a sudden, that the Ghost had warned him of a visitation when the bell tolled one. He resolved to lie awake until the hour was past; and, considering that he could no more go to sleep than go to Heaven, this was perhaps the wisest resolution in his power.

The quarter was so long, that he was more than once convinced he must have sunk into a doze unconsciously, and missed the clock. At length it broke upon his listening ear.

"Ding, dong!"

"A quarter past," said Scrooge, counting.

"Ding dong!"

"Half past!" said Scrooge.

"Ding dong!"

"A quarter to it," said Scrooge.

"Ding dong!"

"The hour itself," said Scrooge, triumphantly, "and nothing else!"

He spoke before the hour bell sounded, which it now did with a deep, dull, hollow, melancholy One. Light flashed up in the room upon the instant, and the curtains of his bed were drawn.

The curtains of his bed were drawn aside, I tell you, by a hand. Not the curtains at his feet, nor the curtains at his back, but those to which his face was addressed. The curtains of his bed were drawn aside; and Scrooge, starting up into a half-recumbent attitude, found himself face to face with the unearthly visitor who drew them: as close to it as I am now to you, and I am standing in the spirit at your elbow.

It was a strange figure[5]—like a child: yet not so like a child as like an old man, viewed through some supernatural medium, which gave him the appearance of having receded from the view, and being diminished to a child's proportions. Its hair, which hung about its neck and down its back, was white as if with age; and yet the face had not a wrinkle in it, and the tenderest bloom was on the skin. The arms were very long and muscular; the hands the same, as if its hold were of uncommon strength. Its legs and feet, most delicately formed, were, like those upper members, bare. It wore a tunic of the purest white, and round its waist was bound a lustrous belt, the sheen of which was beautiful. It held a branch of fresh green holly in its hand; and, in singular contradiction of that wintry emblem, had its dress trimmed with summer flowers. But the strangest thing about it was, that from the crown of its head there sprung a bright clear jet of light, by which all this was visible; and which was doubtless the occasion of its using, in its duller moments, a great extinguisher[6] for a cap, which it now held under its arm.

Even this, though, when Scrooge looked at it with increasing steadiness, was not its strangest quality. For as its belt sparkled and glittered now in one part and now in another, and what was light one instant, at another time was dark, so the figure itself fluctuated in its distinctness: being now a thing with one arm, now with one leg, now with twenty legs, now a pair of legs without a head, now a head without a body: of which dissolving parts, no outline would be visible in the dense gloom wherein they melted away. And in the very wonder of this, it would be itself again; distinct and clear as ever.

"Are you the Spirit, sir, whose coming was foretold to me?" asked Scrooge.

"I am."

The voice was soft and gentle. Singularly low, as if instead of being so close beside him, it were at a distance.

"Who, and what are you?" Scrooge demanded.

"I am the Ghost of Christmas Past."

"Long Past?" inquired Scrooge: observant of its dwarfish stature.

"No. Your past."

Perhaps, Scrooge could not have told anybody why, if anybody could have asked him; but he had a special desire to see the Spirit in his cap; and begged him to be covered.

"What!" exclaimed the Ghost, "Would you so soon put out, with worldly hands, the light I give? Is it not enough that you are one of those whose passions made this cap, and force me through whole trains of years to wear it low upon my brow!"

Scrooge reverently disclaimed all intention to offend or any knowledge of having willfully bonneted[7] the Spirit at any period of his life. He then made bold to inquire what business brought him there.

"Your welfare," said the Ghost.

Scrooge expressed himself much obliged, but could not help thinking that a night of unbroken rest would have been more conducive to that end. The Spirit must have heard him thinking, for it said immediately:

"Your reclamation, then. Take heed."

It put out its strong hand as it spoke, and clasped him gently by the arm. "Rise. And walk with me."

It would have been in vain for Scrooge to plead that the weather and the hour were not adapted to pedestrian purposes; that the bed was warm, and the thermometer a long way below freezing; that he was clad but lightly in his slippers, dressing-gown, and nightcap; and that he had a cold upon him at that time. The grasp, though gentle as a woman's hand, was not to be resisted. He rose: but finding that the Spirit made towards the window, clasped his robe in supplication.

"I am mortal," Scrooge remonstrated, "and liable to fall."

"Bear but a touch of my hand there," said the Spirit, laying it upon his heart, "and you shall be upheld in more than this."

As the words were spoken, they passed through the wall, and stood upon an open country road, with fields on either hand. The city had entirely vanished. Not a vestige of it was to be seen. The darkness and the mist had vanished with it, for it was a clear, cold, winter day, with snow upon the ground.

"Good Heaven!" said Scrooge, clasping his hands together, as he looked about him. "I was bred in this place. I was a boy here."

The Spirit gazed upon him mildly. Its gentle touch, though it had been light and instantaneous, appeared still present to the old man's sense of feeling. He was conscious of a thousand odors floating in the air, each one connected with a thousand thoughts, and hopes, and joys, and cares long, long, forgotten.

"Your lip is trembling," said the Ghost. "And what is that upon your cheek?"

Scrooge muttered, with an unusual catching in his voice, that it was a pimple; and begged the Ghost to lead him where he would.

"You recollect the way?" inquired the Spirit.

"Remember it!" cried Scrooge with fervor—"I could walk it blindfold."

"Strange to have forgotten it for so many years," observed the Ghost. "Let us go on."

They walked along the road, Scrooge recognizing every gate, and post, and tree; until a little market-town appeared in the distance, with its bridge, its church, its ruined castle,[8] and winding river. Some shaggy ponies now were seen trotting towards them with boys upon their backs, who called to other boys in country gigs and carts, driven by farmers. All these boys were in great spirits, and shouted to each other, until the broad fields were so full of merry music, that the crisp air laughed to hear it.

"These are but shadows of the things that have been," said the Ghost. "They have no consciousness of us."

The jocund travelers came on; and as they came, Scrooge knew and named them every one. Why was he rejoiced beyond all bounds to see them. Why did his cold eye glisten, and his heart leap up as they went past? Why was he filled with gladness when he heard them give each other Merry Christmas, as they parted at cross-roads and-bye ways, for their several homes? What was Merry Christmas to Scrooge? Out upon merry Christmas! What good had it ever done to him?

"The school is not quite deserted," said the Ghost. "A solitary child, neglected by his friends, is left there still."

Scrooge said he knew it. And he sobbed.

They left the high-road, by a well-remembered lane, and soon approached a mansion[9] of dull red brick, with a little weathercock-surmounted cupola, on the roof, and a bell hanging in it. It was a large house, but one of broken fortunes; for the spacious offices were little used, their walls were damp and mossy, their windows broken, and their gates decayed. Fowls clucked and strutted in the stables; and the coach-houses and sheds were over-run with grass. Nor was it more retentive of its ancient state, within; for entering the dreary hall, and glancing through the open doors of many rooms, they found them poorly furnished, cold, and vast. There was an earthy savor in the air, a chilly bareness in the place, which associated itself somehow with too much getting up by candle-light, and not too much to eat.

They went, the Ghost and Scrooge, across the hall, to a door at the back of the house. It opened before them, and disclosed a long, bare, melancholy room, made barer still by lines of plain deal forms[10] and desks. At one of these, a lonely boy was reading[11] near a feeble fire; and Scrooge sat down upon a form, and wept to see his poor forgotten self as he used to be.

Not a latent echo in the house, not a squeak and scuffle from the mice behind the paneling, not a drip from the half-thawed water-spout in the dull yard behind, not a sigh among the leafless boughs of one despondent poplar, not the idle swinging of an empty store-house door, no, not a clicking in the fire, but fell upon the heart of Scrooge with a softening influence, and gave a freer passage to his tears.

The Spirit touched him on the arm, and pointed to his younger self, intent upon his reading. Suddenly a man, in foreign garments: wonderfully real and distinct to look at: stood outside the window, with an ax stuck in his belt, and leading by the bridle an ass laden with wood.

"Why, it's Ali Baba!"[12] Scrooge exclaimed in ecstasy. "It's dear old honest Ali Baba. Yes, yes, I know. One Christmas time, when yonder solitary child was left here all alone, he did come, for the first time, just like that. Poor boy. And Valentine,"[13] said Scrooge, "and his wild brother, Orson; there they go. And what's his name,[14] who was put down in his drawers, asleep, at the Gate of Damascus; don't you see him? And the Sultan's Groom turned upside down by the genii; there he is upon his head. Serves him right. I'm glad of it. What business had he to be married to the Princess."

To hear Scrooge expending all the earnestness of his nature on such subjects, in a most extraordinary voice between laughing and crying; and to see his heightened and excited face; would have been a surprise to his business friends in the city, indeed.

"There's the Parrot!"[15] cried Scrooge. "Green body and yellow tail, with a thing like a lettuce growing out of the top of his head; there he is! Poor Robin Crusoe, he called him, when he came home again after sailing round the island. "Poor Robin Crusoe, where have you been, Robin Crusoe?" The man thought he was dreaming, but he wasn't. It was the Parrot, you know. There goes Friday, running for his life to the little creek! Halloa! Hoop! Hallo!"

Then, with a rapidity of transition very foreign to his usual character, he said, in pity for his former self, "Poor boy!" and cried again.

"I wish," Scrooge muttered, putting his hand in his pocket, and looking about him, after drying his eyes with his cuff: "but it's too late now."

"What is the matter?" asked the Spirit.

"Nothing," said Scrooge. "Nothing. There was a boy singing a Christmas Carol at my door last night. I should like to have given him something: that's all."

The Ghost smiled thoughtfully, and waved its hand: saying as it did so, "Let us see another Christmas!"

Scrooge's former self grew larger at the words, and the room became a little darker and more dirty. The panels shrank,[16] the windows cracked; fragments of plaster fell out of the ceiling, and the naked laths were shown instead; but how all this was brought about, Scrooge knew no more than you do. He only knew that it was quite correct; that everything had happened so; that there he was, alone again, when all the other boys had gone home for the jolly holidays.

He was not reading now, but walking up and down despairingly.

Scrooge looked at the Ghost, and with a mournful shaking of his head, glanced anxiously towards the door.

It opened; and a little girl, much younger than the boy, came darting in, and putting her arms about his neck, and often kissing him, addressed him as her "Dear, dear brother."

"I have come to bring you home, dear brother!" said the child, clapping her tiny hands, and bending down to laugh. "To bring you home, home, home!"

"Home, little Fan?"[17] returned the boy.

"Yes!" said the child, brimful of glee. "Home, for good and all. Home, forever and ever. Father is so much kinder than he used to be, that home's like Heaven! He spoke so gently to me one dear night when I was going to bed, that I was not afraid to ask him once more if you might come home; and he said Yes, you should; and sent me in a coach to bring you. And you're to be a man!" said the child, opening her eyes, "and are never to come back here; but first, we're to be together all the Christmas long, and have the merriest time in all the world."

"You are quite a woman, little Fan!" exclaimed the boy.

She clapped her hands and laughed, and tried to touch his head; but being too little, laughed again, and stood on tiptoe to embrace him. Then she began to drag him, in her childish eagerness, towards the door; and he, nothing loth to go, accompanied her.

A terrible voice in the hall cried. "Bring down Master Scrooge's box, there!" And in the hall appeared the schoolmaster[18] himself, who glared on Master Scrooge with a ferocious condescension, and threw him into a dreadful state of mind by shaking hands with him. He then conveyed him and his sister into the veryiest old well of a shivering best-parlour that ever was seen, where the maps upon the wall, and the celestial and terrestrial globes in the windows, were waxy with cold. Here he produced a decanter of curiously light wine,[19] and a block of curiously heavy cake, and administered installments of those dainties to the young people: at the same time, sending out a meagrer servant to offer a glass of "something" to the postboy,[20] who answered that he thanked the gentleman, but if it was the same tap as he had tasted before, he had rather not. Master Scrooge's trunk being by this time tied on to the top of the chaise,[21] the children bade the schoolmaster good-bye right willingly; and getting into it, drove gaily down the garden sweep,[22] the quick wheels dashing the hoar-frost and snow from off the dark leaves of the evergreens like spray.

"Always a delicate creature, whom a breath might have withered," said the Ghost. "But she had a large heart!"

"So she had," cried Scrooge. "You're right. I'll not gainsay it, Spirit. God forbid!"

"She died a woman," said the Ghost, "and had, as I think, children."

"One child," Scrooge returned.

"True," said the Ghost. "Your nephew! And she died giving him life; just as, I believe, your mother died giving you life."[23]

Scrooge seemed uneasy in his mind; and answered briefly, "Yes."

Although they had but that moment left the school behind them, they were now in the busy thoroughfares of a city, where shadowy passengers passed and repassed; where shadowy carts and coaches battle for the way, and all the strife and tumult of a real city were. It was made plain enough, by the dressing of the shops, that here too it was Christmas time again; but it was evening, and the streets were lighted up.

The Ghost stopped at a certain warehouse door, and asked Scrooge if he knew it.

"Know it!" said Scrooge. "Was I apprenticed here?"

They went in. At sight of an old gentleman in a Welsh wig, sitting behind such a high desk, that if he had been two inches taller he must have knocked his head against the ceiling, Scrooge cried in great excitement:

"Why, it's old Fezziwig! Bless his heart; it's Fezziwig alive again!"

Old Fezziwig laid down his pen, and looked up at the clock, which pointed to the hour of seven.[24] He rubbed his hands; adjusted his capacious waistcoat; laughed all over himself, from his shows to his organ of benevolence;[25] and called out in a comfortable, oily, rich, fat, jovial voice:

"Yo ho, there! Ebenezer! Dick!"

Scrooge's former self, now grown a young man, came briskly in, accompanied by his fellow-prentice.

"Dick Wilkins, to be sure," said Scrooge to the Ghost. "Bless me, yes. There he is. He was very much attached to me, was Dick. Poor Dick. Dear, dear."

"Yo ho, my boys!" said Fezziwig. "No more work tonight. Christmas Eve, Dick. Christmas, Ebenezer. Let's have the shutters up," cried old Fezziwig, with a sharp clap of his hands, "before a man can say Jack Robinson!"[26]

You wouldn't believe how those two fellows went at it. They charged into the street with the shutters—one, two, three—had them up in their places—four, five, six—barred them and pinned then—seven, eight, nine—and came back before you could have got to twelve, panting like race-horses.

"Hilli-ho!" cried old Fezziwig, skipping down from the high desk, with wonderful agility. "Clear away, my lads, and let's have lots of room here. Hilli-ho, Dick! Chirrup, Ebenezer."

Clear away! There was nothing they wouldn't have cleared away, or couldn't have cleared away, with old Fezziwig looking on. It was done in a minute. Every movable was packed off, as if it were dismissed from public life for evermore; the floor was swept and watered, the lamps were trimmed, fuel was heaped upon the fire; and the warehouse was as snug, and warm, and dry, and bright a ball-room, as you would desire to see upon a winter's night.

In came a fiddler with a music-book, and went up to the lofty desk, and made an orchestra of it, and tuned like fifty stomach-aches. In came Mrs. Fezziwig, one vast substantial smile. In came the three Miss Fezziwigs, beaming and lovable. In came the six young followers whose hearts they broke. In came all the young men and women employed in the business. In came the housemaid, with her cousin, the baker. In came the cook, with her brother's particular friend, the milkman. In came the boy from over the way, who was suspected of not having board enough from his master; trying to hide himself behind the girl from next door but one, who was proved to have had her ears pulled by her mistress. In they all came, one after another; some shyly, some boldly, some gracefully, some awkwardly, some pushing, some pulling; in they all came, anyhow and everyhow. Away they all went, twenty couple at once; hands half round and back again the other way; down the middle and up again; round and round in various stages of affectionate grouping; old top couple always turning up in the wrong place; new top couple starting off again, as soon as they got there; all top couples at last, and not a bottom one to help them. When this result was brought about, old Fezziwig, clapping his hands to stop the dance, cried out, "Well done!" and the fiddler plunged his hot face into a pot of porter,[27] especially provided for that purpose. But scorning rest, upon his reappearance, he instantly began again, though there were no dancers yet, as if the other fiddler had been carried home, exhausted, on a shutter, and he were a branD-new man resolved to beat him out of sight, or perish.

There were more dances, and there were forfeits,[28] and more dances, and there was cake, and there was negus,[29] and there was a great piece of Cold Roast, and there was a great piece of Cold Boiled, and there were mince-pies, and plenty of beer. But the great effect of the evening came after the Roast and Boiled, when the fiddler (an artful dog, mind! The sort of man who knew his business better than you or I could have told it him!) struck up "Sir Roger de Coverley."[30] Then old Fezziwig stood out to dance with Mrs. Fezziwig. Top couple too; with a good stiff piece of work cut out for them; three or four and twenty pair of partners; people who were not to be trifled with; people who *would* dance, and had no notion of walking.

But if they had been twice as many—ah, four times—old Fezziwig would have been a match for them, and so would Mrs. Fezziwig. As to *her*, she was worthy to be his partner in every sense of the term. If that's not high praise, tell me higher, and I'll use it. A positive light appeared to issue from Fezziwig's calves. They shone in every part of the dance like moons. You couldn't have predicted, at any given time, what would have become of them next. And when old Fezziwig and Mrs. Fezziwig had gone all through the dance; advance and retire, both hands to your partner, bow and curtsey, corkscrew, thread-the-needle, and back again to your place; Fezziwig "cut,"[31] and cut so deftly, that he appeared to wink with his legs, and came upon his feet again without a stagger.

When the clock struck eleven, this domestic ball broke up. Mr. and Mrs. Fezziwig took their stations, one on either side of the door, and shaking hands with every person individually as he or she went out, wished him or her a Merry Christmas. When everybody had retired but the two prentices, they did the same to them; and thus the cheerful voices died away, and the lads were left to their beds; which were under a counter in the back-shop.

During the whole of this time, Scrooge had acted like a man out of his wits. His heart and soul were in the scene, and with his former self. He corroborated everything, remembered everything, enjoyed everything, and underwent the strangest agitation. It was not until now, when the bright faces of his former self and Dick were turned from them, that he remembered the Ghost, and became conscious that it was looking full upon him, while the light upon its head burnt very clear.

"A small matter," said the Ghost, "to make these silly folks so full of gratitude."

"Small!" echoed Scrooge.

The Spirit signed to him to listen to the two apprentices, who were pouring out their hearts in praise of Fezziwig: and when he had done so, said, "Why! Is it not! He has spent but a few pounds of your mortal money: three or four perhaps. Is that so much that he deserves this praise?"

"It isn't that," said Scrooge, heated by the remark, and speaking unconsciously like his former, not his latter, self. "It isn't that, Spirit. He has the power to render us happy or unhappy; to make our service light or burdensome; a pleasure or a toil. Say that his power lies in words and looks; in things so slight and insignificant that it is impossible to add and count them up: what then? The happiness he gives, is quite as great as if it cost a fortune."

He felt the Spirit's glance, and stopped.

"What is the matter?" asked the Ghost.

"Nothing in particular," said Scrooge.

"Something, I think?" the Ghost insisted.

"No," said Scrooge, "No. I should like to be able to say a word or two to my clerk just now! That's all."

His former self turned down the lamps as he gave utterance to the wish; and Scrooge and the Ghost again stood side by side in the open air.

"My time grows short," observed the Spirit. "Quick!"

This was not addressed to Scrooge, or to any one whom he could see, but it produced an immediate effect. For again Scrooge saw himself. He was older now; a man in the prime of life. His face had not the harsh and rigid lines of later years; but it had begun to wear the signs of care and avarice. There was an eager, greedy, restless motion in the eye, which showed the passion that had taken root, and where the shadow of the growing tree would fall.

He was not alone, but sat by the side of a fair young girl in a mourning-dress: in whose eyes there were tears, which sparkled in the light that shone out of the Ghost of Christmas Past.

"It matters little," she said, softly. "To you, very little. Another idol has displaced me; and if it can cheer and comfort you in time to come, as I would have tried to do, I have no just cause to grieve."

"What Idol has displaced you?" he rejoined.

"A golden one."[32]

"This is the even-handed dealing of the world!" he said. "There is nothing on which it is so hard as poverty; and there is nothing it professes to condemn with such severity as the pursuit of wealth!"

"You fear the world too much," she answered, gently. "All your other hopes have merged into the hope of being beyond the chance of its sordid reproach. I have seen your nobler aspirations fall off one by one, until the master-passion, Gain, engrosses you. Have I not?"

"What then?" he retorted. "Even if I have grown so much wiser, what then? I am not changed towards you."

She shook her head.

"Am I?"

"Our contract is an old one. It was made when we were both poor and content to be so, until, in good season, we could improve our worldly fortune by our patient industry. You *are* changed. When it was made, you were another man."

"I was a boy," he said impatiently.

"Your own feeling tells you that you were not what you are," she returned. "I am. That which promised happiness when we were one in heart, is fraught with misery now that we are two. How often and how keenly I have thought of this, I will not say. It is enough that I *have* thought of it, and can release you from our engagement."[33]

"Have I ever sought release?"

"In words? No. Never."

"In what, then?"

"In a changed nature; in an altered spirit; in another atmosphere of life; another Hope as its great end. In everything that made my love of any worth or value in your sight. If this had never been between us," said the girl, looking mildly, but with steadiness, upon him; "tell me, would you seek me out and try to win me now? Ah, no!"

He seemed to yield to the justice of this supposition, in spite of himself. But he said with a struggle," "You think not?"

"I would gladly think otherwise if I could," she answered, "Heaven knows. When *I* have learned a Truth like this, I know how strong and irresistible it must be. But if you were free today, tomorrow, yesterday, can even I believe that you would choose a dowerless girl[34]—you who, in your very confidence with her, weigh everything by Gain: or, choosing her, if for a moment you were false enough to your one guiding principle to do so, do I not know that your repentance and regret would surely follow? I do; and I release you. With a full heart, for the love of him you once were."

He was about to speak; but with her head turned from him, she resumed.

"You may—the memory of what is past half makes me hope you will—

have pain in this. A very, very brief time, and you will dismiss the recollection of it, gladly, as an unprofitable dream, from which it happened well that you awoke. May you be happy in the life you have chosen."

She left him, and they parted.

"Spirit!" said Scrooge, "show me no more! Conduct me home. Why do you delight to torture me?"

"One shadow more!" exclaimed the Ghost.

"No more!" cried Scrooge! "No more, I don't wish to see it! Show me no more!"

But the relentless Ghost pinioned him in both his arms, and forced him to observe what happened next.

They were in another scene and place; a room, not very large or handsome, but full of comfort. Near to the winter fire sat a beautiful young girl, so like that last that Scrooge believed it was the same, until he saw *her*, now a comely matron, sitting opposite her daughter. The noise in this room was perfectly tumultuous, for there were more children there, than Scrooge in his agitated state of mind could count; and, unlike the celebrated herd in the poem,[35] they were not forty children conducting themselves like one, but every child was conducting itself like forty. The consequences were uproarious beyond belief; but no one seemed to care; on the contrary, the mother and daughter laughed heartily, and enjoyed it very much; and the latter, soon beginning to mingle in the sports, got pillaged by the young brigands most ruthlessly. "What would I not have given to one of them! Though I never could have been so rude, no, no! I wouldn't for the wealth of all the world have crushed that braided hair, and torn it down; and for the precious little shoe, I wouldn't have plucked it off, God bless my soul! To save my life. As to measuring her waist in sport, as they did, bold young brood, I couldn't have done it; I should have expected my arm to have grown round it for a punishment, and never come straight again. And yet I should have dearly liked, I own, to have touched her lips; to have questioned her, that she might have opened them; to have looked upon the lashes of her downcast eyes, and never raised a blush; to have let loose waves of hair, an inch of which would be a keepsake beyond price: in short, I should have liked, I do confess, to have had the lightest licence of a child, and yet to have been man enough to know its value."

But now a knocking at the door was heard, and such a rush immediately ensued that she with laughing face and plundered dress was borne towards it—the center of a flushed and boisterous group, just in time to greet the father, who came home attended by a man laden with Christmas toys and presents. Then the shouting and the struggling, and the onslaught that was made on the defenseless porter. The scaling him with chairs for ladders to dive into his pockets, despoil him of brown-paper parcels, hold on tight by his cravat, hug him round his neck, pommel his back, and kick his legs in irrepressible affection. The shouts of wonder and delight with which the development of every package was received. The terrible announcement that the baby had been taken in the act of putting a doll's frying-pan into his mouth, and was more than suspected of having swallowed a fictitious turkey, glued on a wooden platter. The immense relief of finding this a false alarm. The joy, and gratitude, and ecstasy. They are all indescribable alike. It is enough that by degrees the children and their emotions got out of the parlor, and by one stair at a time, up to the top of the house; where they went to bed, and so subsided.

And now Scrooge looked on more attentively than ever, when the master of the house, having his daughter leaning fondly on him, sat down with her and her mother at his own fireside; and when he thought that such another creature, quite as graceful and as full of promise, might have called him father, and been a spring-time in the haggard winter of his life, his sight grew very dim indeed.

"Belle," said the husband, turning to his wife with a smile, "I saw an old friend of yours this afternoon."

"Who was it?"

"Guess!"

"How can I? Tut, don't I know," she added in the same breath, laughing as he laughed. "Mr. Scrooge."

"Mr. Scrooge it was. I passed his office window; and as it was not shut up, and he had a candle inside, I could scarcely help seeing him. His partner lies upon the point of death, I hear; and there he sat alone. Quite alone in the world, I do believe."

"Spirit!" said Scrooge in a broken voice, "remove me from this place."

"I told you these were shadows of the things that have been," said the Ghost. "That they are what they are, do not blame me!"

"Remove me!" Scrooge exclaimed, "I cannot bear it!"

He turned upon the Ghost, and seeing that it looked upon him with a face, in which in some strange way there were fragments of all the faces it had shown him, wrestled with it.

"Leave me! Take me back. Haunt me no longer!"

In the struggle, if that can be called a struggle in which the Ghost with no visible resistance on its own part was undisturbed by any effort of its adversary, Scrooge observed that its light was burning high and bright; and dimly connecting that with its influence over him, he seized the extinguisher-cap, and by a sudden action pressed it down upon its head.

The Spirit dropped beneath it, so that the extinguisher covered its whole form; but though Scrooge pressed it down with all his force, he could not hide the light,[36] which streamed from under it, in an unbroken flood upon the ground.

He was conscious of being exhausted, and overcome by an irresistible drowsiness; and, further, of being in his own bedroom. He gave the cap a parting squeeze, in which his hand relaxed; and had barely time to reel to bed, before he sank into a heavy sleep.

Stave Two Footnotes:

1 According to Hearn's research (referencing Gwen Majors): St. Andrews Undershaft Church, at the corner of Leadenhall Street and St. Mary Avenue.

2 Repeating watch or clock (invented about 1676).

3 If a bill of exchange was not presented by the third day, it would not be honored, and the money would consequently be lost.

4 After the Panic of 1837, many states repudiated their bonds, thus dramatically weakening American credit around the world.

5 Hearn feels the reason for Leech's not illustrating the First Spirit was because Dickens was so ambiguous about it himself; More than 2000 years old but young, like the Germanic *Christkindl*, or *Christkind*, which is usually portrayed by a girl; but also like Kris Kringle, more an older man, such as St. Nicholas or Santa Claus.

6 That there is need for an extinguisher implies a candle-like figure.

7 A pun with a double meaning: both knocking someone's hat down over the eyes or snuffing out a candle with a bonnet (or cap).

8 Hearn reveals that Dickens had included the castle reference in his first manuscript (thus making it evident he was referring to his childhood home: Medway River, Strood, Chatham, and Rochester), but for some reason, deleated it.

9 According to Hearn, this was the Wellington Academy where Dickens received a brief year-and-a-half education before leaving at fifteen. A counterpart is in *David Copperfield* as well.

10 Long, unpainted, unvarnished pine benches.

11 Dickens, being a sickly boy, more often thannot, read while his classmates were playing.

12 Dickens is now in a childish dreamworld, where figures in the books he read were as real as any he knew outside of books. He loved *The Arabian Nights* as a child.

13 *The History of the Two Valyannte Brethren* (1495), translated by Henry Watson into English in 1565 (Heam).

14 Bedridden Hassan, from *The Arabian Nights*.

15 From *Robinson Crusoe*, which Dickens read over and over again as a child.

16 A way of expressing the rapid passage of time.

17 Dickens also had a sister named Fanny, who, two years older than he, would die at the age of thirty-eight (see Dickens biography in the introduction), five years after *A Christmas Carol* was written.

18 Dickens, like most schoolchildren of his day, experienced bery little kindness in school. Many of the schoolmasters were, in fact, sadistic.

19 Hearn, referncing *Punch*, notes that it was customary at English boarding schools for masters to offer "half-baked cake and home-made wine" to departing students.

20 Driver of the carriage.

21 Carriage drawn by one horse.

22 Curve of the driveway through the grounds.

23 Apparently, Dickens, in his public readings, may have implied that both women died young, in childbirth—or shortly after—and since that time, in stage, photogplay, and film portrayals of the story, it has occasionally been incorporated into the text.

24 Businesses were usually open until 9:00 P.M.

25 Phrenologists, diving the brain into forty parts, positioned "benevolence" in the forehead, according to Hearn.

26 Heam notes that the name came from a seventeenth-century comic song, based on a real person who'd arrive at friends' homes and leave before he could even be announced.

27 A cheap popular ale.

28 By the early nineteenth century, forfeit payment was usually taken in kisses rather than in coins.

29 A drink made of wine, hot water, sugar, nutmeg, and lemon juice.

30 Hearn notes that this very popular country dance (dating back to the Normans) was incredibly complicated, only the best dancers being able to do it without a misstep. For good reason, it was generally the last dance of the evening. Dickens himself loved to dance the "Sir Roger de Coverley."

31 A fancy dance step in which a dancer, leaping into the air, alternates his feet (one in front of the other) before touching ground.

32 See Exodus 32.

33 Hearn notes that in his later public readings, to make it clear to audiences what the agreement was, Dickens added the word "engagement."

34 Apparently, her parents had recently died, leaving her nothing for a dowry.

35 "Written in March" (1802), by William Wordsworth.

36 Hearn feels the significance here is that, try as he may, Scrooge cannot snuff out—or forget—the lessons the Spirit has taught him. And this First Spirit, essentially a radiant effervescent candle, is a symbol for memory, which can be fully extinguished only by death.

THE EXTINGUISHER

Stave Three:

The Second of the Three Spirits

Awaking in the middle of a prodigiously tough snore, and sitting up in bed to get his thoughts together, Scrooge had no occasion to be told that the bell was again upon the stroke of One. He felt that he was restored to consciousness in the right nick of time, for the especial purpose of holding a conference with the second messenger dispatched to him through Jacob Marley's intervention. But, finding that he turned uncomfortably cold when he began to wonder which of his curtains this new specter would draw back, he put them every one aside with his own hands, and lying down again, established a sharp look-out all round the bed. For, he wished to challenge the Spirit on the moment of its appearance, and did not wish to be taken by surprise, and made nervous.

Gentlemen of the free-and-easy[1] sort, who plume themselves on being acquainted with a move or two,[2] and being usually equal to the time of day,[3] express the wide range of their capacity for adventure by observing that they are good for anything from pitch-and-toss to manslaughter; between which opposite extremes, no doubt, there lies a tolerably wide and comprehensive range of subjects. Without venturing for Scrooge quite as hardily as this, I don't mind calling on you to believe that he was ready for a good broad field of strange appearances, and that nothing between a baby and rhinoceros would have astonished him very much.

Now, being prepared for almost anything, he was not by any means prepared for nothing; and, consequently, when the Bell struck One, and no shape appeared, he was taken with a violent fit of trembling. Five minutes, ten minutes, a quarter of an hour went by, yet nothing came. All this time, he lay upon his bed, the very core and center of a blaze of ruddy light, which streamed upon it when the clock proclaimed the hour; and which, being only light, was more alarming than a dozen ghosts, as he was powerless to make out what it meant, or would be at; and was sometimes apprehensive that he might be at that very moment an interesting case of spontaneous combustion, without having the consolation of knowing it. At last, however, he began to think—as you or I would have thought at first; for it is always the person not in the predicament who knows what ought to have been done in it, and would unquestionably have done it too—at last, I say, he began to think that the source and secret of this ghostly light might be in the adjoining room, from whence, on further tracing it, it seemed to shine. This idea taking full possession of his mind, he got up softly and shuffled in his slippers to the door.

The moment Scrooge's hand was on the lock, a strange voice called him by his name, and bade him enter. He obeyed.

It was his own room. There was no doubt about that. But it had undergone a surprising transformation. The walls and ceiling were so hung with living green,[4] that it looked a perfect grove; from every part of which, bright gleaming berries glistened. The crisp leaves of holly, mistletoe, and ivy reflected back the light, as if so many little mirrors had been scattered there; and such a mighty blaze went roaring up the chimney, as that dull petrifaction of a hearth had never known in Scrooge's time, or Marley's, or for many and many a winter season gone. Heaped up on the floor, to form a kind of throne, were turkeys, geese, game, poultry, brawn,[5] great joints of meat, sucking-pigs,[6] long wreaths of sausages, mince-pies, plum-puddings, barrels of oysters, red-hot chestnuts, cherry-cheeked apples, juicy oranges, luscious pears, immense twelfth-cakes,[7] and seething bowls of punch,[8] that made the chamber dim with their delicious steam. In easy state upon this couch, there sat a jolly Giant,[9] glorious to see, who bore a glowing torch, in shape not unlike Plenty's horn,[10] and held it up, high up, to shed its light on Scrooge, as he came peeping round the door.

"Come in!" exclaimed the Ghost. "Come in, and know me better, man."

Scrooge entered timidly, and hung his head before this Spirit. He was not the dogged Scrooge he had been; and though the Spirit's eyes were clear and kind, he did not like to meet them.

"I am the Ghost of Christmas Present," said the Spirit. "Look upon me."

Scrooge reverently did so. It was clothed in one simple green robe, or mantle, bordered with white fur. This garment hung so loosely on the figure, that its capacious breast[11] was bare, as if disdaining to be warded or concealed by any artifice. Its feet, observable beneath the ample folds of the garment, were also bare; and on its head it wore no other covering than a holly wreath, set here and there with shining icicles. Its dark brown curls were long and free; free as its genial face, its sparkling eye, its open hand, its cheery voice, its unconstrained demeanor, and its joyful air. Girded round its middle was an antique scabbard; but no sword was in it, and the ancient sheath was eaten up with rust.[12]

"You have never seen the like of me before!" exclaimed the Spirit.

"Never," Scrooge made answer to it.

"Have never walked forth with the younger members of my family; meaning (for I am very young) my elder brothers born in these later years?" pursued the Phantom.

"I don't think I have," said Scrooge. "I am afraid I have not. Have you had many brothers, Spirit?"

"More than eighteen hundred,"[13] said the Ghost.

"A tremendous family to provide for," muttered Scrooge.

The Ghost of Christmas Present rose.

"Spirit," said Scrooge submissively, "conduct me where you will. I went forth last night on compulsion, and I learnt a lesson which is working now. Tonight, if you have aught to teach me, let me profit by it."

"Touch my robe."

Scrooge did as he was told, and held it fast.

Holly, mistletoe, red berries, ivy, turkeys, geese, game, poultry, brawn, meat, pigs, sausages, oysters, pies, puddings, fruit, and punch, all vanished instantly. So did the room, the fire, the ruddy glow, the hour of night, and they stood in the city streets on Christmas morning, where (for the weather was severe) the people made a rough, but brisk and not unpleasant kind of music, in scraping the snow from the pavement in front of their dwellings, and from the tops of their houses, whence it was mad delight to the boys to see it come plumping down into the road below, and splitting into artificial little snow-storms.

The house fronts looked black enough, and the windows blacker, contrasting with the smooth white sheet of snow upon the roofs, and with the dirtier snow upon the ground; which last deposit had been ploughed up in deep furrows by the heavy wheels of carts and wagons; furrows that crossed and recrossed each other hundreds of times where the great streets branched off, and made intricate channels, hard to trace in the thick yellow mud and icy water. The sky was gloomy, and the shortest streets were choked up with a dingy mist, half thawed, half frozen, whose heavier particles descended in shower of sooty atoms, as if all the chimneys in Great Britain had, by one consent, caught fire, and were blazing away to their dear hearts' content. There was nothing very cheerful in the climate or the town, and yet was there an air of cheerfulness abroad that the clearest summer air and brightest summer sun might have endeavored to diffuse in vain.

For, the people who were shoveling away on the housetops were jovial and full of glee; calling out to one another from the parapets, and now and then exchanging a facetious snowball—better-natured missile far than many a wordy jest—laughing heartily if it went right and not less heartily if it went wrong. The poulterers' shops were still half open, and the fruiterers' were radiant in their glory. There were great, round, pot-bellied baskets of chestnuts, shaped like the waistcoats of jolly old gentlemen, lolling at the doors, and tumbling out into the street in their apoplectic opulence. There were ruddy, brown-faced, broad-girthed Spanish Friars, and winking from their shelves in wanton slyness at the girls as they went by, and glanced demurely at the hung-up mistletoe. There were pears and apples, clustered high in blooming pyramids; there were bunches of grapes, made, in the shopkeepers' benevolence to dangle from conspicuous hooks, that people's mouths might water gratis as they passed; there were piles of filberts, mossy and brown, recalling, in their fragrance, ancient walks among the woods, and pleasant shufflings ankle deep through withered leaves; there were Norfolk Biffins,[14] squab and swarthy, setting off the yellow of the oranges and lemons, and, in the great compactness of their juicy persons, urgently entreating and beseeching to be carried home in paper bags and eaten after dinner.

The very gold and silver fish,[15] set forth among these choice fruits in a bowl, though members of a dull and stagnant-blooded race, appeared to know that there was something going on; and, to a fish, went gasping round and round their little world in slow and passionless excitement.

The Grocers! Ooh the Grocers'! Nearly closed, with perhaps two shutters down, or one; but through those gaps such glimpses. It was not alone that the scales descending on the counter made a merry sound, or that the twine and roller parted company so briskly, or that the canisters were rattled up and down like juggling tricks, or even that the blended scents of tea and coffee were so grateful to the nose, or even that the raisins were so plentiful and rare, the almonds so extremely white, the sticks of cinnamon so long and straight, the other spices so delicious, the candied fruits so caked and spotted with molten sugar as to make the coldest lookers-on feel faint and subsequently bilious. Nor was it that the figs were moist and pulpy, or that the French plums blushed in modest tartness from their highly-decorated boxes, or that everything was good to eat and in its Christmas dress; but the customers were all so hurried and so eager in the hopeful promise of the day, that they tumbled up against each other at the door, clashing their wicker baskets wildly, and left their purchases upon the counter, and came running back to fetch them, and committed hundreds of the like mistakes, in the best humor possible; while the Grocer and his people were so frank and fresh that the polished hearts with which they fastened their aprons behind might have been their own, worn outside for general inspection, and for Christmas daws to peck at if they chose.[16]

But soon the steeples called good people all, to church and chapel, and away they came, flocking through the streets in their best clothes, and with their gayest faces. And at the same time there emerged from scores of bye-streets, lanes, and nameless turnings, innumerable people, carrying their dinners to the bakers' shops. The sight of these poor revelers appeared to interest the Spirit very much, for he stood with Scrooge beside him in a baker's doorway, and taking off the covers as their bearers passed, sprinkled incense[17] on their dinners from his torch. And it was a very uncommon kind of torch, for once or twice when there were angry words between some dinner-carriers who had jostled each other, he shed a few drops of water on them from it, and their good humor was restored directly. For they said, it was a shame to quarrel upon Christmas Day. And so it was. God love it, so it was.

In time the bells ceased, and the bakers were shut up; and yet there was a genial shadowing forth of all these dinners and the progress of their cooking, in the thawed blotch of wet above each baker's oven; where the pavement smoked as if its stones were cooking too.

"Is there a peculiar flavor in what you sprinkle from your torch?" asked Scrooge.

"There is. My own."

"Would it apply to any kind of dinner on this day?" asked Scrooge.

"To any kindly given. To a poor one most."

"Why to a poor one most?" asked Scrooge.

"Because it needs it most."

"Spirit," said Scrooge, after a moment's thought, "I wonder you, of all the beings in the many worlds about us, should desire to cramp these people's opportunities of innocent enjoyment."

"I!" cried the Spirit.

"You would deprive them of their means of dining every seventh day, often the only day on which they can be said to dine at all," said Scrooge. "Wouldn't you?"

"I!" cried the Spirit.

"You seek to close these places on the Seventh Day,"[18] said Scrooge. "And it comes to the same thing."

"I seek!" exclaimed the Spirit.

"Forgive me if I am wrong. It has been done in your name, or at least in that of your family," said Scrooge.

"There are some upon this earth of yours," returned the Spirit, "who lay claim to know us, and who do their deeds of passion, pride, ill-will, hatred, envy, bigotry, and selfishness in our name, who are as strange to us and all our kith and kin, as if they had never lived. Remember that, and charge their doings on themselves, not us."

Scrooge promised that he would; and they went on, invisible, as they had been before, into the suburbs of the town. It was a remarkable quality of the Ghost (which Scrooge had observed at the baker's), that notwithstanding his gigantic size, he could accommodate himself to any place with ease; and that he stood beneath a low roof quite as gracefully and like a supernatural creature, as it was possible he could have done in any lofty hall.

And perhaps it was the pleasure the good Spirit had in showing off this power of his, or else it was his own kind, generous, hearty nature, and his sympathy with all poor men, that led him straight to Scrooge's clerk's; for there he went, and took Scrooge with him, holding to his robe; and on the threshold of the door the Spirit smiled, and stopped to bless Bob Cratchit's[19] dwelling with the sprinkling of his torch. Think of that. Bob had but fifteen "bob" a week himself; he pocketed on Saturdays but fifteen copies of his Christian name; and yet the Ghost of Christmas Present blessed his four-roomed house![21]

Then up rose Mrs. Cratchit, Cratchit's wife, dressed out but poorly in a twice-turned gown, but brave in ribbons, which are cheap and make a goodly show for sixpence; and she laid the cloth, assisted by Belinda Cratchit, second of her daughters, also brave in ribbons; while Master Peter Cratchit plunged a fork into the saucepan of potatoes, and getting the corners of his monstrous shirt collar (Bob's private property, conferred upon his son and heir in honor of the day) into his mouth, rejoiced to find himself so gallantly attired, and yearned to show his linen in the fashionable Parks. And now two smaller Cratchits, boy and girl, came tearing in, screaming that outside the baker's they had smelt the goose, and known it for their own; and basking in luxurious thoughts of sage and onion, these young Cratchits danced about the table, and exalted Master Peter Cratchit to the skies, while he (not proud, although his collars nearly choked him) blew the fire, until the slow potatoes bubbling up, knocked loudly at the saucepan-lid to be let out and peeled.

"What has ever got your precious father then?" said Mrs. Cratchit. "And your brother, Tiny Tim?[22] And Martha warn't as late last Christmas Day by half-an-hour."

"Here's Martha, mother," said a girl, appearing as she spoke.

"Here's Martha, mother!" cried the two young Cratchits. "Hurrah! There's such a goose, Martha!"

"Why, bless your heart alive, my dear, how late you are!" said Mrs. Cratchit, kissing her a dozen times, and taking off her shawl and bonnet for her with officious zeal.

"We'd a deal of work to finish up last night," replied the girl, "and had to clear away this morning, mother."

"Well. Never mind so long as you are come," said Mrs. Cratchit. "Sit ye down before the fire, my dear, and have a warm,[23] Lord bless ye."

"No, no. There's father coming," cried the two young Cratchits, who were everywhere at once. "Hide, Martha, hide!"

So Martha hid herself, and in came little Bob, the father, with at least three feet of comforter exclusive of the fringe, hanging down before him; and his threadbare clothes darned up and brushed, to look seasonable; and Tiny Tim upon his shoulder. Alas for Tiny Tim, he bore a little crutch, and had his limbs supported by an iron frame.

"Why, where's our Martha?" cried Bob Cratchit, looking round.

"Not coming," said Mrs. Cratchit.

"Not coming!" said Bob, with a sudden declension in his high spirits; for he had been Tim's blood horse all the way from church, and had come home rampant. "Not coming upon Christmas Day?"

Martha didn't like to see him disappointed, if it were only in joke; so she came out prematurely from behind the closet door, and ran into his arms, while the two young Cratchits hustled Tiny Tim, and bore him off into the wash-house, that he might hear the pudding singing in the copper.[24]

"And how did little Tim behave?" asked Mrs. Cratchit, when she had rallied Bob on his credulity, and Bob had hugged his daughter to his heart's content.

"As good as gold," said Bob, "and better. Somehow he gets thoughtful sitting by himself so much, and thinks the strangest things you ever heard. He told me, coming home, that he hoped the people saw him in the church,[25] because he was a cripple, and it might be pleasant to them to remember upon Christmas Day, who made lame beggars walk, and blind men see."[26]

Bob's voice was tremulous when he told them this, and trembled more when he said that Tiny Tim was growing strong and hearty.

His active little crutch was heard upon the floor, and back came Tiny Tim before another word was spoken, escorted by his brother and sister to his stool before the fire; and while Bob, turning up his cuffs—as if, poor fellow, they were capable of being made more shabby—compounded some hot mixture in a jug with gin and lemons, and stirred it round and round and put it on the hob to simmer; Master Peter, and the two ubiquitous young Cratchits went to fetch the goose, with which they soon returned in high procession.

Such a bustle ensued that you might have thought a goose the rarest of all birds; a feathered phenomenon, to which a black swan was a matter of course—and in truth it was something very like it in that house. Mrs. Cratchit made the gravy (ready beforehand in a little saucepan) hissing hot; Master Peter mashed the potatoes with incredible vigor; Miss Belinda sweetened up the apple-sauce; Martha dusted the hot plates; Bob took Tiny Tim beside him in a tiny corner at the table; the two young Cratchits set chairs for everybody, not forgetting themselves, and mounting guard upon their posts, crammed spoons into their mouths, lest they should shriek for goose before their turn came to be helped. At last the dishes were set on, and grace was said. It was succeeded by a breathless pause, as Mrs. Cratchit, looking slowly all along the carving-knife, prepared to plunge it in the breast; but when she did, and when the long expected gush of stuffing issued forth, one murmur of delight arose all round the board, and even Tiny Tim, excited by the two young Cratchits, beat on the table with the handle of his knife, and feebly cried Hurrah!

There never was such a goose. Bob said he didn't believe there ever was such a goose cooked. Its tenderness and flavor, size and cheapness, were the themes of universal admiration. Eked out by apple-sauce and mashed potatoes, it was a sufficient dinner for the whole family; indeed, as Mrs. Cratchit said with great delight (surveying one small atom of a bone upon the dish), they hadn't ate it all at last. Yet every one had had enough, and the youngest Cratchits in particular, were steeped in sage and onion to the eyebrows. But now, the plates being changed by Miss Belinda, Mrs. Cratchit left the room alone—too nervous to bear witnesses—to take the pudding up and bring it in.

Suppose it should not be done enough? Suppose it should break in turning out? Suppose somebody should have got over the wall of the back-yard, and stolen it,[27] while they were merry with the goose—a supposition at which the two young Cratchits became livid. All sorts of horrors were supposed.

Hallo! A great deal of steam! The pudding was out of the copper. A smell like a washing-day. That was the cloth. A smell like an eating-house and a pastrycook's next door to each other, with a laundress's next door to that. That was the pudding. In half a minute Mrs. Cratchit entered—flushed, but smiling proudly—with the pudding, like a speckled cannon-ball, so hard and firm, blazing in half of half-a-quartern[28] of ignited brandy, and bedight[29] with Christmas holly stuck into the top.

Oh, a wonderful pudding! Bob Cratchit said, and calmly too, that he regarded it as the greatest success achieved by Mrs. Cratchit since their marriage. Mrs. Cratchit said that now the weight was off her mind, she would confess she had had her doubts about the quantity of flour.

Everybody had something to say about it, but nobody said or thought it was at all a small pudding for a large family. It would have been flat heresy to do so. Any Cratchit would have blushed to hint at such a thing.

At last the dinner was all done, the cloth was cleared, the hearth swept, and the fire made up. The compound in the jug being tasted, and considered perfect, apples and oranges were put upon the table, and a shovel-full of chestnuts on the fire. Then all the Cratchit family drew round the hearth, in what Bob Cratchit called a circle, meaning half a one; and at Bob Cratchit's elbow stood the family display of glass. Two tumblers, and a custard-cup without a handle.

These held the hot stuff from the jug, however, as well as golden goblets would have done; and Bob served it out with beaming looks, while the chestnuts on the fire sputtered and cracked noisily. Then Bob proposed:

"A Merry Christmas to us all, my dears. God bless us."

Which all the family re-echoed.

"God bless us every one!" said Tiny Tim, the last of all.

He sat very close to his father's side upon his little stool. Bob held his withered little hand in his, as if he loved the child, and wished to keep him by his side, and dreaded that he might be taken from him.

"Spirit," said Scrooge, with an interest he had never felt before, "tell me if Tiny Tim will live."[30]

"I see a vacant seat," replied the Ghost, "in the poor chimney-corner, and a crutch without an owner, carefully preserved. If these shadows remain unaltered by the Future, the child will die."

"No, no," said Scrooge. "Oh, no, kind Spirit. Say he will be spared."

"If these shadows remain unaltered by the Future, none other of my race," returned the Ghost, "will find him here. What then? If he be like to die, he had better do it, and decrease the surplus population."

Scrooge hung his head to hear his own words quoted by the Spirit, and was overcome with penitence and grief.

"Man," said the Ghost, "if man you be in heart, not adamant, forbear that wicked can't until you have discovered What the surplus is, and

Where it is. Will you decide what men shall live, what men shall die? It may be, that in the sight of Heaven, you are more worthless and less fit to live than millions like this poor man's child. Oh God! To hear the Insect on the leaf pronouncing on the too much life among his hungry brothers in the dust."

Scrooge bent before the Ghost's rebuke, and trembling cast his eyes upon the ground. But he raised them speedily, on hearing his own name.

"Mr. Scrooge!" said Bob; "I'll give you Mr. Scrooge, the Founder of the Feast!"

"The Founder of the Feast indeed!" cried Mrs. Cratchit, reddening. "I wish I had him here. I'd give him a piece of my mind to feast upon, and I hope he'd have a good appetite for it."

"My dear," said Bob, "the children. Christmas Day."

"It should be Christmas Day, I am sure," said she, "on which one drinks the health of such an odious, stingy, hard, unfeeling man as Mr. Scrooge. You know he is, Robert. Nobody knows it better than you do, poor fellow."

"My dear," was Bob's mild answer, "Christmas Day."

"I'll drink his health for your sake and the Day's," said Mrs. Cratchit, "not for his. Long life to him. A merry Christmas and a happy new year!—he'll be very merry and very happy, I have no doubt!"

The children drank the toast after her. It was the first of their proceedings which had no heartiness. Tiny Tim drank it last of all, but he didn't care twopence for it. Scrooge was the Ogre of the family. The mention of his name cast a dark shadow on the party, which was not dispelled for full five minutes.

After it had passed away, they were ten times merrier than before, from the mere relief of Scrooge the Baleful being done with. Bob Cratchit told them how he had a situation in his eye for Master Peter, which would bring in, if obtained, full five-and-sixpence weekly. The two young Cratchits laughed tremendously at the idea of Peter's being a man of business; and Peter himself looked thoughtfully at the fire from between his collars, as if he were deliberating what particular investments he should favor when he came into the receipt of that bewildering income. Martha, who was a poor apprentice at a milliner's, then told them what kind of work she had to do, and how many hours she worked at a stretch, and how she meant to lie abed tomorrow morning for a good long rest; tomorrow being a holiday she passed at home. Also how she had seen a countess and a lord some days before, and how the lord was much about as tall as Peter; at which Peter pulled up his collars so high that you couldn't have seen his head if you had been there. All this time the chestnuts and the jug went round and round; and by-and-by they had a song, about a lost child traveling in the snow, from Tiny Tim, who had a plaintive little voice, and sang it very well indeed.

There was nothing of high mark in this. They were not a handsome family; they were not well dressed; their shoes were far from being waterproof; their clothes were scanty; and Peter might have known, and very likely did, the inside of a pawnbroker's.[31] But, they were happy, grateful, pleased with one another, and contented with the time; and when they faded, and looked happier yet in the bright sprinklings of the Spirit's torch at parting, Scrooge had his eye upon them, and especially on Tiny Tim, until the last.

By this time it was getting dark, and snowing pretty heavily; and as Scrooge and the Spirit went along the streets, the brightness of the roaring fires in kitchens, parlors, and all sorts of rooms, was wonderful. Here, the flickering of the blaze showed preparations for a cozy dinner, with hot plates baking through and through before the fire, and deep red curtains, ready to be drawn to shut out cold and darkness. There all the children of the house were running out into the snow to meet their married sisters, brothers, cousins, uncles, aunts, and be the first to greet them. Here, again, were shadows on the window-blind of guests assembling; and there a group of handsome girls, all hooded and fur-booted, and all chattering at once, tripped lightly off to some near neighbor's house; where, woe upon the single man who saw them enter—artful witches, well they knew it—in a glow.

But, if you had judged from the numbers of people on their way to friendly gatherings, you might have thought that no one was at home to give them welcome when they got there, instead of every house expecting company, and piling up its fires half-chimney high. Blessings on it, how the Ghost exulted. How it bared its breadth of breast, and opened its capacious palm, and floated on, outpouring, with a generous hand, its bright and harmless mirth on everything within its reach. The very lamp-lighter, who ran on before dotting the dusky street with specks of light, and who was dressed to spend the evening somewhere, laughed out loud-ly as the Spirit passed, though little kenned the lamplighter that he had any company but Christmas.

And now, without a word of warning from the Ghost, they stood upon a bleak and desert moor, where monstrous masses of rude stone were cast about, as though it were the burial-place of giants;[32] and water spread itself wheresoever it listed—or would have done so, but for the frost that held it prisoner; and nothing grew but moss and furze,[33] and coarse rank grass. Down in the west the setting sun had left a streak of fiery red, which glared upon the desolation for an instant, like a sullen eye, and frowning lower, lower, lower yet, was lost in the thick gloom of darkest night.

"What place is this?" asked Scrooge.

"A place where miners live,[34] who labor in the bowels of the earth," returned the Spirit. "But they know me. See."

A light shone from the window of a hut, and swiftly they advanced towards it. Passing through the wall of mud and stone, they found a cheerful company assembled round a glowing fire. An old, old man and woman, with their children and their children's children, and another generation beyond that, all decked out gaily in their holiday attire. The old man, in a voice that seldom rose above the howling of the wind upon the barren waste, was singing them a Christmas song—it had been a very old song when he was a boy—and from time to time they all joined in the chorus. So surely as they raised their voices, the old man got quite blithe and loud; and so surely as they stopped, his vigor sank again.

The Spirit did not tarry here, but bade Scrooge hold his robe, and passing on above the moor, sped—whither. Not to sea? To sea. To Scrooge's horror, looking back, he saw the last of the land, a frightful range of rocks, behind them; and his ears were deafened by the thundering of water, as it rolled and roared, and raged among the dreadful caverns it had worn, and fiercely tried to undermine the earth.

Built upon a dismal reef of sunken rocks, some league or so from shore, on which the waters chafed and dashed, the wild year through, there stood a solitary lighthouse.[35] Great heaps of sea-weed clung to its base, and storm-birds—born of the wind one might suppose, as sea-weed of the water—rose and fell about it, like the waves they skimmed.

But even here, two men who watched the light had made a fire, that through the loophole in the thick stone wall shed out a ray of brightness on the awful sea. Joining their horny hands over the rough table at which they sat, they wished each other Merry Christmas in their can of grog; and one of them: the elder, too, with his face all damaged and scarred with hard weather, as the figure-head of an old ship might be: struck up a sturdy song that was like a Gale in itself.

Again the Ghost sped on, above the black and heaving sea—on, on—until, being far away, as he told Scrooge, from any shore, they lighted on a ship. They stood beside the helmsman at the wheel, the look-out in the bow, the officers who had the watch; dark, ghostly figures in their several stations; but every man among them hummed a Christmas tune, or had a Christmas thought, or spoke below his breath to his companion of some bygone Christmas Day, with homeward hopes belonging to it. And every man on board, waking or sleeping, good or bad, had had a kinder word for another on that day than on any day in the year; and had shared to some extent in its festivities; and had remembered those he cared for at a distance, and had known that they delighted to remember him.

It was a great surprise to Scrooge, while listening to the moaning of the wind, and thinking what a solemn thing it was to move on through the lonely darkness over an unknown abyss, whose depths were secrets as profound as Death: it was a great surprise to Scrooge, while thus engaged, to hear a hearty laugh. It was a much greater surprise to Scrooge to recognize it as his own nephew's and to find himself in a bright, dry, gleaming room, with the Spirit standing smiling by his side, and looking at that same nephew with approving affability.

"Ha, ha!" laughed Scrooge's nephew. "Ha, ha, ha!"

If you should happen, by any unlikely chance, to know a man more blest in a laugh than Scrooge's nephew, all I can say is, I should like to know him too. Introduce him to me, and I'll cultivate his acquaintance.

It is a fair, even-handed, noble adjustment of things, that while there is infection in disease and sorrow, there is nothing in the world so irresistibly contagious as laughter and good-humor. When Scrooge's nephew laughed in this way: holding his sides, rolling his head, and twisting his face into the most extravagant contortions: Scrooge's niece, by marriage, laughed as heartily as he. And their assembled friends being not a bit behindhand, roared out lustily.

"Ha, ha! Ha, ha, ha, ha!"

"He said that Christmas was a humbug, as I live!" cried Scrooge's nephew. "He believed it too."

"More shame for him, Fred." said Scrooge's niece, indignantly. Bless those women; they never do anything by halves. They are always in earnest.

She was very pretty: exceedingly pretty. With a dimpled, surprised-looking, capital face; a ripe little mouth, that seemed made to be kissed—as no doubt it was; all kinds of good little dots about her chin, that melted into one another when she laughed; and the sunniest pair of eyes you ever saw in any little creature's head. Altogether she was what you would have called provoking,[36] you know; but satisfactory, too. Oh perfectly satisfactory!

"He's a comical old fellow," said Scrooge's nephew, "that's the truth: and not so pleasant as he might be. However, his offenses carry their own punishment, and I have nothing to say against him."

"I'm sure he is very rich, Fred," hinted Scrooge's niece. "At least you always tell me so."

"What of that, my dear?" said Scrooge's nephew. "His wealth is of no use to him. He don't do any good with it. He don't make himself comfortable with it. He hasn't the satisfaction of thinking—ha, ha, ha!—that he is ever going to benefit us with it."

"I have no patience with him," observed Scrooge's niece. Scrooge's niece's sisters, and all the other ladies, expressed the same opinion.

"Oh, I have," said Scrooge's nephew. "I am sorry for him; I couldn't be angry with him if I tried. Who suffers by his ill whims? Himself, always. Here, he takes it into his head to dislike us, and he won't come and dine with us. What's the consequence? He don't lose much of a dinner."

"Indeed, I think he loses a very good dinner," interrupted Scrooge's niece. Everybody else said the same, and they must be allowed to have been competent judges, because they had just had dinner; and, with the dessert upon the table, were clustered round the fire, by lamplight.

"Well. I'm very glad to hear it," said Scrooge's nephew, "because I haven't great faith in these young housekeepers. What do you say, Topper?"

Topper had clearly got his eye upon one of Scrooge's niece's sisters, for he answered that a bachelor was a wretched outcast, who had no right to express an opinion on the subject. Whereat Scrooge's niece's sister—the plump one with the lace tucker: not the one with the roses—blushed.

"Do go on, Fred," said Scrooge's niece, clapping her hands. "He never finishes what he begins to say. He is such a ridiculous fellow."

Scrooge's nephew reveled in another laugh, and as it was impossible to keep the infection off; though the plump sister tried hard to do it with aromatic vinegar; his example was unanimously followed.

"I was only going to say," said Scrooge's nephew, "that the consequence of his taking a dislike to us, and not making merry with us, is, as I think, that he loses some pleasant moments, which could do him no harm. I am sure he loses pleasanter companions than he can find in his own thoughts, either in his moldy old office, or his dusty chambers. I mean to give him the same chance every year, whether he likes it or not, for I pity him. He may rail at Christmas till he dies, but he can't help thinking better of it—

I defy him—if he finds me going there, in good temper, year after year, and saying Uncle Scrooge, how are you. If it only puts him in the vein to leave his poor clerk fifty pounds, that's something; and I think I shook him yesterday."

It was their turn to laugh now at the notion of his shaking Scrooge. But being thoroughly good-natured, and not much caring what they laughed at, so that they laughed at any rate, he encouraged them in their merriment, and passed the bottle joyously.

After tea they had some music. For they were a musical family, and knew what they were about, when they sung a Glee[37] or Catch,[38] I can assure you: especially Topper, who could growl away in the bass like a good one, and never swell the large veins in his forehead, or get red in the face over it. Scrooge's niece played well upon the harp; and played among other tunes a simple little air (a mere nothing: you might learn to whistle it in two minutes), which had been familiar to the child who fetched Scrooge from the boarding-school, as he had been reminded by the Ghost of Christmas Past. When this strain of music sounded, all the things that Ghost had shown him, came upon his mind; he softened more and more; and thought that if he could have listened to it often, years ago, he might have cultivated the kindnesses of life for his own happiness with his own hands, without resorting to the sexton's spade that buried Jacob Marley.

But they didn't devote the whole evening to music. After a while they played at forfeits; for it is good to be children sometimes, and never better than at Christmas, when its mighty Founder was a child himself. Stop. There was first a game at blind-man's buff. Of course there was. And I no more believe Topper was really blind than I believe he had eyes in his boots. My opinion is, that it was a done thing between him and Scrooge's nephew; and that the Ghost of Christmas Present knew it. The way he went after that plump sister in the lace tucker, was an outrage on the credulity of human nature. Knocking down the fire-irons, tumbling over the chairs, bumping against the piano, smothering himself among the curtains, wherever she went, there went he. He always knew where the plump sister was. He wouldn't catch anybody else. If you had fallen up against him (as some of them did), on purpose, he would have made a feint of endeavoring to seize you, which would have been an affront to your understanding, and would instantly have sidled off in the direction of the plump sister. She often cried out that it wasn't fair; and it really was not. But when at last, he caught her; when, in spite of all her silken rustlings, and her rapid flutterings past him, he got her into a corner whence there was no escape; then his conduct was the most execrable. For his pretending not to know her; his pretending that it was necessary to touch her head-dress, and further to assure himself of her identity by pressing a certain ring upon her finger, and a certain chain about her neck; was vile, monstrous. No doubt she told him her opinion of it, when, another blind-man being in office, they were so very confidential together, behind the curtains.

Scrooge's niece was not one of the blind-man's buff party, but was made comfortable with a large chair and a footstool, in a snug corner, where the Ghost and Scrooge were close behind her. But she joined in the forfeits, and loved her love to admiration with all the letters of the alphabet.[39] Likewise at the game of How, When, and Where,[40] she was very great, and to the secret joy of Scrooge's nephew, beat her sisters hollow: though they were sharp girls too, as could have told you. There might have been twenty people there, young and old, but they all played, and so did Scrooge, for, wholly forgetting the interest he had in what was going on, that his voice made no sound in their ears, he sometimes came out with his guess quite loud, and very often guessed quite right, too; for the sharpest needle, best Whitechapel,[41] warranted not to cut in the eye, was not sharper than Scrooge; blunt as he took it in his head to be.

The Ghost was greatly pleased to find him in this mood, and looked upon him with such favor, that he begged like a boy to be allowed to stay until the guests departed. But this the Spirit said could not be done.

"Here's a new game," said Scrooge. "One half hour, Spirit, only one."

It was a Game called Yes and No,[42] where Scrooge's nephew had to think of something, and the rest must find out what; he only answering to their questions yes or no, as the case was. The brisk fire of questioning to which he was exposed, elicited from him that he was thinking of an animal, a live animal, rather a disagreeable animal, a savage animal, an animal that growled and grunted sometimes, and talked sometimes, and lived in London, and walked about the streets, and wasn't made a show of, and wasn't led by anybody, and didn't live in a menagerie, and was never killed in a market, and was not a horse, or an ass, or a cow, or a bull, or a tiger, or a dog, or a pig, or a cat, or a bear. At every fresh question that was put to him, this nephew burst into a fresh roar of laughter; and was so inexpressibly tickled, that he was obliged to get up off the sofa and stamp. At last the plump sister, falling into a similar state, cried out:

"I have found it out! I know what it is, Fred! I know what it is!"

"What is it?" cried Fred.

"It's your Uncle Scrooge!"

Which it certainly was. Admiration was the universal sentiment, though some objected that the reply to "Is it a bear?" ought to have been "Yes," inasmuch as an answer in the negative was sufficient to have diverted their thoughts from Mr. Scrooge, supposing they had ever had any tendency that way.

"He has given us plenty of merriment, I am sure," said Fred, "and it would be ungrateful not to drink his health. Here is a glass of mulled wine ready to our hand at the moment; and I say, 'Uncle Scrooge!'"

"Well! Uncle Scrooge!" they cried.

"A Merry Christmas and a Happy New Year to the old man, whatever he is," said Scrooge's nephew. "He wouldn't take it from me, but may he have it, nevertheless. Uncle Scrooge!"

Uncle Scrooge had imperceptibly become so gay and light of heart, that he would have pledged the unconscious company in return, and thanked them in an inaudible speech, if the Ghost had given him time. But the whole scene passed off in the breath of the last word spoken by his nephew; and he and the Spirit were again upon their travels.

Much they saw, and far they went, and many homes they visited, but always with a happy end. The Spirit stood beside sick beds, and they were cheerful; on foreign lands, and they were close at home; by struggling men, and they were patient in their greater hope; by poverty, and it was rich. In almshouse, hospital, and jail, in misery's every refuge, where vain man in his little brief authority had not made fast the door and barred the Spirit out, he left his blessing, and taught Scrooge his precepts.

It was a long night, if it were only a night; but Scrooge had his doubts of this, because the Christmas Holidays appeared to be condensed into the space of time they passed together. It was strange, too, that while Scrooge remained unaltered in his outward form, the Ghost grew older, clearly older. Scrooge had observed this change, but never spoke of it, until they left a children's Twelfth Night party,[43] when, looking at the Spirit as they stood together in an open place, he noticed that its hair was grey.

"Are spirits' lives so short?" asked Scrooge.

"My life upon this globe, is very brief," replied the Ghost. "It ends tonight."

"Tonight!" cried Scrooge.

"Tonight at midnight. Hark! The time is drawing near."

The chimes were ringing the three quarters past eleven at that moment.

"Forgive me if I am not justified in what I ask," said Scrooge, looking intently at the Spirit's robe, "but I see something strange, and not belonging to yourself, protruding from your skirts. Is it a foot or a claw?"

"It might be a claw, for the flesh there is upon it," was the Spirit's sorrowful reply. "Look here."

From the foldings of its robe, it brought two children; wretched, abject, frightful, hideous, miserable. They knelt down at its feet, and clung upon the outside of its garment.

"Oh, Man, look here! Look, look, down here!" exclaimed the Ghost.

They were a boy and a girl. Yellow, meager, ragged, scowling, wolfish; but prostrate, too, in their humility. Where graceful youth should have filled their features out, and touched them with its freshest tints, a stale and shriveled hand, like that of age, had pinched, and twisted them, and pulled them into shreds. Where angels might have sat enthroned, devils lurked, and glared out menacing. No change, no degradation, no perversion of humanity, in any grade, through all the mysteries of wonderful creation, has monsters half so horrible and dread.

Scrooge started back, appalled. Having them shown to him in this way, he tried to say they were fine children, but the words choked themselves, rather than be parties to a lie of such enormous magnitude.

"Spirit, are they yours?" Scrooge could say no more.

"They are Man's," said the Spirit, looking down upon them. "And they cling to me, appealing from their fathers. This boy is Ignorance. This girl is Want.[44] Beware them both, and all of their degree, but most of all beware this boy, for on his brow I see that written which is Doom, unless the writing be erased. Deny it!" cried the Spirit, stretching out its hand towards the city. "Slander those who tell it ye. Admit it for your factious purposes, and make it worse. And abide the end."

"Have they no refuge or resource?" cried Scrooge.

"Are there no prisons?" said the Spirit, turning on him for the last time with his own words. "Are th[45]ere no workhouses?"

The bell struck twelve.

Scrooge looked about him for the Ghost, and saw it not. As the last stroke ceased to vibrate, he remembered the prediction of old Jacob Marley, and lifting up his eyes, beheld a solemn Phantom, draped and hooded, coming, like a mist along the ground, towards him.

Stave Three Footnotes:

1 Sporting type—someone who likes to smike, drink, roister, gamble.

2 Wordly.

3 Ready for whatever happens.

4 Evergreens.

5 Boar flesh.

6 Not more than four weeks old (often roasted whole).

7 A large pastry frosted and highly decorated (usually served on Twelfth Night/Epiphany). Inside is a bean or coin, and whoever bites down on the prize becomes king or queen of the celebration.

8 Probably wassail.

9 Similiar to Father Christmas.

10 Cornucopia.

11 Traditionally, the center of emotion.

12 Father Christmas is often depicted in armor. Dickens suggests by the empty scabbard and rust that Christ and Christian goodwill conquer all.

13 To be exact: 1,842.

14 A cooking apple with a red-rust skin.

15 Carp.

16 A tradition dating back to medieval times—wearing one's heart on a sleeve—but it also meant "for folks to find fault with" (according to Hearn).

17 One of the gifts of the Magi to the Christ Child.

18 Sir Andrew Agnew tried a number of times in the 1830s to institute a Sunday Blue Law, closing bakeries and other places where food was available.

19 Hearn points out that "cratch" is an old English word for "creche"; but his name also suggests the scratching quill pens in those days.

20 A Cockney word for a shilling (12 pence); taken from "baubee," a debased Scottish coin. Hearn (referencing C.Z. Barnett) notes that Cratchit's Christmas dinner (seven shillings for the goose, five for the pudding, three for the onions, sage, and oranges) represented nearly a full week's wages for him.

21 Dickens lived in a similar four-room house as a child in Camden Town. Hearn notes that the six Cratchit children correspond in age and sex to the six in Dicknes' family: Fanny, Charles, Letitia, Frederick, Harriet, and Alfred (Martha, Peter, belinda, boy, girl, Tiny Tim).

22 Earlier to be named "Little Fred" after Dickens's brother Alfred. In October 1843, while visiting his sister Fan and her invalid son, Harry Burnett, in Manchester, Dickens found the inspiration for Tiny Tim. Later,

Hearn reminds us, when the boy died youg, Dickens used him again as the lost boy: Paul Dombey.

23 A state of gradually warming up.

24 A boiler (used for washing clothes).

25 St. Stephen's Church in Camden Town.

26 John 5, Mark 8.

27 This all too frequently happened in that district.

28. One quarter of a pint.

29 Adorned; dressed.

30 Hearn notes that this exchange was not in the original manuscript; however, Dickens, while reading his galleys, felt it important to offer some hope for Tiny Tim's survival, so he added these lines.

31 As a child, Dickens was invariably the one sent to pawn family goods in order to have enough food in the house to eat.

32 Setting: the coase of Cornwall, the traditional stting for the "Jack the Giant Killer" story.

33 Gorse.

34 Land's End, Cornwall—most likely, the Botallick Mine.

35 Probably Longships Lighthouse.

36 Provocative

37 A musical composition for three or more voices (usually light or secular).

38 A comic canon (or round) for three or more voices (each singing a different line simultaneously).

39 A parlor game: "I love my love with an A," each player having to complete sentences with each letter of the alphabet. The game was also used to teach children the alphabet.

40 A game of forfeits, in which each player in turn must ask, "How do you like it?" "When do you like it?" "Where do you like it?"

41 A London district known for making needles.

42 Dickens loved this game.

43 In Dickens' time, the Christmas season lasted until Epiphany. The Dickens family always loved the Twelfth Night parties their father put on for them.

44 Through these two children, Dickens hoped readers of the story would commit themselves to making a difference in the lives of poor children. His inspiration came from the terrible schools for poor—or "ragged"—children, and so many more were in slums, mines, chimneys (see William Blake's "The Chimney Sweeper"), and prisons.

45 The hour corresponds to the Twelfth Day of Christmas. Hearn notes that while the first two Ghosts appeared at one (the beginning of the day), the black-shrouded Ghost appears at twelve, the traditional bewitching hour.

IGNORANCE AND WANT

Stave Four:

The Last of the Spirits

The Phantom[1] slowly, gravely, silently approached. When it came, Scrooge bent down upon his knee; for in the very air through which this Spirit moved it seemed to scatter gloom and mystery.

It was shrouded in a deep black garment, which concealed its head, its face, its form, and left nothing of it visible save one outstretched hand. But for this it would have been difficult to detach its figure from the night, and separate it from the darkness by which it was surrounded.

He felt that it was tall and stately when it came beside him, and that its mysterious presence filled him with a solemn dread. He knew no more, for the Spirit neither spoke nor moved.

"I am in the presence of the Ghost of Christmas Yet To Come?" said Scrooge.

The Spirit answered not, but pointed downward with its hand.

"You are about to show me shadows of the things that have not happened, but will happen in the time before us," Scrooge pursued. "Is that so, Spirit?"

The upper portion of the garment was contracted for an instant in its folds, as if the Spirit had inclined its head. That was the only answer he received.

Although well used to ghostly company by this time, Scrooge feared the silent shape so much that his legs trembled beneath him, and he found that he could hardly stand when he prepared to follow it. The Spirit paused a moment, as observing his condition, and giving him time to recover.

But Scrooge was all the worse for this. It thrilled him with a vague uncertain horror, to know that behind the dusky shroud there were ghostly eyes intently fixed upon him, while he, though he stretched his own to the utmost, could see nothing but a spectral hand and one great heap of black.

"Ghost of the Future!" he exclaimed, "I fear you more than any specter I have seen. But as I know your purpose is to do me good, and as I hope to live to be another man from what I was, I am prepared to bear you company, and do it with a thankful heart. Will you not speak to me?"

It gave him no reply. The hand was pointed straight before them.

"Lead on," said Scrooge. "Lead on. The night is waning fast, and it is precious time to me, I know. Lead on, Spirit."

The Phantom moved away as it had come towards him. Scrooge followed in the shadow of its dress, which bore him up, he thought, and carried him along.

They scarcely seemed to enter the city; for the city rather seemed to spring up about them, and encompass them of its own act. But there they were, in the heart of it; on Change, amongst the merchants; who hurried up and down, and chinked the money in their pockets, and conversed in groups, and looked at their watches, and trifled thoughtfully with their great gold seals; and so forth, as Scrooge had seen them often.

The Spirit stopped beside one little knot of business men. Observing that the hand was pointed to them, Scrooge advanced to listen to their talk.

"No," said a great fat man with a monstrous chin," I don't know much about it, either way. I only know he's dead."

"When did he die?" inquired another.

"Last night, I believe."

"Why, what was the matter with him?" asked a third, taking a vast quantity of snuff out of a very large snuff-box. "I thought he'd never die."

"God knows," said the first, with a yawn.

"What has he done with his money?" asked a red-faced gentleman with a pendulous excrescence[2] on the end of his nose that shook like the gills of a turkey-cock.

"I haven't heard," said the man with the large chin, yawning again. "Left it to his company, perhaps. He hasn't left it to me. That's all I know."

This pleasantry was received with a general laugh.

"It's likely to be a very cheap funeral," said the same speaker; "for upon my life I don't know of anybody to go to it. Suppose we make up a party and volunteer?"

"I don't mind going if a lunch is provided," observed the gentleman with the excrescence on his nose. "But I must be fed, if I make one."

Another laugh.

"Well, I am the most disinterested among you, after all," said the first speaker," for I never wear black gloves,[3] and I never eat lunch. But I'll offer to go, if anybody else will. When I come to think of it, I'm not at all sure that I wasn't his most particular friend,[4] for we used to stop and speak whenever we met. Bye, bye."

Speakers and listeners strolled away, and mixed with other groups. Scrooge knew the men, and looked towards the Spirit for an explanation.

The Phantom glided on into a street. Its finger pointed to two persons meeting. Scrooge listened again, thinking that the explanation might lie here.

He knew these men, also, perfectly. They were men of aye business: very wealthy, and of great importance. He had made a point always of standing well in their esteem: in a business point of view, that is; strictly in a business point of view.

"How are you?" said one.

"How are you?" returned the other.

"Well!" said the first. "Old Scratch[5] has got his own at last, hey."

"So I am told," returned the second. "Cold, isn't it?"

"Seasonable for Christmas time. You're not a skater, I suppose?"

"No. No. Something else to think of. Good morning."

Not another word. That was their meeting, their conversation, and their parting.

Scrooge was at first inclined to be surprised that the Spirit should attach importance to conversations apparently so trivial; but feeling assured that they must have some hidden purpose, he set himself to consider what it was likely to be. They could scarcely be supposed to have any bearing on the death of Jacob, his old partner, for that was Past, and this Ghost's province was the Future. Nor could he think of any one immediately connected with himself, to whom he could apply them. But nothing doubting that to whomsoever they applied they had some latent moral for his own improvement, he resolved to treasure up every word he heard, and everything he saw; and especially to observe the shadow of himself when it appeared. For he had an expectation that the conduct of his future self would give him the clue he missed, and would render the solution of these riddles easy.

He looked about in that very place for his own image; but another man stood in his accustomed corner, and though the clock pointed to his usual time of day for being there, he saw no likeness of himself among the multitudes that poured in through the Porch. It gave him little surprise, however; for he had been revolving in his mind a change of life, and thought and hoped he saw his new-born resolutions carried out in this.

Quiet and dark, beside him stood the Phantom, with its outstretched hand. When he roused himself from his thoughtful quest, he fancied from the turn of the hand, and its situation in reference to himself, that the Unseen Eyes were looking at him keenly. It made him shudder, and feel very cold.

They left the busy scene, and went into an obscure part of the town, where Scrooge had never penetrated before, although he recognized its situation, and its bad repute. The ways were foul and narrow; the shops and houses wretched; the people half-naked, drunken, slipshod, ugly. Alleys and archways, like so many cesspools, disgorged their offenses of smell, and dirt, and life, upon the straggling streets; and the whole quarter reeked with crime, with filth, and misery.

Far in this den of infamous resort, there was a low-browed, beetling[6] shop, below a pent-house roof,[7] where iron, old rags, bottles, bones, and greasy offal, were bought. Upon the floor within, were piled up heaps of rusty keys, nails, chains, hinges, files, scales, weights, and refuse iron of all kinds. Secrets that few would like to scrutinize were bred and hidden in mountains of unseemly rags, masses of corrupted fat,[8] and sepulchers of bones. Sitting in among the wares he dealt in, by a charcoal stove, made of old bricks, was a grey-haired rascal, nearly seventy years of age; who had screened himself from the cold air without, by a frowsy curtaining of miscellaneous tatters, hung upon a line; and smoked his pipe in all the luxury of calm retirement.

Scrooge and the Phantom came into the presence of this man, just as a woman with a heavy bundle slunk into the shop. But she had scarcely entered, when another woman, similarly laden, came in too; and she was closely followed by a man in faded black, who was no less startled by the sight of them, than they had been upon the recognition of each other. After a short period of blank astonishment, in which the old man with the pipe had joined them, they all three burst into a laugh.

"Let the charwoman[9] alone to be the first!" cried she who had entered first. "Let the laundress alone to be the second; and let the undertaker's man alone to be the third. Look here, old Joe, here's a chance. If we haven't all three[10] met here without meaning it!"

"You couldn't have met in a better place," said old Joe, removing his pipe from his mouth. "Come into the parlor. You were made free of it long ago, you know; and the other two an't strangers. Stop till I shut the door of the shop. Ah. How it skreeks. There an't such a rusty bit of metal in the place as its own hinges, I believe; and I'm sure there's no such old bones here, as mine. Ha, ha! We're all suitable to our calling, we're well matched. Come into the parlor. Come into the parlor."

The parlor was the space behind the screen of rags. The old man raked the fire together with an old stair-rod[11] and, having trimmed his smoky lamp (for it was night), with the stem of his pipe, put it in his mouth again.

While he did this, the woman who had already spoken threw her bundle on the floor, and sat down in a flaunting manner on a stool; crossing her elbows on her knees, and looking with a bold defiance at the other two.

"What odds,[12] then. What odds, Mrs. Dilber." said the woman. "Every person has a right to take care of themselves. He always did."

"That's true, indeed," said the laundress. "No man more so."

"Why then, don't stand staring as if you was afraid, woman; who's the wiser? We're not going to pick holes in each other's coats,[13] I suppose?"

"No, indeed," said Mrs. Dilber and the man together. "We should hope not."

"Very well, then!" cried the woman. "That's enough. Who's the worse for the loss of a few things like these? Not a dead man, I suppose."

"No, indeed," said Mrs. Dilber, laughing.

"If he wanted to keep them after he was dead, a wicked old screw," pursued the woman, "why wasn't he natural in his lifetime? If he had been, he'd have had somebody to look after him when he was struck with Death, instead of lying gasping out his last there, alone by himself."

"It's the truest word that ever was spoke," said Mrs. Dilber. "It's a judgment on him."

"I wish it was a little heavier judgment," replied the woman; "and it should have been, you may depend upon it, if I could have laid my hands on anything else. Open that bundle, old Joe, and let me know the value of it. Speak out plain. I'm not afraid to be the first, nor afraid for them to see it. We know pretty well that we were helping ourselves, before we met here, I believe. It's no sin. Open the bundle, Joe."

But the gallantry of her friends would not allow of this; and the man in faded black, mounting the breach first,[14] produced his plunder. It was not extensive. A seal or two, a pencil-case, a pair of sleeve-buttons, and a brooch of no great value,[15] were all. They were severally examined and appraised by old Joe, who chalked the sums he was disposed to give for each upon the wall, and added them up into a total when he found there was nothing more to come.

"That's your account," said Joe, "and I wouldn't give another sixpence, if I was to be boiled for not doing it. Who's next?"

Mrs. Dilber was next. Sheets and towels, a little wearing apparel, two old-fashioned silver teaspoons, a pair of sugar-tongs, and a few boots. Her account was stated on the wall in the same manner.

"I always give too much to ladies. It's a weakness of mine, and that's the way I ruin myself," said old Joe. "That's your account. If you asked me for another penny, and made it an open question, I'd repent of being so liberal and knock off half-a-crown."

"And now undo my bundle, Joe," said the first woman.

Joe went down on his knees for the greater convenience of opening it, and having unfastened a great many knots, dragged out a large and heavy roll of some dark stuff.

"What do you call this?" said Joe. "Bed-curtains?"

"Ah!" returned the woman, laughing and leaning forward on her crossed arms. "Bed-curtains."

"You don't mean to say you took them down, rings and all, with him lying there?" said Joe.

"Yes I do," replied the woman. "Why not?"

"You were born to make your fortune," said Joe," and you'll certainly do it."

"I certainly shan't hold my hand, when I can get anything in it by reaching it out, for the sake of such a man as he was, I promise you, Joe," returned the woman coolly. "Don't drop that oil upon the blankets, now."

"His blankets?" asked Joe.

"Whose else's do you think?" replied the woman. "He isn't likely to take cold without them, I dare say."

"I hope he didn't die of any thing catching. Eh?" said old Joe, stopping in his work, and looking up.

"Don't you be afraid of that," returned the woman. "I an't so fond of his company that I'd loiter about him for such things, if he did. Ah. You may look through that shirt till your eyes ache; but you won't find a hole in it, nor a threadbare place. It's the best he had, and a fine one too. They'd have wasted it, if it hadn't been for me."

"What do you call wasting of it?" asked old Joe.

"Putting it on him to be buried in, to be sure," replied the woman with a laugh. "Somebody was fool enough to do it, but I took it off again. If calico an't good enough for such a purpose, it isn't good enough for anything. It's quite as becoming to the body. He can't look uglier than he did in that one."

Scrooge listened to this dialogue in horror. As they sat grouped about their spoil, in the scanty light afforded by the old man's lamp, he viewed them with a detestation and disgust, which could hardly have been greater, though they demons, marketing the corpse itself.

"Ha, ha!" laughed the same woman, when old Joe, producing a flannel bag with money in it, told out their several gains upon the ground. "This is the end of it, you see. He frightened every one away from him when he was alive, to profit us when he was dead. Ha, ha, ha!"

"Spirit," said Scrooge, shuddering from head to foot. "I see, I see. The case of this unhappy man might be my own. My life tends that way, now. Merciful Heaven, what is this?"

He recoiled in terror, for the scene had changed, and now he almost touched a bed: a bare, uncurtained bed: on which, beneath a ragged sheet, there lay a something covered up, which, though it was dumb, announced itself in awful language.

The room was very dark, too dark to be observed with any accuracy, though Scrooge glanced round it in obedience to a secret impulse, anxious to know what kind of room it was. A pale light, rising in the outer air, fell straight upon the bed; and on it, plundered and bereft, unwatched, unwept, uncared for, was the body of this man.

Scrooge glanced towards the Phantom. Its steady hand was pointed to the head. The cover was so carelessly adjusted that the slightest raising of it, the motion of a finger upon Scrooge's part, would have disclosed the face. He thought of it, felt how easy it would be to do, and longed to do it; but had no more power to withdraw the veil than to dismiss the specter at his side.

Oh cold, cold, rigid, dreadful Death, set up thine altar here, and dress it with such terrors as thou hast at thy command: for this is thy dominion. But of the loved, revered, and honored head, thou canst not turn one hair to thy dread purposes, or make one feature odious. It is not that the hand is heavy and will fall down when released; it is not that the heart and pulse are still; but that the hand was open, generous, and true; the heart brave, warm, and tender; and the pulse a man's. Strike, Shadow, strike. And see his good deeds springing from the wound, to sow the world with life immortal!

No voice pronounced these words in Scrooge's ears, and yet he heard them when he looked upon the bed. He thought, if this man could be raised up now, what would be his foremost thoughts. Avarice, hard-dealing, griping cares. They have brought him to a rich end, truly.

He lay, in the dark empty house, with not a man, a woman, or a child, to say that he was kind to me in this or that, and for the memory of one kind word I will be kind to him. A cat was tearing at the door, and there was a sound of gnawing rats beneath the hearth-stone. What they wanted in the room of death, and why they were so restless and disturbed, Scrooge did not dare to think.

"Spirit," he said, "this is a fearful place. In leaving it, I shall not leave its lesson, trust me. Let us go."

Still the Ghost pointed with an unmoved finger to the head.

"I understand you," Scrooge returned, "and I would do it, if I could. But I have not the power, Spirit. I have not the power."

Again it seemed to look upon him.

"If there is any person in the town, who feels emotion caused by this man's death," said Scrooge quite agonized, "show that person to me, Spirit, I beseech you."

The Phantom spread its dark robe before him for a moment, like a wing; and withdrawing it, revealed a room by daylight, where a mother and her children were.

She was expecting someone, and with anxious eagerness; for she walked up and down the room; started at every sound; looked out from the window; glanced at the clock; tried, but in vain, to work with her needle; and could hardly bear the voices of the children in their play.

At length the long-expected knock was heard. She hurried to the door, and met her husband; a man whose face was careworn and depressed, though he was young. There was a remarkable expression in it now; a kind of serious delight of which he felt ashamed, and which he struggled to repress.

He sat down to the dinner that had been boarding for him by the fire; and when she asked him faintly what news (which was not until after a long silence), he appeared embarrassed how to answer.

"Is it good." she said, "or bad?"—to help him.

"Bad," he answered.

"We are quite ruined."

"No. There is hope yet, Caroline."

"If he relents," she said, amazed, "there is. Nothing is past hope, if such a miracle has happened."

"He is past relenting," said her husband. "He is dead."

She was a mild and patient creature if her face spoke truth; but she was thankful in her soul to hear it, and she said so, with clasped hands. She prayed forgiveness the next moment, and was sorry; but the first was the emotion of her heart.

"What the half-drunken woman whom I told you of last night, said to me, when I tried to see him and obtain a week's delay; and what I thought was a mere excuse to avoid me; turns out to have been quite true. He was not only very ill, but dying, then."

"To whom will our debt be transferred?"

"I don't know. But before that time we shall be ready with the money; and even though we were not, it would be a bad fortune indeed to find so merciless a creditor in his successor. We may sleep tonight with light hearts, Caroline."

Yes. Soften it as they would, their hearts were lighter. The children's faces hushed, and clustered round to hear what they so little understood, were brighter; and it was a happier house for this man's death. The only emotion that the Ghost could show him, caused by the event, was one of pleasure.

"Let me see some tenderness connected with a death," said Scrooge; "or that dark chamber, Spirit, which we left just now, will be forever present to me."

The Ghost conducted him through several streets familiar to his feet; and as they went along, Scrooge looked here and there to find himself, but nowhere was he to be seen. They entered poor Bob Cratchit's house; the dwelling he had visited before; and found the mother and the children seated round the fire.

Quiet. Very quiet. The noisy little Cratchits were as still as statues in one corner, and sat looking up at Peter, who had a book before him. The mother and her daughters were engaged in sewing. But surely they were very quiet.

"And he took a child, and set him in the midst of them."[16]

Where had Scrooge heard those words? He had not dreamed them. The boy must have read them out, as he and the Spirit crossed the threshold. Why did he not go on?

The mother laid her work upon the table, and put her hand up to her face.

"The color hurts my eyes," she said.

The color?[17] Ah, poor Tiny Tim.

"They're better now again," said Cratchit's wife. "It makes them weak by candle-light; and I wouldn't show weak eyes to your father when he comes home, for the world. It must be near his time."

"Past it rather," Peter answered, shutting up his book. "But I think he's walked a little slower than he used, these few last evenings, mother."

They were very quiet again. At last she said, and in a steady, cheerful voice, that only faltered once:

"I have known him walk with—I have known him walk with Tiny Tim upon his shoulder, very fast indeed."

"And so have I," cried Peter. "Often."

"And so have I," exclaimed another. So had all.

"But he was very light to carry," she resumed, intent upon her work, "and his father loved him so, that it was no trouble—no trouble. And there is your father at the door!"

She hurried out to meet him; and little Bob in his comforter—he had need of it, poor fellow—came in. His tea was ready for him on the hob, and they all tried who should help him to it most. Then the two young Cratchits got upon his knees and laid, each child a little cheek, against his face, as if they said, "Don't mind it, father. Don't be grieved."

Bob was very cheerful with them, and spoke pleasantly to all the family. He looked at the work upon the table, and praised the industry and speed of Mrs. Cratchit and the girls. They would be done long before Sunday, he said.

"Sunday. You went today, then, Robert?" said his wife.

"Yes, my dear," returned Bob. "I wish you could have gone. It would have done you good to see how green a place it is. But you'll see it often. I promised him that I would walk there on a Sunday. My little, little child!" cried Bob. "My little child!"

He broke down all at once. He couldn't help it. If he could have helped it, he and his child would have been farther apart perhaps than they were.

He left the room, and went upstairs into the room above, which was lighted cheerfully, and hung with Christmas. There was a chair set close beside the child, and there were signs of someone having been there, lately. Poor Bob sat down in it, and when he had thought a little and composed himself, he kissed the little face. He was reconciled to what had happened, and went down again quite happy.

They drew about the fire, and talked; the girls and mother working still. Bob told them of the extraordinary kindness of Mr. Scrooge's nephew, whom he had scarcely seen but once, and who, meeting him in the street that day, and seeing that he looked a little—"just a little down you know," said Bob, inquired what had happened to distress him. "On which," said Bob, "for he is the pleasantest-spoken gentleman you ever heard, I told him. 'I am heartily sorry for it, Mr. Cratchit,' he said, 'and heartily sorry for your good wife.' By-the-bye, how he ever knew that, I don't know."

"Knew what, my dear?"

"Why, that you were a good wife," replied Bob.

"Everybody knows that," said Peter.

"Very well observed, my boy!" cried Bob. "I hope they do. 'Heartily sorry,' he said, 'for your good wife. If I can be of service to you in any way,' he said, giving me his card, 'that's where I live. Pray come to me.' Now, it wasn't," cried Bob," for the sake of anything he might be able to do for us, so much as for his kind way, that this was quite delightful. It really seemed as if he had known our Tiny Tim, and felt with us."

"I'm sure he's a good soul," said Mrs. Cratchit.

"You would be surer of it, my dear," returned Bob, "if you saw and spoke to him. I shouldn't be at all surprised mark what I say, if he got Peter a better situation."

"Only hear that, Peter," said Mrs. Cratchit.

"And then," cried one of the girls, "Peter will be keeping company with someone,[18] and setting up for himself."

"Get along with you!" retorted Peter, grinning.

"It's just as likely as not," said Bob, "one of these days; though there's plenty of time for that, my dear. But however and when ever we part from one another, I am sure we shall none of us forget poor Tiny Tim—shall we—or this first parting that there was among us."

"Never, father!" cried they all.

"And I know," said Bob, "I know, my dears, that when we recollect how patient and how mild he was; although he was a little, little child; we shall not quarrel easily among ourselves, and forget poor Tiny Tim in doing it."

"No, never, father!" they all cried again.

"I am very happy," said little Bob, "I am very happy!"

Mrs. Cratchit kissed him, his daughters kissed him, the two young Cratchits kissed him, and Peter and himself shook hands. Spirit of Tiny Tim, thy childish essence was from God.

"Specter," said Scrooge, "something informs me that our parting moment is at hand. I know it, but I know not how. Tell me what man that was whom we saw lying dead."

The Ghost of Christmas Yet To Come conveyed him, as before— though at a different time, he thought: indeed, there seemed no order in these latter visions, save that they were in the Future—into the resorts of business men, but showed him not himself. Indeed, the Spirit did not stay for anything, but went straight on, as to the end just now desired, until besought by Scrooge to tarry for a moment.

"These courts," said Scrooge, "through which we hurry now, is where my place of occupation is, and has been for a length of time. I see the house. Let me behold what I shall be, in days to come."

The Spirit stopped; the hand was pointed elsewhere.

"The house is yonder," Scrooge exclaimed. "Why do you point away?"

The inexorable finger underwent no change.

Scrooge hastened to the window of his office, and looked in. It was an office still, but not his. The furniture was not the same, and the figure in the chair was not himself. The Phantom pointed as before.

He joined it once again, and wondering why and whither he had gone, accompanied it until they reached an iron gate. He paused to look round before entering.

A churchyard.[19] Here, then, the wretched man whose name he had now to learn, lay underneath the ground. It was a worthy place. Walled in by houses; overrun by grass and weeds, the growth of vegetation's death,[20] not life; choked up with too much burying; fat with repleted appetite.[21] A worthy place!

The Spirit stood among the graves, and pointed down to One. He advanced towards it trembling. The Phantom was exactly as it had been, but he dreaded that he saw new meaning in its solemn shape.

"Before I draw nearer to that stone to which you point," said Scrooge, "answer me one question. Are these the shadows of the things that Will be, or are they shadows of things that May be, only?"

Still the Ghost pointed downward to the grave by which it stood.

"Men's courses will foreshadow certain ends, to which, if persevered in, they must lead," said Scrooge. "But if the courses be departed from, the ends will change. Say it is thus with what you show me."

The Spirit was immovable as ever.

Scrooge crept towards it, trembling as he went; and following the finger, read upon the stone of the neglected grave his own name, EBENEZER SCROOGE.

"Am I that man who lay upon the bed?" he cried, upon his knees.

The finger pointed from the grave to him, and back again.

"No, Spirit! Oh no, no!"

The finger still was there.

"Spirit!" he cried, tight clutching at its robe, "hear me. I am not the man I was. I will not be the man I must have been but for this intercourse. Why show me this, if I am past all hope?"

For the first time the hand appeared to shake.

"Good Spirit," he pursued, as down upon the ground he fell before it: "Your nature intercedes for me, and pities me. Assure me that I yet may change these shadows you have shown me, by an altered life."

The kind hand trembled.

"I will honor Christmas in my heart, and try to keep it all the year. I will live in the Past, the Present, and the Future. The Spirits of all Three shall strive within me. I will not shut out the lessons that they teach. Oh, tell me I may sponge away the writing on this stone!"

In his agony, he caught the spectral hand. It sought to free itself, but he was strong in his entreaty, and detained it. The Spirit, stronger yet, repulsed him.

Holding up his hands in a last prayer to have his fate aye reversed, he saw an alteration in the Phantom's hood and dress. It shrunk, collapsed, and dwindled down into a bedpost.

Stave Four Footnotes:

1 The Third Ghost is, of course, Death. Hearn notes that Christmas comes at the end—or death—of a year, and that the birth of Christ is itself a reminder of the crucifixion—as pointed out in the spiritual I *Wonder as I wander.* "How Jesus the Savior was born for to die."

2 A hanging wart.

3 Given to those who attended English funerals.

4 Hearn points out what an insult this represents from a supposed friend: not to attend the funeral even when bribed to do so by a set of gloves and a free meal.

5 The devil.

6 Projecting; overhanding.

7 A roof sloping up a wall.

8 Grease, drippings, and kitchen waste were purchased and resold: the grease for candles and soap, the drippings as a butter substitute.

9 A temporary servant (hired by the day) to do odd housework. this one most liely was hired by the person who was settling the estate.

10 Reminiscent of the three ghoulish witches in Macbeth.

11 A brass har that keeps stair carpets down.

12 Means "What does it matter?"

13 Means "to have a quarrel."

14 Means "taking the lead."

15 Found by this undertaker's assistant on the body or in the clothes he put on the body.

16 One of Dickens's favorite Bible passages (Matthew 18:2, Mark 9:36), and he amplified them in his bood The Life of Our Lord (1849).

17 Mrs. Cratchit and the girls are sewing their mourning clothes.

18 Of marrying age.

19 All Hallows Staining, Star Alley, off Mark Lane, in the Langborn Ward (Hearn referencing Gwen Major).

20 Weeds and rank grass kill off all other vegetation.

21 Dickens is being ironic in so describing a graveyard.

Stave Five:

The End of It

Yes! And the bedpost was his own. The bed was his own, the room was his own. Best and happiest of all, the Time before him was his own, to make amends in!

"I will live in the Past, the Present, and the Future!" Scrooge repeated, as he scrambled out of bed. "The Spirits of all Three shall strive within me. Oh Jacob Marley! Heaven, and the Christmas Time be praised for this. I say it on my knees, old Jacob, on my knees!"

He was so fluttered and so glowing with his good intentions, that his broken voice would scarcely answer to his call. He had been sobbing violently in his conflict with the Spirit, and his face was wet with tears.

"They are not torn down!" cried Scrooge, folding one of his bed-curtains in his arms, "they are not torn down, rings and all. They are here—I am here—the shadows of the things that would have been, may be dispelled. They will be! I know they will."

His hands were busy with his garments all this time; turning them inside out, putting them on upside down, tearing them, mislaying them, making them parties to every kind of extravagance.

"I don't know what to do!" cried Scrooge, laughing and crying in the same breath; and making a perfect Laocoön[1] of himself with his stockings. "I am as light as a feather, I am as happy as an angel, I am as merry as a schoolboy. I am as giddy as a drunken man. A merry Christmas to everybody! A happy New Year to all the world! Hallo here! Whoop! Hallo!"

He had frisked into the sitting-room, and was now standing there, perfectly winded.

"There's the saucepan that the gruel was in!" cried Scrooge, starting off again, and frisking round the fireplace. "There's the door, by which the Ghost of Jacob Marley entered. There's the corner where the Ghost of Christmas Present sat. There's the window where I saw the wandering Spirits. It's all right, it's all true, it all happened. Ha ha ha!"

Really, for a man who had been out of practice for so many years, it was a splendid laugh, a most illustrious laugh. The father of a long, long line of brilliant laughs.

"I don't know what day of the month it is," said Scrooge. "I don't know how long I've been among the Spirits. I don't know anything. I'm quite a baby. Never mind. I don't care. I'd rather be a baby. Hallo! Whoop! Hallo here!"

He was checked in his transports by the churches ringing out the lustiest peals he had ever heard. Clash, clang, hammer; ding, dong, bell! Bell, dong, ding; hammer, clang, clash! Oh, glorious, glorious!

Running to the window, he opened it, and put out his head. No fog, no mist; clear, bright, jovial, stirring, cold; cold, piping for the blood to dance to; Golden sunlight; Heavenly sky; sweet fresh air; merry bells. Oh, glorious. Glorious!

"What's today?" cried Scrooge, calling downward to a boy in Sunday clothes, who perhaps had loitered in to look about him.

"Eh?" returned the boy, with all his might of wonder.

"What's today, my fine fellow?" said Scrooge.

"Today?" replied the boy. "Why, Christmas Day."

"It's Christmas Day!" said Scrooge to himself. "I haven't missed it. The Spirits have done it all in one night. They can do anything they like. Of course they can. Of course they can. Hallo, my fine fellow!"

"Hallo!" returned the boy.

"Do you know the Poulterer's, in the next street but one, at the corner?" Scrooge inquired.

"I should hope I did," replied the lad.

"An intelligent boy!" said Scrooge. "A remarkable boy! Do you know whether they've sold the prize Turkey that was hanging up there—Not the little prize Turkey: the big one?"

"What, the one as big as me?" returned the boy.

"What a delightful boy!" said Scrooge. "It's a pleasure to talk to him. Yes, my buck."

"It's hanging there now," replied the boy.

"Is it?" said Scrooge. "Go and buy it."

"Walk-ER!"² exclaimed the boy.

"No, no," said Scrooge, "I am in earnest. Go and buy it, and tell them to bring it here, that I may give them the direction where to take it. Come back with the man, and I'll give you a shilling. Come back with him in less than five minutes and I'll give you half-a-crown."

The boy was off like a shot. He must have had a steady hand at a trigger who could have got a shot off half so fast.

"I'll send it to Bob Cratchit's!" whispered Scrooge, rubbing his hands, and splitting with a laugh. "He shan't know who sends it. It's twice the size of Tiny Tim. Joe Miller³ never made such a joke as sending it to Bob's will be!"

The hand in which he wrote the address was not a steady one, but write it he did, somehow, and went down-stairs to open the street door, ready for the coming of the poulterer's man. As he stood there, waiting his arrival, the knocker caught his eye.

"I shall love it, as long as I live!" cried Scrooge, patting it with his hand. "I scarcely ever looked at it before. What an honest expression it has in its face. It's a wonderful knocker....Here's the Turkey. Hallo! Whoop! How are you? Merry Christmas!"

It was a Turkey! He never could have stood upon his legs, that bird. He would have snapped them short off in a minute, like sticks of sealing-wax.

"Why, it's impossible to carry that to Camden Town," said Scrooge. "You must have a cab."

The chuckle with which he said this, and the chuckle with which he paid for the Turkey, and the chuckle with which he paid for the cab, and the chuckle with which he recompensed the boy, were only to be exceeded by the chuckle with which he sat down breathless in his chair again, and chuckled till he cried.

Shaving was not an easy task, for his hand continued to shake very much; and shaving requires attention, even when you don't dance while you are at it. But if he had cut the end of his nose off, he would have put a piece of sticking-plaster over it, and been quite satisfied.

He dressed himself all in his best, and at last got out into the streets. The people were by this time pouring forth, as he had seen them with the Ghost of Christmas Present; and walking with his hands behind him, Scrooge regarded every one with a delighted smile. He looked so irresistibly pleasant, in a word, that three or four good-humored fellows said, "Good morning, sir. A merry Christmas to you." And Scrooge said often afterwards, that of all the blithe sounds he had ever heard, those were the blithest in his ears.

He had not gone far, when coming on towards him he beheld the portly gentleman, who had walked into his counting-house the day before, and said, "Scrooge and Marley's, I believe." It sent a pang across his heart to think how this old gentleman would look upon him when they met; but he knew what path lay straight before him, and he took it.

"My dear sir," said Scrooge, quickening his pace, and taking the old gentleman by both his hands. "How do you do. I hope you succeeded yesterday. It was very kind of you. A merry Christmas to you, sir!"

"Mr. Scrooge?"

"Yes," said Scrooge. "That is my name, and I fear it may not be pleasant to you. Allow me to ask your pardon. And will you have the goodness"—here Scrooge whispered in his ear.

"Lord bless me!" cried the gentleman, as if his breath were taken away. "My dear Mr. Scrooge, are you serious?"

"If you please," said Scrooge. "Not a farthing less. A great many backpayments are included in it, I assure you. Will you do me that favor?"

"My dear sir," said the other, shaking hands with him. "I don't know what to say to such munificence."

"Don't say anything please," retorted Scrooge. "Come and see me. Will you come and see me?"

"I will!" cried the old gentleman. And it was clear he meant to do it.

"Thank you," said Scrooge. "I am much obliged to you. I thank you fifty times. Bless you!"

He went to church, and walked about the streets, and watched the people hurrying to and fro, and patted children on the head, and questioned beggars, and looked down into the kitchens of houses, and up to the windows, and found that everything could yield him pleasure. He had never dreamed that any walk—that anything—could give him so much happiness. In the afternoon he turned his steps towards his nephew's house.

He passed the door a dozen times, before he had the courage to go up and knock. But he made a dash, and did it:

"Is your master at home, my dear?" said Scrooge to the girl. Nice girl. Very.

"Yes, sir."

"Where is he, my love?" said Scrooge.

"He's in the dining-room, sir, along with mistress. I'll show you up-stairs, if you please."

"Thank you. He knows me," said Scrooge, with his hand already on the dining-room lock. "I'll go in here, my dear."

He turned it gently, and sidled his face in, round the door. They were looking at the table (which was spread out in great array); for these young housekeepers are always nervous on such points, and like to see that everything is right.

"Fred!" said Scrooge.

Dear heart alive, how his niece by marriage started. Scrooge had forgotten, for the moment, about her sitting in the corner with the footstool, or he wouldn't have done it, on any account.

"Why bless my soul!" cried Fred," who's that?"

"It's I. Your uncle Scrooge. I have come to dinner. Will you let me in, Fred?"

Let him in! It is a mercy he didn't shake his arm off. He was at home in five minutes. Nothing could be heartier. His niece looked just the same. So did Topper when he came. So did the plump sister when she came. So did every one when they came. Wonderful party, wonderful games, wonderful unanimity, wonderful happiness!

But he was early at the office next morning[4]. Oh he was early there. If he could only be there first, and catch Bob Cratchit coming late! That was the thing he had set his heart upon.

And he did it; yes, he did. The clock struck nine. No Bob. A quarter past. No Bob. He was full eighteen minutes and a half behind his time. Scrooge sat with his door wide open, that he might see him come into the tank.

His hat was off, before he opened the door; his comforter too. He was on his stool in a jiffy; driving away with his pen, as if he were trying to overtake nine o'clock.

"Hallo," growled Scrooge, in his accustomed voice, as near as he could feign it. "What do you mean by coming here at this time of day?"

"I'm very sorry, sir," said Bob. "I *am* behind my time."

"You are?" repeated Scrooge. "Yes. I think you are. Step this way, if you please."

"It's only once a year, sir," pleaded Bob, appearing from the tank. "It shall not be repeated. I was making rather merry yesterday, sir."

"Now, I'll tell you what, my friend," said Scrooge, "I am not going to stand this sort of thing any longer. And therefore," he continued, leaping from his stool, and giving Bob such a dig in the waistcoat that he staggered back into the tank again; "and therefore I am about to raise your salary!"

Bob trembled, and got a little nearer to the ruler. He had a momentary idea of knocking Scrooge down with it, holding him, and calling to the people in the court for help and a strait-waistcoat.

"A merry Christmas, Bob," said Scrooge, with an earnestness that could not be mistaken, as he clapped him on the back. "A merrier Christmas, Bob, my good fellow, than I have given you for many a year. I'll raise your salary, and endeavor to assist your struggling family, and we will discuss your affairs this very afternoon, over a Christmas bowl of smoking bishop, Bob. Make up the fires, and buy another coal-scuttle before you dot another "i", Bob Cratchit!"

Scrooge was better than his word. He did it all, and infinitely more; and to Tiny Tim, who did not die, he was a second father. He became as good a friend, as good a master, and as good a man, as the good old city knew, or any other good old city, town, or borough, in the good old world. Some people laughed to see the alteration in him, but he let them laugh, and little heeded them; for he was wise enough to know that nothing ever happened on this globe, for good, at which some people did not have their fill of laughter in the outset; and knowing that such as these would be blind anyway, he thought it quite as well that they should wrinkle up their eyes in grins, as have the malady in less attractive forms. His own heart laughed: and that was quite enough for him.

He had no further intercourse with Spirits, but lived upon the Total Abstinence Principle[5] ever afterwards; and it was always said of him, that he knew how to keep Christmas well, if any man alive possessed the knowledge. May that be truly said of us, and all of us! And so, as Tiny Tim observed, God Bless Us, Every One!

Stave Five Footnotes:

1 A reference to the famous Roman statue of the fifth century depicting this Trojan priest and his two sons being strangled by serpents. According to Hearn, this was not in the original text, but Dickens, as he was reading the galleys, thought it would be a perfect way to describe Scrooge's contortions with his socks.

2 A Cockney expression of surprise, incredulity, and sometimes disbelief.

3 A popular but illiterate comic actor (1684-1738). the dramatist John Mottley collected the actor's purported jokes and sayings and published them as Joe Miller's Jests (1739), which was—according to Hearn—a jest in itself, as Miller didn't come up with any of them. As a result, almost any joke or jest from then on was attributed to the actor.

4 St. Stephen's Day (Boxing day), when gifts were normally given to those who had provided services during the year.

5 The abstinence from alcohol spirits is used here by Dickens as a pun in referring to supernatural ones.

AFTERWORD

DISCUSSION WITH PROFESSOR WHEELER
(For Formal School, Home School and Book Club Discussions)

First of all, permit me to define my perception of the role of the teacher. I believe that the ideal teaching relationship involves the teacher and the student, both looking in the same direction, and both with a sense of wonder. A teacher is not an important person dishing out rote learning to an unimportant person. I furthermore do not believe that a Ph.D. automatically brings with it omniscience, despite the way some of us act. In discussions, I tell my students beforehand that my opinions and conclusions are no more valid than theirs, for each of us sees reality from a different perspective.

Now that my role is clear, let's continue. The purpose of the discussion section of the series is to encourage debate, to dig deeper into the books than would be true without it and to spawn other questions that may build on the ones I begin with here. If you take advantage of this section, you will be gaining just as good an understanding of the book as you would were you actually sitting in one of my classroom circles.

As you read this book, record your thoughts and reactions each day in a journal. Also, an unabridged dictionary is almost essential in completely understanding the text. If your vocabulary is to grow, something else is needed besides the dictionary: vocabulary cards. Take a stack of 3 x 5 cards, and write the words you don't know on one side and their definitions on the other, with each word used in a sentence. Every time you stumble on words you are unsure of—and I found quite a number myself!—make a card for it. Continually go over these cards; and keep all, except those you never miss, in a card file. You will be amazed at how fast your vocabulary will grow!

The Introduction Must Be Read Before
Beginning Next Section

QUESTIONS TO DEEPEN
YOUR UNDERSTANDING

Stave One: Marley's Ghost

1. The statement "Scrooge's name was good upon the Exchange" means that while Scrooge may have been stingy and bitter, he was perceived as being ethical. His name stood for something. In Dickens' day, one's name meant a great deal. Dishonoring it dishonored the entire family and was perceived as being worse than death itself. If one's father or mother died with unpaid debts—even if that person had declared bankruptcy—the surviving children felt an obligation to repay every penny.

   Today, honor is an attribute to which we pay little attention. Listen to any TV talk show and you will hear individuals "telling all" just to gain notice, notoriety and money.

   And, worse yet, our legal system has encouraged us to believe that if something is legal that means it must also be right. Is that always true? Give some examples.

   Discuss what it means to "have a good name," to be considered trustworthy and dependable, to have bankers declare that your word is all the security they need. What has been lost since the time a person's word and handshake were enough to seal a contract? How is our society different today? Why do you think things have changed?

2. Scrooge is the ultimate miser. We learn in Scripture and in life that God has a way of balancing out what we do and say. In other words, the way we treat others is how we'll be treated—usually compounded. One does not have to believe in God for this principle to be operative: Sooner or later, life comes full circle.

Scrooge, during the course of this drama, discovers that truth. The Third Spirit graphically reveals the tragic results of a self-centered life. Each time you come across a statement in the book that has to do with generosity, giving, service to others, write it down; then, at the end, compare them and arrive at conclusions. Finally, discuss what lessons you feel Dickens intended us to gain from the story.

3. Dickens implies that each of us carries our own "weather" with us. Do you feel that is true? If so, what can we do about it in our own interactions with people?

4. Scrooge's nephew plays a significant role in the story. Note that he does not weary of doing good: Every Christmas, he wishes his crusty uncle a merry Christmas and invites him home to share the holiday with his family. Eventually, when Scrooge's heart is softened, these persistent attempts to be friendly and kind bear fruit.

   What does this say to us in terms of our interactions with others? How should we behave toward those who do not respond kindly or graciously toward our overtures of friendship? Is there ever a situation in which a person should not be treated with kindness and respect? Explain.

   Is it possible that too many of us demand instant gratification? Are we unwilling for God to take our kind words and acts and use them to gradually break down walls of resistance? What should we do about it?

5. Is it true, as Fred maintains, that people tend to treat each other differently during the Christmas season? If it is true, give some examples of how people, including ourselves, do this. Is that a good thing or a bad thing? Should we treat people the "Christmas way" all year round? Why?

6. The two gentlemen who ask Scrooge to donate to the poor play a key role in the book. Explain what that role is and how it affects Scrooge.

Discuss the role of giving, of tithing, in our lives. Should there be guidelines?

Should we first research an organization before we give (to see if they are illegitimate or top-heavy—in other words, with a disproportionate percentage of the money raised used for management overhead rather than for the ostensible cause)? Is that good stewardship? What is stewardship?

7. Does supporting established charities mean we no longer need to give in cases of individual need? We've all been approached, from time to time, by panhandlers—people we are certain will use the requested "food" money for liquor, drugs or tobacco. How should we respond?

I make it a policy to never turn anyone down completely—I always will give something. Even when I am almost certain it will be misused. The important thing is to respond to the request with both love and respect, remembering that Christ would have died for the person asking for help. In every interaction I have, from day to day, I try to remember to be kind to each of our Lord's sheep.

Discuss, at length, the exciting and challenging issue of philanthropy.

8. Scrooge refers to the poor and needy as the "surplus population." Like Scrooge, certain groups in our society believe over population will eventually destroy our planet if something isn't done to control the birth rate. Is there a golden mean? Explain.

9. Do we sometimes act like ostriches, sticking our heads in the sand to avoid seeing others' needs? Do we say, in effect, "As long as I don't know for sure what's going on, I'm not accountable for following through and helping out"? If so, what should we do about it?

10. Scrooge pays Cratchit as little as possible. For that, we scorn Scrooge. Later on, when Scrooge becomes generous, we praise him. Having

said that, why is it that so many professed Christians are perceived to be such tightwads when it comes to being generous with their employees? One would think that, of all people, Christians would be the most generous! What can we do to correct this tendency or perspective?

11. In the story, Dickens repeatedly comes back to accountability; the concept that each of us, like it or not, is our brother's keeper; that, if we walk through life thinking only of ourselves, it will be virtually impossible for us to be happy or feel blessed. Discuss.

12. Marley tells Scrooge that, as a result of each day's acts and words, we forge links in a chain that we must drag around with us for eternity after we die. C. S. Lewis, in that monumental little book *Mere Christianity*, puts it a little differently. He points out that each decision, act and conversation makes a "mark on the soul." Singly, these marks are not very significant, but over time they tend to cluster, and these clusters become habits, and habits evolve into character, and character eventually determines one's eternal destiny.

Compare the two metaphors in terms of the impact on the choices we make every moment of our lives, keeping in mind the truth that, every day, either we are moving toward being nobler creatures who are more in tune with the divine or we are going in the opposite direction.

13. One of the most powerful quotations in the book is this one: "'Business!' cried the Ghost, wringing its hands again. 'Mankind was my business. The common welfare was my business; charity, mercy, forbearance and benevolence were all my business. The details of my trade were but a drop of water in the comprehensive ocean of my business.'"

Think about what Marley says here: Basically, we could establish an international corporation and become a household name; yet, if we aren't being our brother's keeper on a daily basis, our success and fame avail us nothing. Do you think that's true? Why or why not?

Afterword

If that concept is true, what is Dickens saying to us about our priorities, especially our tendency to equate success with money and possessions rather than with qualities of the heart? Discuss.

Stave Two: The First of the Three Spirits

14. When Scrooge re-experiences his past, for the first time we note good qualities in him. Dickens himself, in writing *Carol*, was using his own past as a way of arriving at the truth about himself. How important is it that we periodically journey back to our past experiences? What should we look for there? To what kind of past experiences does the Second Ghost take Scrooge? What would be our own counterparts to them?

15. Discuss this strange paradox: Scrooge strongly resists leaving his past once he gets there—almost as strongly as he resisted remembering the past in the first place! Only after vicariously re-experiencing the kindness he received from others when he was young does Scrooge see how inhumanely he treats people now. Looking at it from a different angle: It was not verbal sermons that changed his heart; it was physical sermons, represented by kind acts, that make the difference. We impact others by the lives we lead, not merely by the words we speak.

16. In his biography in the introduction, Dickens, in rediscovering his childhood self, also rediscovers how much books meant to him as a child. Discuss how much is lost in life by the failure to fall in love with good books. How much is lost in the mind by failure to grow in our reading? How much do we cripple our potential in life by failing to read good books?

17. Perhaps the saddest words in this story are these: "It's too late now." For most of us, these words are likely to come to mind when we are at the funerals of friends and loved ones, as we realize that the kind words we might have said, the kind things we might have done are all moot now: no more useful to us than the three-day banknote Scrooge worries about on the fourth day.

Kalidasa, one of India's greatest poets, addressed that human problem in a 1,500-year-old poem called "Salutation to the Dawn." It is a poem that had a major impact on my life years ago and continues to have today. At my urging, many of my students have memorized it, and since then, many have told me it has changed their lives.

The essence of Kalidasa's message is this: Every day is in itself a miniature lifetime, with a beginning, a middle and an end. Energy devoted to yesterday and tomorrow is energy wasted, for regret and worry are futile. Only as we concentrate on today, the one timeframe we can do anything about, can we make a success of our lives. The beauty of the message is this: Once we are able to hold our heads high and face God with our today's, saying, "Lord, if you were to judge my life by today, I would be content, for I've tried to be a good steward. I've tried to use wisely the time you've entrusted to me. I've tried to grow, and I've tried to minister to those sheep of Yours that I came into contact with today," will we be able to cease regretting yesterday and worrying about tomorrow.

Since this poem ties in so perfectly with *A Christmas Carol,* I am including it in its entirety, for you to memorize, assimilate and live by:

Salutation to the Dawn

Look to this day!
For it is life, the very life of life.
In its brief course
Lie all the verities and realities of your
existence—
The bliss of growth,
The glory of action,
The splendor of achievement.
For yesterday is already a dream
And tomorrow is only a vision,
But today well lived

Makes every yesterday a dream of happiness
And every tomorrow a vision of hope.
Look well, therefore, to this day!
Such is the salutation to the dawn.

Discuss the significance of the concepts in the poem.

18. In receiving his sister Fran's kindness again, in retrospect, Scrooge
sees his own self-centeredness in a new light—again, by contrast.
Too often we ignore the love and kindness expressed, from day to
day, in our own families. What can we do about it?

19. The scene with Fezziwig vividly brings home to Scrooge the fact that
he has been a terrible boss to Cratchit. Scrooge experiences something
else at Fezziwig's that he had lost: the ability to carpe diem (seize the
day)—to gain joy out of every nuance, every moment, of every day;
hence, the changed life in the fifth stave (what, in King James language
is termed "the abundant life"). How incredible that Christians, of all
people, should walk around morosely, as if there were no God and the
world had caved in on them! Discuss.

20. In re-experiencing his own broken engagement, Scrooge realized
how much he had lost in throwing away Bell's love. "And for what?"
he now asks himself. Scrooge realized that there was a price to pay
for his being too busy and too selfish to marry and have children: a
lonely old age.

Discuss the roles of marriage, family and children in our lives.

Stave Three: The Second of the Three Spirits

21. If there is one word that capsulizes this book, it is kindness, one of
the most crucial and far-reaching qualities in God's universe.
Without it, life is sad and miserable, both for the person who fails
to practice the quality and for those who come into contact with
that person. From the story, discuss instances of the presence or

absence of kindness and the difference it makes. Note that the Second Ghost sprinkles that "gift" on people passing by.

22. What does the Cratchit scene accomplish in the book? How—and why—does Scrooge change as he watches them celebrate Christmas together? Who in the family softens Scrooge's heart the most? Why? What are the lessons we can gain from that truth.

23. At Fred's house, the people are having a rollicking good time. How is Scrooge changed by what he sees and hears? What causes these changes? What should be the significance to us? For instance, what should be the role of play in our lives?

Stave Four: The Last of the Spirits

24. This stave is, by far, the most devastating of all. All the action leads into it, and Scrooge must at last face his moment of truth. Note how Dickens pulls it off: Rather than telling about Scrooge's demise through passive narration, he drops the reader into separate, apparently unrelated, conversations with people on the street. One has the feeling of actually being there, listening in and having to pull the information together oneself.

Discuss this aspect of writing—that is, letting dialogue, rather than narration, carry the story. What does each of these conversations contribute to the whole? Study each one carefully and compare.

25. Note how Dickens is a master at being able to arrive at the personality essence of an individual by just honing in on dialogue. Study each character in the book, even those who are only given a few lines; then see if you can construct a core of individuality out of that. In our own writing, how can we learn from Dickens in this respect?

26. As the stave progresses, how does Dickens orchestrate increasing horror on the part of Scrooge?

27. What is accomplished by the return to the Cratchit family?

28. What is accomplished by the fact that the Third Ghost is mute—says not a word?

29. Starting with the Third Ghost, analyze the role of each ghost in the overall scheme of the book. How is each one different? What does each contribute to the whole?

Stave Five: The End of It

30. Describe (starting from the first stave and moving toward the end) how Scrooge changes during the course of the story. What causes the biggest changes? Do they occur all at once or gradually? After doing that, compile two character studies: Scrooge at the beginning and Scrooge at the end. Compare them. Do you feel the changes are justified by the action and the dialogue? Explain.

31. Discuss the impact of the story. What was the overall effect on you? Do you feel this effect will be short-lived? Or do you feel it will affect the way you treat others for a long time? Explain and discuss.

The
Christmas Angel

By

Abbie Farwell Brown

Introduction and Afterword

by

Joe Wheeler

TABLE OF CONTENTS

INTRODUCTION

ABBIE FARWELL BROWN AND
THE CHRISTMAS ANGEL

I have always loved Christmas stories—especially the heart-tugging kind. And, let's face it, sentiment and Christmas belong together. Of all the seasons of the year, the heart is the most open to love, empathy, kindness, forgiveness, generosity, and change . . . at Christmas.

Thousands of authors have written stories about Christmas, but sadly, most of them are shallow, sterile, and un-moving. These stories may be technically brilliant, but if they fail to engage the heart, I view them as failures.

Only a few have written "great" Christmas stories, and even fewer have written "great" Christmas books (usually novelette length rather than full book length, as Christmas books are rarely very long). And of those few *special* Christmas books which percolate to the top, very few manage to stay there, but gradually, over time, sink down into that vast subterranean sea of forgotten books. To stay alive, season after season, generation after generation, presupposes a magical ingredient no critic-scientist has ever been able to isolate. *The Christmas Carol, Miracle on 34th Street, Its a Wonderful Life,* and *The Other Wise Man* have made it. In recent years, *The Best Christmas Pageant Ever* by Barbara Robinson (1972) and Richard Paul Evans' *The Christmas Box* (1993) have so far evidenced staying power, but only time will reveal whether they will stay there.

But, none of this precludes comebacks. Literature and public taste are, after all, cyclical, thus even during authors' lifetimes, reputations roll along on roller-coasters, undulating up and down as public tastes and demands change. No one remains *hot* forever. But sometimes certain works brazenly dig into our memories and impudently refuse to leave. Which brings us to Abbie Farwell Brown.

It was some years ago when I first "met" her. My wife and I were wandering around New England at the height of fall colors. While browsing in a used book-store, Connie discovered an old book—and short—with the intriguing title of *The Christmas Angel.* She brought it over to me and asked if I was familiar with it or with the author. I was not, but on the strength of the wonderful woodcut illustrations, we bought it. Upon our return home, I unpacked it, then sat down to read it—and *LOVED* it.

The Christmas Angel

So here it is. I don't often creep out far enough on limbs to risk getting sawed off, but I shall make an exception for *The Christmas Angel*. It has all the enduring qualities that have kept *The Christmas Carol* at the top for over a century and a half—in fact, one reader told me that she even prefers it over *The Christmas Carol*. It is one of those rarities: a book that should be loved equally by all generations—from small children to senior citizens. I can see it being filmed; and I can see it becoming a Christmas tradition: unthinkable to get through a Christmas season without reading it out loud to the family once again.

Since the story is divided into 15 short chapters, it would lend itself to being spread out during the Advent or the Twelve days of Christmas.

And, unquestionably, the Reginald Birch illustrations add a very special dimension to the book.

When Christ wished to hammer home a point, He told a story, a parable, an allegory. This is just such a story. But, coupled with that is something else: it is one of the most memorable and poignant angel stories I have ever read. And it is amazing how many people today are rediscovering angel stories!

In this story, the angel's "target" is Miss Terry—a bitter, cold, bigoted, and unforgiving old woman. As with Dickens' Scrooge, in her life, virtually all sentiment, caring, and love had been discarded, then trampled on, in her morose journey through the years. And now, at Christmas, but one tie to her past remains, one key that might unlock her cell of isolation: her childhood box of toys.

She determines to burn them—*every last one.*

ABOUT THE INTRODUCTION

For decades, one of the few absolutes in my literature classes has been this: *Never read the introduction before reading the book!* Those who ignored my thundering admonition lived to regret their disobedience. Downcast, they would come to me and say, "Dr. Wheeler, I confess that I read the introduction first, and it wrecked the book for me. I couldn't enjoy the story, because all the way through, I saw it through someone *else's eyes*. I don't agree with the editor on certain points, but those conclusions are in my head, and now I don't know *what* I think!"

Given that God never created a human clone, no two of us will ever perceive reality in exactly the same way—and no two of us ever should! Therefore, no matter how educated, polished, brilliant, insightful, or eloquent the teacher might be, don't ever permit that person to tell you how to think or respond, for that is a violation of the most sacred thing God gives us—our individuality.

My solution to the introduction problem was to split it in two: an introduction, to whet the appetite for, and enrich the reading of, the book; and an afterword, to generate discussion and debate *after* the reader has arrived at his or her own conclusions about the book and is ready to challenge my (the teacher's) perceptions.

ABOUT THE ILLUSTRATIONS

How fleeing fame is! For well over half a century, *St. Nicholas Magazine* was the premier children's magazine in America, and its editor, Mary Mapes Dodge, a household name. Almost as famous during the last quarter of the nineteenth century and first quarter of the twentieth was artist Reginald Birch, whose illustrations appeared in virtually every issue of *St. Nicholas Magazine*, and in many children's books as well. His romanticized Little Lord Fauntleroy look—Birch did the illustrations for the original book—dominated contemporary children's art just as much as Norman Rockwell would after him.

Readers of this series will already be familiar with Birch because of the memorable half-tone illustrations he did for Louisa May Alcott's *Little Men*. These however are woodcuts, among the finest Birch ever did, completely capturing the mood and characters in this remarkable story.

ABOUT THE AUTHOR

Abbie Farwell Brown
(1881-1927)

No matter what my birth may be,
       No matter where my lot is cast
I am the heir in equity
       Of all the wondrous past.

The art, the science, and the lore
       Of all the ages long since dust,
The wisdom of the world in store
       Is mine, all mine, in trust.

The beauty of the living earth,
       The power of the golden sun,
The present, whatsoever my birth,
       I share with everyone.

As much as any man, am I
       The owner of the working day,
Mine are the minutes as they fly
       To save or throw away.

And mine the future to be greater
       Unto the generation new
I help to shape it with my breath
       Mine as I think or do.

Present and past my heritage
       The future laid in my control,
No matter what my name or age
       I am a master-soul.

          —Abbie Farwell Brown, "The Heritage," 1919,
          archived in the Schlesinger Library of Radcliffe

The Christmas Angel

Without question, this biography has proved to be the hardest one yet to research and write. In fact, for a time, I had all but resigned myself to there being no life sketch of her at all! But we persisted, and finally struck pay dirt: The Schlesinger Library of Radcliffe College at Harvard University houses all that apparently exists of Abbie Farwell Brown's papers.

Thus to Cambridge, Massachusetts I journeyed, and found my way to the white-porticoed Schlesinger Library of Radcliffe, Brown's alma mater. They take very good care of the three small boxes of her papers.

Barbara Haber (Head Curator of books and manuscripts), and Wendy Thomas were especially helpful and kind to me, not only helping me with manuscripts and archival materials but also launching me out upon the Internet. Extremely helpful in conceptualizing Miss Brown's story is the life synopsis, written by Jo Ann Abraham Reiss, and Carolyn Ticknor's splendid eulogy, "Carolyn Ticknor's Estimate of Abbie Farwell Brown," March 23, 1927, Boston newspaper column (both archived in the Schlesinger Library of Radcliffe.) If this modest biography is effective, Barbara Haber and her equally helpful associates made what you are now reading possible. So, bless them!

There is no biography to work from. Even though Brown was a faithful diarist, only two diaries survive—and they are more travelogue than diary. Neither did her letters survive her, of which she wrote thousands. I might have known this would be so, for in a column she wrote (under a pseudonym) in 1898, when she was only 27, are these prophetic words: "I shall have a big bonfire tonight on my open hearth. I have been looking over piles and heaps of old letters this morning, sorting them out and trying to decide which were really worth keeping and which had served their brief purpose and were better metamorphosed into ashes."

As a result of no diaries, and no letters to speak of, I am forced to write a very different kind of life sketch. I will have to let her own words do the speaking; thoughts will prevail over actions.

A NEW ENGLAND PRINCESS

The blood royal of America is *Mayflowerian*. Many other ships brought settlers, in the earliest days, to places such as St. Augustine, Roanoke, Jamestown, Baltimore, Philadelphia, and New Amsterdam, but only The *Mayflower* registers in the American consciousness as the first, as the true beginning of things.

The little girl who cried her way into Boston's Brahmanic Beacon Hill, thirteen generations later, carried in her tiny veins the bluest blood in New England. Her father, Benjamin Farwell Brown, was descended from Isaac Allerton, a *Mayflower* settler, who had served as assistant governor of the Plymouth Colony. Her mother, Clara Neal Brown, came from a family of New Hampshire pioneers who had set-tled and named the town of Exeter. For ten generations, not one of little Abbie's ancestors had lived outside New England. Her lineage included Cavaliers, Roundheads, Puritans, Church of Englanders, explorers, adventurers, sailors, farmers, leaders (including Captain Myles Standish), merchants, and writers, and reached all the way back to William the Conqueror. Abbie herself, with good rea-son, was called a "bluestocking."

She was born on August 21 of 1871 in the family home at 41 West Cedar Street. Everyone cooperated: the doctor arrived at half past three, the nurse around four, and Abbie—weighing eight pounds—before five. The robust appetite she was born with would quickly grow into an appetite for all life, all experience, all nature.

MY LITTLE CHAIR

> I had a little arm-chair once; 'twas very, very small,
> So no one else, but only I, could sit in it at all,
> And by the open fireplace I'd watch the sparks arise,
> While in the glowing embers came strange pictures to my eyes,—
> My chin upon my chubby hand, my elbow on my knee,
> And sitting in the little chair just big enough for me.
>
> I saw fair towers and battlements, with moat and drawbridge too,
> And fairy knights and ladies from the world my fancy knew,
> And in the coals great caverns yawned, whence fiery dragons came,
> With breath of sparks and cinders black and eyes of hot red flame.
> Oh, they were very wonderful, the sights I used to see
> When sitting in that little chair just big enough for me.

The Christmas Angel

But now the magic spell is gone, and sadly, all in vain,
I look into the fire to see those pictures bright again;
But with the little chair I fear I have outgrown them all,
For one can only see the fairy world when one is small.
And as the fire cracks and snaps I long once more to be
A child, and in the little chair just big enough for me.

—Abbie Farwell Brown, "My Little Chair,"
archived in the Schlesinger Library of Radcliffe

Her mother, educated at Hampton Academy, artistic, and an award-winning author herself, shaped her childhood, and that of her one sibling, Ethel. Looking back on those early days, Abbie observed, "I cannot remember when I did not write. My mother was always very clever with her pen and pencil. When my sister and I were tiny girls our mother started a little home paper for us. We called it The *Catkin*, being fond, as we all were, of cats. We wrote jingles and scraps of prose." ("Young Women Who Uphold Our Literary Fame Belong to the Galaxy of Stars," *Sunday Boston Herald*, January 10, 1904). Sometimes their mother illustrated it, but more often Abbie and Ethel did. Amazingly, these copies of The *Catkin*, now close to a century and a quarter old, survived. What an experience it was, after having read about them, to open a folder in the Schlesinger Library and pull out these hand-written, hand-illustrated family magazines. The paper being of high rag content, the illustrations look as if they could have been sketched only a short time ago, rather than but thirteen to fifteen years after the Civil War.

Her mother, having connections with leading magazines of the day, encouraged the little girls to set their sights high at a very early age. Thus both girls became known by readers of the greatest children's magazine of the age, *St. Nicholas* (Abbie writing and Ethel illustrating), while they were still in their early teens.

Abbie's formal schooling began at Bowdoin School, where she graduated as valedictorian in 1886 at the age of fourteen. Already we can see in that valedictory, her concern for all life; indeed her perception of the interconnectedness of life:

> *Everything in nature is made for a purpose. The smallest living creature has its mission. The tiniest grain of sand has its part in forming the vast sea beds which sustain the weight of the ocean. The frail insect living but an hour fulfills its mission, and the largest animal on earth can do no more. The flowers,—have they not all missions? Does not one gladden our*

hearts with its beauty, another yield sweet perfume to please us, and another save our lives as a medicine?

Then may we not each have a purpose, a higher motive, something more than to be content merely to drag along from day to day getting enough to eat and drink?

May we not, like the columbine which, dressed in bright colors and dancing gaily on its slender stem, brightens and lends life to the grey old rock against which it grows, may we not lighten the burdens of some other human being like ourselves, perhaps less fortunate than we, but still a fellow creature, and needing comfort like us?

(excerpted from Brown's 1886 Valedictory,
Bowdoin School, archived in the Schlesinger Library of Radcliffe.)

Abbie may have not at this time fully realized her calling in life, nevertheless this valedictory clearly telegraphs what her life and ministry to those less fortunate than she would be all about. Note that her illustrations, her metaphoric imagery, comes straight from nature. That would always be so even after she reached full artistic maturity. Already she was developing the rhythm and beat that would give her prose and poetry such power and poignancy. Rather ironic, isn't it, that this child of one of America's greatest cities should draw almost exclusively from the rural and from nature for her subject matter and imagery.

Almost no author is able to retain childhood perspective once childhood is past. Elizabeth Goudge is one of the only such writers I have ever known who has been able to retain the lens of childhood after growing up. Abbie Farwell Brown is another, as we shall see. But "My Little Chair" reveals to us that it wasn't easy, retaining that low-to-the-ground perspective. Her unique italicized asides enable her to carry on dual conversations with her readers.

POINTS OF VIEW

When beating drums and tramping feet
With crowds of people fill the streets,
Oh how they run and push and cry

The   To watch the soldiers passing by!
procession   But though I stand on tiptoe tall,
invisible.   The grown-ups make a solid wall.
Oh, it is very sad to be
So little that one cannot see!

The Christmas Angel

I hear the bands of music play,
And see some banners move away.
The soldiers pass and soon are gone,
And I have seen not even one!   *Selfish*
The people must forget, I know,   *big*
That they were children long ago.   *folk!*
How splendid it must feel to be
So big that one can always see!

But sometimes when the grown-ups come
To see my play house here at home,
And when I try to show the rest
The things I like the very best,—   *Blind*
The truly things one has to "play,"—   *big*
They only look around and say,   *folk!*
"I can't see any castle there!"
Or "Where's the Princess?" "How?" and
"Where?"

Oh, does it not seem very queer
When I can see them plainly here,
Big people who could view so well
The long procession, and could tell   *Good*
What uniform the soldiers wore,   *to*
Can't see things on the nursery floor?   *be*
How dreadful it must feel to be   *little!*
So big and old one cannot see!

—Abbie Farwell Brown, from *A Pocketful of Posies*, 1902

Is childhood an accumulation of weeks, months, and years? Is it a state of mind? What we *do* know is that children perceive life differently than adults do. Brown's view was perhaps best articulated during a newspaper interview: "Children could write juvenile masterpieces if grown people wouldn't prod them with models. . . . The trouble with most of the literature that is being written for children is that the writers know too much and admit that they know it.

"Most authors don't look at a cow as a child looks at a cow—horns and tail and a meadowy smell—but they must invariably see a dairy.

"Many writers turn to writing child stuff as a last resort of the editorial incompetent; whereas to get down on one's knees and take a waist-high view of life is a

184

kind of literary acrobatics possible only to the patient" (excerpted from undated newspaper clipping, "Child Classics Seen By Author," archived in the Schlesinger Library of Radcliffe.)

Following graduation from Bowdoin, Abbie enrolled in Boston Girls' Latin School[1], where she gave birth to, organized, and edited the school paper, *The Jabberwock*, thereby showing her love for Lewis Carroll's "Alice" books. It was during these years that Josephine Preston Peabody, descendant of another prominent New England family, came into her life. Josephine would not only become one of the nation's best known Boston poets, but she would also become the closest and dearest friend Abbie would ever know, a true soul sister.

These were full years for Abbie, as she was ever in the center of whatever activities were going on: be they dances, Dickens carnivals, banquets, masques and plays, parades, prize drills, or calisthenics. Along the way she somehow found time to add to her growing national recognition as an author by her submissions to magazines such as *St. Nicholas*. *The Jabberwock* saw most of these literary labors first, however. In 1891, Abbie was elected President of her graduating class.

Then came Radcliffe, then and now one of the most prestigious women's colleges in America. She attended there during the years 1891-2 and 1893-4, taking, as always, a most active part in campus dramatics and literary affairs, and continuing to find homes for her poems and stories.

AN IMMUNE

From all accounts, the talented Miss Brown was lovely, and always the center of a flock of devoted admirers, men *and* women. Clearly, she had many opportunities to marry, but took advantage of none of them—in fact, she would live her entire life in the house on West Cedar Street in which she was born.

Since she left no revealing diary entries or letters, in terms of her romantic relationships, we are forced to look for clues in her writings, always a dangerous thing to do, for one's fictional world does not necessarily mirror the author's actual life. One poem especially, written during her first year at Radcliffe, quite likely was autobiographical.

SIC TRANSIT

> I had a castle in the air
> With towers tall and pillars fair
> And filled with treasures rich and rare,
> > And there my fancy free
> > Dwelt long in ecstasy.
>
> My castle fell but yesterday.
> My dreams have vanished quite away.
>
> Upon the sand I wrote a name,
> The name of one whose true love came
> To set my life in love's sweet frame
> > Brief picture, fair and sweet
> > Of happiness, complete.
>
> The name I wrote but yesterday
> The morning's tide has wiped away.
>
> I picked a wild rose by the sea,
> I thought its beauty bloomed for me,
> And took it with me tenderly
> > Its petals were so fair
> > Its perfume rich and rare—
>
> The rose I picked but yesterday
> I find now fades quite away.
>
> > > —Abbie Farwell Brown, archived in the
> > > Schlesinger Library of Radcliffe

The Christmas Angel

Revealing glimpses into her dating and social life during these years are seen through the prism of the most self-revealing prose she ever wrote, the fascinating series of articles she wrote for the *St. Louis Globe-Democrat*, under the pseudonym of Jean Neal, during 1898-9. Taken as a whole, they reveal much about women of her time.

In her "Burning Old Letters," it is clear that she has received a lot of letters from men over the years. Of them she observes, "A man . . . never for a moment forgets to whom he is writing. He is conscious of his audience and of himself in relation to it. He does not talk himself out as he would in conversation—where indeed he has the advantage of the average girl in unconscious ease and lack of affectation. But he tries so hard to be adequate. He is not spontaneous; he does not write for the pleasure of it, but only when he has something particular to say is he at his best."

But not always does she find men so self-conscious and stilted: "But when a man who is really worth while forgets his audience and loses his consciousness that he is writing a letter, then indeed are his eagerly scrawled pages worth while. Then, when he is genuine and sincere, he is apt also to be more impressive in diction, more forceful in idea and more apt in illustration. I love best of all to correspond with a man on those terms."

In "The Old and the New Valentine," she castigates men for showing so little imagination in their courting: "Men have no imagination nowadays; that's the trouble. . . . It is not the girls' fault that there is so little romance in the world. Indeed, it is they who keep alive what little there is extant; and in their secret souls they mourn because there is no more. . . ."

In "Women and War," written during the Spanish-American War, she notes that "All the world loves a lover, as we know; but from time immemorial all the lassies have loved the soldier laddie. And even though they have no time to look upon us, we watch them off and out of sight with our hearts in our eyes." In "The Summer Man," also written during that war, she resignedly admits that women, when available men are few, so spoil the few men who show up at summer resorts that those men tend to become despots.

In "Picnics and Picnics," she maintains that no more than half of those invited to a picnic should be female; males are essential to the success of such an activity.

"May Day" is a holiday she yearns for as it once was celebrated, but now, she sighs, it has fallen "into disrepute only since men have become too busy and prosaic and commonplace to appreciate it."

But, of them all, she gave herself away most in "Engagement of One's

Friends." First of all, she labels herself an "immune" (immunity from marrying), declaring, "I think I am an immune myself; at least, no microbe has as yet fixed his cold claw on me—and I have been repeatedly exposed." But then, mixing her signals, she admits that "It is a queer feeling to receive the announcement of an old friend's engagement; queerer still, if once upon a time you might have had the opportunity to write your name in place of that other hers. It has been said, I think, that no woman relishes the idea of losing a devotion once hers to command: still less to see it transferred to another woman. . . . We don't wish it ours again—we could have had it in the first place if we had wanted it. But there certainly is a queer little feeling of pique and almost of jealousy that there should be consolation in the world for the loss of us."

But, she submits, there are compensations to singlehood: "Chaperoned by one's juniors, if one happens to have the gift of looking younger than is possible, one can go on, in season and out of season, having the good times which fall only to the lot of bachelor maids. . . . We are envied often, we immunes. . . . Nowadays there is no obloquy attached to the state of spinsterhood—it is quite the fashion to prolong girlhood to the utmost bounds; there is always a chance to change one's mind before it is too late, in case the right one should come along."

Apparently, for her, the right one never did.

A 'WANDERING

The snow-white ships that sail the sea	*If only*
Are like adventurous birds, to me.	
They spread their wings and fly afar	*I*
To foreign lands where wonders are;	
Where gondolas ply up and down	*could*
The byways of a fairy town;	
Where gloomy mountain caverns hold	*be*
Forgotten stores of robber gold;	
Where tigers in the jungle roam,	*a*
And curious creatures are at home;	
Where lovely castles gleam in Spain;	
Where camels in a winding train	*bird*
Bear treasures from Aladdin's land	
and Across the desert's yellow sand;	
Where painted mosques with towers high	
Point to the magic eastern sky;	

fly.   Where mystic lamps turn night to day;
Where tinkling rainbow fountains play;
Where giants lived, and dragons, too,
Where fairy fancies might come true;
Where everything is quaint and queer,
So different from now and here!
All tinted amethyst and gold,
And nothing new, but ever old.

Oh   Oh, pennies would be useless there,
But golden sequins are to spare,

my!   And jingling ducats buy such things
As children's dreaming never brings.

Oh, snow-white ships that sail the sea,
Great birds, do lend your wings to me,
And bear me happily some day
To those bright wonders far away!

—Abbie Farwell Brown, "Snow-White Ships,"
from *A Pocketful of Posies*, 1902

After having dreamed of going abroad for many years, in 1899 Brown made up part of a traveling foursome self-labeled "The Bachelor Girls," and sailed to Europe. Fortunately, she wrote a series of travel sketches for the *St. Louis Globe-Democrat*; in them is revealed much more of her reactions, impressions, and personality than the diary entries do.

"EDINBURGH, SCOTLAND, July 10—It is a bewildering experience for four unsquired dames, little used to traveling, to find themselves stranded in a foreign city . . . with no prospect of finding a lodging for their weary bones [the visit of the Prince of Wales was attracting such crowds that all the available rooms were booked]. At last an angelic maid in the inevitable black gown, white cap and dainty apron of the Scottish chambermaids, gave us faint hope of obtaining an attic room. The quartet fell upon her neck in tearful joy, and accepted any terms, any condition of condensed living—even four in a bed or two in a bath tub was better than renting the cab for the night, as we were desperately contemplating. . . ."

Of the food, she was less than ecstatic: "We cannot get used to the bad coffee, cold bread and meat for breakfast, nor to the overdone beef and uncanny broths at dinner, with the lack of napkins, tea and ice water."

But, oh, the Highland soldier! "Anything more peacocky and dazzling than his six feet of kilt, tartan, bear skin, white coat, gaiters and tattooed knees, would be hard to find. Eh, but he is bonnie and I find my hairt sair taken wi' a' his glory. We saw a regiment of him being drilled at the castle yesterday, and it was like a moving kaleidoscope of color. He is very callous, however, and casts an eye neither to right nor left to notice the admiring lasses who wilt along his path."

The historical sites really meant the most to her. Places like Holyrood Castle:

> We passed into Holyrood with many a tremor of pity for the poor Queen Mary, who seems so specially identified with it. It is a grand place, but very gloomy and sad—not wholly with memories, but because of the architecture of those days and the lack of airy lighting. Mary's apartments, with the little secret stair leading down to Darnley's room, contain many mementos of the ill-fated Queen, and seem full of her presence. Her royal bed, canopied in oak and faded crimson damask, stands close by the door of the little supper room where Rizzio was seized dining with her. The conspirators entered by her secret stair and dragged the poor, beautiful, much-loved youth out at a side door. A sinister spot in the corridor is pointed out as being dyed in his blood. It does no harm to believe the legend unless one is too sensitive to bear the shock which sight of that faint shadow of a stain conveys (excerpted from Jean Neal's [Brown's pseudonym] "Bachelor Girls in Scotland," St. Louis Globe-Democrat, July 30, 1899).

Reluctantly leaving Edinburgh, the quartet moved on to Melrose Abbey, Durham, York, Canterbury, Birmingham, Warwick, and Stratford. Then it was on to London, via Kenilworth Castle: "What a joy dear old, smutty, damp, gray London is. . . . Not so strange nor quaint nor grand nor beautiful, perhaps, as what we have seen in many of our wanderings, but every turn of every street brings us up short upon some thrilling site or association: every other corner bears a name which brings our hearts up into our mouths with a queer thump of recognition and greeting. Every little church—and they are thick in London as mosquitoes in New Jersey—has its legend or its sacred shrine of some bookmaking friend, to whom we never come so near in time or place or spirit as now. The very stones beneath one's feet seem to cry out the names of those who have trodden them in times past, and in the thickest whir of traffic one feels the spirit of things which happened long ago."

Everywhere they found memories of Dickens, in "the dirtiest alley in London, Tom All Alone's pathetic graveyard, and in the Old Curiosity Shop."

191

The brooding Tower of London was quite another story! "The tower filled us with gloom. One could hardly look to enjoy a happy morning in these grim surroundings." In all their many pilgrimages, they did not forget the great British Museum. Above all, they did not forget Westminster Abbey. Three times Brown returned to its Poets' Corner, there to commune and dream.

Not surprisingly, given Brown's love of flowers, she rhapsodized over an endearing trait of Londoners: "We hardly met a man in the morning who had not a posy or boutonniere in his lapel; they always seemed to have time for this little grace, and are not ashamed of being considered effeminate if caught buying flowers on the street. And what delightful flowers they are—how cheap and plentiful! They go by us in little donkey carts heaped high like a huge nosegay, with roses, mignonette, lavender, pinks, violets. Everyone seems fond of them, and everyone seems to consider flowers as one of the actual necessities of life" (excerpted from Brown's "Bachelor Girls in London," *St. Louis Globe-Democrat*, November 19, 1899).

Sadly, the girls bade farewell to London and headed to the Lorna Doone country, Bideford, Salisbury, and the land of Jane Austen; traveling by horse and carriage.

A ship then took them across the windy English Channel to Antwerp and Amsterdam. Germany was next. At Cologne's shrine of St. Ursula and the Eleven Thousand Virgins, Brown came face to face with the question: How much is legend and how much is truth? Responding, she admitted, "But we wanted to believe it all—it is really much easier to believe everything than to be a skeptic in the atmosphere of so much obvious age and gorgeous faith; and the chamber was a very holy place to us. . . . And after all, whether the legend be true or no . . . , the sentiment which they have inspired through all these hundreds of years is a touching and beautiful thing, and the floor worn by countless pilgrims' feet, and the cold metal kissed by so many earnest lips, have surely become sacred in their own right."

As for cathedrals and castles, she announced, tongue in cheek, that "If when we reach our native shores we are not able to build for ourselves a cathedral and a ruined castle, it will prove that we are singularly unobservant. I have seen so many of both these specimens of ancient architecture that I feel as if I could make either with both eyes shut. After climbing to the top of Cologne Cathedral, the second tallest building in the world, I believe, oh, how my legs did ache! And after a glorious day on the Rhine, whisking by countless castles of every pattern and variety, to say nothing of a special visit to Heidelberg Castle, with careful inspection of every dungeon and battlement, I feel that I have acquired the cathe-dral-castle recipe. But I won't give it away. It's too precious" (excerpted from Brown's "Bachelor Girls in Kaiser William's Country," *St. Louis Globe-Democrat*, October 8, 1899).

Switzerland and the Alps were next. Hordes of Cookies (tourists led by Cook guides) were everywhere, each with chamois beard and eldelweiss-bedecked-hat and notched alpenstock cane, induced them to sing a popular tourist ditty often:

> "I would not be a Cookie,
>   Nor with the Cookies stand,
>   The edelweiss on my forehead,
>   An alpenstock in my hand."

Not that they hadn't tried to fit in but their alpenstocks were "continually poking into the eyes of porters and of drivers and fellow travelers, and (worst of all) of us." Besides that, they were always being left somewhere. Oh yes, and mak-ing them the laughingstock of whoever was around. So they were not at all bro-ken-hearted when a porter walked away with the alpenstocks in Geneva, and never brought them back.

But, never to be forgotten was Zermatt and the Matterhorn. "Ah, what a glo-rious day that was—my birthday—and spent in a heavenly meadow, pink with alpine lilies in the shadow of that great sky-biting tooth. My birthday cake was a plummy mountain frosted with snow; the loveliest of alpine flowers in countless varieties garlanded the feast, and a brilliant peak, one for each year of my life, stood up for candles all about. It was the best birthday party I ever had. . . ."

In those days, travel in the mountains was not for the faint of heart. They traveled in horse-drawn diligences ("like open victorias, with an extra seat above behind the driver"). "Our road to Chamonix over the famous Tete Noir Pass is a ticklish experience for weak nerves. . . . Such dizzy precipices sheering down into gorges of jagged, hard rock, with rushing torrents at the bottom. We would go under an arch of rock, through a black hole of a tunnel, and emerge to find the horses' hoofs clinging to the very edge of the cliff, at a right-angle of the road" (excerpted from Brown's "Bachelor Girls in the Alps," *St. Louis Globe-Democrat*, October 22, 1899).

Then it was Paris! The shopping was both wonderful and addictive. But, as to the cabmen ". . . who take basest advantage of our not being able to argue in vol-uble French. Of all misguided and gallows-bound rogues the French cabman is the most to be anathematized. We found his species civil in England, bland in Belgium, dull in Holland, obstinate in Germany, and guileful in Switzerland. But in Paris he is villainy itself. Not only does he unmercifully beat his horse as I have never seen horses abused elsewhere, not only does he drive so carelessly that the wheels of your cabriolet are forever becoming entangled with the other cabs which pass in the night, not only does he smoke bad cigars whose smoke puffs into your face, and swears horrid French, swears at every one he encounters—but he charges you for overtime and weeps if you refuse his unrighteous demands. And of all unendurable horrors a weeping thief is the worst. . . ."

As to the city itself, "You can't tell what may happen in Paris at any minute, we have this feeling continually in this joyous, reckless, clean and sparkling city, which has bathed in blood so often. Everything looks new and fresh as if just made; and the most cheerful places of all are the sights of wholesale murders and awful crimes" (excerpted from "Bachelor Girls in Paris," *St. Louis Globe-Democrat*, November 5, 1899).

Finally, exhausted from the unrelenting pace of their sight-seeing, they crossed the Channel to England. Windsor Castle, where Queen Victoria resided, was their last destination. Brown climbed high up into the castle tower; far away, she could see Eton College and the spire of Stoke Pogis Church, "where 'Elegy in a Country Churchyard' was born and where Gray lies buried." She wrapped up her life-changing trip with these words: "It makes one feel queer to stand by the grave of Kings. One cannot help feeling a little sense of triumph in one's life and power and youth, realizing how much better it is to be a live dog than a dead lion.

"For, is it not far more satisfactory to be looking forward to a joyous sea trip to good old America, with a turkey dinner and jolly American cooking at its end, than to be lying there in royal state, shorn of one's head, or with a bullet through one's heart, amid all the pride, pomp and circumstance of knightly gear and golden shields and rampant lions?

"And now to pack my trunk" (excerpted from "Bachelor Girls at Windsor Castle," *St. Louis Globe-Democrat*, December 3, 1899; other references are from Brown's trip journal, archived in the Schlesinger Library of Radcliffe.)

LITTLE BROTHERS

Like
Hiawatha.

I wish I knew the simple words
To talk with Fish and Beasts and Birds!
We call them "dumb" because they speak
A tongue not English, French, or Greek;

Animals
are
not
dumb!

But they are wiser far than we,
And often grieve, it seems to me,
Because we folk of Tailor-Land
Can't answer them nor understand.

We
are
dull.

How pleasant it would be to stray
About the woods and fields all day,
Conversing with them, high and low,
Of matters that one wants to know.

Tree-
top
tales.

I should learn very curious things
From Brother Bird who loaned his wings
To bear me up into the sky,
Till never child had soared so high!

Water-
wonders.

And Brother Fish would teach the maze
Of ripple-paths and water-ways;

Would tell me fishy tales, and show
What fishermen can never know.

Four-
footed
fun.
Big eyes!
Big teeth!
Red tongues!

Then Brother Beast would make me wise
With secrets which a man would prize.
The bigger Beasts would walk beside,
And bear me when I chose to ride;
They would defend me from the foe,
And teach the safest way to go.
The little ones would find me food,
And bring me news of bad and good;
And I should love them, oh! so well,

But kind
to me.

And they would know, for I could tell.
So I should be their little King,
To share their life in everything.

All this I cannot do, indeed;
But it is 'most as good to read,

The Christmas Angel

I shall   All cuddled in some cosy nook,
play   Of Mowgli in the Jungle Book;
Mowgli.   Of Mowgli who, it seems to me,
               Is what one most would like to be!
               —Abbie Farwell Brown, from *A Pocketful of Posies,* 1902

The twenty-eight-year-old dreamer who returned home to Boston on the eve of a new century was not at all the same person who had left five months before. Before, she had only read about these things in books, now she had seen and experienced them first-hand: castles and cathedrals, dungeons and gardens, knightly armor and blood-stained axe, the "Venus de Milo" and the "Mona Lisa." In Europe, legend perceived as truth had forced her to reevaluate what was real and what was not.

Only a little over a month after her ship carried her home in time for Thanksgiving, midnight bells rang in a new century. And fourteen months later, January 22, 1901, Victoria, empress of a quarter of mankind, was dead. She had come to the throne way back in 1837, and had mourned her husband Albert's death for forty long years.

On the streets of America, most of the world's automobiles—some 8,000—competed with some ten million bicycles and eighteen million horses and mules. The world, it was changing.

But Miss Brown was not much concerned with the technology of this new age: the automobile, the ever-faster trains, the airplane, each resulting in an ever-faster pace of life. Ideas generated by the long trip whirled relentlessly in her head, giving her no peace until they were dealt with. First and foremost was her first book with Houghton Mifflin, *The Book of Saints and Friendly Beasts* (1900), inspired by what she discovered in England's Chester Cathedral: carved in its choir stalls were scenes depicting the life of St. Werburg. Obviously, the product of meticulous and extensive research, within the book's covers she explored the symbiotic relationship between certain men, women, and the animal world, starting way back with St. Francis who knew that "all the creatures are our little brothers, ready to meet half way those who will but try to understand."

All of these stories deal with men and women, boys and girls, who, at least according to legend, had both the inclination and the ability to reach across the communication chasm which normally separates man from animal, human from non-human.

No book Brown ever wrote has proven more popular than this; even today, Brown aficionados diligently seek it out.

However, another of Brown's books has exercised the same staying power (at least in the used book market) as its illustrious predecessor: *The Lonesomest Doll* (1902), the story of a friendship between a sheltered child queen (Clothilde) and a gatekeeper's daughter (Nichelte). The catalyst is a doll so beautiful and valuable that she is neither played with nor loved. So popular has it been, in fact, that several decades later, it was reissued, featuring Arthur Rackham illustrations.

A Pocketful of Posies (1902) and *Fresh Posies* (1908) featured the best of Brown's early poetry, especially those written primarily for children.

Another powerful book for young people was her *In the Days of Giants: A Book of Norse Tales* (1902), in which she retells such fascinating Scandinavian myths. Altogether, a deeply moving book about the Norse gods, Brown tells each story simply, movingly, and beautifully. It reads like the Fall of Eden or Camelot, with Loki, the scheming Lucifer or the plotting Mordred, who brought sorrow and darkness to the world—and an end to joyous Valhalla. Balder, the Norse Prometheus or Christ figure, was beloved by C. S. Lewis, who borrowed more from Norse mythology than from any other. So splendidly written is this book that it remained a standard on children's library shelves several generations after it was first published.

The Curious Book of Birds (1903) humanizes birds, much as does Kipling in his *Jungle Book* and Thornton Burgess in his beloved stories. Brown ranged far in seeking out folk stories: some from the ancient world (mostly European), some from the Orient, some from Africa, and some from Native American lore.

The Flower Princess (1904) is actually a quartet of stories. "The Flower Princess," the story of a beautiful princess who determines to marry only someone who loves flowers as much as she does (unquestionably, one could validly substitute Abbie Farwell Brown as the Princess and not lose a nuance, so great was her personal love for flowers); "The Little Friend," a Christmas "inasmuch" story, was later published as a separate book; "The Mermaid's Child" is a Cain and Abel type narrative, with a humanized mer-child sacrificed by a jealous brother. Interestingly enough, a stork acts as the all-seeing mediator and judge in the story. "The Ten Blowers" is the supreme example of farcical slapstick humor in Brown's canon. Altogether, a remarkable book!

Next came two related books: *Brothers and Sisters* (1906), and *Friends and Cousins* (1907). In the first book, many of the stories feature the same children, and each story intertwines action, suspense, and Judeo-Christian values. Some of the stories take place in a child's fairyland world and some of them take place on a very real island off the Maine coast. So popular were the Maine island stories that Brown brought the protagonists back again in her *Friends and Cousins*. The dominant theme in all the stories is integrity—not in a preachy sense but in an undergirding sense.

John of the Woods (1909) is a wonderful adaptation spinning off from *The Book of Saints and Friendly Beasts*. The hero, John, is a battered orphan boy who flees his tormenters by escaping into the Italian forests. His life is saved by John the Hermit, a St. Francis-type who all the animals and birds of the forest love. After John matures, the sanctuary of the forest is desecrated by a hunting king and prince, determined to slay at will. From that moment on, the idyl ceases and suspense sets in. It is thereafter virtually unputdownable! In a very special sense, this is a pre-modern, pro-environment book, preaching the interconnectedness of all life and the need to protect all of God's creatures.

The Christmas Angel (1910) was, of course, her first great Christmas book.

With these almost yearly books taking much of her time, Brown still managed to find time to write a steady stream of poetry, short stories, and plays. According to Jo Ann Abraham Reiss, "she had a special gift for writing poetry appropriate to a musical setting, and for years was commissioned by Silver, Burdett & Company to contribute lyrics for songs in their Progressive Music Series. Collaborating with the composer Mabel W. Daniels, she won a Girl Scout competition for "On the Trail," which was adopted as the official song of the Girl Scouts." Beginning in 1902, she somehow also found time to serve as an editor of the "Young Folks Library," a twenty volume series published by Hall & Locke, as well as return to Europe again and again. (Reiss sketch archived in the Schlesinger Library of Radcliffe.)

She was fortunate in that she wrote and published during what is called the Golden Age of Children's Literature. But the tradition she represents best can be traced back through Howard Pyle, Andrew Lang, Nathaniel Hawthorne, Washington Irving, the Brothers Grimm, and Hans Christian Andersen, authors who reinterpreted mythology and legends especially for children.

THE INK WELL

My bottle of ink once said to me—
"Did you but know, could you but see
The wonderful stories all distilled
With which my inkiness is filled.

They are swimming around, a million words
To tell of fanciful beasts and birds,

Introduction

Fairies, pirates, girls and boys,
Treasure ships and beautiful toys.

You go fishing around with a pen
Catching a little tale now and then
But there they lurk, a million more,
That nobody ever caught before."

Then I shook that ink and stirred it well,
I fished. And what do you think befell?
A wee little minnow was all that bit,
But I hauled him out. And this is it.

—Abbie Farwell Brown, archived in the
Schlesinger Library of Radcliffe

The years continued to sweep by, and the "golden-haired, petite (she was only 5'3"), piquant-faced little authoress" kept mighty busy. ("Peace With a Sword," February 1918 news clipping is archived in the Schlesinger Library of Radcliffe.)

It was during this second decade of the new century that Brown grew more reflective, perhaps sensing she might not live a long life.

She became more concerned about her legacy—not merely her poems, short stories, plays, lyrics, and books, but her insights into the world children live in, and the role the written and spoken word ought to play in their lies. Not only did she write about these two areas of intense concern, but she lectured all over the country about them as well.

Four lectures had to do with "The Child and the Book." In them, she maintained that growth in spirituality, imagination, empathy and taste was best achieved indirectly, through books, agreeing completely with Tennyson.

"For truth in closest words shall fail,
When truth embodied in a tale
Shall enter in at lowly doors!"
(from *In Memorium*)

Preschoolers.

Her first talk had to do with children ages one through four. Her first concern had to do with the overall atmosphere of the home: "Books are the heart of the house—keep them lying about. The living room ought to be the book room, but even in the nursery there ought to be a book shelf. The overriding goal during these crucial first four years ought to be to make a book-lover of the child, and to develop the child's vocabulary."

The Story Hour she considered supremely important, and emphasized telling stories, reading stories aloud, cozy book-reading corners, bedtime stories, the impact of regular habit in this respect, and the long-term impact of story-related memories.

As for the physical book, she urged parents to inculcate reverence for it, to teach children to be careful in their book-handling, to encourage curiosity, to not cheapen books by too great numbers of them, and to teach them how books are made. Her list of no-no-nevers, consisted of these: Don't buy for small children books that are (1) ugly, (2) poorly printed, (3) poorly bound, (4) inadequately illustrated, (5) incorporate overly shiny paper, (6) are too heavy.

Children Ages Four to Seven.

Action is more important now. Boys and girls are still alike interest-wise. This is not an age for children to tell the stories, but for parents to. During this age, their sense of right and wrong is rapidly developing, as is the conscience. Emphasize manners, kindness, generosity, sympathy, empathy, and truthfulness. Curiosity is being awakened, and they'll have *lots* of questions. They are ready for true stories and facts of nature, and imagination-development, but it is important to discriminate between facts and imagination. This is excellent age for fairy tales, fables, myths, legends, heroes, lessons of good and evil, simple truths of life, justice, retribution. Brown point out that "nature and fairy lore are not incompatible; love of fairy world being the beginning of imagination in the child."

In poetry, you should now move from the simple to poetry with a meaning. In religious works, read the Scriptures aloud so as to communicate beauty of words; also read from *Pilgrim's Progress* and from legends of saints and good people. Be morally indirect rather than too preachy.

Children Ages Seven to Twelve.

Major changes occur during these years. They are now of school age. The imagination really flowers during this period! Areas to be emphasized include conscience, social virtues, curiosity, precepts, and imagination. Interest-wise, boys and girls now begin to diverge. There should be twofold development: spiritual and practical. They are beginning to react as they observe, are sensitive to suggestions, and are increasingly self-conscious. They have a growing antipathy to overt moralizing, desiring instead *Deeds, not words!* In reading, they are intrigued by slang, and increasingly enjoy shocking by choice of words.

Introduction

Their individuality is continuing to flower: *Feed the strongest interest!* Since this is the age of hero worship (especially for boys), feed them stories of chivalry, adventure, clan-spirit, pirates, and secrecy. Girls, on the other hand, are growing more responsible and sentimental, and can be so over-conscientious. They are ready for brave girls and gentle boys (Joan of Arc, Galahad). Thus boys and girls need to be addressed differently now, but encourage sympathy and empathy so they don't despise or put down the other. A good age for historic girls' and historic boys' series. Both the ideal and the practical need to be emphasized, especially the love of beauty, strength, and nobility.

Important to be reading the Bible out loud, as well as religious magazines; emphasize Bible heroes and saintly individuals. The best way to internalize chivalry, bravery, sacrifice, loyalty, and devotion, however, is through romances.

Poetry-wise, *there is no danger of too much!* Building on Field and Riley, stir in Whittier, Arnold, Robin Hood type ballads, Longfellow (especially *Hiawatha*), Tennyson, Holmes (the humorous ones), Shakespeare (re-told); same for Chaucer. *Soak the modern child with poetry!*

Brown, quoting from *St. Nicholas Magazine,* sums up this section in these words:

> *If they have good taste and good*
> *moral standards at age Twelve—they*
> *will not be easily lost.*

Boys and Girls Ages Twelve to Sixteen.

During these years, they continue to develop a sense of responsibility; and their ability to think and reason is strengthened. It is an age of *doing.* A sense of individuality becomes obvious. It is time to encourage honesty, loyalty, and generosity in girls, and kindness, delicacy, tact, and self-sacrifice in boys. Boys of this age love the sturdy virtues of danger, strength, pirates, secrecy, clan-spirit, and athletic books. They tend to gravitate toward objective things. Girls, on the other hand, tend to gravitate toward the sentimental, romantic, morbid, introspective, and the subjective. Again, *girls will read the boys' books—not vice-versa.* They share a common love of romance and adventure, but boys are fascinated by the practical and hate sentiment, whereas the girls are more dreamy.

This is a crucial age for developing standards of life, behavior: *character.* Introducing them to good biography is crucial at this age. History and travel broadens their interests, and citizenship can be inculcated through books like *Man Without a Country.*

The Christmas Angel

It is extremely important that poetry not be neglected during this age. They are ready for heavier things now—*The Great Ones!* Avoid edited, condensed versions—*they are not very real*—and *stick to the complete text.*

Brown summed up this section with this statement:

"Classics are read before 13—or never" (excerpted from "The Child and the Book" lecture notes, archived in the Schlesinger Library of Radcliffe.)

Brown also lectured on the subject of poetry. First of all, she noted that poetry is ruined for many children because of adult emphasis on artificiality in elocution ("imitation, rather than imagination.") All art requires imagination. Make poetry fun, such as she did in her "The Candy Lion":

Harmless	A CANDY Lion's very good
and	Because he cannot bite,
sweet-	Nor wander roaring for his food,
tempered	Nor eat up folks at night.

But though it's very nice for me,
    It's not so nice for him;   *Fades*
For every day he seems to be   *away*
More shapeless and more slim.   *somehow*

And first, there's no tail any more;   *Why! Why!*
   —And next, he has no head;
And then,—he's just a candy Roar,   *So, you*
And might as well be dead.   *eat Him up.*

—Abbie Farwell Brown,
from Brown's *Pocketful of Posies*, 1902

A writer who can make poetry fun for children is special indeed—but one who can be informative and educational without losing the impishness and whimsy . . . is a *master!* Note her poem "The Spoiled Violin," in this respect:

I know a little family,   *Viol*
   A family of Strings;   *Family.*
Viol is their ancient name,—
   They are the quaintest things!

Their family resemblances   *Good*
   Are very, very strong,   *voices,*

They haven't any hands nor feet,   *too.*
   But oh, their necks are long!

Bass Viol is the big Papa,   *Papa*
Who stands against the wall;   *and*
And Mother 'Cello, soft and sweet,   *Mamma.*
Near by, is 'most as tall.

Next there is sister Viola
(Who used to be a twin),   *Sister and*
But crowding in before them all   *little Brother.*
Is little Violin.

Mamma has often said to me—   *Seen,*
I'm sure of every word—   *not*
That when the grown-up people speak,   *not heard.*
I must be seen, not *heard.*

"Gr-r-r!"   But in the family of Strings
growls   It is not so at all,
Bass Viol.   For Father only mumbles things
              Up there against the wall;

"Tum-te-dum!"   And Mother 'Cello's voice is low,
"Teedle-dee!"   And Viola's is thin,
"P-r-r-r,   But always louder than the rest
squeak-squeak!   Talks little Violin.

Tra-la-la-oh!   He interrupts them when he likes;
Tra-la-la-oh,   They cannot keep him still.
squeak-squeak!   He runs and quavers, laughs and whines;
Pr-r-r-r,   His voice is high and shrill.

zim, zim, zim!"   No matter who was speaking first,
                 No matter what they play,
Rude boy!   The Violin just pitches in
              And always has his say.

I'd spank   If I were Violin's Papa,—
him,   Bass Viol, six feet high,—

203

The Christmas Angel

I would not let my silly son
Think he was big as I.

If I were Mrs. 'Cello, too,
wouldn't   I'd bring him up to be
you?   A nice, well-mannered Violin,
Seen and not heard—like me.

—Abbie Farwell Brown, from
A Pocketful of Posies, 1902

As for her books published during the second decade of the century, her second Christmas book, *Their City Christmas*, was published in 1912. While it is a good book, it lacks the power of *The Christmas Angel*. The story is about a fisherman's family on a Maine island and their relationship to the affluent family that vacations in Maine during the summer, but lives in Boston the rest of the time; now, at Christmas, the city children invite the island twins to Boston for the Christmas holidays. Homely values permeate the story.

The Lucky Stone (1914) is a wondrous book! The plot has to do with a delightful orphan named Maggie who yearns for love, beauty, and the opportunity to escape the ugly world of tenements for the outdoors; a beautiful "princess" who has everything money can buy but is bored and lonely; a teacher-social worker who befriends Maggie and longs for serenity and an unarticulated dream woman. The catalyst is "The Lucky Stone." It is a book to fall in love with!

Kisington Town (1915) is unlike any book I ever met—based on a rather wild premise that there could be a city-state where all the really important people are affiliated with the city library! Well, an evil tyrant, Red Rex, attacks the city, and its destruction appears certain. The only person who can possibly save it is the boy Harold, who just happens to be a master story-teller, of the caliber of Scheherazade of *Arabian Nights*.

Rock of Liberty (1918) is a patriotic cantata based on a poem she wrote titled "Peace With a Sword." She wrote it to generate patriotism and encourage young men and women to volunteer to help beat back the "barbarians" in World War I. A year earlier, the work had been set to music and performed by Boston's Handel and Haydn Society.

Heart of New England (1920) is a remarkable tribute to the tough hardscrabble world of her ancestors, New England. It is her most patriotic book. Brown strongly empathized with the true unsung heroes in New England history: the women who suffered so much but received little credit for it. "Pilgrim Mothers," the fourth poem in the collection, is one of the finest and most moving poems she ever wrote:

> Now thank God for the women
> Who dared the perilous sea
> With our adventurous ancestors,
> To bear them company!
>
> They sailed, they knew not whither,
> They came, nor questioned why,
> But that the man-folk whom they loved
> Without their care would die.
>
> Babies newly born they carried,
> And bairns with wavering feet;
> But never a cow was there for milk,
> And never a stove for heat.
>
> Through icy waves they landed,
> They washed in frozen streams;
> They shivered through the nights of dread
> With horror in their dreams.
>
> Through toil and want and danger
> High-hearted they could wait;
> They lived and died for the commonweal,
> And mothered a nursling State.
>
> They had no voice in meeting.
> No vote in pact of law;
> But of their flesh and blood is built
> Our strength for peace and war.
>
> Thank God for the brave women
> Of a hard three-hundred years!
> Have they not earned a nation's trust
> Through sacrifice and tears?

—Abbie Farwell Brown, from *Heart of New England*, 1920

Under the Rowan Tree (1926) is an anthology of eighteen loosely related stories written at various stages of Brown's career. Unfortunately, the collection lacks cohesiveness and focus.

We are still searching for copies of a number of her books, so they can be evaluated and described. They are: *Notable Trees about Boston* (1900), *The Curious Book of Birds* (1903), *The Star Jewels and Other Wonders* (1905), *Tales of the Red Children* (1909), *The Boy Mozart* (1910), *Songs of Sixpence* (1914), *Surprise House* (1917), *Round Robin* (1921), and *The Lights of Beacon Hill* (1922).

Meanwhile, her stories, poetry, and plays continued to be published by the nation's major magazines, and her name recognition continued to grow.

THE SILVER STAIR

I traveled by the path of Pain
Unto the gate of Day
But Love has besought me back again
So I retraced my way.

To live and love and labor still
And finish it may be
Some special task my Father's will
Has set aside for me.

—Abbie Farwell Brown, "The Traveler Returned,"
archived in the Schlesinger Library of Radcliffe

The Great War was at last over and the boys had come home—except for the thousands buried under white crosses "over there." Prosperity came sweeping back, and America entered a new age, acclaimed as the savior of Europe.

But there in the venerable Brown home on Beacon Hill, life went on pretty much as usual. The pattern of her life now established, its images and colors clear, her days and nights settled into a fairly predictable routine. She exercised vigorously, playing tennis and golf, walked a great deal, bicycled, and danced. She loved to put on (and attend) parties of all kinds, be they advertising parties, valentine parties, ghost parties, dramatic vignettes from life parties, or just-because parties. Picnics with the right company were always a joy. And how she loved to travel, to wander abroad, and then to wander home. In fact, she labeled traveling as the only sure cure for weather-induced blues. "Of course, some more than others are slaves to the whims of the sun, rain and wind. I confess to being that most sensitive of unpractical scientific instruments, the human barometer. As the sun smiles, so do I. When it rains I am like the 'sorry little pig.' With mouth drawn down at the corners and with a hatred of my fellow man in my bosom. On these days life is not popular with me, and my spirits sink way down below freezing point into the bulb of despair." But, even during such dismal days, just the thought of travel was enough to un-wilt her leaves (excerpted from Brown's "A Sure Cure for the Blues," *St. Louis Globe-Democrat,* January 29, 1899).

But lest we be left with too gloomy a picture of her, normally she was the most joyful of human beings. In fact, she submitted that every day ought to be celebrated as an anniversary of something, not just the usual national holidays. In "Anniversaries That Thrill," she raved about "What a kaleidoscopic variety of color is offered by a whole year of days, no two alike, each one famous for some event of time, remote or near." Perhaps it might be an anniversary of a famous battle that changed the course of history. "How near it brings us to history, to the people who lived and fought and died those many years ago, when we think that upon a morning, very like this, mayhap, so many people opened their eyes all unknowing on a day which was to make a milestone in the world's annals—and at night of that same day so many eyes were closed to open no more."

But, almost as thrilling to her, was to open her eyes and greet an anniversary having to do with a favorite author. Then there are the many festivals of the church. Each is a day of days, distinct, replete with tradition, romance, legend, literature and fancy; that each brings to mind its own vivid pictures, its own wealth of suggestion and its own charm for the ensuing hours. . . . "We will scatter fern seed on St. John's Eve, and become invisible, so that we can see the fairies' pranks unobserved. We will go a-Maying, and also note before that on April 19 it is Primrose Day, and we must wear the yellow dainties, playing we are in England. We will eat goose at Michaelmas and hot cross buns on Good Friday, and we will observe the saints' days, each in its due time, for many of the legends are very beautiful, and it is well to know them."

In her case, of course, she has jotted down the birth dates of family or friends—but far more importantly, she has filled her book with anniversaries of writers, musicians, painters, anyone who beautified the earth. When the natal day of a great writer arrives, she greets it with one of his or her quotations. In short, Brown maintains that, with such daily riches at hand, it ought to be impossible to become blasé or disillusioned (excerpted from Brown's "Anniversaries That Thrill," *St. Louis Globe-Democrat,* March 5, 1899).

The Christmas Angel

While she loved the serenity of the countryside, the mountains, rivers, and seas, she was also very much a city woman, reveling in its amenities, its concerts, its plays, its lectures, its art exhibits, its formal dining, its sidewalk cafes, its opportunities to participate in great events.

Not the least of her many contributions had to do with her untiring leadership roles within the New England literary community. Not only was she an active member of the Boston Authors' Club, the Boston Drama League, and the Poetry Society of America, she was also a charter member of the New England Poetry Club—in fact it had been organized at her home in 1915, and she was serving as its President at the time of her death in 1927 (Reiss, 249).

Caroline Ticknor, author, editor, and playwright, member of one of New England's most illustrious publishing families, and one of Brown's closest friends, categorized her a "Poet and Friend; or rather one should say Friend and Poet, so vital was her contribution in the field of sympathy and friendship. Wherever she touched other lives she gave herself so generously and freely, that what she was, almost obscured the many things that she did. Yet her accomplishments were manifold, and she excelled in all that she attempted. Her books of prose and verse, her work upon the platform, her clubs, her college, her church, her country, to each she gave unstintingly its rightful share of her well-balanced life, discharging each responsibility with equal zeal, and doing everything with her whole heart. Yet, while she gave ungrudgingly to many interests, she was above all else a poet, whose exquisite productions placed her in the front ranks of our American poets.

"Especially will her sprightly and sparkling verses for little people remain a never-failing source of joy to the young readers, singing straight from her heart into their own, brimming with fun and frolic, sweet, wholesome, and inspiring, she speaks with the authority of one who knows the fairies and understands the language of the "little brothers" of the animal creation. So truly was she at home in fairyland and elfland that she might well have been herself the Queen of the Fairies, or an imprisoned Dryad. "One cannot read her poem, 'Sylvia' without instant assurance that there she flashed a searchlight upon herself:

> Sylvia is always gay,
> When she winged to earth one day,
> Through the wonders of the sky,
> She caught a star as she flew by,
> Green and gold and amethyst,
> In her tiny baby fist,
> And hid it in her little breast

Introduction

As a secret unconfessed.
Like a jeweled lantern she
Shines for all the world to see,
In her eyes the sparkle beams,
From her burnished hair it gleams;
Radiant all she does and says,
All her pretty, twinkling ways—
Just because she dared to leaven
Lifetime with a bit of heaven,
Sylvia! Without your spark
Oh, the journey would be dark.

—Abbie Farwell Brown, archived in the
Schlesinger Library of Radcliffe (Ticknor, March 23, 1927)

In 1924, her tribute to America's first great composer, *The Boyhood of Edward MacDowell* (who had lived close to the Brown home) was published. She subtitled it "A Boy Who Never Grew Up." Concentrating on his Quaker childhood and youthful study in Europe, rather than adult traumas, still she managed to bring his memorable life story full circle. It is a moving tribute to a great man!

The Silver Stair (1926) was destined to be the last book she saw through to completion. Reading the poems in the collection it is clear she sensed the tides of her life were running back out to that greater sea. There is much here about the ocean, autumn, and old age—and little here for children. It seems obvious that she knew her pixie grace was gone forever, that God was calling her home, for her *joie du vivre* is noticeably in short supply—and all that was left was the putting out to sea with the withdrawing tide, and the darkening west.

The Lantern and Other Plays for Children (1928) was published posthumously. In it are four plays: *The Lantern*, a play set during the American Revolution, with the heroic role carried by the child Barbara. *Rhoecus* is a haunting poem involving Rhoecus, lover of the woods who tries to keep a five-hundred-year-old monarch of the forest from being chopped down; Chloe, the rather insensitive daughter of the determined woodsman; and the tormented Dryad, forced to make a life-changing decision. *The Wishing Moon* has to do with children seeking extraordinary powers on St. John's Eve; and *The Little Shadows* is a dramatized version of Stevenson's shadow poem. It is a splendid collection! The fact that it was republished half a century later testifies to the enduring qualities of these plays.

Very little is said about the role of her father in her life; clearly, he was a man of business, concentrating his considerable energies in the family company which dealt with whale oil and candles. But her mother was the guiding beacon of her life, and enjoyed a long life. Abbie would dedicate *The Silver Stair* collection to her mother, bringing her life and career full circle back to the woman who gave birth to it all.

No doubt the daughter assumed her mother's longevity would be her heritage as well, but alas! It was not to be. It came suddenly, out of a cloudless sky, to this daughter of New England, this lover of life in all its many dimensions.

It seemed she was just entering into the flood-tide of her fame and influence. Carolyn Ticknor noted that, "Those who were present at that triumphal gathering, a few months since, where to a host of friends she read selections from her latest book, *The Silver Stair*, will not forget the warmth of the ovation tendered by that enthusiastic audience composed of personal friends and lovers of her books.

"And to the poet it was a joyful climax to her years of steadily ascending literary achievement. Serene, lovely, and glad almost to tears, the title of her book, *The Silver Stair*, seemed to mark the ascent on which she paused prepared for further flight." (Ticknor, March 23, 1927).

The title of this last book was taken from one of Brown's most powerful poems by that same title, having to do with twin sisters, one born with a longing for the hills and the other one for the sea. Brown had used the image earlier in her wondrous story, "The Mermaid Necklace," twenty years before. ."In that story, written during the morning of her life, the Silver Stair was a resplendent ladder, connecting sea to sky.

Hardly had the glow of her triumph faded when the terrible blow landed: she who had always reveled in the visual, approaching each dawn with the child-like joy of a child, was going *blind!* How could she possibly face a life devoid of light? The answer was not long in coming:

IN THE DARK

> In the dark I lie and think
> Of the glory in a day;
> Of the sunshine and the shade,
> All the color, soft or gay.
>
> I can see it better now
> As I lie with curtained eyes.
> Oh, the rainbow and the moon:
> Oh, the opal of the skies!
>
> How the poppies glow and thrill,
> How the pigeon-feathers shine!
> I will weave them into dreams,

I will make them ever mine.
All the wonder of a wave,
All the magic of a tree,
I shall wear them in my soul
When these eyes no longer see.

—Abbie Farwell Brown, from *Heart of New England*, 1920

The rest of the story was chronicled movingly, and with a broken heart, by her friend: "Out of the threatening dark she emerged hopefully, ready to meet the issue undaunted, ready to follow the gleaming of that inner torch, which should shed life upon her interrupted work.

And then the second summons sounded, to lay aside that work. . . . With equal courage she faced the final edict which called her to the conflict with pain and mortal illness, and bade her lay aside her pen, even when life seemed sweetest, and most full of opportunity. With fortitude and faith she met this final test, hopefully, prayerfully, still trusting the beneficence of the Eternal One, her guiding star.

"And so she climbed the 'Silver Stair' and vanished from our sight, to live forever in our hearts" (Ticknor, March 23, 1927).

The last poem in *The Silver Stair* is one that must have raised eyebrows when it was published—after all, she was only 55. Did she know something, or sense something, her readers didn't know? It almost seems so:

THE BOOK OF ME

I do not know the history that lies
Beyond the present page; I may not peer
Further than where one sets the marker here,
At this day's chapter. Not with childish eyes
Shall I anticipate the next surprise,
Nor flutter through the leaves in hope or fear,
To learn the story's end, however near,
And foil the Author's loving mysteries.

There may be pain, unbearable if guessed
Through waiting hours; but soon forgotten, blent
Into the plot whereby I live and look.
There must be joy—no story so unblessed
As to miss that. I trust and am content;
Until a solemn *Finis* ends the book.

—Abbie Farwell Brown, from *The Silver Stair*, 1926

The Christmas Angel

Typical of letters pouring in to the family after her swift passing is this one from friend and Boston luminary Vida O. Scudder: "We who love radiant Abbie mourn with you; why, the whole city mourns with you, I think. I do not know any one whose loss would be so generally felt; her sweet wholesomeness, her vital charm, her inexhaustible sympathies, endeared her everywhere and illumined every circle in which she moved—I suppose even in paradise it was felt that Abbie was needed so much that she must be called there!" (letter to Ethel Brown, archived in the Schlesinger Library of Radcliffe.)

Joseph Leininger Wheeler, Ph.D.
The Grey House
Conifer, Colorado

THE WORKS OF ABBIE FARWELL BROWN

MAGAZINES

This magazine listing is very incomplete, consequently I am hoping collectors of Abbie Farwell Brown will fill me in with copies of missing entries so we can update our readers in future printings.

1891   "A Topsy-Turvy Piece," *Woman's Home Companion*, September

1892   "A Clover," *Harvard Advocate*, May 18

1893   "Luck" (poem), *New England Magazine*, November

1894   "The Burying of the Hatchet," *New England Magazine*, July
"Valentine: Sweet, Has the Snowdrop Blossomed?" (poem), *New England Magazine*, March.

1895   "Haunted House" (poem), *New England Magazine*, May "A New Evening's Entertainment," *Ladies' Home Journal*, January (illustrated by Charles Gibson)
"For an Evening Party—The Advertising Game," *Ladies' Home Companion*, April 15
"A Dish of Tea," *Peterson's Magazine*, August
"A Ghost Party," *Ladies' Home Companion*, October 1

1896   "Love's Calendar" (poem), *New England Magazine*, March
"Valentine: If Twere Spring" (poem), *New England Magazine*, March
"As Luck Would Have It," *The Housewife*, June
"When Churchyards Yawn," *Boston Post*, September 15

1897   "A Valentine Party," *Woman's Home Companion*, February
"New England Valentine" (poem), *New England Magazine*, February
"The Indian Spring" (poem), *New England Magazine*, June
"Indian Pipes" (poem), *New England Magazine*, August
"His Adopted Friend," *Woman's Home Companion*, September
"In the Fog," *The Housewife*, September
"Rosemary" (poem), *New England Magazine*, November
"A Christmas Gift," *Woman's Home Companion*, December

1898   "His Freshman Romance," *Woman's Home Companion*, January

"Moods" (poem), *New England Magazine*, January
"Burning Old Letters," (Jean Neal, pseudonym), *St. Louis Globe-Democrat*, January 23
"A Defense of the Tea Habit" (Jean Neal, pseudonym), *St. Louis Globe-Democrat*, January 30
"The Old and New Valentine" (Jean Neal, pseudonym), *St. Louis Globe-Democrat*, February 13
"Women's Clubs" (Jean Neal, pseudonym), *St. Louis Globe-Democrat*, February 20
"A Home Run," *Vogue*, March 17
"I Did Not Know" (poem), *New England Magazine*, April
"The Modern Girl and Athletics" (Jean Neal, pseudonym), *St. Louis Globe-Democrat*, April 11
"Pastoral" (poem), *New England Magazine*, May
"A Painted Conscience," *St. Louis Globe-Democrat*, May 1
"A Defense of the Diary" (Jean Neal, pseudonym), *St. Louis Globe-Democrat*, May 22
"The Minions of Fashion" (Jean Neal, pseudonym), *St. Louis Globe-Democrat*, May 29
"The Tour of the Four," *The Ladies' World*, June
"Tryst" (poem), *New England Magazine*, July
"From Sandal to Shoe" (Jean Neal, pseudonym), *St. Louis Globe-Democrat*, July 3
"Women and the War" (Jean Neal, pseudonym), *St. Louis Globe-Democrat*, July 10
"The Summer Man" (Jean Neal, pseudonym), *St. Louis Globe-Democrat*, July 31
"Picnics and Picnics" (Jean Neal, pseudonym), *St. Louis Globe-Democrat*, October 2

1899   "Mind Reader," *New England Magazine*, January
"A Sure Cure for the Blues" (Jean Neal, pseudonym), *St. Louis Globe-Democrat*, January 29
"Sarcophagus" (poem), *New England Magazine*, February
"The Way of Ruth," *New England Magazine*, March
"Anniversaries That Thrill" (Jean Neal, pseudonym), *St. Louis Globe-Democrat*, March 5

"The Man Who Played the Cymbals," *The Interior,* March 9

"May Day" (Jean Neal, pseudonym), *St. Louis Globe-Democrat,* April 30

"The Brotherless Girl" (Jean Neal, pseudonym), *St. Louis Globe-Democrat,* May 7

"The Engagement of One's Gentleman Friends" (Jean Neal, pseudonym), *St. Louis Globe-Democrat,* June 11

"Bachelor Girls in Scotland" (Jean Neal, pseudonym), *St. Louis Globe-Democrat,* July 30

"A Sisterly Office," *The Household,* August

"Bachelor Girls in the Land of Canals and Windmills" (Jean Neal, pseudonym), *St. Louis Globe-Democrat,* September 10

"Bachelor Girls in Kaiser William's Country" (Jean Neal, pseudonym), *St. Louis Globe-Democrat,* October 8

"Bachelor Girls in the Alps" (Jean Neal, pseudonym), *St. Louis Globe-Democrat,* October 22

"Bachelor Girls in Paris" (Jean Neal, pseudonym), *St. Louis Globe-Democrat,* November 5

"Bachelor Girls in London" (Jean Neal, pseudonym), *St. Louis Globe-Democrat,* November 19

"Bachelor Girls in Windsor Castle" (Jean Neal, pseudonym), *St. Louis Globe Democrat,* December 3

1900   "Faring Down the World" (poem), *New England Magazine,* January

"Ballad of the Little Page" (poem), *St. Nicholas,* February

"In a Library" (poem), *St. Nicholas,* March

"Crab Tree," *Munsey,* April

"Not at Home" (poem), *New England Magazine,* April

"Blessed Privilege" (poem), *New England Magazine,* July

"Notable Trees About Boston," *New England Magazine,* July

"The Barn Stormers," *The Ladies' World,* July

"The Seven Sleepers of Ephesus," *The Churchman,* July 28

"The Children's Crusade," *Radcliffe Magazine,* December

1901   "Family Reunion" (poem), *St. Nicholas,* September

"The Little Cassandra Turkey," *The Interior,* November 21

"Christmas Stories of the Saints," *Lippincott,* December

1902   "The Dissolving of a Partnership," *The Ladies' World*, September
        "Neighbors," *Lippincott*, November
        "Salaun, the Witless," *The Churchman*, November 1

1903   "Beauty of Antiquity," *New England Magazine*, May
        "Old Ipswich Town," *New England Magazine*, June

1905   "The Mermaid Necklace," *The Churchman*, February 4, 11
        "City Roofs" (poem), *Harper*, April
        "The Yankee Balloon," *The Churchman*, July 1

1906   "The Faun Boys," *The Churchman*, January 20, 27
        "Wanderlust" (poem), *Harper*, February
        "Memory of Deacon Poole," *New England Magazine*, March
        "The Dark Room," *The Churchman*, March 18
        "The Educated Cat," *Good Housekeeping*, September
        "Pages of J.T.T." (poem), *Poet Lore*, September

1907   "The Neighbor's Baby," *American Baby*, February
        "This Sorry Scheme of Things" (poem), *Harper*, March
        "Fireflies" (poem), *New England Magazine*, August
        "Wonder Garden," *St. Nicholas*, September
        "Thankful Cats," *The Churchman*, November 23

1908   "The Prize-Winner," *The Churchman*, January 11, 18, February 8, 15
        "An Inconsistent Romance," *New England Magazine*, February
        "To the Rescue," *The Congregationalist and the Christian World*,
        November 28
        "The Cheerful Winters, A Christmas Story," *The Congregationalist
        and the Christian World*, December 19

1910   "Mr. Bear's Party," *Kindergarten Review*, October
        "Bubbles" (poem), *Woman's Home Companion*, November

1911   "King's Pie" (poem), *St. Nicholas*, January
        "Tree City" (poem), *St. Nicholas*, May
        "Fisherman" (poem), *Good Housekeeping*, June
        "Windows" (poem), *Outlook*, July

"Writing for Children," *The Writer*, September
"The Book and the Child," *Home Progress*, November
"Island Twins," *Woman's Home Companion*, (series begins in December)

1912   "Island Twins," *Woman's Home Companion*, (series ends in April)
"Transfigured" (poem), *Lippincott*, June
"Rose Perennial" (poem), *Literary Digest*, June
"The Adventures of Jim, and John and Jane," *Denison Manufacturing Company*, no month

1913   "Child's Poetry-books," *Home Progress*, January
"The Dog Who Kept His Eyes Open," *Congregationalist*, February 6
"Heritage" (poem), *Outlook*, March
"Answers to Home Progress Questions Concerning Child Management," *Home Progress*, April
"Bells That Brought Fairy Gold," *Woman's Home Companion*, June
"Well-Wishing" (poem), *Woman's Home Companion*, July
"An Inherited Tradition," *Sunday Magazine*, December 14

1914   "Mystery of Enchanted Oval," *Boston Post*, January 25
"The Lucky Stone," *St. Nicholas*, January, February, March, April, May, June, July
"Button, Button," *The Companion*, February 5
"Magic Shoes," *Delineator*, June
"A Star for Cadie," *Associated Sunday Magazine*, July 12
"Luck-pluck" (poem), *St. Nicholas*, September

1915   "Where the Arrow Pointed," *Sunday School Advocate*, November 13, 20, 27, December 4, 11, 18, 26

1916   "The Goldfish Globe," *The Classmates*, January 15
"Sparrow" (poem), *St. Nicholas*, July
"The Sewing Circle," *The Churchman*, July 22

1917   "Concerning Halves" (poem), *Harper*, June
"Secret" (poem), *St. Nicholas*, June
"Cross-current" (poem), *Bellman*, December 15

1918   "Plume" (poem), *Bookman,* January
       "Maids and Mushrooms" (poem), *Bookman,* May
       "Knights" (poem), *Harper,* September
       "Fairy Ring" (poem), *Bellman,* September 8

1919   "Sylvia" (poem), *Ladies' Home Journal,* January
       "Every Day for a Hero" (poem), *St. Nicholas,* March
       "From the Canteen" (poem), *Delineator,* November
       "Mushrooms or Fairy Cats?" (poem), *Woman's Home Companion,* December

1920   "Pilgrims' Plymouth," *Delineator,* June
       "Names" (poem), *Atlantic,* June
       (same), *Literary Digest,* June 12
       "Pilgrim Mothers" (poem), *Woman's Home Companion,* October
       "Frightened Path" (poem), *Current Opinion,* November
       "Scarecrow" (poem), *Current Opinion,* November
       "Pirate Treasure" (poem), *Literary Digest,* November 6

1921   "Low Tide" (poem), *North American,* August
       "The Tramper" (poem), *Christian Endeavor World,* November 1

1923   "Wild Grape" (poem), *Atlantic,* March
       "Josephine Peabody, the Piper," *Bookman,* May
       "Grandser" (poem), *Literary Digest,* July 21
       "Robin the Thief" (poem), *St. Nicholas,* August

1925   "Dahlia" (poem), *Garden Monthly,* April
       "Amy Lowell" (poem), *Literary Digest,* June 6

1926   "Ancient Humor" (poem), *Bookman,* February
       "The Wonderful Arrow," *Children's Hour,* March
       "Heroines" (poem), *St. Nicholas,* June
       "Weather Vane" (poem), *Woman's Home Companion,* July
       "Road Past the Dressmaker's House" (poem), *Woman's Home Companion,* October

1927   "To a Gloomy Poet" (poem), *Boston Transcript*, March 12, also
        appeared in *Contemporary Verse*, March

STORIES—NO DATE
"Winged Boots," *The Young Churchman*
"The Yellow Day," *The Housewife*, (serial)
"The Square Fairies," *Sunday Magazine* of the *Sunday Post*

BOOKS
1900   *The Book of Saints and Friendly Beasts* (Boston: Houghton Mifflin)
        Notable Trees About Boston (Boston: Houghton Mifflin)

1901   *The Lonesomest Doll* (Boston: Houghton Mifflin)
        (1928: Reprinted with the Arthur Rackham illustrations)

1902   *In the Days of Giants: A Book of Norse Tales* (Boston: Houghton
        Mifflin)
        A Pocketful of Posies (Boston: Houghton Mifflin)

1903   *The Curious Book of Birds* (Boston: Houghton Mifflin)

1904   *The Flower Princess* (Boston: Houghton Mifflin)

1905   *The Star Jewels and Other Wonders* (Boston: Houghton Mifflin)

1906   *Brothers and Sisters* (Boston: Houghton Mifflin)

1907   *Friends and Cousins* (Boston: Houghton Mifflin)

1908   *Fresh Posies* (Boston: Houghton Mifflin)

1909   *John of the Woods* (Boston: Houghton Mifflin)
        Tales of the Red Children (publisher not known; collab. with Jack
        Bell Mackintosh)

1910   *The Christmas Angel* (Boston: Houghton Mifflin)
        The Boy Mozart (Boston: Parker, Baker and Taylor Publishing Co.)

The Christmas Angel

1912   *Their City Christmas* (Boston: Houghton Mifflin)

1914   *The Lucky Stone* (Boston: Houghton Mifflin)
            Songs of Sixpence (Boston: Houghton Mifflin)

1915   *Kisington Town* (Boston: Houghton Mifflin)

1917   *Surprise House* (Boston: Houghton Mifflin)

1918   *Rock of Liberty* ["Peace with a Sword"] (Music by Rossetter G. Cole.
            Boston: Arthur P. Schmidt Co.)
1920   *Heart of New England* (Boston: Houghton Mifflin)

1921   *Round Robin* (E. P. Dutton & Company)
1922   *The Lights of Beacon Hill* (Boston: Houghton Mifflin)

1924   *The Boyhood of Edward MacDowell* (New York: Frederick A. Stokes)

1926   *The Silver Stair* (Boston: Houghton Mifflin)
            Under the Rowan Tree (Boston: Houghton Mifflin)

1928   *The Lantern and Other Plays* (Boston: Houghton Mifflin; reprinted
            by Core Collection Books in 1978)

1960   *The Little Friend* (excerpted from *The Flower Princess;* Boston:
            Houghton Mifflin)

Although many sources were used for this list of works, special thanks and appreciation are due the staff of the Schlesinger Library of Radcliffe College at Harvard University

1

THE PLAY BOX

At the sound of footsteps along the hall Miss Terry looked up from the letter which she was reading for the sixth time. "Of course I would not see him," she said, pursing her lips into a hard line. "Certainly not!"

A bump on the library door, as from an opposing knee, did duty for a knock.

"Bring the box in here, Norah," said Miss Terry, holding open the door for her servant, who was gasping under the weight of a packing-case. "Set it down on the rug by the fireplace. I am going to look it over and burn up the rubbish this evening."

She glanced once more at the letter in her hand, then with a sniff tossed it upon the fire.

"Yes'm," said Norah, as she set down the box with a thump. She stooped once more to pick up something which had fallen out when the cover was jarred open. It was a pink papier-mâché angel, such as are often hung from the top of Christmas trees as a crowning symbol. Norah stood holding it between thumb and finger, staring amazedly. Who would think to find such a bit of frivolity in the house of Miss Terry!

Her mistress looked up from the fire, where the bit of writing was writhing painfully, and caught the expression on Norah's face.

"What have you there?" she asked, frowning, as she took the object into her own hands. "The Christmas Angel!" she exclaimed under her breath. "I had quite forgotten it." Then as if it burned her fingers she thrust the little figure back into the box and turned to Norah brusquely. "There, that's all. You can go now, Norah," she said.

"Yes'm," answered the maid. She hesitated. "If you please'm, it's Christmas Eve."

"Well, I believe so," snapped Miss Terry, who seemed to be in a particularly bad humor this evening. "What do you want?"

Norah flushed; but she was hardened to her mistress's manner. "Only to ask if I may go out for a little while to see the decorations and hear the singing."

"Decorations? Singing? Fiddlesticks!" retorted Miss Terry, poker in hand. "What decorations? What singing?"

"Why, all the windows along the street are full of candles," answered Norah, "rows of candles in every house, to light the Christ Child on his way when he comes through the city tonight."

"Fiddlesticks!" again snarled her mistress.

"And choir-boys are going about the streets, they say, singing carols in front of the lighted houses," continued Norah enthusiastically. "It must sound so pretty!"

"They had much better be at home in bed. I believe people are losing their minds!"

"Please'm, may I go?" asked Norah again.

Norah had no puritanical[1] traditions to her account. Moreover she was young and warm and enthusiastic. Sometimes the spell of Miss Terry's somber house threatened her to the point of desperation. It was so this Christmas Eve; but she made her request with apparent calmness.

"Yes, go along," answered her mistress ungraciously.

"Thank you, 'm," said the servant demurely, but with a brightening of her blue eyes. And presently the area door banged behind her quick-retreating footsteps.

"H'm! Didn't take her long to get ready!" muttered Miss Terry, giving the fire a vicious poke. She was alone in the house, on Christmas Eve, and not a man, woman, or child in the world cared. Well, it was what she wanted. It was of her own doing. If she had wished—

She sat back in her chair, with thin, long hands lying along the arms of it, gazing into the fire. A bit of paper there was crumbling into ashes. Alone on Christmas Eve! Even Norah had some relation with the world outside. Was there not a stalwart officer waiting for her on the nearest corner? Even Norah could feel a simple childish pleasure in candles and carols and merriment, and the old, old superstition.

"Stuff and nonsense!" mused Miss Terry scornfully. "What is our Christmas, anyway? A time for shopkeepers to sell and for foolish folks to kill themselves in buying. Christmas spirit? No! It is all humbug—all self-ishness, and worry; an unwholesome season of unnatural activities. I am glad I am out of it. I am glad no one expects anything of me—nor I of any one. I am quite independent; blessedly independent of the whole foolish business. It is a good time to begin clearing up for the new year. I'm glad I thought of it. I've long threatened to get rid of the stuff that has been accumulating in that corner of the attic. Now I will begin."

She tugged the packing-case an inch nearer the fire. It was like Miss Terry to insist upon that nearer inch. Then she raised the cover. It was a box full of children's battered toys, old-fashioned and quaint; the toys in vogue thirty—forty—fifty years earlier, when Miss Terry was a child. She gave a reminiscent sniff as she threw up the cover and saw on the under side of it a big label of pasteboard unevenly lettered.

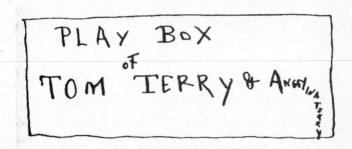

"Humph!" she snorted. There was a great deal in that "humph." It meant: Yes, Tom's name had plenty of room, while poor little Angelina had to squeeze in as well as she could. How like Tom! This accounted for everything, even to his not being in his sister's house this very night. How unreasonable he had been!

Miss Terry shrugged impatiently. Why think of Tom tonight? Years ago he had deliberately cut himself adrift from her interests. No need to think of him now. It was too late to appease her. But here were all these toys to be got rid of. The fire was hungry for them. Why not begin?

Miss Terry stooped to poke over the contents of the box with lean, long fingers. In one corner thrust up a doll's arm; in another, an animal's tail pointed heavenward. She caught glimpses of glitter and tinsel, wheels and fragments of unidentifiable toys.

"What rubbish!" she said. "Yes, I'll burn them all. They are good for nothing else. I suppose some folks would try to give them away, and bore a lot of people to death. They seem to think they are saving something, that way. Nonsense! I know better. It is all foolishness, this craze for giving. Most things are better destroyed as soon as you are done with them. Why, nobody wants such a truck as this. Now, could any child ever have cared for so silly a thing?" She pulled out a faded jumping-jack, and regarded it scornfully. "Idiotic! Such toys are demoralizing for children— weakens their minds. It is a shame to think how every one seems bound to spoil children, especially at Christmastime. Well, no one can say that I have added to the shameful waste."

Miss Terry tossed the poor jumping-jack on the fire, and eyed his last contortions with grim satisfaction.

But as she watched, a quaint idea came to her. She was famous for eccentric ideas.

"I will try an experiment," she said. "I will prove once and for all my point about the 'Christmas spirit.' I will drop some of these old toys out on the sidewalk and see what happens. It may be interesting."

2

JACK-IN-THE-BOX

Miss Terry rose and crossed two rooms to the front window, looking out upon the street. A flare of light almost blinded her eyes. Every window opposite her along the block, as far as she could see, was illuminated with a row of lighted candles across the sash. The soft, unusual glow threw into relief the pretty curtains and wreaths of green, and gave glimpses of cozy interiors and flitting happy figures.

"What a waste of candles!" scolded Miss Terry. "Folks are growing terribly extravagant."

The street was white with snow which had fallen a few hours earlier, piled in drifts along the curb of the little-traveled terrace. But the sidewalks were neatly shoveled and swept clean, as became the eminently respectable part of the city where Miss Terry lived. A long flight of steps, with iron railing at the side, led down from the front door, upon which a silver plate had for generations in decorous flourishes announced the name of Terry.

Miss Terry returned to the play box and drew out between thumb and finger the topmost toy. It happened to be a wooden box, with a wire hasp for fastening the cover. Half unconsciously she pressed the spring, and a hideous Jack-in-the-box sprang out to confront her with a squeak, a leering smile, and a red nose. Miss Terry eyed him with disfavor.

"I always did hate that thing," she said. "Tom was continually frightening me with it, I remember." As if to be rid of unwelcome memories she shut her mouth tight, even as she shut Jack back into his box, snapping the spring into place. *This will do to begin with*, she thought. She crossed to the window, which she opened quickly, and tossed out the box, so that it fell squarely in the middle of the sidewalk. Then closing the window and turning down the lights in the room behind her, Miss Terry hid in the folds of the curtains and watched to see what would happen to Jack.

The street was quiet. Few persons passed on either side. At last she spied two little ragamuffins approaching. They seemed to be Jewish lads of the newsboy class, and they eyed the display of candles appraisingly. The smaller boy first caught sight of the box in the middle of the sidewalk.

"Hello! Wot's dis?" he grunted, making a dash upon it.

"Gee! Wot's up?" responded the other, who was instantly at his elbow.

"Gwan! Lemme look at it."

The smaller boy drew away and pressed the spring of the box eagerly. Ping! Out popped the Jack into his astonished face; whereupon he set up a guffaw.

"Give it here!" commanded the bigger boy.

"Naw! You let it alone! It's mine!" asserted the other, edging away along the curbstone. "I saw it first. You can't have it."

"Give it here. I saw it first myself. Hand it over, or I'll smash you!"

The bigger boy advanced threateningly.

"I won't!" the other whimpered, clasping the box tightly under his jacket.

He started to run, but the bigger fellow was too quick for him. He pounced across the sidewalk, and soon the twain were struggling in the snowdrift, pummeling one another with might and main.

"I told you so!" commented Miss Terry from behind the curtain. "Here's the first show of the beautiful Christmas spirit that is supposed to be abroad. Look at the little beasts fighting over something that neither of them really wants!"

Just then Miss Terry spied a blue-coated figure leisurely approaching.

At the same moment an instinct seemed to warn the struggling urchins.

"Cop!" said a muffled voice from the pile of arms and legs, and in an instant two black shadows were flitting down the street; but not before the bigger boy had wrenched the box from the pocket of the little chap.

"So that is the end of experiment number one," quoth Miss Terry, smiling grimly. "It happened just about as I expected. They will be fighting again as soon as they are out of sight. They are Jews; but that doesn't make any difference about the Christmas spirit. Now let's see what becomes of the next experiment."

3

THE FLANTON DOG

She returned to the play box by the fire, and rummaged for a few minutes among the tangled toys. Then with something like a chuckle she drew out a soft, pale creature with four wobbly legs.

"The Flanton Dog!" she said. "Well, I vow! I had forgotten all about him. It was Tom who coined the name for him because he was made of Canton flannel."

She stood the thing up on the table as well as his weak legs would allow, and inspected him critically. He certainly was a forlorn specimen. One of the black beads which had served him for eyes was gone. His ears, which had originally stood up saucily on his head, now drooped in limp dejection. One of them was a mere shapeless rag hanging by a thread. He was dirty and discolored, and his tail was gone. But still he smiled with his red-thread mouth and seemed trying to make the best of things.

"What a nightmare!" said Miss Terry contemptuously. "I know there isn't a child in the city who wants such a wretched-looking thing. Why, even the animal rescue folks would give the boys a 'free shot' at that. This isn't going to bring out any Christmas spirit," she sneered. "I will try it and see."

Once more she lifted the window and tossed the dog to the sidewalk. He rolled upon his back and lay pathetically with crooked legs yearning upward, still smiling. Hardly had Miss Terry time to conceal herself behind the curtain when she saw a figure approaching, airily waving a stick.

"No ragamuffin this time," she said. "Hello! It is that good-for-nothing young Cooper fellow from the next block. They say he is a millionaire. Well, he isn't even going to see the Flanton Dog."

The young man came swinging along, debonairly; he was whistling under his breath. He was a dapper figure in a long coat and a silk hat, under which the candles lighted a rather silly face. When he reached the spot in the sidewalk where the Flanton Dog lay, he paused a moment looking down. Then he poked the object with his stick. On the other side of the street a mother and her little boy were passing at the time. The child's eyes caught sight of the dog on the sidewalk, and he hung back, watching to see what the young man would do to it. But his mother drew him after her. Just then an automobile came panting through the snow. With a quick movement Cooper picked up the dog on the end of his stick and tossed it into the street, under the wheels of the machine. The child across the street uttered a howl of anguish at the sight. Miss Terry herself was surprised to feel a pang shoot through her as the car passed over the queer old toy. She retreated from the window quickly.

"Well, that's the end of Flanton," she said with half a sigh. "I knew that fellow was a brute. I might have expected something like that. But it looked so...so..." She hesitated for a word, and did not finish her sentence, but bit her lip and sniffed cynically.

4

THE NOAH'S ARK

"Now, what comes next?" Miss Terry rummaged in the box until her fingers met something odd-shaped, long, and smooth-sided. With some difficulty she drew out the object, for it was of good size.

"H'm! The old Noah's ark," she said. "I wonder if all the animals are in there."

She lifted the cover, and turned out into her lap the long-imprisoned animals and their round-bodied chief. Mrs. Noah and her sons had long since disappeared. But the ark-builder, hatless and one-armed, still presided over a menagerie of sorry beasts. Scarcely one could boast of being a quadruped. To few of them the years had spared a tail. From their close resemblance in their misery, it was not hard to believe in the kinship of all animal life. She took them up and examined them curiously one by one. Finally she selected a shapeless slate-colored block from the mass. "This was the elephant," she mused. "I remember when Tom stepped on him and smashed his trunk. 'I guess I'm going to be an expressman when I grow up,' he said, looking sorry. Tom was always full of his jokes. Now I'll try this and see what happens to the ark on its last voyage."

Just then there was a noise outside. An automobile honked past, and Miss Terry shuddered, recalling the pathetic end of the Flanton Dog, which had given her quite a turn.

"I hate those horrid machines!" she exclaimed. "They seem like juggernaut. I'd like to forbid their going through this street."

She crowded the elephant with Noah and the rest of his charge back into the ark and closed the lid. "I can't throw this out of the window," she reflected. "They would spill. I must take it out on the sidewalk. Land! The fire's going out! That girl doesn't know how to build fires so they will keep."

She laid the Noah's ark on the table, and going to the closet tugged out several big logs, which she arranged geometrically. About laying fires, as about most other things, Miss Terry had her own positive theories. Taking the bellows in hand she blew furiously, and was presently rewarded with a brisk blaze. She smiled with satisfaction, and trotted upstairs to find her red knit shawl. With this about her shoulders she was prepared to brave the December cold. Down the steps she went, and deposited the ark discreetly at their foot; then returned to take up her position behind the curtains.

There were a good many people passing, but they seemed too preoccupied to glance down at the sidewalk. They were nearly all hurrying in one direction. Some were running in the middle of the street.

"They are in a great hurry," sniffed Miss Terry disdainfully. "One would think they had something really important to do. I suppose they are going to hear the singing. Fiddlesticks!"

A man hastened by under the window; a woman; two children, a boy and a girl, running and gesticulating eagerly. None of them noticed the Noah's ark lying at the foot of the steps.

Miss Terry began to grow impatient. "Are they all blind?" she fretted. "What is the matter with them? I wish somebody would find the thing. I am tired of seeing it lying there."

She tapped the floor impatiently with her slipper. Just then a woman approached. She was dressed in the most uncompromising of mourning, and she walked slowly, with bent head, never glancing at the lighted windows on either side.

"She will see it," commented Miss Terry. And sure enough, she did. She stopped at the doorway, drew her skirts aside, and bent over to look at the strange-shaped box at her feet. Finally she lifted it. But immediately she shivered and acted so strangely that Miss Terry thought she was about to break the toy in pieces on the steps or throw it into the street. Evidently she detested the sight of it.

Just then up came a second woman with two small boys hanging at her skirts. They were ragged and sick-looking. There was something about the expression of even the tiny knot of hair at the back of the woman's head which told of anxious poverty. With envious curiosity she hurried up to see what a luckier mortal had found, crowding to look over her shoulder. The woman in black drew haughtily away and clutched the Noah's ark with a gesture of proprietorship.

Go away! This is my affair. Miss Terry read her expression and sniffed. "There is the Christmas spirit coming out again," she said to herself. "Look at her face!"

The black-gowned woman prepared to move on with the toy under her arm. But the second woman caught hold of her skirt and began to speak earnestly. She pointed to the Noah's ark, then to her two children. Her eyes were beseeching. The little boys crowded forward eagerly. But some wicked spirit seemed to have seized the finder of the ark. Angrily she shook off the hand of the other woman, and clutching the box yet more firmly under her arm, she hurried away. Once, twice, she turned and shook her head at the ragged woman who followed her. Then, with a savage gesture at the two children, she disappeared beyond Miss Terry's straining eyes. The poor woman and her boys followed forlornly at a distance.

"They really wanted it, that old Noah's ark!" exclaimed Miss Terry in amazement. "I can scarcely believe it. But why did that other creature keep the thing? I see! Only because she found they cared for it. Well, that is a happy spirit for Christmas time, I should say! Humph! I did not expect to find anything quite so mean as that!"

5

MIRANDA

Miss Terry returned to the fireside, fumbled in the box, and drew out a doll. She was an ugly, old-fashioned doll, with bruised waxen face of no particular color. Her mop of flaxen hair was straggling and uneven, much the worse for the attention given by generations of moths. She wore a faded green silk dress in the style of Lincoln's day, and a primitive bonnet, evidently made by childish hands. She was a strange, dead-looking figure, with pale eyelids closed, as Miss Terry dragged her from the box. But when she was set upright the lids snapped open and a pair of bright blue eyes looked straight into those of Miss Terry. It was so sudden that the lady nearly gasped.

"Miranda!" she exclaimed. "It is old Miranda! I have not thought of her for years." She held the doll at arm's length, gazing fixedly at her for some minutes.

"I cannot burn her," she muttered at last. "It would seem almost like murder. I don't like to throw her away, but I have vowed to get rid of these things tonight. And I'll do it, anyway. Yes, I'll make an experiment of her. I wonder what sort of trouble she will cause."

Not even Miss Terry could think of seeing old Miranda lying exposed to the winter night. She found a piece of paper, rolled up the doll in a neat package, and tied it with red string. It was, to look upon, entirely a tempting package. Once more she stole down the steps and hesitated where to leave Miranda: not on the sidewalk—for some reason that seemed impossible. But near the foot of the flight of steps leading to the front door she deposited the doll. The white package shone out plainly in the illuminated street. There was no doubt that it would be readily seen.

With a quite unexplainable interest, Miss Terry watched to see what would happen to Miranda. She waited for some time. The street seemed deserted. Miss Terry caught the faint sound of singing. The choristers were passing through a neighboring street, and doubtless all wayfarers within hearing of their voices were following in their wake.

She was thoroughly interested in her grim joke, but she was becoming impatient. Were there to be no more people passing by? Must the doll stay there unclaimed until morning? Presently she became aware of a child's figure drawing near. It was a little girl of about ten, very shabbily dressed, with tangled yellow curls hanging over her shoulders. There was something familiar about her appearance, but Miss Terry could not say what it was. She came hurrying along the sidewalk with a preoccupied air, and seemed about to pass the steps without seeing the package lying there. But just as she was opposite the window, her eye caught the gleam of the white paper. She paused. She looked at it eagerly; it was such a tempting package, both as to its size and shape! She went closer and bent down to examine it. She took it into her bare little hands and seemed to squeeze it gently. There is no mistaking the contours of a doll, however well it may be enveloped in paper wrappings. The child's eyes grew more and more eager. She glanced behind her furtively; she looked up and down the street. Then with a sudden intuition she looked straight ahead, up the flight of stairs.

Miss Terry read her mind accurately. She was thinking that probably the doll belonged in that house; some one must have dropped the package while going out or in. Would she ring the bell and return it? Miss Terry had not thought of that possibility. But she shook her head and her lip curled. "Return it? Of course not! Ragged children do not usually return promising packages which they have found—even on Christmas Eve. Look now!"

Once more the child glanced stealthily behind her, up and down the street. Once more she looked up at the dark house before her, the only black spot in a wreath of brilliancy. She did not see the face peering at her through the curtains, a face which scanned her own half wistfully. What was to become of Miranda? The little girl thrust the package under her ragged coat and ran away down the street as fast as her legs could take her.

"A thief!" cried Miss Terry. "That is the climax. I have detected a child taking what she knew did not belong to her, on Christmas Eve! Where are all their Sunday School lessons and their social improvement classes? I knew it! This Christmas spirit that one hears so much about is nothing but an empty sham. I have proved it to my satisfaction tonight. I will burn the rest of these toys, every one of them, and then go to bed. It is too disgusting! She was a nice-looking child, too. Poor old Miranda!"

With something like a sigh Miss Terry strode back to the fire, where the play box stood gaping. She had made but a small inroad upon its heaped-up treasures. She threw herself listlessly into the chair and began to plough through the things in her box. Broken games and animals, dolls' dresses painfully tailored by unskilled fingers, disjointed members—sorry relics of past pleasures—one by one Miss Terry seized them between disdainful thumb and finger and tossed them into the fire. Her face showed not a qualm at parting with these childhood treasures; only the stern sense of a good housekeeper's duty fulfilled. With queer contortions the bits writhed on the coals, and finally flared into dissolution, vanishing up chimney in a shower of sparks to the heaven of spent toys.

SHE LOOKED UP AND DOWN THE STREET

6

THE CHRISTMAS ANGEL

Almost at the bottom of the box Miss Terry's fingers closed about a small object. Once more she drew out the papier-mâché angel which had so excited the wonder of Norah when once before that evening it had come to light.

Miss Terry held it up and looked at it with the same expression on her face, half tender, half contemptuous. "The Christmas Angel!" she murmured involuntarily, as she had done before. And again there flashed through her mind a vivid picture.

It was the day before Christmas, fifty years earlier. She and her brother Tom were trimming the Christmas tree in this very library. She saw Tom, in a white piqué suit with short socks that were always slipping down his fat legs. She saw herself in a white dress and blue ribbons, pouting in a corner. They had been quarreling about the Christmas tree, disputing as to which of them should light the first candle[2] when the time arrived. Then their mother came to them smiling, a sweet-faced lady who seemed not to notice the red faces and the tears. She put something into Tom's hand saying, "This is the Christmas Angel of peace and goodwill. Hang it on the tree, children, so that it may shed a blessing on all who come here to give and to receive."

How lovely and pink it looked in Tom's hand! Little Angelina had thought it the most beautiful thing she had ever seen—and holy, too, as if it had some blessed charm. Fiddlesticks! What queer fancies children have!

241

YOU HANG IT ON THE TREE, ANGELINA

Miss Terry remembered how a strange thrill had crept through Angelina as she gazed at it. Then she and Tom looked at each other and were ashamed of their quarrel. Suddenly Tom held out the Angel to his sister. "You hang it on the tree, Angelina," he said magnanimously. "I know you want to."

But she—little fool!—she too had a fit of generosity.

"No, you hang it, Tom. You're taller," she said.

"I'll hang it at the very top of the tree!" he replied, nothing loath. Eagerly he mounted the stepladder, while Angelina watched him enviously, thinking how clumsy he was, and how much better she could do it.

How funny and fat Tom had looked on top of the ladder, reaching as high as he dared! The ladder began to wobble, and he balanced precariously, while Angelina clutched at his fat ankles with a scream of fright. But Tom said:

"Ow! Angelina, let go my ankles! You hurt! Now don't scream. I shan't fall. Don't you know that this is the Christmas Angel, and he will never let me get hurt on Christmas Eve?"

Swaying wildly on one toe Tom had clutched at the air, at the tree itself—anywhere for support. Yet, almost as if by a miracle, he did not fall. And the Christmas Angel was looking down from the very top of the tree.

Miss Terry laid the little pink figure in her lap and mused. "Mother was wise!" she sighed. "She knew how to settle our quarrels in those days. Perhaps if she had still been here things would have gone differently. Tom might not have left me for good. For good." She emphasized the words with a nod as if arguing against something.

Again she took up the Christmas Angel and looked earnestly at it. Could it be that tears were glistening in her eyes? Certainly not! With a sudden sniff and jerk of the shoulders she leaned forward, holding the angel towards the fire. This should follow the other useless toys. But something seemed to stay her hand. She drew back, hesitated, then rose to her feet.

"I can't burn it," she said. "It's no use, I can't burn it. But I don't want to see the thing around. I will put this out on the sidewalk, too. Possibly this may be different and do some good to somebody."

The Christmas Angel

She wrapped the shawl about her shoulders and once more ran down the steps. She left the angel face upward in the middle of the sidewalk, and retreated quickly to the house. As she opened the door to enter, she caught the distant chorus of fresh young voices singing in a neighboring square:

"Angels from the realms of glory,
Wing your flight o'er all the earth."

When she took her place behind the curtain she was trembling a little, she could not guess why. But now she watched with renewed eagerness. What was to be the fate of the Christmas Angel? Would he fall into the right hands and be hung upon some Christmas tree ere morning? Would he. . .

Miss Terry held her breath. A man was staggering along the street toward her. He whistled noisily a vulgar song, as he reeled from curb to railing, threatening to fall at every step. A drunken man on Christmas Eve! Miss Terry felt a great loathing for him. He was at the foot of the steps now. He was close upon the angel. Would he see it, or would he tread upon it in his disgusting blindness?

Yes—no! He saw the little pink image lying on the bricks, and with a lurch forward bent to examine it. Miss Terry flattened her nose against the pane eagerly. She expected to see him fall upon the angel bodily. But no; he righted himself with a whoop of drunken mirth.

"Angel!" she heard him croak with maudlin accent. "Pink angel, begorrah![3] What doin' 'ere, eh? Whoop! Go back to sky, angel!" and lifting a brutal foot he kicked the image into the street. Then with a shriek of laughter he staggered away out of sight.

Miss Terry found herself trembling with indignation. The idea! He had kicked the Christmas Angel—the very angel that Tom had hung on their tree! It was sacrilege, or at least—Fiddlesticks! Miss Terry's mind was growing confused. She had a sudden impulse to rescue the toy from being trampled into filthiness. The fire was better than that.

She hurried down the steps into the street, forgetting her shawl. She sought in the snow and snatched the pink morsel to safety. Straight to the fire she carried it, and once more held it out to the flames. But again she found it impossible to burn the thing. Once, twice, she tried. But each time something seemed to snatch back her wrist. At last she shrugged impatiently and laid the angel on the mantelpiece beside the square, old marble clock, which marked the hour of half-past eight.

"Well, I won't burn it tonight," she reflected. "Somehow, I can't do it just now. I don't see what has got into me! But tomorrow I will. Yes, tomorrow I will."

She sat down in the armchair and fumbled in the old play box for the remaining scraps. There were but a few meaningless bits of ribbon and gauze, with the end of a Christmas candle, the survivor of some past festival, burned on some tree in the past. All these but the last she tossed into the fire, where they made a final protesting blaze. The candle end fell to the floor unnoticed.

"There! That is the last of the stuff," she exclaimed with grim satisfaction, shaking the dust from her black silk skirt. "It is all gone now, thank Heaven, and I can go to bed in peace. No, I forgot Norah. I suppose I must sit up and wait for her. Bother the girl! She ought to be in by now. What can she find to amuse her all this time? Christmas Eve! Fiddlesticks! But I have got rid of a lot of rubbish tonight, and that is worth something."

She sank back in her chair and clasped her hands over her breast with a sigh. She felt strangely weary. Her eyes sought the clock once more, and doing so rested upon the Christmas Angel lying beside it. She frowned and closed her eyes to shut out the sight with its haunting memories and suggestions.

BEFORE THE FIRE

Suddenly there was a volume of sound outside, and a great brightness filled the room. Miss Terry opened her eyes. The fire was burning red; but a yellow light, as from thousands of candles, shone in at the window, and there was the sound of singing—the sweetest singing that Miss Terry had ever heard.

> "An Angel of the Lord came down,
> And glory shone around."

The words seemed chanted by the voices of young angels. Miss Terry passed her hands over her eyes and glanced at the clock. But what the hour was she never noticed, for her gaze was filled with something else. Beside the clock, in the spot where she had laid it a few minutes before, was the Christmas Angel. But now, instead of lying helplessly on its back, it was standing on rosy feet, with arms outstretched toward her. Over its head fluttered gauzy wings. From under the yellow hair which rippled over the shoulders two blue eyes beamed kindly upon her, and the mouth widened into the sweetest smile.

"Peace on earth to men of goodwill!" cried the angel, and the tone of his speech was music, yet quite natural and thrilling.

Miss Terry stared hard at the angel and rubbed her eyes, saying to herself, "Fiddlesticks! I am dreaming!"

But she could not rub away the vision. When she opened her eyes the angel still stood tiptoe on the mantel-shelf, smiling at her and shaking his golden head.

"Angelina!" said the angel softly; and Miss Terry trembled to hear her name thus spoken for the first time in years. "Angelina, you do not want to believe your own eyes, do you? But I am real; more real than the things you see every day. You must believe in me. I am the Christmas Angel."

"I know it." Miss Terry's voice was hoarse and unmanageable, as of one in a nightmare. "I remember."

"You remember!" repeated the Angel. "Yes; you remember the day when you and Tom hung me on the Christmas tree. You were a sweet little girl then, with blue eyes and yellow curls. You believed the Christmas story and loved Santa Claus. Then you were simple and affectionate and generous and happy."

"Fiddlesticks!" Miss Terry tried to say. But the word would not come.

"Now you have lost the old belief and the old love," went on the angel. "Now you have studied books and read wise men's sayings. You understand the higher criticism, and the higher charity, and the higher egoism. You don't believe in mere giving. You don't believe in the Christmas spirit—you know better. But are you happy, dear Angelina?"

Again Miss Terry thrilled to the sound of her name so sweetly spoken; but she answered nothing. The angel replied for her.

"No, you are not happy because you have cut yourself off from the things that bring folk together in peace and goodwill at this holy time. Where are your friends? Where is your brother tonight? You are still hard and unforgiving to Tom. You refused to see him today, though he wrote so boyishly, so humbly and affectionately. You have not tried to make any soul happy. You don't believe in me, the Christmas Spirit."

There is such a word as Fiddlesticks, whatever it may mean. But Miss Terry's mind and tongue were unable to form it.

"The Christmas spirit!" continued the angel. "What is life worth if one cannot believe in the Christmas spirit?"

With a powerful effort Miss Terry shook off her nightmare sufficiently to say, "The Christmas spirit is no real thing. I have proved it tonight. It is not real. It is a humbug!"

"Not real? A humbug?" repeated the angel softly. "And you have proved it, Angelina, this very night?"

Miss Terry nodded.

"I know what you have done," said the angel. "I know very well. How keen you were! How clever! You made a test of chance, to prove your point."

Again Miss Terry nodded with complacency.

"What knowledge of the world! What grasp of human nature!" commented the angel, smiling. "It is like you mere mortals to say, 'I will make my test in my own way. If certain things happen, I shall foresee what the result must be. If certain other things happen, I shall know that I am right.' Events fall out as you expect, and you smile with satisfaction, feeling your wisdom justified. It ought to make you happy. But does it?"

Miss Terry regarded the angel doubtfully.

"Look now!" he went on, holding up a rosy finger. "You are so nearsighted! You are so unimaginative! You do not dream beyond the thing you see. You judge the tale finished while the best has yet to be told. And you stake your faith, your hope, your charity upon this blind human judgment—which is mere chance!"

Miss Terry opened her lips to say, "I saw—" but the angel interrupted her.

"You saw but the beginning," he said. "You saw but the first page of each history. Shall I turn over the leaves and let you read what really happened? Shall I help you to see the whole truth instead of a part? On this night holy truth, which is of Heaven, comes for all men to see and to believe. Look!"

8

JACK AGAIN

The Christmas Angel gently waved his hand to and fro. Gradually, as Miss Terry sat back in her chair, the library grew dark; or rather, things faded into an indistinguishable blur. Then it seemed as if she were sitting at a theatre gazing at a great stage. But at this theatre there was nothing about her, nothing between her and the place where things were happening.

First she saw two little ragamuffins quarreling over something in the snow. She recognized them. They were the two Jewish boys who had picked up the Jack-in-the-box. An officer appeared, and they ran away, the bigger boy having possession of the toy; the smaller one with fists in his eyes, bawling with disappointment.

Miss Terry's lips curled with the cynical disgust which she had felt when first witnessing this scene. But a sweet voice—and she knew it was the angel's—whispered in her ear, "Wait and see!"

She watched the two boys run through the streets until they came to a dark corner. There the little fellow caught up with the other, and once more the struggle began. It was a hard and bloody fight. But this time the victory was with the smaller lad, who used his fists and feet like an enraged animal, until the other howled for mercy and handed over the disputed toy.

"Whatcher want it fer, Sam?" he blubbered as he saw it go into the little fellow's pocket.

"Mind yer own business! I just want it," answered Sam surlily.

"Betcher I know," taunted the bigger boy.

"Betcher yer don't."

"Do!"

"Don't!"

Another fight seemed imminent. But wisdom prevailed with Sammy. He would not challenge fate a third time. "Come on, then, and see," he grunted.

And Ike followed. Off the two trudged, through the brilliantly lighted streets, until they came to a part of the city where the ways were narrower and dark.

"Huh! Knowed you was comin' here," commented Ike as they turned into a grim, dirty alley.

Little Sam growled, "Didn't!" apparently as a matter of habit.

"Did!" reasserted Ike. "Just where I was comin' myself."

Sam turned to him with a grin.

"Was yer now? By—! Ain't that funny? I thought of it right off."

"Sure. Same here!"

They both burst into a guffaw and executed an impromptu double-shuffle of delight. They were at the door of a tenement house with steep stairs leading into darkness. Up three flights pounded the two pairs of heavy boots, till they reached a half-open door, whence issued the clatter of a sewing-machine and the voices of children. Sam stood on the threshold grinning debonairly, with hands thrust into his pockets. Ike peered over his shoulder, also grinning.

It was a meagre room into which they gazed, a room the chief furniture of which seemed to be babies. Two little ones sprawled on the floor. A third tiny tot lay in a broken-down carriage beside the door. A pale, ill-looking woman was running the machine. On the cot bed was crumpled a fragile little fellow of about five, and a small pair of crutches lay across the foot of the bed.

When the two boys appeared in the doorway, the woman stopped her machine and the children set up a howl of pleasure. "Sammy! Ikey" cried the woman, smiling a wan welcome, as the babies crept and toddled toward the newcomers. "Where ye come from?"

"Been to see the shops and the lights in the swell houses," answered Sammy with a grimace. "Gee! Ain't they wastin' candles to beat the band!"

"Enough to last a family a whole year," muttered Ike with disgust.

The woman sighed. "Maybe they ain't wasted exactly," she said. "How I'd like to see 'em! But I got to finish this job. I told the chil'ren they mustn't expect anything this Christmas. But they are too little to know the difference anyway; all but Joe. I wish I had something for Joe."

"I got something for Joe," said Sammy unexpectedly.

The face of the pale little cripple lighted.

"What is it?" he asked eagerly. "Oh, what is it? A real Christmas present for me?"

"Naw! It ain't a Christmas present," said Sam.

"We don't care anything about Christmas," volunteered Ikey with a grin.

Sam looked at him with a frown of rebuke.

"It's just a present," he said. And it didn't cost a cent. I didn't buy it. I—we found it!"

"Found it in the street?" Joe's eyes shone.

"Yah!" the boys nodded.

"Oh, it is a Christmas present!" cried Joe. "Santa Claus must have dropped it there for me, because he knew we hadn't any chimney in this house, and he sent you kind, kind boys to bring it to me."

The two urchins looked sideways at each other, but said nothing. Presently Sam drew out the box from his pocket and tried to thrust it into Ike's hand. "You give it to 'em," he said. "You're the biggest."

"Naw! You give it. You found it," protested Ike.

"Ah, g'wan!"

"Big fool!"

There was a tussle, and it almost seemed as if the past unpleasantness was to be repeated from an opposite cause. But Joe's voice settled the dispute.

"Oh, Sammy, please!" he cried. "I can't wait another minute. Do please give it to me now!"

At these words Sam stepped forward without further argument and laid the box on the bed in front of the little cripple. The babies crowded about. The mother left her machine and stood smiling faintly at the foot of the bed.

Joe pressed the spring. Ping! Out sprang the Jack-in-the-box, with the same red nose, the same leer, the same roguish eyes which had surprised the children of fifty years ago.

Jack was always sure of his audience. My! How they screamed and begged Joe to "do it again." And as for Joe, he lay back on his pillow and laughed and laughed as though he would never stop. It was the first Jack any of them had ever seen.

Tears stood in the mother's eyes. "Well," she said, "it's as good as a play to see him. Joe hasn't laughed like that for months. You boys have done him lots of good. I wouldn't wonder if it helped him get well! If you was Christians I'd say you showed the real Christmas spirit. But—perhaps ye do, all the same! I dunno!"

Sam and Ike were so busy playing with the children that they did not hear.

Gradually the tenement house faded and became a blur before Miss Terry's eyes. Once more she saw the mantelshelf before her and the Christmas Angel with outstretched arms waving to and fro. "You see!" he said. "You did not guess all the pleasure that was shut up in that box with old Jack, did you?"

Miss Terry shook her head.

"And you see how different it all was from what you thought. Now let us see what became of the Canton-flannel dog."

"The Flanton Dog." Miss Terry amended the phrase under her breath. It seemed so natural to use Tom's word.

"Yes, the Flanton Dog," the angel smiled. "What do you think became of him?"

"I saw what became of him," said Miss Terry. "Bob Cooper threw him under an automobile, and he was crushed flatter than a pancake."

"Then you left the window," said the angel. "In your human way you assumed that this was the end. But wait and see."

Once more the room darkened and blurred, and Miss Terry looked out upon past events as upon a busy, ever-shifting stage.

PING! OUT SPRANG THE JACK-IN-THE-BOX

BOB COOPER SAVES THE BABY

9

THE DOG AGAIN

She saw the snowy street, into which, from the tip of his stick, Bob Cooper had just tossed the Flanton Dog. She saw, what she had not seen before, the woman and child on the opposite side of the street. She saw the baby stretch out wistful hands after the dog lying in the snow. Then an automobile honked past, and she felt again the thrill of horror as it ran over the poor old toy. At the same moment the child screamed, and she saw it point tearfully at the Flanton tragedy. The mother, who had seen nothing of all this, stopped and spoke to him reprovingly.

"What's the matter, Johnnie?" she said. "Sh! Don't make such a noise. Here we are at Mrs. Wales's gate, and you mustn't make a fuss. Now be a good boy and wait here till Mother comes out."

She rang the area bell and stood basket in hand, waiting to be admitted. But Johnnie gazed at one spot in the street, with eyes full of tears, and with now and then a sob gurgling from his throat. He could not forget what he had seen.

The door opened for the mother, who disappeared inside the house, with one last command to the child: "Now be a good boy, Johnnie. I'll be back in half a minute."

Hardly was she out of sight when Johnnie started through the snowdrift toward the middle of the street. With difficulty he lifted his little legs out of the deep snow; now and then he stumbled and fell into the soft mass. But he rose only the more determined upon his errand, and kept his eyes fixed on the wreck of the Flanton Dog.

Bob Cooper, who was idly strolling up and down the block, smoking a cigarette, as he watched the flitting girlish shadows in a certain window opposite, saw the child's frantic struggles in the snow and was intensely amused. "Bah Jove!" he chuckled. "I believe he's after the wretched dawg that I tossed over there with my stick. Fahncy it!" And carelessly he puffed a whiff of smoke.

At last the baby boy reached the middle of the street and stooped to pick up the battered toy. It was flattened and shapeless, but the child clasped it tenderly and began to coo softly to it.

"Bah Jove!" repeated Cooper. "Fahncy caring so much about anything! Poor kid! Perhaps that is all the Christmas he will have." He blew a thoughtful puff through his nose. "Christmas Eve!" The thought flashed through his mind with a new appeal.

Just then came a sudden "Honk, honk!" An automobile had turned the corner and was coming up at full speed. It was the same machine which had passed a few minutes earlier in the opposite direction.

"Hi there!" Cooper yelled to the child. But the latter was sitting in the snow in the middle of the street, rocking back and forth, with the Flanton Dog in his arms. There was scarcely time for action. Bob dropped his cigarette and his cane, made one leap into the street and another to the child, and by the impact of his body threw the baby into the drift at the curb. With a horrified honk the automobile passed over the young man, who lay senseless in the snow.

He was not killed. Miss Terry saw him taken to his home close by, where his broken leg was set and his bruises attended to. She saw him lying bandaged and white on his bed when the woman and her child were brought to see him. Johnnie was still clasping closely the unlucky Flanton Dog.

"Well, Kid," said the young man feebly, "so you saved the dog, after all."

"Oh sir!" cried the poor woman, weeping. "Only to think that he would not be here now but for you. What a Christmas that would have been for me! You were so good, so brave!"

"Oh, rot!" protested Bob faintly. "Had to do it; my fault anyway; Christmas Eve—couldn't see a kid hurt on Christmas Eve."

He called the attendant and asked for the pocketbook which had been in his coat at the time of the accident. Putting it into the woman's hand, he said, "Good-by. Get Johnnie something really jolly for Christmas. I'm afraid the dog is about all in. Get him a new one."

But Johnnie refused to have a new dog. It was the poor, shapeless Flanton animal which remained the darling of his heart for many a year.

All this of past and future Miss Terry knew through the angel's power. When once more the library lightened, and she saw the pink figure smiling at her from the mantel, she spoke of her own accord.

"It was my fault, because I put the dog in the way. I caused all that trouble."

"Trouble?" said the angel, puzzled. "Do you call it trouble? Do you not see what it has done for that heartless youth? It brought his good moment. Perhaps he will be a different man after this. And as for the child; he was made happy by something that would otherwise have been wasted, and he has gained a friend who will not forget him. Trouble! And do you think you did it?" He laughed knowingly.

"I certainly did," said Miss Terry firmly.

"But it was I, yes I, the Christmas Spirit, who put it into your head to do what you did. You may not believe it, but so it was. You too, even you, Angelina, could not quite escape the influence of the Christmas Spirit, and so these things have happened. But now let us see what became of the third experiment."

10

NOAH AGAIN

In the street of candles, a woman dressed all in black had picked up the poor old Noah's ark and was looking at it wildly. She was a widow who had just lost her only child, a little son, and she was in a state of morbid bitterness bordering on distraction.

When the second woman with the two little ones came up and begged for the toy, something hard and sullen and cruel rose in the widow's heart, and she refused angrily to give up the thing. She hated those two boys who had been spared when her own was taken. She would not make them happy.

"No, you shall not have it" she cried, clutching the Noah's ark fiercely. "I will destroy it."

The poor woman and the children followed her wistfully. The little boys were crying. They were cold and hungry and disappointed. They had come so near to something pleasant. They had almost been lucky; but the luck had passed over their heads to another.

The woman in mourning strode on rapidly, the thoughts within her no less black than the garments which she wore. She hated the world; she hated the people who lived in it. She hated Christmastime, when every one seemed merry except herself. And yes, yes! Most of all she hated children. She clenched her teeth wickedly; her mind reeled.

Suddenly, somewhere, a chorus of happy voices began to sing the words of an old carol:

The Christmas Angel

"Holy night! Peaceful night!
All is dark save the light,
Yonder where they sweet vigil keep,
O'er the Babe who in silent sleep
Rests in heavenly peace."

Softly and sweetly the childish voices ascended from the street. The woman in black stopped short, breathing hard. She saw the band of choristers standing in a group on the sidewalk and in the snow, their hats pulled down over their eyes, their collars turned up around their ears, their hands deep in pockets. In their midst rose the tall wooden cross carried by a little fellow with yellow hair. They sang as simply and as heartily as a flock of birds out in the snow.

The woman gave a great sob. Her little lad had been a choir boy—perhaps these were his one-time comrades. The second verse of the carol rang out sweetly:

"Holy night! Peaceful night!
Only for shepherds' sight
Came blest visions of angel throngs,
With their loud Hallelujah songs,
Saying, Jesus is come!"

Suddenly it seemed to the distracted mother that her own boy's voice blended with those others. He, too, was singing in honor of that Child. Happy and ever young, he was bidding her rejoice in the day which made all childhood sacred. And for his sake she had been hating children!

With a sudden revulsion of feeling she turned to see what had become of the poor mother and her boys. They were not far behind, huddling in the shadow. The black-cloaked woman strode quickly up to them. They shrank pitifully at her approach, and she felt the shame of it. They were afraid of her!

"Here," she said, thrusting the Noah's ark into the hands of the larger boy. "Take it. It belongs to you."

The child took it timidly. The mother began to protest thanks. Trying to control the shake in her voice, the dark lady spoke again. "Have you prepared a Christmas for your children?"

The woman shook her head. "I have nothing," she sighed. "A roof over our heads, that's all."

"Your husband?"

"He died a month ago."

So other folk had raw sorrows, too. The mourner had forgotten that.

"There is no one expecting you at home?" Again the woman shook her head dolefully. "Come with me," said the dark lady impulsively. "You shall be my guests tonight. And tomorrow I will make a Christmas for the children. The house shall put off its shadow. I, too, will light candles. I have toys,"— her voice broke—"and clothing; many things, which are being wasted. That is not right! Something led you to me, or me to you; something—perhaps it was an angel—whoever dropped that Noah's ark in the street. An angel might do that, I believe. Come with me."

The woman and her sons followed her, rejoicing greatly in the midst of their wonder.

There were tears in the eyes through which Miss Terry saw once more the Christmas Angel. She wiped them hastily. But still the angel seemed to shine with a fairer radiance.

"You see!" was all he said. And Miss Terry bowed her head. She began to understand.

11

MIRANDA AGAIN

Once more, on the wings of vision, Miss Terry was out in the snowy street. She was following the fleet steps of a little girl who carried a white-paper package under her arm. Miss Terry knew that she was learning the fate of her old doll, Miranda, whom her own hands had thrust out into a cold world.

Poor Miranda! After all these years to become the property of a thief! Mary was the little thief's name. Hugging the tempting package close, Mary ran and ran until she was out of breath. Her one thought was to get as far as possible from the place where the bundle had lain. For she suspected that the steps where she had found it led up to the doll's home. That was why in her own eyes also she was a little thief. But now she had run so far and had turned so many corners that she could not find her way back if she would. There was triumph in the thought. Mary chuckled to herself as she stopped running and began to walk leisurely in the neighborhood with which she was more familiar.

She pinched the package gently. Yes, there could be no doubt about it. It was a doll—not a very large doll; but Mary reflected that she had never thought she would care for a large doll. Undoubtedly it was a very nice one. Had she not found it in a wealthy part of the city, on the steps of a mansion? Mary gloated over the doll as she fancied it; with real hair, and eyes that opened and shut; with four little white teeth, and hands with dimples in the knuckles. She had seen such dolls in the windows of the big shops. But she had never hoped to have one for her very own.

"Maybe it will have on a blue silk dress and white kid shoes, like that one I saw this morning!" she mused rapturously.

She pinched the spot where she fancied the doll's feet ought to be.

"Yes, she's got shoes, sure enough! I bet they're white, too. They feel white. Oh, what fun I shall have with her,"—she hugged the doll fondly—"if Uncle and Aunt don't take her away!"

The sudden thought made her stand still in horror. "They sold Mother's little clock for rum," she said bitterly. "They sold the ring with the red stone that Father gave me on my birthday when I was seven. They sold the presents that I got at Sunday School last year. Oh, wouldn't it be dreadful it they should sell my new doll! And I know they will want to if they see her." She squeezed the bundle closer with the prescient pang of parting.

"Maybe they'll be out somewhere." With this faint hope she reached the tenement and crept up the dingy stairs. She peeped in at the door. Alas! Her uncle and aunt were in the kitchen, through which she had to pass. They had company; some dirty-looking men and women, and there were a jug and glasses on the table before them. Mary's heart sank, but she nodded bravely to the company and tried to slip through the crowd to the other room. But her aunt was quick to see that she carried something under her coat.

"What you got there? A Christmas present?" she sneered.

Mary flushed. "No," she said slowly, "just something I found."

"Found? Hello, what is it? A package!"

Her uncle advanced and snatched it from her.

"Please," pleaded Mary, "please, I found it. It is mine. I think it is only a doll."

"A doll! Huh! Who needs a doll?" hiccupped her uncle. "We want something more to drink. We'll sell it—"

A bellow of laughter resounded through the room. The paper being torn roughly away, poor Miranda stood revealed in all her faded beauty.

The pallid waxen face, straggling hair, and old-fashioned dress presented a sorry sight to the greedy eyes which had expected to find something exchangeable for drink. A sorry sight she was to Mary, who had hoped for something so much lovelier. A flush of disappointment came into her cheek, and tears to her eyes.

"Here, take your old doll," said her uncle roughly, thrusting it into her arms. "Take your old doll and get away with her. If that's the best you can find you'd better steal something next time."

Steal something! Had she not in fact stolen it? Mary knew very well that she had, and she flushed pinker yet to think what a fool she had made of herself for nothing. She took the despised doll and retreated into the other room, followed by a chorus of jeers and comments. She banged the door behind her and sat down with poor Miranda on her knees, crying as if her heart would break. She had so longed for a beautiful doll! It did seem too cruel that when she found one it should turn out to be so ugly. She seized poor Miranda and shook her fiercely.

"You horrid old thing!" she said. "Ain't you ashamed to fool me so? Ain't you ashamed to make me think you was a lovely doll with pretty clo'es and white kid shoes? Ain't you?"

She shook Miranda again until her eyeballs rattled in her head. The doll fell to the floor and lay there with closed eyes. Her face was pallid and ghastly. Her bonnet had fallen off, and her hair stuck out wildly in every direction. Her legs were doubled under her in the most helpless fashion. She was the forlornest figure of a doll imaginable. Presently Mary drew her hands away from her eyes and looked down at Miranda. There was something in the doll's attitude as she lay there which touched the little girl's heart. Once she had seen a woman who had been injured in the street—she would never forget it. The poor creature's eyes had been closed, and her face, under the fallen bonnet, was of this same pasty color. Mary shuddered. Suddenly she felt a warm rush of pity for the doll.

"You poor old thing!" she exclaimed, looking at Miranda almost tenderly. "I'm sorry I shook you. You look so tired and sad and homesick! I wonder if somebody is worrying about you this minute. It was very wicked of me to take you away—on Christmas Eve, too! I wish I had left you where I found you. Maybe some little girl is crying now because you are lost."

Mary stooped and lifted the doll gently upon her knees. As she took Miranda up, the blue eyes opened and seemed to look full at her. Miranda's one beauty was her eyes. Mary felt her heart grow warmer and warmer toward the quaint stranger.

"You have lovely eyes," she murmured. "I think after all you are almost pretty. Perhaps I should grow to like you awfully. You are not a bit like the doll I hoped to have; but that is not your fault." A thought made her face brighten. Why, if you had been a beautiful doll they would have taken you away and sold you for rum. Her face expressed utter disgust. She hugged Miranda close with a sudden outburst of affection. "Oh, you dear old thing!" she cried. "I am so glad you are—just like this. I am so glad, for now I can keep you always and always, and no one will want to take you away from me."

She rocked to and fro, holding the doll tightly to her heart. Mary was not one to feel a half passion about anything. "I will make you some new dresses," she said, fingering the old-fashioned silk with a puzzled air. "I wonder why your mother dressed you so queerly? She was not much of a sewer if she made this bonnet!" Scornfully she took off the primitive bonnet and smoothed out the tangled hair. "I wonder what you have on underneath," she said.

With gentle fingers she began to undress Miranda. Off came the green silk dress with its tight "basque" and overskirt. Off came the ruffled petticoat and little chemise edged with fine lace. And Miranda stood in shapeless, kid-bodied ugliness, which stage of evolution the doll of her day had reached.

But there was something more. Around her neck she wore a ribbon; on the ribbon was a cardboard medal; and on the medal a childish hand had scratched these words:

Miranda Terry.
If lost, please return her to her mother,
Angelina Terry,
87 Overlook Terrace.

It was such a card as Miss Terry herself had worn in the days when her mother had first let her and Tom go out on the street without a nurse.

Mary stared hard at the bit of cardboard. Eighty-seven Overlook Terrace! Yes, that was where she had found the doll. She remembered now seeing the name on a street corner. Miranda; what a pretty name for a doll! Angelina Terry; so that was the name of the little girl who had lost Miranda. Angelina must be feeling very sorry now. Perhaps she was crying herself to sleep, for it was growing late.

Her two girl cousins came romping into the bedroom. They had been having a hilarious evening.

"Hello, Mary!" they cried. "We heard about your great find!"

"Playing with your old doll, are you? Goin' to hang up her stockin' and see if Santa Claus will fill it?"

"Huh! Santa Claus won't come to this house, I guess!"

Mary had almost forgotten that it was Christmas Eve. There had been nothing in the house to remind her. Perhaps Angelina Terry had hung up a stocking for Miranda at 87 Overlook Terrace. But there would be no Miranda to see it the next morning.

Her cousins teased her for some time, while they undressed, and Mary grew sulky. She sat in her corner and said very little. But eventually the room grew quiet, for the girls slept easily. Then Mary crept into her little cot with the doll in her arms. She loved Miranda so much that she would never part with her, no indeed; not even though she now knew where Miranda belonged. Eighty-seven Overlook Terrace! The figures danced before her eyes maliciously. She wished she could forget them. And the thought of Angelina Terry kept coming to her. Poor Angelina!

She ain't "poor Angelina'" argued Mary to herself. She's rich Angelina.

Doesn't she live in a big house in the swell part of the city? I s'pose she has hundreds of dolls, much handsomer than Miranda, and lots of other toys. I guess she won't miss this one queer old doll. I guess she'd let me keep it if she knew I hadn't any of my own. I guess it ought to be my doll. Anyway, I'm going to keep her. I don't believe Angelina loves Miranda so much as I do.

She laid her cheek against the doll's cold waxen one and presently fell asleep.

But she slept uneasily. In the middle of the night she awoke and lay for hours tossing and unhappy in the stuffy little room. The clock struck one, two, three. At last she gave a great sigh, and cuddling Miranda in her arms turned over, with peace in her heart.

"I will play you are mine, my very own dollie, for just this one night," she whispered in Miranda's ear. "Tomorrow will be Christmas Day, and I will take you back to your little mother, Angelina Terry. I can't do a mean thing at Christmas time—not even for you, dear Miranda."

Thereupon she fell into a peaceful sleep.

12

THE ANGEL AGAIN

"Will she bring it back?" asked Miss Terry eagerly, when once more she found herself under the gaze of the Christmas Angel. He nodded brightly.

"Tomorrow morning you will see," he said. "It will prove that all I have shown you is really true."

"A pretty child," said Miss Terry musingly. "A very nice child indeed. I believe she looks very much as I used to be myself."

"You see, she is not a thief after all; not yet," said the angel. "What a pity that she must live in that sad home, with such terrible people! A sensitive child like her, craving sympathy and affection—what chance has she for happiness? What would you yourself have been in surroundings like hers?"

"Yes, she is very like what I was. Of course I shall let her keep the doll."

Miss Terry hesitated. The angel looked at her steadily and his glance seemed to read her half-formed thoughts.

"Surely," he said. "It seems to belong to her, does it not? But is this all? I wonder if something more does not belong to her."

"What more?" asked Miss Terry shortly.

"A home!" cried the angel.

Miss Terry groped in her memory for a scornful retort which she had once been fond of using, but there was no such word to be found. Instead there came to her lips the name, "Mary."

The angel repeated it softly, "Mary. It is a blessed name," he said. "Blessed is the roof that shelters a Mary in her need."

There was a long silence, in which Miss Terry felt new impulses stirring within her; impulses drawing her to the child whose looks recalled her own childhood. The angel regarded her with beaming eyes. After some time he said quietly, "Now let us see what became of your last experiment."

Miss Terry started. It seemed as if she had been interrupted in pleasant dreaming. "You were the last experiment," she said. "I knew what became of you. Here you are!"

"Yet many more have happened than you guessed," replied the angel meaningfully. "I have tried to show you how often that is the case. Look again."

Without moving from her chair Miss Terry seemed to be looking out on her sidewalk, where, so it seemed, she had just laid the pink figure of the angel. She saw the drunken man approach. She heard his coarse laugh; saw his brutal movement as he kicked the Christmas symbol into the street. In sick disgust she saw him reel away out of sight. She saw herself run down the steps, rescue the angel, and bring it into the house. Surely the story was finished. What more could there be?

But something bade her vision follow the steps of the wretched man. Down the street he reeled, singing a blasphemous song. With a whoop he rounded a corner and ran into a happy party which filled sidewalk and street, as it hurried in the direction from which he came. Good-naturedly they jostled him against the wall, and he grasped a railing to steady himself as they swept by. It was the choir on their way to carol in the next street. Before them went the cross-bearer, lifting high his simple wooden emblem.

The eyes of the drunken man caught sight of this, and wavered. The presence of the crowd conveyed no meaning to his dazed brains. But there was something in the familiar symbol which held his vision. He looked, and crossed himself, remembering the traditions of his childhood. Some of the boys were humming as they went the stirring strains of an ancient Christmas march known to all nations; a carol which began, some say, as a rousing drinking chorus.

The familiar strain touched some chord in the sodden brain. The man gave a feeble whinny, trying to follow the melody. He pulled himself together and lurched forward in a sudden impulse to join the band of pilgrims. But by the time he had taken three steps they had vanished, miraculously, as it seemed to him.

"Begorra, they're gone!" he cried. "Who were they? Were they rale folks? What was it they was singin'?"

He sank back helplessly on a flight of steps. "Ve-ni-te a-do-re-mus!" he croaked in a quavering basso. And his tangled mind went through strange processes. Suddenly, there came to him in a flash of exaggerated memory the figure of the Christmas Angel which not ten minutes earlier he had kicked into the street. A pious horror fell upon him.

"Mither o' mercy!" he cried, again crossing himself. "What have I been an' done? It was a howly image; an' what did I do to ut? Lemme go back an' find ut, an' take ut up out av the street."

Greatly sobered by his fear, he staggered down the block and around the corner to the steps of Miss Terry's house.

"This is the place," he mused. "I know ut; here's where the frindly lam'post hild me in its arrums. I rimimber there was a dark house forninst me. Here's where ut lay on the sidewalk, all pink an' pretty. An' I kicked ut into the street! Where is ut now? Where gone? Howly Mither! Here's the spot where ut fell, look now! The shape of uts little body and the wings of ut in the snow. But 'tis gone intirely!" He rubbed his eyes and crossed himself again. "'Tis flown away," he muttered. "'Tis gone back to Hiven to tell Mary Mither o' the wicked thing I done this night. Oh, 'tis a miracle that's happened! An' oh! The wicked man I am, drunk and disorderly on the howly eve!"

> "O come, all ye faithful,
> Joyful and triumphant!"

Once more he heard the familiar strain taken up lustily by many voices.

"Hear all the world singin' on the way to Bethlehem!" he said, and the stupor seemed to leave his brain. He no longer staggered.

HE GRASPED A RAILING TO STEADY HIMSELF

"I'll run an' join 'em, an' I won't drink another drop this night." He looked up at the starry sky. "Maybe the angel hears me. Maybe he'll help me to keep straight tomorrow. It might be my Guardian Angel himsilf that I treated so! Saints forgive me!"

With head bowed humbly, but no longer reeling, he moved away towards the sound of music.

"You were his Guardian Angel," said Miss Terry, when once more she saw the figure on the mantel-shelf. And she spoke with reverent gentleness.

The angel smiled brightly. "The Christmas Spirit is a guardian angel to many," he said. "Never again despise me, Angelina. Never again make light of my influence."

"Never again," murmured Miss Terry half unconsciously. "I wish it were not too late—"

"It is never too late," said the Christmas Angel eagerly, as if he read her unspoken thought. "Oh, never too late, Angelina."

13

THE CHRISTMAS CANDLE

Suddenly there was a sound—a dull reverberating sound. It seemed to Miss Terry to come from neither north, south, east, nor west, but from a different world. Ah! She recognized it now. It was somebody knocking on the library door.

Miss Terry gave a long sigh and drew herself up in her chair. "It must be Norah just come back," she said to herself. "I had forgotten Norah completely. It must be shockingly late. Come in," she called, as she glanced at the clock.

She rubbed her eyes and looked again. A few minutes after nine! She had thought it must be midnight!

Norah entered to find her mistress staring at the mantel where the clock stood. She saw lying beside the clock the pink Angel which had fallen from the box as she brought it in—the box now empty by the fire.

"Law, Miss," she said, "have you burned them all up but him? I'm glad you saved him, he's so pretty."

"Norah," said Miss Terry with an effort, "is that clock right?"

"Yes'm," said Norah. "I set it this morning. I came back as soon as I could, Miss," she added apologetically.

"It isn't that," answered Miss Terry, drawing her hand across her forehead dazedly. "I did not mind your absence. But I thought it must be later."

"Oh, no, I wouldn't stay out any later when you was alone here, Miss," said Norah penitently. "I felt ashamed after I had gone. I ought not to have left you so—on Christmas Eve. But oh, Miss! The singing was so beautiful, and the houses looked so grand with the candles in the windows. It is like a holy night indeed!"

Miss Terry stooped and picked up something from the floor. It was the bit of candle-end which had escaped the holocaust.

"Are the candles still lighted, Norah?" she asked, eyeing the bit of wax in her hand.

"Yes'm, some of them," answered the maid. "It is getting late, and a good many have burned out. But some houses are still as bright as ever."

"Perhaps it is not too late, then," murmured Miss Terry, as if yielding a disputed point. "Let us hurry, Norah."

She rose, and going to the mantelshelf gently took up the figure of the Angel, while Norah looked on in amazement.

"Norah," said Miss Terry, with an eagerness which made her voice tremble, "I want you to hang the Christmas Angel in the window there. I, too, have a fancy to burn a candle tonight. If it is not too late I'd like to have a little share in the Christmas spirit."

Norah's eyes lighted. "Oh, yes'm," she said. "I'll hang it right away. And I'll find an empty spool to hold the candle."

She bustled briskly about, and presently in the window appeared a little device unlike any other in the block. Against the darkness within, the figure of the Angel with arms outstretched towards the street shone in a soft light from the flame of a single tiny candle such as blossom on Christmas trees.

It caught the attention of many home-goers, who said, smiling, "How simple! How pretty! How quaint! It is a type of the Christmas spirit which is abroad tonight. You can feel it everywhere, blessing the city."

For some minutes before the candle was lighted, a man muffled in a heavy overcoat had been standing in a doorway opposite Miss Terry's house. He was tall and grizzled and his face was sad. He stared up at the gloomy windows, the only oblongs of blackness in the illuminated block, and he shivered, shrugging his shoulders.

"The same as ever!" he said to himself. "I might have known she would never change. Anyone else, on Christmas Eve, after the letter I wrote her, would have softened a little. But I might have known. She is hard as nails! Of course, it was my fault in the first place to leave her as I did. But when I acknowledged it, and when I wrote that letter on Christmas Eve, I thought Angelina might feel differently." He looked at his watch. "Nearly half-past nine," he muttered. "I may as well go home. She said she wanted to be let alone; that Christmas meant nothing to her. I don't dare to call—on my only sister! I suppose she is there all alone, and here I am all alone, too. What a pity! If I saw the least sign—"

Just then there was the spark of a match against the darkness framed in by the window opposite. A hand and arm shone in the flicker of light across the upper sash. A tiny spark, tremulous at first, like a bird alighting on a frail branch, paused, steadied, and became fixed. In the light of a small taper the man caught a glimpse of a pale, long face in a frame of silver hair. It faded into the background. But above the candle he now saw, with arms outstretched it seemed toward himself, a pink little angel with gauzy wings.

The man's heart gave a leap. Sudden memories thronged his brain, making him almost dizzy. At last they formulated into one smothered cry. "The Christmas Angel! It is the very same pink angel that Angelina and I used to hang on our Christmas tree!"

In three great leaps, like a schoolboy, he crossed the street and ran up the steps of Number 87. The Christmas Angel seemed to smile with ineffable sweetness as he gave the bell a vigorous pull.

14

TOM

Miss Terry was leaning on the mantel-shelf looking into the fire, when the bell pealed furiously. She started and turned pale.

"Lord 'a mercy!" responded Norah, who was still admiring the effect of the window-decoration. "What's that? Who can be calling here tonight, making such a noise?"

"Go to the door, Norah," said Miss Terry with a strange note in her voice. "It may be some one to see me. It is not too late."

"Yes'm," said Norah, obedient but bewildered.

Presently the library door opened and a figure strode in; a tall, broad-shouldered man in a fur overcoat. For a moment he stood just inside the door, hesitating. Miss Terry took two steps forward from the fire-place.

"Tom!" she said faintly. "You came—after all!"

"After all, Angelina," he said. "Yes, because I saw that," he waved his hand toward the window. "That gave me courage to come in. It is our Christmas Angel. I remember all about it. Does it mean anything, Angelina?"

Miss Terry held out a moment longer. Then she faltered forward. "O Tom!" she sobbed, as she felt his brotherly, strong arms about her. "O Tom! And so he has brought you back to me, and me to you!"

"He? Angelina girl, who?" He smoothed her silver hair with rough, kind fingers.

"Why, the Christmas Angel; our Guardian Angel, Tom. All these years I kept him in the play box, and I was going to burn him up. But I couldn't

281

do it, Tom. How wonderful it is!"

They sat down before the fire and she began to tell him the whole story. But she interrupted herself to send for Norah, who came to her, mystified and half scandalized by the greeting which she had seen those two oldsters exchange.

"This is my brother Tom, Norah, who has come back," she said. "I believe it is not too late to make some preparation for Christmas Day. The stores will still be open. Run out and order things for a grand occasion, Norah. And—O Norah!" a sudden remembrance came to her. "If you have time, will you please get some toys and pretty things such as a little girl would like; a little girl of about ten, with my complexion—I mean, with yellow hair and blue eyes. We may have a little guest tomorrow."

"Yes'm," said Norah, moving like one in a dream.

"A guest?" exclaimed Tom. And Miss Terry told him about Mary.

"I love little girls," said Tom, "especially little girls with yellow hair and blue eyes, such as you used to have, Angelina."

"You will like Mary, then," said Miss Terry, with a pretty pink flush of pleasure in her cheeks.

"I shall like her, if she comes," amended Tom, who, man-like, received with reservations the account of a vision vouchsafed not unto him.

"She will come," said Miss Terry with her old positiveness, glancing towards the window where the Christmas Angel hung.

Then arose the sound of singing outside the house. The passing choristers had spied the quaint window, now the only one in the street which remained lighted:

"When Christ was born of Mary free,
In Bethlehem, in that fair citye,
Angels sang with mirth and glee,
In Excelsis Gloria!"

15

CHRISTMAS DAY

And Mary came. The brother and sister were at breakfast—the happiest which either of them had known for years—when there came a timid pull at the front-door bell. Miss Angelina laid down her knife and fork and looked across the table at Tom.

"She has come. Mary has come," she said. "Norah, if it is a little girl with a package under her arm, bring her in here."

"Yes'm!" gasped Norah, who believed she was living in a dream where everything was topsy-turvy. When had a child last entered Miss Terry's dining-room!

Norah disappeared and presently returned ushering in a little girl of ten, with blue eyes and yellow hair. Under her arm she carried a white-paper package, very badly wrapped.

Miss Terry exchanged with her brother a glance which said, *I told you so!* The child seemed bashful and afraid to speak; no wonder!

Tom's kind heart yearned to her. "Good morning! Wish you a merry Christmas, Mary!" he said smiling.

The child gave a start. "Why, how did you know my name?" she cried.

Tom looked confused. How indeed did he know? But Miss Angelina, with a readiness that surprised herself, came to his rescue.

"We were talking of a little girl named Mary," she said. "And you look just like her. What did you come for, dear?"

The little girl hung her head and turned crimson.

"I—I came to see Angelina Terry," she whispered. "I—I've got a doll that belongs to her."

There was a pause, then Miss Terry said, "Well, go on."

"I—I found her on the steps of this house last night, and I ought to have brought her right here then. But I didn't. I took her home. I hope Angelina was not very unhappy last night."

Miss Terry smiled upon Tom, who gave a kind, low laugh.

"No," said Miss Terry. "Angelina did not worry about her lost doll. She was thinking about something else—the nicest Christmas present that ever anybody had. But you were a good girl to bring back the doll."

"No, I'm not a good girl," said Mary, and her voice trembled. "I was a wicked girl. I meant to keep Miranda for myself, because I thought she would be a lovely big doll. And when I found she was old and homely, somehow I still wanted to keep her. But it was stealing, and I couldn't. Please, will you give her to Angelina, and tell her I am so sorry?" She took Miranda out of the wrapping and held her toward Miss Terry without looking at the doll. It was as if she were afraid of being tempted once more.

Miss Terry did not take the doll.

"I am Angelina," she said. "The doll was mine."

"You! Angelina!" the child's face was full of bewilderment. Mechanically she drew Miranda to her and clasped her close.

"Yes, I am Angelina, and that was my doll Miranda," said Miss Terry gently. "Thank you for returning her. But Mary—your name is Mary?" The child nodded. "Suppose I wanted you to keep her for me, what would you say?"

Mary's eyes still dwelt upon Miss Terry with a puzzled look. This gray-haired Angelina was so different from the one she had pictured. She did not answer the question. Miss Terry drew the child to a chair beside her.

"Tell me all about yourself, Mary," she said.

After some coaxing and prompting from what they already guessed, Mary told the story of her sad little life.

She was an orphan recently left to the care of her uncle and aunt, who had received her grudgingly. They were her sole relatives, and the shame of their degraded lives was plain through the outlines of the vague picture which Mary sketched of them.

"You do not love them, Mary?" asked Miss Terry kindly.

"No," answered the child. "They always speak crossly to me. When they have been drinking they beat me."

Tom rose from the table with a muttered word and began to pace the floor. His blue eyes were full of tears.

"Mary," said Miss Terry, "will the people at home be worried if you do not come back to dinner?"

MARY RETURNS THE DOLL

Mary shook her head wonderingly. "No," she said. "They will not care. I am often away on holidays. I go to the Museums."

"Then I want you to stay with us today," said Miss Terry. "We are going to have a Christmas celebration, and we need you for a guest. Will you stay, you and Miranda?"

Mary looked down at the doll in her arms, and up at the two kind faces bent toward her. "Yes," she said impulsively, "I will stay. How good you are! I don't want to go home."

"Don't go home!" burst out Tom. "Stay with us always and be our little girl."

Mary looked from one to the other, half frightened at the new idea. Miss Terry bent and pecked at her cheek, with a thrill at the new sensation.

"Yes, we mean it," she said, and her voice was almost sweet. "We believe that the Christmas Angel has brought you to us, Mary. You have the Christmas name. But you seem to us like the little girl we both knew best, little Angelina with blue eyes and yellow hair, who was Miranda's mother. Will you stay with us, Mary Angelina? Would you like to stay?

Mary looked up with a wistful smile. "You are so good!" she said again. "I wish I could stay. But Uncle and Aunt are so—I am afraid of what they might do to us all. If they thought you wanted me, they would not let me go."

"I will fix Uncle and Aunt," said Tom, going for his coat. "Leave them to me. I know an argument that settles uncles and aunts of that sort. You need not go back to their house, I promise you, Mary, my dear."

Mary gave a great sigh of relief. "Oh, I am so glad!" she said. "It was such a wicked house. And here it is so good!"

"Good!" Miss Terry echoed the word with a sigh. "Come with me, Mary," she said.

She led her little guest through the hall to the library, where a great fire was blazing, with sundry mysterious packages in white paper piled on the table beside it. But Miss Terry did not stop at the fireplace. She drew Mary to the window which looked out on the sidewalk. Above the lower sash Mary saw the remains of a burned-out Christmas candle; and over it hung a pink papier-mâché angel stretching out open arms toward her.

"This is the Christmas Angel, Mary," said Miss Terry. "He is as old as Miranda—"

"He is as old as Christmas," interrupted Tom, looking in from the hall.

"When we were children, Tom and I, we hung him on our Christmas tree," went on Miss Terry. "We think he brought you to us. We believe he has changed the world for us—has brought us peace, goodwill, and happiness. He is going to be the guardian angel of our house. You must love him, Mary."

"How beautiful he is!" said Mary reverently. "His face shines like the Baby's that I saw once in the Church. Oh, Miss Angelina! He is like the Christ-Child himself!"

"Call me Aunt Angelina," said Miss Terry with a quick breath.

"Aunt Angelina," cried the child, throwing her arms about Miss Terry's neck.

Tom came and put his great furry coat-sleeves about them both. "And Uncle Tom," he said.

"Dear Uncle Tom!" whispered the child shyly.

There were tears in the eyes of all three.

"Now we shall live happy ever after," said Tom.

And the Christmas Angel beamed upon them.

Endnotes

Introduction:

1   Latin schools were liberal arts oriented but with a classical literature—especially Latin—base. Students in those days rarely learned any other contemporary language besides English.

Chapter One:

1   The Puritans banned all Christmas celebrations during the Commonwealth Period in England.

Chapter Six:

2   In pre-electric light times, candles were placed on branches for Christmas illumination and atmosphere—obviously, the fire danger was high.

3   Irish expression meaning "It's a fine day!"

DISCUSSION WITH PROFESSOR WHEELER

(For Formal School, Home School, and Book Club Discussions)

First of all, permit me to define my perception of the role of the teacher. I believe that the ideal teaching relationship involves the teacher and the student, both looking in the same direction, and both with a sense of wonder. A teacher is not an important person dishing out rote learning to an unimportant person. I furthermore do not believe that a Ph.D. automatically brings with it omniscience, despite the way some of us act. In discussions, I tell my students beforehand that my opinions and conclusions are no more valid than theirs, for each of us sees reality from a different perspective.

Now that my role is clear, let's continue. The purpose of the discussion section of the series is to encourage debate, to dig deeper into the books than would be true without it and to spawn other questions that may build on the ones I begin with here. If you take advantage of this section, you will be gaining just as good an understanding of the book as you would were you actually sitting in one of my classroom circles.

As you read this book, record your thoughts and reactions each day in a journal. Also, an unabridged dictionary is almost essential in complete-ly understanding the text. If your vocabulary is to grow, something else is needed besides the dictionary: vocabulary cards. Take a stack of 3 x 5 cards, and write the words you don't know on one side and their definitions on the other, with each word used in a sentence. Every time you stumble on words you are unsure of—and I found quite a number myself!—make a card for it. Continually go over these cards; and keep all, except those you never miss, in a card file. You will be amazed at how fast your vocabulary will grow!

Afterword

The Introduction Must Be Read Before Beginning the Next Section.

QUESTIONS TO DEEPEN YOUR UNDERSTANDING

Chapter 1. The Play Box

1. Beginning sentences and paragraphs often make or break a book. In this book, Abbie Farwell Brown drops us right into dialogue and action in progress. What does this first paragraph accomplish, in terms of your desire to read on, or to close the book and leave the rest of the book unread?

2. Pay particular attention to how Brown fleshes out her characters. On five-by-eight-inch cards (one for each character in book), chart out the evolution of each character, starting with Miss Terry and Norah. First impressions (both in real life and in literature) are so powerful that they might as well be carved in marble. Flat characters, as we know, remain frozen in their created state; round characters refuse such imprisonment and smash their way through to freedom. Which characters do you feel are flat in the book? Which are round?
    Sometimes we arrive at our initial judgment on the basis of what the author says about a given character; and sometimes the author steps back into the shadows and lets the character's words and body language carry their own freight. Which method do you feel works the best? Why?

3. Unquestionably, where Christmas stories and books are concerned, every one of them is compared—consciously or unconsciously—to the great original of the genre, Dickens' 1843 mas-

terpiece, *The Christmas Carol.* Since this is so, start out at the very beginning noting similarities and differences, and weighing their relative effectiveness. In other words, just because a work may achieve icon status, that does not mean that it is therefore immune to all future challenges to its preeminence. Which one moves you most deeply? Which one's persuasiveness is harder to resist? Are their methodologies different? Are the two plots similar? Or are there significant differences? Continue to compare through each chapter, then arrive at overall conclusions at the book's end.

4. "Alone on Christmas Eve"—what is the impact of that line? Why is it harder to be alone at Christmas Eve than at other times? Or is it?

5. What do you think Miss Terry means by labeling "candles, carols, and merriment" as mere superstition? How do her scornful Christmas-related musings compare to Scrooge's in The Christmas Carol?

6. Note how the size of Tom's long-ago lettering, compared to her own, only reinforces Miss Terry's determination to have nothing to do with her long-estranged brother. Could it be human nature to skew everything, all evidence, all documentation, in the direction of our predetermined course of action? If that is true, why is it?

7. What is the significance of Miss Terry's first name, in light of the overall story?

8. Old toys today bring small fortunes at antique shows. Is that perceived "value" as significant as the toys' esoteric value? Why? Do you agree with Miss Terry's contention that "Most things are better destroyed as soon as you are done with them"? Or do

you feel there are valid reasons to hold on to them for purely sentimental reasons? Why?

Chapter 2. Jack-in-the-box

9. Until recent times, houses tended to be lived in by generation after generation of the same families. What would it be like to live in a house that your ancestors had been born in, lived in, and died in? Would you prefer that to shifting from house to house as we do today? What are the benefits of visiting the houses where famous people once lived?

10. Have you ever owned a Jack-in-the-box? Have you ever wanted to? How do you react to Jack's leaping out of the box?

11. How early do we acquire the urge to possess something? Is it a good trait? A bad trait? Are there any dangers connected with it? Discuss.

12. Does Miss Terry appear to be a bigot? Does she appear to like those of Jewish descent? Since Jews don't believe in Christmas, how does she relate the fighting of the two ragamuffins to that Christian holiday? As the story progresses, watch to see if this initial negative perception persists.

Chapter 3. The Flanton Dog

13. Preconceptions—we all have them. What preconceptions does Miss Terry have about the "dapper figure in a long coat and a silk hat"? Hold them until later in the book so as to see if her preconceptions turn out to be on the mark.

14. Ironic, isn't it, that Miss Terry, who has determined to burn up her old toys, nevertheless feels "a pang shoot through her" as an automobile drives over the battered old toy dog. Can you make sense out of that?

Chapter 4. The Noah's Ark

15. Why is it, do you think, that so few toys survive intact? Are they deliberately mistreated, or does it just "happen"?

16. Prior to our age, when someone died, surviving family wore black as a symbol of mourning, for weeks, months, years—sometimes for life. Do you think we ought to go back to such a tradition? Give reasons.

17. To what perversity in our makeup do we owe our valuing only what others value, desiring only what others desire, and considering as worthless only what others consider worthless? What point is Brown trying to make (with the two women) about human nature? Is this a condition which we can overcome? How?

Chapter 5. Miranda

18. Compare the role Brown's old toys have in her story to that of "real-life" people in Scrooge's youth, in *The Christmas Carol.* Is one device more effective than the other (or only different)? Also study comparative impact on the two protagonists: Ebenezer Scrooge and Angelina Terry.

19. If the eyes are the windows of the soul, what is the effect on Miss Terry of Miranda's eyes? Why would burning her seem like murder? And why did she wrap her in paper when she had failed to do so with the other toys?

20. Why do you feel Miss Terry can now heave the rest of the toys into the fire without any of the reservations she had earlier in the evening's experiments? Would you have felt the same way? Why?

Chapter 6. The Christmas Angel

21. How many of life's troubles, do you think, are caused by our own determination to be first? Why do we insist on such preeminence? And when such rivalry once rears its malevolent head among siblings, oftentimes life-long alienation, bitterness, and tragedy is the result, just as it happened between Tom and Angelina. Have you noted similar cases or experienced them yourself? With what results?

22. In what way did Miss Terry feel her mother had been wise fifty years before?

23. Why did Miss Terry rescue the Christmas Angel from the muddy street, and why did she find it impossible to toss it into the fire as she had so many other toys?

24. Were you surprised that the Christmas Angel was male? Look in the Bible and see what it says about angels being male or females. Why do so many people assume angels are male?

Chapter 7. Before the Fire

25. What do you think is symbolized behind the tradition of placing an angel at the top of each Christmas tree?

26. What do you believe is meant by these words: "Now you have lost the old belief and the old love. . . . Now you have studied

books and read wise men's sayings. You understand the higher criticism, and the higher charity, and the higher egoism. You don't believe in mere giving. You don't believe in the Christmas spirit—you know better"?

27. As the story continues, try to gain a concept of the full meaning of "Christmas spirit" as used in the book.

Chapter 8. Jack Again

28. What did Miss Terry learn in the rest of the Jack-in-the-box story (especially where appearances and circumstantial evidence are concerned)?

Chapter 9. The Dog Again

29. Why is it, do you think, that toys have greater reality to children than they do to adults? How is that borne out in this chapter?

30. Just as was true of the fabled "velveteen rabbit," Johnny refuses a new replacement for the battered old dog. Why is it that a child would reject a new and perfect dog, preferring to stay with the crippled old one?

31. All that happens to us is a matter of perspective: We may perceive it as tragic whereas in reality the act may result in wonderful and unexpected things happening to us. How is this truth brought home to Miss Terry?

Chapter 10. Noah Again

32. How difficult it must be to look out from behind bars of pain to people outside who are happy! That is the widow's plight here. Does the reality of her anguish make it easier to forgive her for her selfish act?

33. What role do the carol singers have in this book? How does their singing contribute to the story? Which characters are impacted by it? How?

34. What is your perception of the role of angels in our lives? Do you think an angel might minister through a papier-mâché counterpart?

Chapter 11. Miranda Again

35. What do you think Brown meant by this line? "Once more, on the wings of vision, Miss Terry was out on the snowy street"? Do you believe a Higher Power may choose to communicate with us through dreams or visions? Have you ever known personally of such communication? Discuss.

36. "Mary was not one to feel a half passion about anything"— what a thing to say! How about you? If you had to choose between a friend known for "half passions" and a friend known for "full passions," which one would you rather have? Why?

37. In this chapter, Mary rationalizes for all she's worth in order to avoid taking Miranda back. Do we rationalize? For what reasons? How about you—do you rationalize? If so, are you able to convince your inner self that all is well in spite of it? Is Mary's

The Christmas Angel

rationalizing strong enough to convince her questioning conscience? Has your conscience ever kept you awake? Discuss.

Chapter 12. The Angel Again

38. What is the significance of the name of the little girl who finds Miranda in this story? Does her name make a difference to Miss Terry?

39. To all appearances, the drunkard who kicked the Christmas Angel into the street was a hopeless case, and Miss Terry scorned him. What does she now discover about her quick judgment of him? Do we do this sort of holier-than-thou thing very often? Why? What can we do to change such snap judgments?

Chapter 13. The Christmas Candle

40. How does this section compare to the counterpart in *The Christmas Carol*? How much time has passed since Norah left?

41. What is the significance of Angelina Terry's placing the angel in her window? What is the significance to the grizzled man watching from across the street?

Chapter 14. Tom

42. How does Angelina's Christmas Angel and her Guardian Angel blur together? Does her brother believe her story?

Chapter 15. Christmas Day

43. How does the coming of Mary bring Angelina and Tom full circle?

44. What is the overall impact of the book on you?

45. How effective are the concluding lines?

ABOUT THE EDITOR

Joe Wheeler, Ph.D., is considered to be one of America's leading anthologizers of stories, and has written or edited 53 books, including the *Great Stories Remembered* series, the *Heart to Heart* series, and the best selling *Christmas in My Heart* series. He is Emeritus Professor of English at Columbia Union College in Takoma Park, Maryland; Co-founder and Executive Director of the Zane Grey's West Society; and General Editor at Focus on the Family. Dr. Wheeler and his wife, Connie, currently reside in Conifer, Colorado.

"Joe Wheeler is America's Keeper of the Story"

—Dr. James Dobson